STRIKE OF THE HAWK

It was coming too fast and vicious, even for me. I could not imagine an AXE agent selling out. A double agent. Of all the organizations in the world, I had naïvely believed that AXE was incorruptible. "Who is the agent?" I asked, controlling my anger. "For all I know, it could be you," Hawk said without emotion. "Your next job is to find the double agent and correct him, or her. After that, you take care of Cronin and make peace with all the syndicate people. You're high on their kill list. And so am I."

PLUS A FULL LENGTH
BONUS BOOK:
DOUBLE IDENTITY

NICK CARTER IS IT!

"Nick Carter out-Bonds James Bond."
—*Buffalo Evening News*

"Nick Carter is America's #1 espionage agent."
—*Variety*

"Nick Carter is razor-sharp suspense."
—*King Features*

"Nick Carter is extraordinarily big."
—*Bestsellers*

"Nick Carter has attracted an army of addicted readers . . . the books are fast, have plenty of action and just the right degree of sex . . . Nick Carter is the American James Bond, suave, sophisticated, a killer with both the ladies and the enemy."
—*The New York Times*

NC-A

From The Nick Carter Killmaster Series

Dedicated to The Men of the
Secret Services of the
United States of America

A Killmaster Spy Chiller

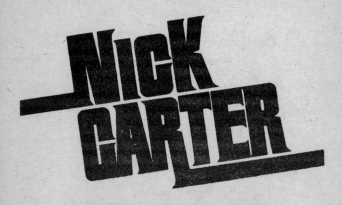

NICK CARTER

STRIKE OF THE HAWK

PLUS A SPECIAL BONUS BOOK
DOUBLE IDENTITY
A CLASSIC NICK CARTER ADVENTURE

CHARTER
NEW YORK

A DIVISION OF CHARTER COMMUNICATIONS INC.
A GROSSET & DUNLAP COMPANY

STRIKE OF THE HAWK

DOUBLE IDENTITY

Charter Books
A Division of Charter Communications Inc.
A Grosset & Dunlap Company
360 Park Avenue South
New York, New York 10010

2 4 6 8 0 9 7 5 3 1
Manufactured in the United States of America

STRIKE OF THE HAWK

Chapter One

I had them.

For six weeks, I had chased them from Tripoli, to Tobruk, to Baghdad, to Amir, to Calcutta, to Kuala Lumpur, to Sydney, to Honolulu, to San Francisco, to New York, to Miami, to Caracas, to Rio, to Lisbon, to London, to Bonn, to Paris, back again to Tripoli and now to Corsica where it would be all over in a matter of minutes.

Forty-two days and nights, around the world, and at least one body for each day. That didn't count the two lying behind me in individual pools of blood, or the twenty guards outside the wall. The last two, sprawled on the dark lawn in front of the syndicate safehouse on the northern shore of the French island, had died so silently that not even the katydids in nearby palms stopped making their harsh lovecalls.

Thte razor-sharp stiletto, which I call Hugo and which is probably the most famous knife in the world, had slit their throats with such ease that the killing had done nothing to psych me up for the final coup.

Now, I stood at the side of the big mansion, listening to the low roar of the Mediterranean. My left hand was on the cooling metal of the main air shaft which sucked air to the men hiding three levels down. The house itself was empty. They had all gone below, bolting doors behind them, knowing that I was coming.

The two guards had been left on the grounds in a faint hope that one of them at least would stop me.

1

Nobody stops Nick Carter. That's me, top agent for AXE. If the past forty-two days had not convinced them of the truth of my brash statement, my next act certainly would.

My fingers slid around the metal pipe, looking for the screws or bolts that held on the protective cover. There were none; the cover was welded on.

I dropped to my knees and inspected the tiny slots just beneath the cap's mushroom top. High tensile steel. The syndicate did things right. The safehouse was impenetrable, or so its builders thought.

I glanced at my digital watch, a present from my boss following my last assignment. It was now ten minutes until midnight. The Polaris submarine, carrying my boss, David Hawk, would surface at exactly midnight, lie two miles off the northern shore of Corsica for precisely ten minutes, then leave, with or without me.

And it would take ten minutes to reach the rubber liferaft, yank the small motor into life and chug through the rolling waves to the sub.

And the goddam airpipe had a cap that was welded on.

I had already taken the small gas bomb that I carry just behind my testicles from its pouch and had put it on the grass beside the pipe. All I had to do was pull one tiny pin and drop the bomb into the pipe. Within seconds, the lethal gas would be sucked into the safehouse's air-conditioning system.

Seconds after that, the remaining twelve men of the NOTCH syndicate would choke in agony eliminating the masterminds of a plot to kill ninety percent of the world's population with Bubonic plague. The air system of the safehouse was built to filter out plague germs, but it would not touch the secret chemical used in my gas bomb. Pierre—that was what I fondly called the bomb—would penetrate any filtering system. If, that is, I could get the lousy cap off the pipe so Pierre could do his job.

The seconds were humming away silently.

A hand grenade—it was the only solution. It would make a hell of a lot of noise and would warn the men below. I would have to drop Pierre almost immediately after the hand grenade blew off the cap—and this meant that I would have to be close when the grenade went—but it was a chance I had to take. I could be blown to hell, NOTCH would still be in business and, in another six weeks, most of the world would be dead.

Risk. It's a part of the fabric of my soul. I get triple pay for taking risks. And, if I didn't take this particular risk, the twelve men below would have enough time to switch to their emergency air supply—pure oxygen—and the gas bomb would go for nothing.

I fished a grenade out of the strap around my shoulder and taped it to the curving grid pattern of the air-suction pipe letting the pin and handle hang free. I tied a thin strip of nylon twine to the pin and backed to the corner of the house.

Thirty feet away. Too close for safety and too far away for effectiveness with the gas bomb. The bomb had to be dropped at almost the same instant the men below became aware that their air system was being endangered.

Sweat began to bead on my forehead. It literally poured down my sides. I finally looked at the watch and swore aloud.

It was three minutes until midnight.

I had to catch that submarine or all kinds of other hell would break loose on the beautiful island of Corsica.

Sharply at midnight, just when the submarine would be surfacing, a member of the Corse—the French equivalent of the Mafia—would call Corsican police and report that an American espionage agent had been sent to the island to kill the Corsican governor. The Corse agent would even give the local police my location.

The really funny part, if I felt like laughing, was that the Corse had helped me corner the NOTCH syndicate chiefs in the northshore safehouse. Without their firepower, I would never had killed off the twenty NOTCH guards outside the wall and driven the dozen top men into the bowels of the safehouse.

Then, why would a member of the Corse call the police and feed them such a lie?

Easy. The Corse wanted me out of their territory. They had helped me only to repay an old favor, one I had done for them years ago. Once the favor was repaid, they wanted no more of me, or of AXE, or of anyone in the world—including (especially) the French government.

I looked at my watch. One minute until midnight!

It was impossible to go through with my plan and save myself at the same time. It was more than risk now. It was either give up or commit suicide.

Only then, in the final moment of desperation, did it come to me.

The pipe was sucking air into the lower levels of the safehouse. Gas was air. That was it. I ripped the tape from around the grenade, untied the nylon string and taped the gas bomb in the grenade's place. I held my hands around the grid and felt the suction from the air-conditioning pump down below.

Perfect. It would work. Even if only a fourth of Pierre's gas was sucked into the pipe, the twelve men would die.

When I was fifty feet away and felt the hot wind from the ocean on my back, I pulled the string, felt the pin come free and turned to run toward the life raft on the beach.

Suddenly bright lights snapped on all around the high wall that surrounded the landward sides of the safehouse.

Damn the Corse! They had jumped the gun. They had made their call too soon.

"Stop right there, American," a voice boomed from a bullhorn. "We have you covered."

I fired my Luger toward the sound of the bullhorn. A rain of bullets plowed into the well-tailored lawn around me punching up divots. I was pinpointed in light, a hundred yards from the ocean.

I wanted to shout at them: Don't you know I've just saved your lives: Don't you know . . .

A bullet tore into my left side, just above my belt. My side and shoulder went numb.

The Luger boomed again and a light went out.

In a hail of bullets I ran toward the ocean. The moonlight

shone on tiny whitecaps in the water. In the distance—a ghost on the surface of the water—was the submarine.

Holding my side, I zigzagged through bullets till my feet hit sand and I was beyond the lights. But I was still a target for the police guns which barked and chattered in the night. Bullets were hitting the water with that strange, *poik* sound.

As I climbed into the boat and felt my shoes sink into the soft rubber and fabric bottom, I heard feet running across the lawn.

I sprayed four shots from the Luger at the running sounds, then shoved the pistol into my belt. My left arm was useless now, totally paralyzed from the bullet in my side.

The motor caught on the third pull and I was off into the rolling swells. Bullets kept coming, smacking the water all around me. And then someone—not me—got lucky: one of the bullets had put a hole in the air-filled raft.

I aimed the boat toward the silhouette of the big submarine and followed the sound of the hissing. I found the hole and poked my middle finger into it. The hissing stopped, even though bullets still sizzled around me. And, without a hand on the tiller, the life raft was drifting to the right, away from the sub.

With all the effort of my one-hundred and ninety pounds of bone, muscle and adrenalin, I forced my numb left hand to the small motor tiller. I pulled the boat around until it was on a direct course toward the submarine.

The police had lost their bearing on me; their bullets were spitting up water at least a hundred feet to my right.

I was safe. I was home free.

When I was within a hundred yards of the submarine, the little outboard motor whirring valiantly against the rolling ocean, the big ghost moved. It was submerging!

I jerked the tiller to the right to avoid being caught in the suction when the monstrous Polaris went under. In something around ten seconds, it was gone.

There I was, putt-putting in a circle, in a life raft with a leak in it, running out of gas, only two miles off the northern coast of Corsica where everybody, it seemed, wanted me dead, and my only means of escape (or rescue) completely cut off.

Two sets of moving lights appeared off to the west, near the corner of the island. They were the lights of Corsican patrol boats. As N3 with AXE, the most secret ot all the secret organizations in the world, I knew that I could expect no help from David Hawk, the man who received my reports and gave me my orders, or from the government I served.

As the patrol boats came nearer, I sighted movement in the dark water about thirty feet to my right. A bright yellow ring, a lifebuoy, bounced to the surface.

I was abreast of it in a few moments, abandoned the half-dead life raft, and held on to the float for dear life.

It was attached to a strong, insulated line that disappeared beneath the ocean's surface, from which, to my amazement, a tinny voice suddenly emanated.

"Take a deep breath and hang on," it said from a speaker embedded in the cork circle. Even with the noise of the Corsican patrol boats hauling up on my tail, I recognized the voice as Hawk's.

Now the lifebuoy jerked forward so violently that I thought it was going to rip me in two. Water splashed against my face like an unending tidal wave. I turned my head to suck in small gulps of air. Looking back, I saw the big patrol boats circling the life raft. I didn't see them for long. The yellow ring and I were streaking along at thirty knots.

In two minutes, which seemed like two years, I was well out of sight of the patrol boats, still being ripped through the water like bait for a whale. My lungs were bursting for a good, deep injection of air, and the bullet hole in my side felt as though it were being torn open by gigantic, fiery hands.

After perhaps another five minutes of absolute agony, the yellow ring slowed and finally stopped. Exhausted, I clung tightly, leaving the ring snugly anchored over my shoulder. The blasted thing could take off like a jet at any minute.

Hawk seemed to read my mind. "Glad to see that you're still with us," the tinny voice said. I grinned in spite of the pain and fatigue. I bobbed in the water and waited, grinning.

The grin turned into a smile which turned into laughter. I knew that I was just a bit hysterical, but I was laughing for good reason.

It was the irony of my thoughts at that moment. At a time when I should have been thinking of my rescue, and of the successful completion of a mission which saved ninety percent of the earth's population, my thoughts were on sex.

But the feeling went away when I felt hands reaching for me. Even so, there was still a grin on my face as I walked along the big deck of the Polaris sub, heading for the open hatch, safety and my tweed-jacketed, cigar-smoking, no-nonsense boss.

For this mission, I should get at least a month off. The grin was for all the women I would love during that month.

Chapter Two

It was nearly dawn when I came out of the anesthetic. The bullet in my side had lodged against my kidney. If it had come from a more powerful weapon and had been a half inch to the right, I wouldn't be "resting comfortably" in the sick bay of a submarine; I would be rotting on the beach of the north Corsican shore.

The Navy doctor told me how lucky I was. I thanked him and began to sit up.

"Better wait until tomorrow."

"Can't," I said, wincing in pain "Got a report to make."

"It can wait," the doctor said. He raised his left hand and a corpsman slapped a syringe into it. Deftly, the doctor shuttled the syringe into his right hand and gave me a shot of something before I could resist, or even react.

"What the hell was that?" I asked. "I told you . . ."

I told him nothing more for twelve hours. Even then, I had to argue to get him to let me off the cot. At last I made my way down the narrow passageway to the captain's office. The captain, a big, beefy man, smiled at me when the SP opened the door. Hawk was sitting in a chair near the captain's desk. He looked at me passively. No smile of commendation; no scowl of condemnation. You could never tell what Hawk was thinking. At least, I couldn't.

The captain happily left us alone. It was indication of Hawk's great power in Washington that the captain left his own office to us, without complaint; in fact, with some degree of pleasure.

"All right," Hawk said without preamble as he snapped down the button of a small tape recorder on the captain's desk. "Report."

He had not invited me to sit, but my head was spinning. What the hell more could anybody do to me? I took a chair opposite the desk and grinned at my boss, savoring that one moment when Hawk is at his weakest, that moment when he actually *needs* something from someone.

"Report," he said again, his voice toneless, his face tightening a bit.

I sighed. Six weeks of frenetic activity to report and all I wanted to do was sleep, to lie down, to forget. But I began.

After Hawk had sent me to Tripoli in the middle of May to check out a report that a newly-created terrorist group called NOTCH (for Northern Organ To Create Havoc) had begun working in laboratories in various parts of the world and was headquartered in Libya, I had discovered the purpose of the group and the reason for the laboratory work. Each lab team was creating cultures of Bubonic plague. The plan was to innoculate a number of their own people, and to send them on phony assignments to virtually every country in the world. After the six-day incubation period of the disease germs, each innoculated agent would be a walking death trap, spreading Bubonic plague wherever he went.

By the time medical authorities in each nation figured out what was happening, it would be too late. Bubonic plague is so rare today that most medical people can't diagnose it. And unless treatment begins during the first twelve days after a person contracts the plague, no medicine on earth will stop it.

NOTCH had decided to spare the northern part of Africa and the area around the Mediterranean. The people in those areas would be provided another serum, to keep them from getting the disease.

Medical authorities within NOTCH had estimated that the disease, properly spread, would wipe out about ninety percent of the world's population, America's population, for example, would be reduced to about twenty million—from more than two hundred million!

NOTCH agents, specially trained in political and military techniques, would move into each country and take control. The world capital would become Tobruk, although Egyptian authorities were angling to make it Cairo. The Egyptians also wanted to save all other Arab countries, but this could not be accomplished unless Israel was also spared. To knock off Israel, NOTCH leaders were willing to kill more than fifty million Arabs.

When it was all over, NOTCH would not only have political control of the world, it would also be the central agency dealing with all the world's wealth.

"And all plans have been destroyed?" Hawk interrupted.

I nodded. "Along with the laboratories and all traces of the cultures," I added.

"And how did you accomplish it?" He glanced at the recorder, saw that we had plenty of tape, then lit up an incredibly foul-smelling cigar. I was already feeling a bit nauseous from the operation. Now, I was ready to vomit. But I went on.

I told him how I had infiltrated NOTCH by pretending to be a former SS major. I even had my special SS number tatooed in my armpit; I have been able to speak fluent German since I was a child. Once I had learned the overall plan and had stolen a list of laboratories and NOTCH leaders and agents, I had started my own reign of terror.

I blew up laboratories, after first determining that the cultures were not "ripe." I terminated key agents, pursuing them from laboratory to laboratory, whittling them down.

"It was only when I discovered that the highest officials and a few of their flunkies were retreating to the safehouse on Corsica that I used my contacts in the Corse," I said.

"That was a tactical error," Hawk said, exhaling a ring of sickening smoke toward me.

"Perhaps," I said, "but a necessary one. No foreign agent does anything in Corsica without the knowledge and the permission of the Corse."

"True, but you're not just another foreign agent. You're N3."

"They owed me a favor," I said.

Hawk waved his cigar and shook his head. Ashes dropped onto his tweed jacket, but he let them lay. I began to search my pockets for cigarettes, then remembered that the last pack of my special Turkish brand, with my initials in gold on each cigarette, had been ruined during that ripping ride through the ocean.

Without a smile, Hawk took a pack from his jacket pocket and tossed it to me. I grinned, knowing that I was receiving an extremely special favor from the director of AXE. He knew about my cigarettes; he had gone to a lot of trouble to get me a pack.

"Thank you," I said, still grinning.

He grumbled: "It won't become a habit. Now back to the Corse. The Corse owes nobody anything. In fact, as far as they are concerned, you now owe them a favor. A very big favor."

I knew he was right, but my mind didn't want to accept it. My mind told me that I should call it square with the Corse, that someone with a streak of honor in that organization would recall the time I had caught two Corse defectors with four million francs in drug money and had delivered the defectors, along with the money, to a Corse agent in Marseilles. Again, Hawk was reading me.

"The only time the Corse has shown any sign of honor," he said, "was when it fought with the French underground during World War II. Even then, the Corse had its price."

I knew about that. In return for its help to the French, the Corse had received carte blanche to run the drug market, gambling, prostitution and even white slavery in southern France, particularly around Marseilles.

"Well, it's done," I said, savoring my cigarette. "If they call for a favor, I'll simply have to tell them the debt was paid in advance."

Hawk's face tightened and I thought he was going to grin. He didn't. "Go on," he said. "Finish your report."

I finished, bringing him right up to the point three days earlier when I had contacted him for rescue.

"And how did you dispose of the remnants of NOTCH?" he asked.

When I told him he grunted and turned in his chair.

"So, you can't be certain they're dead."

"I'm certain."

He raised an eyebrow. He didn't have to say it: But you didn't wait to see the bodies.

"I didn't want to see the bodies," I said for him. "As it was, I barely escaped having the Corsican police inspect my body."

Worry lines creased his forehead and he punched his cigar out in the captain's shiny ashtray, made from the tail fins of a nuclear torpedo.

"Sir, I don't know what else I could have done."

He remained silent. I started to go over the scene again, but decided what the hell. I'm human. Nick Carter takes every conceivable risk, but Nick Carter is no damned Kamikaze.

Finally, Hawk spoke: "Now, are you convinced?"

"Convinced? Convinced of what?"

"That the Corse does not operate on a favor-for-favor basis. They crossed you, N3. They called the police early because they wanted you dead. They still want you dead."

My nerves came alert. "How do you know that?"

This time, the tight face edged into a grin. It was the deadliest grin I have ever seen on the face of a human.

"Because they also want me dead."

I gulped and sat up straight in the chair, ignoring the sharp pain that ripped through my side.

"Would it be presumptuous of me to ask details on that last little gem of information?"

"It would, but I will provide details. First, tell me about Diane Northrup."

"Oh." I hadn't told him about my escapades with women during the past six weeks. I never told him about the women, and he never mentioned them. But he knew about them. The man was a wizard, a walking computer.

Quickly, very quickly, I told him about meeting Diane Northrup, a big, bosomy blonde, on my initial flight from

New York to Paris, more than six weeks ago. We had spent a couple of days touring the city and sleeping in the cushy beds at George Cinq Hotel. She had turned up again in Calcutta, on her world tour, and we had spent a few memorable nights in that exotic city before I went off to blow up a laboratory and to deal with a few NOTCH people.

"As far as Diane is concerned," I told the boss, "my name is Brad Holland and I'm a public relations man for—"

"As far as Diane Northrup is concerned," Hawk said, his words battering me like nuclear pellets, "your name is Nick Carter, N3, Killmaster for AXE."

Everything went out of me then. But he had more to say. He leaned forward in the chair, snapped off the tape recorder and said in a low, ominous voice: "And, as far as you are concerned from here on out, Diane Northrup is really a woman named Elaine Withers. She is an unwitting agent for the Mafia, the Corse, and every other syndicate involved in drugs. She does not know about NOTCH, or what her real job is. She was recruited by a man named Robert Cronin. Have you heard of him?"

"Of course," I said, lighting up another gold-embossed cigarette. "He's president of a major American drug company with international connections. He's solid and respectable. Sharp, actually."

The horrible grin again, accompanied by a nod.

"He also allowed NOTCH to use his laboratories, although he didn't know what they were up to. His crime has nothing to do with Bubonic plague cultures. His company makes tons of illegal drugs and channels them through the Mafia, the Corse, and others involved in bulk sales of narcotics. You blew up Cronin's laboratories and he wants your hide."

My breath went all the way out. My head spun. I had completed one mission only to trigger another one even more dangerous to me personally.

"Cronin knows about us. He told Miss Withers that his company was on the verge of discovering a cure for glaucoma and that AXE was trying to steal the ingredients for another drug company. He put her on your tail, so to speak.''

"But how does he know so much about us?''

Hawk sighed and said, simply, "One of our agents has sold us out.''

It was coming too fast and too vicious, even for me. I could not imagine an AXE agent selling out. A double agent. Of all the organizations in the world, I had naïvely believed that AXE was incorruptible.

"Who is the agent?'' I asked, controlling my anger.

Hawk shot an arrow of smoke through the tail fins of the captain's ashtray. "For all I know, it could be you,'' he said without emotion.

"Sir!'' I was half out of the chair, full of anger.

He waved me down.

"Your next job,'' he said almost casually, "is to find the double agent in AXE and correct him—or her. After that, you take care of Cronin and make peace with all the syndicate people. So far, Cronin hasn't let the word go public, but it's only a matter of time before everyone involved with him and his illegal drugs will know about AXE. And you'll be high on their kill list.''

I sucked smoke into my lungs and felt my anger rise. "When do I start?''

"You already have. We'll be dumping you at Tangier in a few hours. Elaine Withers—your precious Diane Northrup—is back in Paris. She has made contact with a number of AXE agents, at Cronin's direction. One of them obviously has told her too much. She's the best place to start. We'll see just how much of a charmer you really are.'' He almost grinned. "You have to get there on your own, but I do have some new cover papers for you. Don't blow it, Nick. I have a personal stake in this next mission.''

He took a crumpled piece of paper from his side pocket and gave it to me. I smoothed it out and read the typed message:

"AXE dies, starting with you.''

I looked up at Hawk, searching his eyes for a clue. The eyes were small and blank, revealing nothing.

"Elaine Withers delivered that to me in a sealed envelope

just two days after your little affair in Calcutta. That's why you go to her. Find out how much she knows, how she got her information, then dispose of her.''

He meant ''kill her,'' but Hawk has never given me, or any AXE agent an order to kill.

''Sir, would you mind telling me why you didn't inform me of this note as soon as you received it?''

''Don't mind at all,'' he said. ''You were on a mission that required all your attention—and then some. If you had known about this, you would have been useless against NOTCH. As it is, we may all wind up being useless anyway. Any other questions?''

I shook my head and Hawk went on. ''Cheer up, Nick,'' he said as he inspected the glowing tip of his cigar. ''We've been in worse fixes.''

Suddenly I thought of a question but left without asking it: When?

Chapter Three

At precisely ten p.m., when the lights of the colorful old Moroccan city sparkled in the dark night, the Navy chopper took off from the deck of the surfaced Polaris. Hawk had not come on deck to wish me bon voyage. There isn't a sentimental bone in his body.

He didn't seem to care that I was still wobbly and in pain from the bullet wound and ensuing operation. He didn't seem to care that I was being cut loose in a city known for vicious drug peddlers. He didn't seem to care that, if I were attacked after leaving the protection of the Navy, I would be weak and easy prey to all sorts of enemies.

He wanted results, not excuses. Well, I would give him results. I was well-prepared. My personal arsenal had been refurbished and appropriately cached: my stiletto, Hugo, in its chamois sheath, strapped to my right forearm; Wilhelmina, my 9mm Luger loaded with a clip of nine cartridges, was tucked in a shoulder harness; five extra clips, were stashed flat against my belly. And I had a new gas bomb, smaller and more lethal than earlier AXE issues. I could hardly feel it in the tiny pouch between my legs.

The chopper put down on warm sand ten miles south of the port city—about midway between Tetuán and Rabat. I watched it disappear to the east, where it would cut its running lights, then circle out over the Mediterranean and land God-knew-where.

I was to walk into Tangier and arrange for a flight to Paris.

16

At least that would be the obvious plan. But I rarely did the obvious. Even though only Hawk knew my mission, any seaman aboard the submarine could guess that my initial destination was Tangier—and the chopper pilot would not even have to guess. He would know.

That's why I headed southwest toward Rabat, Morocco's capital on the Atlantic Ocean. South of Rabat was Casablanca, where I would spend some time with Raina Missou, hopefully convalescent time. I needed a few days before taking off for Paris. I needed a few days with Raina, with a friendly face and a warm body. God, what a body.

Even after I left Raina and Casablanca, I would not go directly to Paris. I would take a circuitous route, probably hitting Sicily, Albania, Yugoslavia, Austria, Germany and Luxembourg before even beginning to hone in on France— and Paris.

The best way to find a beehive, I have learned, is to follow the line of the bee after it leaves the flower. There would be no beeline for anyone to follow, if the syndicate boys were trying to find out where I was going.

The best laid plans, however. I had gone only a mile over the sand and rocks of the barren land when I saw the distant lights of a moving vehicle coming directly at me. I moved southward and lay on my belly near the top of a high dune, looking down at what I could now see was a jeep moving ever closer.

When it was within a hundred yards, I squinted in the faint moonlight and made out four passengers. A tall, dignified-looking man sat beside the driver. In the rear were two soldiers with rifles and bayonets projecting toward the starry night sky. I palmed the Luger and waited while, engines laboring and tires crunching, the jeep forged its own road across the dunes. I was on the verge of moving on when, at the last second, the jeep made a sharp right turn and began to bear down on me.

I skittered around the dune, avoiding the bright headlights. The jeep stopped about a hundred feet away and the man in front, obviously an officer, got out. I held the Luger in both hands, aiming directly for the glinting medals on his broad chest.

"Who ever you are and whatever your game is," the officer shouted in flawless English, "you might as well come down. We have you bottled up."

It was then that I heard other sounds. I whirled around and saw jeeps moving toward me from the south, the east and the north.

The officer was not playing any games of bluff tonight.

The big question was, how did they know someone was out on the dark desert? An even bigger question was, did they know who I was? I got no answers just that moment, but I did remember something that chilled me. There was a long-standing battle between Spain and Morocco because of Spanish interests in the North African country—especially the Spanish Sahara—and my passport claimed that I had left from Madrid only three days ago.

I could easily be shot for a Spanish spy. Right out here in the middle of nowhere. Even without the passport, there were my weapons, strange artifacts for the average tourist or businessman to be hauling around.

The other jeeps came to a grinding halt not far from me. One of them, from the east, held me in its bright headlights. I had no choice but to surrender, lie through my teeth and hope that I didn't wind up in a Moroccan prison for a couple of lifetimes.

Just as I was preparing to stand up and place my body and soul at the mercy of what obviously was the Moroccan Army, I heard the screaming roar of planes in the distance. They were not passing jets or even curious pilots trying to inject some excitement into the boredom of required night flying.

They were fighter planes. Evidently they had spotted the headlights of the jeeps and were diving for the kill. I never saw the lights of the six planes because they didn't have them on. But I saw bright tongues of flame from fifty-caliber machine guns in the planes' wings. Then came the large balls of flame from the nose cannons. I saw these a microsecond before I heard the screams from the jeeps and the spattering of bullets on metal, sand and rock.

And then came the earth-jarring booms as the shells from the 20mm cannons exploded in the desert.

"Turn off your lights!" the officer in the first jeep was shouting over and over. "Turn off your lights and shoot them down."

The lights went off and I made my move while the six fighter planes were circling for another run. The pilots didn't need lights now; they already had a good fix on the four jeeps.

I ran down the east side of the dune toward the jeep that had held me in its lights. Two soldiers were dead from machine-gun bullets, an officer was wounded and the driver was merely sitting behind the wheel, stunned into inaction. I hustled the two survivors out of the jeep and hopped into the driver's seat.

As I made the turn, with engine thundering and wheels spitting up rocks, I saw the dark shadows of the planes returning. I floored the gas pedal and shot off westward, my lights out, but still an easy target from above.

Fortunately the fighter planes were too fast for their own good. They were already committed to a run on the same area. By the time their bullets and shells were tearing up a hunk of North Africa and killing more soldiers in the remaining three jeeps, I was tooling off in a southwesterly direction, a good mile from the assault site.

But I knew the planes would come for me.

The jeep was humming along on smooth sand now in the highest possible gear. I ran it flat out for a couple more miles, then turned straight south. I never heard the plane coming behind me; I sensed it. I turned my head just in time to see the first tongues of flame from the wing.

That's when I started the dangerous zigzagging on the roadless sand. The jeep was hitting sixty and each time I jerked on the wheel to avoid bullets from above, the wheels dug in deeply and the jeep almost turned over.

But it didn't turn all the way. When the plane was past me and not one bullet had made its target—me—I jerked the wheel to the right and made a beeline toward the Atlantic coast, heading west again. A straight course would have brought me to the ocean between Rabat and Casablanca, but I would still be stranded, with a long walk to face. When the plane didn't come back, I nudged the jeep southwest and headed for Casablanca.

It was past midnight when I saw the city's lights and found a paved road. The road was empty. I put the jeep into the four-wheel drive, climbed the embankment and moved along smoothly toward the famous port city. I was still a half hour away from the first signs of civilization, so I took time to think.

I knew that Hawk would have fed my report, via the sub's radio, into a computer bank at AXE's headquarters in Washington. All agents used the computer banks to learn what was going on in the world—through the eyes of AXE. I had used it years ago to learn a month ahead of time that a rebel named Fidel Castro was going to launch his final drive to eliminate President Batista. I had used it to learn what was going on with Big Daddy Amin in Uganda, and more recently, to learn about the activities of NOTCH.

The computer bank was designed to keep agents abreast of world developments through reports from other AXE agents. The computers could tell us, almost to the minute, where each agent was located and what his assignment was. Obviously, the agent who had sold out was checking the computer on a regular basis, heard my report and knew that I was being dropped off near Tangier. This agent, as well as Hawk, also knew that I would not do the obvious. That is, I would not go directly into Tangier, as ordered, and arrange a flight to Paris.

The agent had guessed that I would head for Rabat or Casablanca, had alerted the Moroccan Army, or possibly mercenaries who had been in the pay of NOTCH, to have me picked up and efficiently disposed of, to use Hawk's words.

If my deductions were accurate, it would be a simple

chore, once I was back in friendly civilization, to find out which agent was using the AXE computer most often. That would not prove the man to be a double agent, but it would be a starting point.

To avoid further chances—especially since my side was damned near killing me—I left the jeep at a closed gasoline station on the edge of Casablanca. I pulled it behind the station, wedging it between a huge, wrecked truck and a line of junked cars. It might not be found for a week.

As I walked along the deserted streets of the suburbs, I tried to figure out the fighter planes. There was no figuring them, unless perhaps the agent who had warned the Army about me had also warned the Air Force that alien forces were out on the desert south of Tangier. Instead of working two sides of the street, the agent could be trying to work *all* sides of the street, plus the middle, selling information to anybody who would buy.

By sending in the Air Force to attack the Army sent to capture me, the agent was hedging his bet. He knew that I might escape the Army, so he threw in the fighter planes for good measure.

I was developing a pretty sizable dislike—mingled with professional respect—for the AXE agent who had sold out.

And, at the moment, I was beginning to think that my enemies might not have to go to any more trouble to eliminate me: the bandage around my torso was soaked red and the pain stabbed like hot needles. The brief scuffle on the desert had apparently torn out stitches and I was bleeding profusely.

And what had the Navy doctor said? No strenuous activities for a while, then have the bandage changed in five days. Easy for him to say. What doctor anywhere would change the bandage on an obvious bullet wound and not report the incident to local police? I couldn't afford to get mixed up with any more local authorities.

There was one hope: Raina Missou. If she were in her apartment, my immediate problems would be solved. All of them. Raina was a secretary with a small oil export company, but she spent most of her time and talents helping the Moroccan rebels who wanted the Spanish out of the country. With her contacts, Raina Missou could easily find a reliable doctor who would fix up my wound and keep his big mouth shut.

* * *

Raina opened the door a crack and I caught a glimpse of that gorgeous golden—a little sleepy at the moment—face. Raina was part Spanish, part Moroccan and part Chinese, one hell of a delightful combination. She had skin like the surface of unpolished gold, breasts like ripe melons and a sexual drive almost equal to mine.

"Nick," she said as she undid the chain hasp and swung the door all the way open. "Oh, you look like some kind of hell."

"Nice welcome," I replied.

"I mean," she said, stepping back for me to enter the dark apartment, "you look so pale. Are you sick?"

I looked her over good before I strode to a chair and collapsed into it. She wore a diaphanous nightgown that seemed as though it would dissipate under a soft breeze. Outlined against the window, I could see the shape of her body; her high breasts with the dark aureoles of her nipples, her wide hips narrowing into perfectly-shaped legs, her tight little waist, the wedge of dark hair where her legs began.

Raina fixed me a strong scotch on ice, which I gulped down, and I explained part of what had happened. I couldn't wait five days to have the bandage changed. With stitches torn, I needed more than a mere change.

"No problem with that," she said in her mellow, sing-song voice. Her big dark eyes studied my face with curiosity and concern. "Are you certain there are no other problems?"

"Nothing else that can't be handled later," I said, grinning. "Can you swing a doctor?"

She smiled, knowing what could be handled later. "I can swing anything, big man," she said. She went to the telephone, spoke rapidly in Spanish, forgetting that I knew the language well, and talked to a doctor. She was straight. I drank two more scotches and chatted easily with Raina, holding down a rising desire to tumble into her bed with her, before the doctor arrived.

The doctor was small, swarthy and crisp. He had no sense of humor and didn't think anybody else should have one. He did, however, admire the work done by the Navy doctor, and did not appreciate the fact that I had undone much of that good work.

He hit me with a local anesthetic, pulled out all the old stitches and sewed me up again. He outdid himself with the bandage, trying to emulate the skill of the Navy doc. He wound me up so tight that I could hardly breathe.

When he was gone, along with a hundred dollars worth of my Spanish pesos, I turned to Raina. She had watched everything with great concern and I knew that she held a small pistol behind her lovely back. If the doctor had tried anything treacherous, he would have been one dead, humorless doctor.

I went to the bed and took off my boots and trousers. The doctor had already removed my shirt and jacket. I motioned for Raina. She shook her head.

"Not tonight, my wonderful lover. I don't want to have to call the doctor back again. Perhaps in a few days."

"I don't have a few days. Come here. I have a plan."

"No plan," she said. "We wait."

I skimmed out of my jockey shorts and watched her dark eyes as she watched the rising hardness at my middle. I knew her weaknesses, just as she knew mine.

"You dirty dog," Raina said as she turned out the overhead light and moved slowly toward the bed. "That's not a nice thing to do."

"Feels very nice to me," I said. "Make it all feel nicer before the novocaine wears off."

She slid into bed beside me and worked the filmy nightgown over her head. It dropped without a sound on the floor. My hands moved out to cup her swelling breasts and her head went down to kiss me just beneath the bandage. Her head went lower and I lurched upward at the softness of her lips on such a sensitive part of me.

"Is this your plan?" she said between small, darting kisses with her lips and tongue.

"Not quite. Swing over on top. I'll just relax and enjoy it while you do all the work."

She raised her head and looked at me. Soft hands caressed my face and I felt the tips of her breasts brush lightly against my upper chest.

"Just make sure you relax," she ordered.

I didn't. I couldn't. Once her legs were spread across me and I felt her soft wetness, I began to squirm with impatience and ecstasy. She lowered her body and I felt us joining, smoothly, easily, beautifully. She moved from side to side and I began to thrash on the bed. My hands came around her and my fingers dug into her soft, golden buttocks.

Only because all the gods of sex and love seem to be looking out for my welfare did I manage to pull off the sweet interlude of love without doing more damage to my body. Only Raina's immense struggle to please permitted me to survive with a clean bandage and intact stitches. Otherwise, it was an incredible display of lovemaking that left me satiated, delectably tired and dreamily sleepy.

"That was a good plan," Raina murmured. And then she was beside me and I felt safe and cool in the North African night.

Chapter Four

Dawn brought rain and a cooling air. I nestled deeper into the covers and watched while Raina moved about the little apartment fixing *guato*, a Jamaican dish of eggs, mangos and onions—and which tastes like pig brains.

"I have a good friend who can fix up new papers," she said in her sing-song voice as she dropped food into the hot skillet, "but it will take some time. Do you have a name you want to use, or shall I pick one for you?"

"You pick one," I said sleepily. "I think old Hawk knows too well how my mind works. He'd spot any name that I chose."

"How about 'John Smith?'"

"How about something a little more imaginative?"

"All right. Starting soon, you will be Pierre Cantrell."

"No dice," I said, shaking myself back out of sleep that wouldn't be denied. "I have a weapon by the name of Pierre. Hawk would recognize it in a minute."

It was important that I go undercover with an airtight identity that would fool even David Hawk. So far, Robert Cronin and his cronies had figured out my every move, and it was a certain bet that they knew I was heading for Paris. My assignment had been lodged in the computers in Washington. Someone was tapping information from those computers. But there was one thing the computers didn't have: my next undercover identity.

If I could fool David Hawk, I could fool anybody.

They wouldn't have the slightest notion of who to look for in Paris.

"Alex Carson," Raina said gleefully. "That will be your new name. You'll be a tractor salesman. Okay?"

"Okay," I mumbled and drifted off to sleep. It came thickly now, erasing the pain in my side and making the rain on the roof sound far away—and somehow comforting. I could smell the pungent aroma of *guato* cooking on the stove, and then even that was gone.

I dreamed of walking down streets so soft that I could not feel my feet on the pavement. But the sun felt warm on my body and the breeze rumpled my hair pleasantly and the dream went on and on, undulating like ocean waves or Virginia mountains.

When I awoke again, it was night and I was hungry as hell. Raina sat in an easy chair beside the bed, watching me. I felt safe and comfortable and the pain in my side had idled to a tolerable throb.

"You sleep like the dead."

"I am dead, remember?" I said, rubbing my eyes open. "But I've forgotten my new name."

"Alex Carson, but it isn't your name yet." She leaned forward and her breasts shifted inside her loose blouse. "My friend says it will take a day or two to cut new identity papers. You should be plenty rested by then."

I sat up and dropped my feet over the side of the bed. I was surprised when I could feel the cool floor on my feet. In the dream, I could feel nothing down there.

"Yeah, rest," I said, running fingers through my hair to get it out of my eyes. "Rest, food and you, in that order. I've had enough rest for now, but I'm hungrier than a wingless owl. After a quick meal, let's discuss you."

She smiled and got up. In three minutes, she brought in a tray loaded with albacore stuffed with shrimp, papaya juice sweetened with honey, a dozen kinds of pastries and a bottle of wine. I cracked that first and we toasted.

Even as we drank to each other's health, my mind was on David Hawk. In all the years I had worked for that enigmatic and stern boss, I had never seen him quite so tense as he had been aboard the submarine. He had been threatened before, and by formidable forces. But he seemed particularly moved by the threat from Cronin. Perhaps it was because Cronin seemed to have a hold over the Mafia and the Corse. The threat was not just from an American executive gone sour; it was from quarters so inventive and powerful and merciless that no man in his right mind could take it lightly. Sooner or later, unless the threat were removed, it could be made good. Hawk was in tremendous danger, no matter how powerful he might be. He had to strike back—hard and soon.

Wide awake now, I was anxious to get moving. I had to get to Paris, find Diane Northrup/Elaine Withers, and pick her brains for every scrap of information that might lead me to her boss.

"I'm sorry about the delay with your papers," Raina said as I dived into the delicious stuffed fish. "It can't be helped."

"No problem," I said, making my voice light. "If I can't go tomorrow, I'll go the next day. Or the next."

"But you're angry with me."

"I could never be angry with you."

"Yes, you are," she said, frowning her face into deep, bronze wrinkles. "I can tell by the tone of your voice. Why are you so hell-bent to get to Paris?"

I stopped eating and gazed at her lovely face for several seconds. I put my hand on hers and squeezed lightly.

"You know I can't tell you, Raina," I said. "I'm sorry to be so preoccupied, but take my word for it—I really have to get to Paris as soon as possible. It's a matter of life or death to someone very close to me."

"A woman?"

"No," I said. "A very special man. There's nobody on earth like him and this would be a sorry place without him. That's all I can tell you. He's in danger and I have to head off that danger before it moves in for the kill. Do you understand that?"

"Yes." She squeezed my hand. "Go on and eat. I won't

ask questions. You can trust me, as always. Tomorrow, I'll get your new identity papers and help you out of the country. Meanwhile, you sleep.''

The rain was gone with the next dawn. So was my fatigue and my seemingly insatiable need for sleep. Raina was there with a fresh dish of *guato* and I ate it with relish, savoring every bite.

When I was finished with my bath, Raina was gone. Perhaps today, she had said, she would get my papers. But I couldn't wait for the new papers to get the investigation started.

It was important that I find out which agents had used the computer bank immediately following my report to Hawk, and his subsequent filing of that report with Washington. There was a simple method for such checking, but a check at this time was dangerous. It would reveal my whereabouts to the computer—and to anyone checking it.

But I had no choice.

A dilapidated taxi took me into the center of Casablanca. At the central telephone exchange there, a man could make an anonymous telephone call to anyplace in the world and never be noticed. I put two dirham into the coin slot and got the central operator. I gave the code number and waited while the telephone clicked and the voices of colorful Berber tribesmen, in town to wash off the sheep smell and get drunk on coconut wine, rattled around me.

After a full minute, the clicking stopped and a cool, almost mechanical voice said:

"Report."

"No report," I said, feeling foolish because I was actually talking to a machine. "A check."

The voice cracked: "Check, then."

"Require knowledge on who used computer bank on July 22, between hours of 2100 and midnight Moroccan time, whether use was to report or to check on other agents, and whether use was normal or extravagant."

"One moment please," the artificial voice crackled over the telephone.

I waited, watching with some amusement while a big Berber with a turban argued vociferously with a wiry little Frenchman. They were arguing in a mixture of Arabic and French, so I couldn't follow the drift very well. In substance, the argument was over a woman—what else?

"At 2245 July 22, Agent N78 filed report. At 2340, Agent N22 submitted request for check on Agent N3 and one nameless person. First part of check complied with, second part denied and agent admonished because use was extravagant. Further check?"

"No," I said, and almost added a thank you. "Signing off."

"Goodbye."

Outside, I walked slowly and digested the information gleaned from the computer. Agent N78 was a fairly new man with AXE, John Crawford, who was in Australia. N22 was a veteran with AXE, a tough-minded little nam named Dave Snyder. The nameless person mentioned by the computer was none other than David Hawk. I wasn't surprised that N22 had checked on me, and had tried to check on the chief. It was certainly extravagant use, checking on Hawk, but Snyder had been guilty of extravagant use before.

And, it looked as though Snyder was the turncoat agent, the man providing Robert Cronin and his organization with information on my whereabouts.

It was not news that they knew I was in Morocco. It was not really news to me that Snyder was probably the traitor. I had suspected him for months. What *was* news, was his incredible boldness. Snyder, who had just completed an assignment in South Africa was on a month's leave of absence. The last time I checked on him, he was touring diamond mines in the Orange Free State. That was two weeks ago.

The question now was: Where was Snyder, Agent N22?

I didn't want to recheck the computer. It would reveal that

I had made the check on Snyder, directly and implicitly, and I didn't want to do anything to tip their hand that I was suspicious of N22.

As I walked back to Raina Missou's apartment, circling back numerous times to throw off any possible tails, I wondered idly just how long it would be before we taught computers how to kill. One thing I had learned in going up against tremendous odds was that it would be folly to go up against anything as complex and as heartless as a computer. It would be the perfect killing machine because it had no conscience.

Night was hot. Ridiculously so. We pulled a small cot out onto the patio and lay gazing up at the stars and listening to the sounds of the city. Voices rose shrilly, in Spanish, Arabic, French and English—plus a few languages with which I had only a nodding acquaintance. We had made love (with difficulty) as soon as Raina had come home, then she had made a dinner of beef and pork shish kebob with brown rice. Delicious on all counts.

Then the heat wave came in off the North Atlantic and outdid the afternoon sun.

"What's the big holdup on the papers?" I asked again, hiding my irritation as well as possible. "Who's cutting them for me?"

"I can't tell you that, love," she said, tracing a finger down the cleft in my chin and resting the tip on my Adam's apple. "You have your secrets and I have mine. Let's not mingle them, okay?"

"Okay." I knew she wouldn't—and shouldn't—tell me her source for fake identity papers, but I was so irritated that I asked anyway. "That still doesn't explain the holdup."

"These things take time."

I sighed and took a deep gulp of hot air. It was quite unsatisfactory.

"Too much time. A few months ago, you had some cut for me in about four hours."

"They'll be ready early tomorrow," Raina said, moving the finger down my bare chest to my bare belly. "And you have an airline ticket under the name of Alex Carson. By noon, you'll be far out over the Mediterranean, safe from the Moroccan Army and everybody else in North Africa.''

"Let's hope so," I said.

When I awoke just after dawn, Raina had left to get my new papers. I dressed slowly and meticulously, taping Pierre, the gas bomb, neatly behind my testicles, and Wilhelmina, the 9mm Luger, under my arm just above the bandage. Hugo, my stiletto, was strapped tightly to my forearm.

The suit Raina had obtained for me was checkered and loud, just the ticket for a tractor salesman. It made a baggy fit, and that was fine. It covered my weapons well. She returned at 10 a.m. with the papers.

"I would drive you to the airport, my love, but I think it would be better for you to go by taxi. After all, you are supposed to be a salesman, not somebody's lover."

I smiled. "Couldn't I be both?"

"Not this trip," she said, sliding easily into my arms for a farewell kiss. "Perhaps another time when the whole Army isn't looking for you."

"Plus others," I said.

"Yes." She was silent and we kissed. Then: "When will I see you again?"

It seemed as though a dark cloud moved across my mind at that moment. With it came the horrible premonition that I would never see Raina Missou again. Possibly she would be killed, murdered by someone who saw me leaving her flat. Possibly I would be killed, either at the airport by the Army, or in Paris by God-knew-who. I shook off the cloud.

"I'll come this way again," I said. "No matter where I am or what I'm doing, I'll always find the time and the opportunity to come to you, Raina. Didn't you just say that I'm your lover?"

"Yes. Oh yes. Please be careful and please come back soon."

I nodded and left the flat with an old suitcase she had given me. It was a poor item to remember her by.

Chapter Five

As the taxi approached the airport, I should have been warned by the numerous military vehicles parked at intersections and the flyovers of military aircraft. But I was not warned. My mind was ahead, on what I would find in Paris, on Diane Northrup/Elaine Withers, who wittingly or unwittingly was helping to try to destroy me, AXE and David Hawk.

When the taxi sped along the entry ramp to the terminal, past guards and even more vehicles, my mind was on evening when I would be with Diane to get the answers to a number of questions. It was only a two-hour flight to Paris, but I was going first to Algiers. From there, I wasn't certain where I would go to shake off any pursuers, but I knew I wouldn't reach Paris before nightfall.

At the terminal, I tipped generously, giving the driver all my remaining dirham. The driver pocketed the money without acknowledgement and sped away. I saw the source of his haste when I turned with my suitcase and walked into the crowded building. The main concourse and waiting room was filled with soldiers.

They were stopping virtually everyone, checking papers, asking questions. I smiled at them and started across the wide concourse to the El-Moroc flight desk.

"Pardon me, sir," a slim Army captain said as he touched my arm to stop me. "May we see your papers?"

Flanking him were two burly soldiers, each with a stolen Israeli M-27 submachine gun.

"Why, sure," I said jovially, letting a Midwest American twang alter my speech. "What's all the hoopla? Somebody try to get the king again?"

In 1972, several high-ranking Moroccan Air Force fighter pilots had formed a small coup and tried to murder the king. I wasn't trying to be funny. I knew I was in trouble the moment the skinny captain stopped me. Even as I reached for my papers, my hand was itching to get at Wilhelmina, nestled comfortably under my arm. I could get the papers and the gun all in one gesture if I wanted, but I decided to wait. Perhaps the papers would suffice.

The captain studied them for some time. He studied my photo and my face, then read more. The soldiers shifted impatiently from foot to foot and moved nervous, sweaty hands on their automatic weapons.

The captain smiled.

"Everything is in order, Mr. Carson," he said, handing back my phony papers. "Please don't leave the terminal again, though. Stay until your plane leaves."

"Certainly," I replied, remembering to keep the twang. "Say, what's going on, anyway?"

He responded without his smile. "Your guess was closer to the truth than you realize," he said. "We have information that a lunatic American spy was dropped by helicopter near Tangier several days ago."

"A lunatic?"

"Yes," the captain said. "His mission is to murder the king."

"I hope to hell he fails," I said. "I want to come back and sell tractors someday."

"I'm certain he will fail, Mr. Carson," the captain said, smiling again. "And we do need those tractors."

I nodded and moved on toward the desk.

And there stood the biggest obstacle of the day.

Colonel Ahmed Khattabi, one of the men who had put down the revolt of 1972—and a man who knew me well because of my part in that revolt— was standing with other officers near the desk. I had been in Morocco during the 1972 attempt to kill the king, but I had nothing to do with the attempted assassination.

But Colonel Khattabi had been convinced, that I was one of the ringleaders, on assignment from the American government.

He saw me just as I turned to leave the airport.

"Stop that man," his shrill voice cracked in the crowded terminal. "Stop him, he's getting away!"

And I was. I reached the door before anyone could respond to Colonel Khattabi's hysterical screaming. The slim captain was in my path, but I bowled him over and, dropping the suitcase Raina had given me, I plunged through the open doorway.

Outside, soldiers were turning to see what the fuss was all about. Colonel Khattabi's bellowing came through the door and seemed to fill the street.

I snaked my Luger out of its pouch beneath my arm and made for a jeep where two soldiers were idling in the sun. As I ran across the street, I heard the colonel's booming voice behind me. I turned and put one bullet between his eyes.

The shot and the sight of Colonel Khattabi's falling body seemed to galvanize everyone in sight—soldiers and civilians alike.

But the two men beside the jeep brought up their automatic weapons as I rushed toward them.

Wilhelmina boomed twice more and the soldiers crumpled and fell. Just as I swung into the jeep, feeling a stinging pain in my side from the exertion, bullets whanged off the vehicle's bumper. I started the engine and slammed down the gear lever. The tires squealed as the jeep bucked forward in a tight circle. I made a sharp U-turn and dashed out the entrance ramp, going the wrong way against traffic.

An entire fusillade crashed behind me and bullets plunked and whanged and crackled into the seats, metal and windshield of the speeding jeep. Glass shot into the air around my face and I felt the wind directly on me. The windshield was gone.

As I reached the corner of the terminal, a military personnel carrier roared up the ramp from the highway. It was loaded with armed soldiers.

Hitting the brakes, I steered the jeep off the road and across the lawn, heading toward the parking lot. At the same time, I slid my left hand into my trousers and pulled the tiny gas bomb from between my legs. Looking back, I saw that the truck had also left the road and was rumbling after me across the grass.

To the left of the parking lot was a small service road that ran along the highway for a mile or so to a couple of remote hangars. As I headed for that road, I checked the distance between me and the truckload of soldiers, calculated the time it would take them to reach the point where I was at that moment, and pulled the pin on Pierre. I tossed the little bomb over my shoulder and jammed down hard on the gas pedal.

I heard the pop of the bomb and looked back to see the cloud of light blue smoke engulfing the truck.

Perfect timing.

Pierre had gone off ten feet in front of the truck and the driver had rumbled straight into the rising blue cloud of highly lethal gas.

I couldn't hear the gasps and screams of the soldiers. The roar of the jeep's laboring engine was too loud. But the truck never came out of that cloud.

But I was far from safe.

I knew that the word would be out via radio and that soldiers up ahead would be looking for me. As I steered the jeep up the bank to the highway, I started looking for a car to commandeer.

It came before I had gone a mile. It was a black limousine, an American Lincoln Continental. And an important-looking man with a briefcase was in the back seat. I caught up with the limousine, passed it and pulled in fast in front. The driver cursed but braked hard to avoid hitting the jeep.

When we were dead still, I leaped out and ran to the car. Holding the Luger tightly, I gave terse commands in French:

"I need this car. Outside, quickly."

No response. The man and his driver stared at me as

though I had dropped from outer space. Traffic whizzed past. Although I was certain they understood French, I gave them the benefit of the doubt and repeated my commands in Arabic, then English, then Spanish.

It all took only a few seconds, but time seemed to be loping along like a crippled hippopotamus.

When the man and his driver did not respond, I placed the barrel of the Luger directly behind the left ear of the important-looking fellow and repeated my request leaving no doubt about the alternative. The bewildered and frightened pair hurriedly complied.

As I sped away, I could see a whole convoy of military vehicles rumbling out of the airport, more than a mile back.

The Lincoln was soon roaring along at a hundred miles an hour.

I passed four exit ramps and took the fifth. The Lincoln soared down the ramp and into virtually empty streets. The noon rush had not yet started.

After a dozen blocks, I abandoned the Lincoln and ran down a narrow alley to the city's main thoroughfare, which was crowded.

It took me two more hours to wend my way through the heart of the city to Raina Missou's apartment in the south sector.

I was exhausted, my wound was open and bleeding again and the pain was intolerable.

When she opened the door, I passed out in her arms.

The next two days went slowly as hell and I ran up a monstrous debt to the lovely Raina Missou, part Spanish, part Moroccan and part Chinese. Raina brought another doctor to tend to my wound and arranged for a fishing boat to take me out of the country.

And I had to leave. I was out of touch with Hawk, and I knew that time and our enemies would not stand still. Every hour that passed made the danger greater for David Hawk. Even as I waited in Raina's apartment, and soldiers patrolled the streets of Casablanca looking for me, I was fearful that Cronin and Snyder were putting their plot into motion.

"I'll be back to repay you for all this," I told Raina as we rode toward the harbor in the early hours, more than two days after I had escaped with my life at the airport. The streets were almost deserted and I thanked God for that.

"You owe me nothing, my love," she said in her delightful, sing-song voice. She cuddled close in the back seat of the car and I felt her heavy breasts against my arm. "If I had my way, you would stay here forever."

"That sounds nice. I wish it could be so."

I kept my eyes on the driver, a small, swarthy Arab dressed in old khaki clothes. He was trustworthy, Raina had said, as was the captain of the little fishing boat, but I trusted no one.

We reached the harbor without incident and the driver parked in the shadow of a huge warehouse. We sat for several minutes gazing out at the huddled mixture of pleasure boats, freighters, passenger ships, and fishing schooners.

An hour before dawn, a fishing boat chugged into the harbor, eased along a dark pier and cut its engine. I started to get out, but the driver grunted and waved me back. In that moment, he won my trust. Two soldiers, armed with automatic weapons, ran down the dock and streaked out onto the pier. We couldn't hear their conversation, but the skipper of the fishing boat apparently was convincing. After a few minutes, the soldiers went back south along the dock and disappeared into the darkness.

"Now," the driver said.

I kissed Raina goodbye and got out into the shadows.

"*Monsieur*, you must go now. The soldiers will return."

I gripped my Luger tightly under my coat and ran out to the pier. I swung aboard the boat just as the engines rumbled to life. Back toward the warehouse I could see the headlights flicker on the car. The boat eased out into the harbor, speeded up and headed for open sea.

We were going to Lisbon, where I could more or less safely board a plane for Paris.

I simply could not afford to let anything else go wrong now.

During the entire trip to Lisbon, I kept Wilhelmina in my hand, ready to fire the last four bullets at any obstacle, human or otherwise, that got in my way.

Chapter Six

The voyage was so uneventful that I could have slept the whole way. But I stayed awake until I was on the plane to Paris. Then I awoke only when LeBourget was below, surrounded by the almost iridescent triangles of farmland that distinguish the European countryside from America's.

My cover as Alex Carson held up through customs, thanks to Raina's foresight in getting me a Spanish passport, and I was soon in a taxi speeding into the city where Diane Northrup would be staying at the George Cinq Hotel.

Before going to the hotel, I went to a small office on the Champs Elysee, two blocks from the Arc de Triomphe. On the front window of the office, facing the famous boulevard, was the sign:

ALMAGATED PRESS & WIRE SERVICES
Paris Bureau

The man behind the desk in the office barely looked up when I flashed the solid gold card which I had recently been issued by Washington. I wrote out a note for the man. He grunted and nodded toward the back room. I went in and eased into a chair and lifted the telephone receiver.

"Report," the mechanical voice ordered after I had dialed.

In a running—and somewhat monotonous—conversation with the AXE computer in Washington, I reported that Agent N3 had arrived in Paris, then learned that N22 (Dave Snyder) had been checking in regularly, even though he was still on leave. Snyder was speedily becoming more than a suspicion in my mind. Even though the word was not official that he was a counteragent, I knew that I would treat him as one if I saw him. And there was every likelihood that I would see him as soon as he checked the computer again.

When I returned to the front office, the man behind the desk nodded toward a small package on the high counter. I picked it up on my way out, knowing that it would contain three new gas bombs and a dozen clips for my Luger. It was what I had requisitioned on my note when I came in, and the man would have supplied them without question. Standard operating procedure.

The afternoon was balmy but breezy on the boulevard and I couldn't resist the tables and chairs—and bustling, happy activity—of a sidewalk cafe. I sat, ordered a martini, and let my mind relax while I watched people go past on foot and in all manner of vehicles. The Champs Elysee is one of the most fascinating places in the world, although it is only a few blocks long. What the avenue lacks in size, it more than makes up for in intensity and pure excitement.

I finished my drink and walked up to Avenue George V, then down the crowded street to the baroque old hotel. George Cinq. Tall, wide, thick and as comfortable as a ten-year-old bedroom slipper.

I checked in as Alex Carson and the desk clerk gave me the eyebrow treatment. He knew me under a dozen names and was surprised that I was signing in with a new one. I usually rotated the dozen names I use around the world, but danger was so intense now that I had to break out of the mold. I couldn't care less if old acquaintances like desk clerks were surprised.

"Welcome back to the George Cinq, *Monsieur*—ah—Carson," the clerk said, smiling and winking. "I hope your stay this time will be far more enjoyable than the last."

He was referring to a year ago when five thugs hired by a Marseille drug dealer broke into my room, beat me senseless and left me for dead.

I winked back at the clerk.

"It will be," I said. "Do you have a Diane Northrup staying here? Or an Elaine Withers?"

He checked, although I was certain that he had the information on the tip of his French tongue.

"*Oui*," he said with another smile and another wink. "*Mademoiselle* Northrup is in room 1122. I believe *monsieur* knows where the elevator is located."

"I do." I gave him a ten-franc note and returned his wink, then found the tiny elevator that resembled a medieval torture cage.

The elevator clanked and whirred and wheezed, but finally made it to the tenth floor. Once in my room, I slid a new clip into Wilhelmina, taped Pierre behind my balls, stuck two extra clips in my pocket and stashed the remainder of my firepower behind a drawer. Now I was ready for Diane Northrup, or Elaine Withers, and any story she might have for me.

I took the stairs to the next floor and was relieved to find that my side didn't hurt during the climb. The two days of rest at Raina's apartment, followed by another two days on the fishing boat, had allowed me to recover fully.

As I knocked, I checked my watch. It was 3:22 p.m. Diane Northrup opened the door after my second knock. Her eyes glowed with what seemed to be genuine happiness to see me.

"Oh Brad," she squealed. And she was in my arms.

Hard to believe that this woman could be so spontaneous, or that she could blurt out the cover name I had given her, since she obviously knew my real name. It was even harder to believe that, within ten minutes, I might have to beat the truth out of her. She felt great against my body. Her ample bosom crushed against my chest and her wide hips moved hard into mine.

I savored the delicate perfume I remembered from Calcutta, then held her at arm's length to look at her. She had long golden hair and eyes bluer than Mediterranean water at noonday. Her voice was husky and sensuous, her mouth wide and brightly colored with crimson lipstick. Her skin was aglow and was almost translucent with the joy of life.

"Oh, darling Brad," she said, kissing me again. "I heard you were dead."

"Yeah," I said, moving into the room and closing the door. "We have to talk about that, among other things."

"Talk about what?"

"About where you get your information on me and my activities," I said, my eyes flitting around her suite to make certain that we were alone. "And about you passing along information to certain individuals—one in particular."

"Why, Brad," she said, her blue eyes glowing with innocence, "I haven't the slightest idea of what you're talk—"

I slapped her pretty face and almost felt the pain of it on my own cheek.

"Cut it, Elaine," I said. "You should know enough about me by now to realize that I'm not buying. I'm taking. Now, we must have that little talk."

She looked gloomily at me and her eyes seemed to fade into gray. Her fabulous body slumped and she sank heavily into a chair.

"So you know my real name," she said, her voice about to crack. "What else do you know?"

"For starters, I know that you know my real name as well."

As I talked, I moved about the rooms, inspecting closets and the bathroom, then sat opposite the lovely blonde. She was wearing a pale yellow knit dress and she looked good enough to eat. What a damned pity, my mind kept repeating. Very soon, I may be messing up this lovely sight before me, to get the truth.

And she looked so incredibly innocent and harmless. I lit up a gold-embossed cigarette.

"I know that our meeting on that plane to Paris about seven weeks ago was no accident, and that your later appearance in Calcutta was also deliberate. I know that you work for a man named Robert Cronin and that you have been feeding him information on me and several other AXE agents. I know that at least one agent you met has crossed over to Cronin's side—and I have all the proof I need as to which agent has become a traitor. I have to kill him. You're going to help make it easier. You're going to make a lot of things easier.''

She kept shaking her head slowly as I talked, as though my words could not be tolerated, or as though what I said brought out painful truths and memories that she wanted to forget. I stopped to let her say her piece, convinced that she would lie and I would have to commence taking her apart, lovely limb from lovely limb.

''All right, Nick Carter,'' she said, spreading her hands with palms up in a gesture of honesty, a gesture that said she would reveal everything she knew. I hoped she was being straight with me. Otherwise, she would wind up mighty crooked, in body and mind, before I was finished. ''What can I tell you?''

''Start at the beginning,'' I said, crunching out my cigarette and taking another from the case. I let the special cigarette dangle, unlit, while I sniffed the comfortable Turkish aroma. ''Don't leave anything out. You have been on a recruitment campaign for Robert Cronin and I want to know who you have contacted among AXE agents and why Cronin wants to destroy us.''

She shook her head violently. ''That's a tall order for a girl who was nothing more than a secretary a few months ago.''

''You'll have to be a bit more explicit,'' I snapped, leaning forward, swallowing hard and preparing myself for getting the truth by force if necessary.

Diane/Elaine swallowed hard also, then began her story. It had a ring of truth, several rings of truth. A year ago, she had gone to work for Cronin's drug company in its headquarters in New York. She had begun as a secretary to a company vice president, but was quickly promoted to private secretary for the big man himself. Three months ago, Cronin had told her that a number of pharmaceutical salesmen for the company were siphoning off hard drugs and selling them to syndicates for illegal street use.

Cronin then offered her a dream job: to travel around the world to meet those ''salesmen'' and to find out as much as she could about them. All her findings were to be channeled back to Cronin. She was to be extra nice to the so-called salesmen, even to the point of convincing them that she loved them and then sleeping with them.

"I know nothing about AXE, or whatever you call it, and I know nothing about agents," she concluded. "I only know that all of the men I met were like you, involved in some kind of secret activities. But I supposed that the secrecy was because of the danger of the job. I mean, stealing drugs and selling them to syndicate people is hardly the safest thing in the world to do."

"Tell me about the note you delivered to Amalgamated Press and Wire Services in Washington not long after we had been together in Calcutta."

She sat up straight, her pretty mouth open in surprise. She tried to speak, but only her lips and jaw worked. No sounds came out.

"Come on, sweetheart," I said, flexing my right hand in anticipation of a slap of encouragement. "You'll have to do better than that."

"My God, Nick," she said, "that had nothing to do with you—or with whatever it is you do for a living. I had returned to New York to give Mr. Cronin a personal report on our meetings in Paris and Calcutta. When I was finished, he told me to go to Stockholm to meet a salesman named James Lobell. Before I left, he gave me a press release to deliver to Amalgamated in Washington."

"A courier service:" I asked, arching both eyebrows. "Why didn't he just mail it?"

She shrugged her round, supple shoulders and her breasts jiggled in the tight knit dress. "He said it was too important to trust to the mails, and wanted me to deliver it to the head of Amalgamated, personally."

"So you thought you were taking a press release to Washington?"

"Of course. Wasn't it a press release?"

I sat looking at the beautiful woman for a very long time. I have listened to liars and I have listened to innocent people. Generally, I could tell the difference. But not with this girl.

She exuded pure innocence and I was tempted to become a believer. But I had been had that way before. I decided to wait a bit before knocking her lovely body around the room.

"I want the names of all the so-called salesmen you wined and dined and bedded down with, under Cronin's orders."

She blushed. "Nick, I did sleep with several of them, but you know that I love you."

"Sure."

"I really do." She stared at me and tears bubbled into her eyes, threatening to leak down her cheeks.

I waited, suppressing an urge to take her into my arms to comfort her, to tell her that everything was going to be all right. Because everything just might not be all right. She regained her composure, with the help of a handkerchief, and told me the names of the men she had contacted under Cronin's instructions. The list was formidable, headed by Dave Snyder, N22. In fact, she had been with N22 in Cannes only two weeks ago, and had seen him seven different times since beginning her snoop job for Cronin.

"I forgot to tell you one more thing," she said. "I don't know if it's important."

"Let's try it out and see if it's important."

She shifted in her chair and crossed her legs, inadvertently (or perhaps purposely) giving me a tremendous view of her chalk-white thighs. I lit up another cigarette and pretended great calm.

"I was to offer them a chance to get in on a profitable but illegal operation involving drugs," she said. "To find out just how currupt they really were."

"You never offered me any such deal," I said, reviving my suspicions that she was lying through her teeth.

"I know. I intended to, but I decided against it the first time we met."

"Why did you decide against it?"

"I don't really know," she said, shaking her head and gazing directly into my eyes. "There's something about you, Nick, something incorruptible. I knew it would be useless to even try."

"And you reported this back to Cronin?"

"Yes." She lowered her head, as though in shame.

"What about the others? How corruptible did they seem to you?"

"Dave Snyder jumped at the chance. I think he has met with Mr. Cronin, but I don't know for certain. I know that I put him in touch with Mr. Cronin in the New York office."

"And the others?"

She shook her head. "They pretended to be interested, but I suppose they were only trying to find out what my game was. That's my guess. They all seemed straight except Dave Snyder. He seemed downright eager to learn all he could about the deal, and about Mr. Cronin."

"Okay. One more thing." I sat back and smoked while she waited for me to go on. I tried to read her expression, to detect some sign that she was lying. But she sat calmly waiting, her hands folded in her lap. And the hands weren't even perspiring. "That so-called press release you took to Amalgamated in Washington. Do you know that it was a death threat?"

Her eyes widened and her pretty mouth dropped open. She stared at me and made the noiseless, voiceless motions again with her mouth. Then:

"Oh, Nick, you have to be mistaken. Mr. Cronin certainly wouldn't go so far as to kill anyone. Besides, who was he going to kill?"

"*Is* going to kill," I corrected. "The deal is still on. I can't give you details, but it involves an entire organization, starting with the top man. It is a good organization and Cronin has threatened to wipe out every member."

"Is it this AXE you talked about?"

I nodded and watched her face. She seemed genuinely disturbed, genuinely concerned.

"Nick, I don't know anything about AXE or a death threat or agents. What I told you is the truth. If you don't believe me, I suggest you call on Mr. Cronin yourself."

I grinned. "Yeah, he'd like that, wouldn't he? No, baby, I'm not calling on your Mr. Cronin, not in person and not just yet. First, I have to find out if you're telling the truth and if you're willing to work with me.''

She nodded and spread her hands in a gesture of openness.

"I'll do anything you tell me, Nick. And I *am* telling the truth. Do you believe me?"

"We'll soon find out." I took the telephone from the table beside me and handed it to her. "Call your boss in New York," I said. "Tell him that you met with me and that I'm interested in his deal. Tell him I want to arrange a meeting."

We both knew that it would be folly to meet with Robert Cronin. He knew me by reputation, and he knew that I would not become a traitor. Dave Snyder knew it also. All I wanted to do was tip him that I was in Paris, then wait for developments. But I didn't want him to know that I was using myself as bait to draw him, or his associates, into the open.

"Be careful what you say, Diane, or Elaine, whichever name you prefer. You've got to convince him that you believe I'm ready to play turncoat. Okay?"

She nodded and picked up the telephone. After she talked with her boss in New York, I knew that she had been telling me the truth. She did a splendid job. All I had to do was sit back and relax. Results would come before nightfall.

But I did let down.

"Now do you believe me?" Elaine said as we walked arm in arm into the bedroom. She preferred the name Elaine to Diane, because Cronin had chosen the phony name for her. His rationale was that someone might trace Elaine Withers back to him. Now, she didn't trust Cronin or his company, and she truly believed that he was trying to destroy an important organization in the American government, that he was the traitor. She wanted to shed any and all connections with Cronin.

"I believe you," I said as I unzipped the back of her dress and peeled it around her shoulders. The white skin reminded me of balmy Calcutta nights as I stood there holding her soft shoulders and gazing down at the full mounds of her breasts under the pale yellow brassiere.

I slid my hands down her arms and around to cup her

breasts. At the same time, I pressed my groin into her firm
buttocks. Her delicate perfume seemed to surround us and
the thought of having this beautiful and living woman again
filled my head with dreamy thoughts. All danger and pain
and fear seemed far away, far, far away.

In that moment, when I was at my weakest and most
vulnerable, the door crashed open, spilling splinters and
pieces of metal across the floor of the sitting room. Two men
came in with drawn guns. A third stood in the doorway with
an evil grin on his face.

As one man raised his automatic weapon to fire, I pushed
Elaine away from me and went for my Luger, at the same
time leaping back out of the line of fire.

My hand was on Wilhelmina's sturdy butt, my finger on
the trigger. I saw the spits of flame from the muzzle of the
automatic weapon, then heard the chattering. Above this
came the throaty boom of the Luger and the man went down,
firing into the floor.

I caught the second man in my sights just as he was
squeezing the trigger. The Luger and the automatic pistol
went off at the same time, and the man in the doorway made a
flying leap headlong toward the floor.

The bullet from Wilhelmina plunked into his forehead and
he did a slow turn as he went down. I leaped to the bedroom
door and saw the third man scrambling behind a couch,
trying to get his gun out of his holster under his left arm.

I waited for him to get his pistol, then Wilhelmina boomed
twice. He was quiet, but I went into the sitting room to make
sure he was dead. He was.

"It's okay now," I shouted to Elaine Withers. "You can
come up for air. They're all dead."

I heard footsteps in the corridor and knew that I had to get
Elaine Withers and clear out of the hotel. The French police
wouldn't be happy to see either one of us; we would give
them one hell of a puzzle to solve. I really didn't have time to
wonder why men had shown up so quickly after Elaine had
called Cronin in New York. Had they tailed me to the hotel,
or was there a connection between their assault and her

telephone call? I had no time to ponder.

"Elaine:" I called out.

No answer.

Just as a man and a woman appeared at the main door, chattering in French, I ducked back into the bedroom to find out why the woman didn't respond.

My answer was there on the floor, in a widening pool of blood.

Elaine Withers was dead, three bullet wounds in her chest, neck and head.

Even in death, she was beautiful.

I threw a bedspread over her body and went back into the sitting room. People were flocked around the door, so I waved the Luger at them and waded through.

At the elevator, the clerk from the desk saw me and called out: "What happened, *Monsieur*—ah—Carson?"

"Just call the police," I replied as I stepped onto the little cage. "Maybe they can figure it all out."

As the elevator descended, I looked through the grating at the desk clerk. He was grinning.

"I already called the police, *Monsieur* Carter," he said, emphasizing my real name. "Don't you think you should stay and talk with them?"

I shook my head and saved my breath. I was almost out of voice range anyhow. But that grin had told me everything. Soon the desk clerk would spill his guts to the Paris police and I would be a hunted man by both sides of the law.

But to hell with that. I had bigger things to worry about.

Obviously, Cronin and his people were not bashful about striking, hard and quick. The only reason they had not yet hit David Hawk, I figured, was because he was in Washington and it would be difficult to get away with it there.

When I left the George Cinq, I took to alleys, which are plentiful in Paris, and found a small hotel near Avenue Victor Hugo. I used another phony name, knowing that Paris police would receive a copy of the hotel's register and would be looking for both Carson and Carter.

I had just lain back on the hard little bed to begin a quiet mourning of the beautiful Elaine Withers/Diane Northrup when there was a knock on the door. I got up, Luger in hand. An envelope slid under the door and by the time I looked out into the hallway, the messenger had vanished. The message was from Hawk. I could tell because he used the failsafe code—virtually uncrackable without the key, which only two people in the world knew, Hawk and me. Deciphered, it read:

"It has been confirmed that Mr. Snyder has gone bankrupt. He is in Stockholm to settle an old debt. Urgent you go there."

That was AXE language for this: "Snyder is a turncoat; he's in Stockholm to kill our agent there. Stop him."

It was imperative that I get to Sweden to warn James Lobell.

If I could get out of France.

Chapter Seven

The big DC10 dipped its port wing as we approached the city and I looked down at the sparkling islands that make up Stockholm. I have never seen the lovely brick and granite city without thinking of Venice. The thirteen islands that make up Stockholm seem to glitter like stones in an ocean, and water is everywhere—even serving as streets in low-lying areas.

Thousands of boats were moving up and down between the busy islands, serving as taxis and commercial vehicles. And the many bridges and wide streets were filled with people, on foot and in cars and trucks.

The wing leveled off and the jet streaked off to the north, on the edge of Lake Mälaren, to land at an airstrip that is no more than a giant clearing in a forest of pines.

It all seemed so peaceful, yet I knew that Cronin's men—perhaps even Cronin himself—would be there in force. Once they disposed of James Lobell, they would move, in a pack, to another location to eliminate another AXE agent.

Unless I stopped them.

Under most conditions, one AXE agent does not contact another agent directly. That is, we never meet in the flesh. The closest I usually come to other agents is through telephone calls if I cannot learn what I need to learn from them through the computer bank in Washington.

This was an extraordinary situation.

I left the airport, waited until dark and went to James

Lobell's apartment on Staden Island, the heart of Stockholm's old city. He lived in a third-floor flat in a quaint old gabled house that was at least three hundred years old, on a narrow street only a few hundred yards from the water.

"Hey, Nick," he said, spreading his arms as he greeted me at the door, "I haven't seen you in ten years. What in thunder brings our old veteran out to see me?"

"Let's get inside and I'll tell you," I said, looking past him into the apartment to make certain he hadn't already been invaded by Cronin's men.

"What are you looking for, old buddy?" he asked as we moved inside and he closed the door. "Broads or booze?"

Lobell was not a new agent, so he should have known that I would not pay him a visit for broads or booze. It was obvious to me that his loud greeting and convivial comments were a cover. I gazed around the room, inspecting it, and noticed that one window was slightly open.

Lobell followed my gaze and put a finger to his lips, shushing any comment I might make about the window.

"Let me get a jacket from the bedroom," he said loudly. "We'll have to go down the street for a drink. I'm fresh out."

"I don't want a drink," I said, uncertain of what he planned to do. I thought we should check out that open window immediately.

"Of course you do," he said, gripping my arm and guiding me back to the door. He winked, a grim wink. "You must have had a weary trip up here. You need a drink. Come along, old buddy. I know just the place to go."

I didn't protest. We walked down the three flights to the street and James Lobell chatted loudly and amiably as we headed down toward the water. When we were two blocks away, he ducked into an alley and pulled me after him. His voice came in a hoarse whisper.

"You came at a good time, Nick. Somebody has been watching me for days. Just before you arrived, I heard them on the fire escape. When I heard the window being jimmied, I sat and waited. When you knocked, I had my gun in my hand, ready to blast them to hell. What in the world is going on?''

I told him about Robert Cronin and Dave Snyder, and about Elaine Wither's part in the project. He smiled when I mentioned her name, but frowned when I told him that she had been shot during an assault on me. I told him how Hawk had warned me, via the computer, that he, Lobell, also was in trouble.

"Okay," he said finally. "What do we do next?"

"That's easy," I said. "The hunted become the hunters. Let's circle back and watch who is probably right now breaking into your apartment. When they leave, we can follow."

He nodded and led the way to an alley behind his apartment building. We separated then to avoid being caught in a trap. I found refuge in a hedge and settled down with my Luger in my hand to watch his apartment.

The apartment was dark, but I soon saw a flickering light from the window. Flashlight. Someone was in there searching through Lobell's belongings. I saw movement below the fire escape and saw Lobell creeping up behind several garbage cans.

In twenty minutes, the light went off and the window to Lobell's apartment opened wide. Two dark figures came out and down the fire escape. When they rounded the corner and entered the alley, I crouched lower to let them pass. They went silently, moving across the rough cobblestones like two-legged deer.

Lobell came out from behind the cans and motioned for me. We went to the big garage across the alley and got into his car. As we came out of the alley, we saw the men get into a small green Volvo.

"Okay," Lobell said. "Now, all we have to do is make sure they don't spot us."

We cruised all over the small island, then crossed the bridge to the mainland, near the Parliament building. As we gained speed through the more modern section of the city,

Lobell filled me in on what had been happening.

"I just came off an assignment two weeks ago in Libya," he said. "Mostly in the Tobruk area. You know, they're still talking there about an American spy who killed a dozen alleged syndicate men and left two city blocks in flames. You wouldn't know about that, would you?"

"No more than you," I lied.

"Anyway," he said and chuckled, "when I got back, my apartment had been ransacked. The next day, when I went down to the telephone exchange to make my report, I was followed. As time went by, more tails were put on me and once I was stopped in an alley near my apartment by two men who said they wanted directions. They didn't need directions. I could tell by their accent that they were native Stockholmers."

"What did they want, then?"

"To get a closer look at me, I suppose. I gave wrong directions just to see their expressions. They didn't disappoint me. They knew the directions were wrong when a stranger would not have known the difference."

He was silent as we turned a corner, crossed another bridge onto Kungsholmen Island. We passed huge factories and warehouses in this industrial section. The streets were eerily deserted.

"Earlier today," Lobell went on, "I decided to call their bet. I went to a pawn shop and bought a lot of junk and had the pawn broker wrap it in dark paper. When I sneaked the box into the apartment, their curiosity got the better of them, so they came snooping closer. That was when you showed up."

Lobell slowed as the Volvo turned into the driveway of a ball bearing factory. He stopped and we slumped in the front seat, waiting.

"No sense going in there," he said. "This is only a decoy stop. They'll change cars before going to their hideout."

After a long silence, broken only by the clattering of distant machines and the hooting of boats on the eternally-busy Norrstrom, Lobell spoke.

"Nick, you really think they'll get to Hawk?"

"Highly possible," I replied. "They're taking a lot of time and that means they're being very careful and deliberate. And Cronin not only has hired gunmen on his payroll, he has the active support of both the Mafia and the Corse. That makes for an almost unbeatable combination."

Lobell whistled and shook his head in dismay. "My God, what will happen to us? To AXE?"

"If their plan works, Hawk and most AXE agents will die. The government will appoint a new leader, but the new man won't have many people to lead after awhile. Their plan is to nip us all off, you know."

"So," James Lobell said, letting out a full breath and sighing in the dark car. "That means we have to stop them before they get to Hawk."

"Right. Look sharp, my friend, here they come."

A limousine eased out of the factory driveway and we hunched lower in the seat. The limo turned toward us and we both gripped our pistols, waiting for an assault. But the big car moved on past. Lobell waited ten seconds, then started his engine. He made a U-turn and followed the limousine, slowly.

After another hour's drive, the limousine finally stopped at a small hotel on the island of Ostermalm, on a quiet, mostly residential street. Lobell turned off the main street a block past the hotel and parked on a dark street.

"Want to hit them now?" he asked.

"No. We don't know what we would be hitting. Let's stake them out a few days."

Three days later, on a Saturday night, we were ready to hit them. We knew. During our surveillance, we had spotted Robert Cronin and Dave Snyder leaving and entering the little hotel with a bodyguard. Lobell had even gone into the hotel lobby and reported back that Cronin's men had virtually taken over the place.

"This is their headquarters," he said. "They have the top floor for the leaders, and the other two floors for their damned army of thugs."

"So we take a calculated risk in hitting it," I said. "Even if we come out of it with our lives, we may force them to speed up their plans to hit Hawk."

We agreed that the risk was a necessary one.

And so, on Saturday night when the thugs would be relaxed and drinking heavily, we decided to make a two-man assault on the hotel.

We rigged a thin nylon escape line from the top of the hotel to a nearby apartment building. Beyond that building was the river, with plenty of boats for escape. And Lobell arranged for a water taxi to be on hand at the breakwall alongside the river.

We had only to get out of the hotel alive and make it to the boat. We were figuring that Cronin would not be prepared for water pursuit, so we would exact our pound of flesh, eliminating both Cronin and the turncoat agent, then disappear into the cool Swedish night.

The attack plan was simple but Napoleonic in concept. We depended wholly on surprise. And, since Ostermalm was primarily residential, we were far from police headquarters, so would not have to fear immediate police interference. We had no intention of attacking Cronin's army; we wanted only to hit the top floor where the leaders were living, then take off.

James Lobell went up first. I waited in the alley until he signaled from the roof that all was quiet and that our escape line, attached just after nightfall, was still intact.

When I reached the roof, Lobell was crouching in darkness behind an air vent. I joined him and we located the lean-to shed that contained the door and stairway to the top floor below us.

It was so quiet up there that I began to suspect a trap. The hair on the back of my neck raised up, tickling my skin.

"We can't go in that way," I whispered. "Danger signs are lighting my body up like a pinball machine."

"I know what you mean," he replied. "I feel it too."

I didn't want to abort the task, but I also knew that my

warning instinct was almost infallible. It had saved my skin innumerable times.

"All right, Jim," I said. "Let's take the fire escape down to the top floor. It should dump us out into the main corridor. We can strike from there."

Slowly and quietly, we crawled across the dark roof to the fire escape. At the top floor, we jimmied the window and entered the empty corridor. As soon as we were inside, we heard hoarse voices from down the hall.

I moved along the dim corridor and Lobell followed. Another hallway led off to the right, at the end of which were six men standing outside an exit door.

It was the door leading to the roof.

My danger signs had been accurate. We would have been killed as soon as we opened the door from the roof.

Sweat collected under my arms and around my neck, although the corridor was cool. There was a tactical decision to be made. If we attacked the men huddled around the door to the roof, our main quarry—Cronin and Snyder—would be warned. They would get away. However, if we attacked the bedrooms, the thugs would immediately respond and come right down our throats.

But what the hell. I had gone into even worse situations alone. This time, I had another agent to cover my flanks.

"You stay here," I whispered to Lobell. "I'm going to hit one of the bedrooms. As soon as our friends here move, start pumping lead into them. It'll be like shooting . . ."

"Yeah," he whispered tightly. "Like shooting rabbits in a wire cage."

I grinned. "Something like that."

I eased back up the main corridor and picked a door at random. Checking to see that Lobell was ready, I raised my right foot and whacked the door, hard, right beside the doorknob. The door crashed open and I saw three men sitting in easy chairs.

As soon as I opened fire with Wilhelmina, the lights went out and gunshots sounded in the room. Bullets whizzed past me and thunked into the door.

I tossed in a gas bomb and moved swiftly to the next door.

Before I could kick it in, I heard Lobell's powerful Luger open up, followed appropriately by screams and the chattering of automatic weapons.

Then came a tremendous explosion and a flash of fire down the corridor.

Lobell had blown all six men away with a hand grenade.

I didn't have to kick in the second door.

At the moment I felt the concussive pressure from the grenade, the door opened. A heavy man in a black suit stared open-mouthed at me.

I put a bullet smack into that open mouth. The man clutched his throat and stumbled back into the room, knocking over furniture and lamps.

Another rushed out of the bedroom and I dropped him with a single bullet between the eyes.

The suite contained only the two men, neither of them Cronin or Snyder, so I dashed out into the corridor again, just in time to see a burly man open a door down the way, directly behind James Lobell. Lobell was at the main stairway door, pumping bullets from an automatic pistol he apparently had taken from a dead thug.

The man came out of the room, his automatic pistol at the ready. He came slowly, quietly, sneaking up behind the unsuspecting Lobell.

I ran down the corridor and the man turned to face me just as I reached him.

I flexed a muscle in my right arm and Hugo leaped into my hand.

The little knife sank into the man's soft belly and I ripped it up and in, hard. He went down without a sound and I caught his machine pistol in the air.

"Behind you, Nick!" Lobell yelled, turning, but still firing away.

I whirled just as two men took aim on my head with shotguns. I whipped the pistol up and fired without aiming. The gun chattered and the men were cut almost in two. I turned back to Lobell, who had thrown away the machine pistol and was preparing to launch another grenade.

"What the hell is so interesting down those stairs?" I yelled as I reached his side.

"I think the goddam reserves are trying to come up," he said as he backed away from the open door. "Stay back until after that one pops."

On his last word, the grenade went off. The floor bucked under us and two more men, obviously awakened by the furor, stumbled drunkenly out of a room down the hallway. I took careful aim and squeezed the trigger of the automatic weapon. They fell like rag dolls.

"Let's get up to the roof before they reach it from the outside," I said.

"What about Cronin and Snyder?"

"We have to forget them this time. They're not here. Somebody warned these bastards or they wouldn't have been waiting for us. My bet is that Cronin and Snyder, plus all their lieutenants, are holed up on another island, waiting for word that we've been scalped. Let's go."

We made it safely to the roof and started across to where our line was attached. I still had the automatic pistol, but I knew that it was about empty. Just as I was hoping that we wouldn't meet any more of the enemy, two men stepped out from behind an air vent.

I leaped behind another vent, but Lobell attacked with a flying tackle. He caught both men and they all three tumbled in a heap on the dark roof.

I moved up swiftly and, while the men were huffing and cursing trying to free themselves from Lobell, I went to work with the stiletto.

Half sick, weary and still frightened, I stood up and wiped blood from the little knife.

"Pretty damned messy," I said to Lobell who was getting up slowly, "but it saves ammunition."

"And you're going to need it," he said.

Even as he spoke, he commenced firing past me. I turned and fired as five men burst out onto the roof and started toward us. We cut them down in three seconds flat.

"I hope to God that's all of them," Lobell said as we ran across the roof to our escape line. "I don't relish the idea of being pot shot while I'm swinging out over the street."

"Nor do I."

We quickly attached our shiny little pulleys to the line and leaped from the roof, one after the other. As I sailed through the cool, dark air, I heard the racket of automatic weapon fire behind me.

But we made it unscathed. On the other side of the apartment building, we found the fire escape, ran down it to the water's edge and leaped into the waiting water taxi.

"I was just about to get out of here," the boatman said. "What the hell was all that noise back there?"

"Government business," I cracked, flashing my gold card at him. I didn't have to tell him which government.

"Oh," he said. He revved up the engine and pulled out into the river. We headed toward the glittering lights of Norrmalm, the island where most of the city's businesses and theaters were located. I settled back on a soft seat, lit up a gold-embossed cigarette and smoked to settle my nerves. They were leaping about like kittens on an electric chair.

James Lobell situated himself comfortably beside me, the cool wind tossing his blond hair into a bright halo about his head.

"Now that we've got all this adrenalin flowing," he said with a chuckle, "let's not waste it on a drink."

"What do you have in mind?"

"I know a couple of young ladies who aren't doing anything tonight. Okay?"

"Okay."

It was a good idea. Not only would we get laid, but we would have a safe place to spend the night. Either possibility was welcome.

We scored on both counts.

The morning was clear and crisp, almost brittle with vivid

blue skies and sharp sunlight over the water. Kristen moved in the bed beside me and I gazed at her sharp, clear features. She was classic Scandanavian, with eyes as blue as the Swedish sky, hair as soft and golden as the sunlight, and skin as crystal clear and unflawed as the calm waters of the Norrstrom.

And she was as good in bed as she looked.

But all good things come to an end, especially in my business. I wanted to report in and check on Hawk at the same time. I swung my legs out of bed and began to dress. Kristen awoke.

"Where are you going?" she asked in Swedish.

"I'm going for a walk," I said.

"I've heard of people who eat and run," Kristen said, feigning a pout, "but this beats them all."

I patted her face and kissed her full red lips. "Don't worry. I'll be back after a brisk walk along the river. Wait for me."

"All right," she said, sleepy again. She turned over and was almost instantly asleep—the rewards of being a pretty girl not involved in government work.

James Lobell and Alyss were still asleep in her bedroom when I checked.

At the corner, I found a telephone booth and checked my digital watch to calculate the time in Washington. It was 7:04 in Stockholm, so it had to be around midnight in the eastern seaboard of the States. The computer would be awake. I dialed and waited.

"Report," the computer voice crackled over mild static.

"No report," I said. "A check. N3 in Stockholm."

"One moment please."

It was a quick moment. "We did not call, but it is well that you called us. The nameless person is hospitalized."

My nerves went suddenly tense and the hair rose tingling on my neck. I almost blurted out Hawk's name. He was in the hospital? My God, why? I forced calm into my voice.

"Please expand," I said, adopting the impersonal tone of the computer.

"An explosive device," the voice said. "Planted in his automobile."

"When and where?"

"At precisely 10:22 p.m. yesterday, just outside his office."

"Is he all right?"

"Critical."

"Where is he?"

"In the hospital," the computer said, sounding almost cranky.

"Which one?"

"You are being extravagant."

"Sorry," I said, knowing that I had blundered—that it would be extremely dangerous to have that information repeated over long distance telephone. "Anything else?"

"Yes, you are to remain in Europe to find those responsible and you are to dispose of them in the usual manner. That is all."

There was a click. The line was dead. I wanted to get to Washington as soon as possible, but I knew it would be fruitless. Hawk would be in a military hospital under tight security conditions.

As I stepped from the telephone booth, my mind reeling from the impact of the crashing news from the computer, certain truths became self-evident.

Cronin, obviously, was behind the murder attempt on David Hawk, and he did it in retaliation for our evening raid on his stronghold. As we had feared, Lobell and I had speeded up his plans to kill Hawk and start the destruction of AXE. Fortunately, the speeding up caused them to blunder. Hawk was still alive.

And another truth came to me as I walked up the street toward the apartment of the lovely Kristen and Alyss.

Dave Synder, Agent N22, knew that I would immediately contact Washington and learn about the attempt on Hawk's life, learn that the killing had begun. And I knew also that, as I walked along the sun-drenched street in the crisp morning air, Dave Snyder and probably Robert Cronin were watching every move that I made. I swept the nearby apartment buildings with my eyes, staring intently at the bright windows, and knew that I was next on the list.

The bullet could come at any time.

Chapter Eight

For the next three days we were both the hunters and the hunted.

On the first day, Lobell and I were leaving his flat when six mercenaries, well armed and anxious to earn their pay from Cronin, launched an attack from across the street.

The first bullet slammed into the seat of Lobell's car just as we were getting in. I hit the sidewalk on my stomach, but Lobell was caught on the street side of the car. Bullets whanged and clattered on and around the car.

"Open fire, Nick," Lobell yelled above the crash and boom of gunfire. "Cover me so I can get the hell out of here."

I raised from the sidewalk and leaned against the side of the car. As I was hoisting Wilhelmina to the hood, I saw a tongue of flame from the roof of the apartment building.

I squeezed, the Luger boomed three times and a man came sailing down, screaming bloody murder. By the time he hit the sidewalk, I had spotted another gunman and was blazing away while Lobell skittered to safety, right beside me. Some safety. Bullets surrounded us like a veil of falling lead.

But our assailants' eagerness was their downfall. Instead of shooting for the car's fuel tank to blow up our shield—and perhaps us as well—the five remaining gunmen started dashing across the street in a frontal attack.

"You take the left flank, I'll take the right," I murmured to Lobell.

"Check."

We leaned against the car, took careful aim and began pumping lead. Two men fell instantly, two ducked behind parked cars and one charged ahead, his machine pistol chattering like a nest of ground squirrels.

I caught the charging man with a single shot, smack in the throat, and he did a weird death dance in the middle of the street.

Up and down the normally quiet residential street, people were yelling and running for cover. We had brought terror, and they were responding as might be expected. In the distance, a police siren wailed.

"Let's clear out," I said. "We can't afford to get tied up with the cops right now."

"Or at anytime," Lobell commented.

He opened the car door and dived in head first. When he was behind the wheel, I pumped two more shots at the car where the men were hiding, and started to get in. Lobell held a hand grenade out to me.

"Bounce it off the building across the street," he said.

I pulled the pin and lobbed the grenade over the top of the parked car. It struck the building and landed on the sidewalk, out of sight. Lobell started the car and I jumped in. As we pulled away from the curbing, the grenade went off.

Two men screamed, but their screams were cut off by twin explosions as the grenade and the car both went up in shattering bits.

Later that night, after cruising the streets without drawing any fire, we headed toward the apartment of Kristen and Alyss. When we neared their building, a small dark car eased up behind us.

"Oh my God," Lobell said as he squinted into the rearview mirror. "Now, they know about the girls. We don't have a safe place in the whole lousy city."

"Including the one we're in right now," I said.

We lost the tail with a few quick turns and kept on driving until we were in open countryside, beyond the airport. Lobell pulled in at a small inn where we got a room and settled in the cocktail lounge to plan our next move.

We knew that Cronin and Snyder had fled the city, but we had no idea where they had gone. They could be in any of a hundred places I knew about—or a thousand I didn't.

Only one thing was certain: even though they had failed to liquidate David Hawk, they were proceeding with their plan to kill AXE agents, starting with me—and, of course, Lobell. They had left gunmen in Stockholm to eliminate us, and we were methodically killing off those gunmen.

I knew, though, that we were merely skirting around the edges of Cronin's real plan. We were literally and figuratively wandering around in the boondocks while the enemy was taking over the city. In this case, we were playing cat and mouse in Stockholm while Cronin and Snyder were proceeding with their grand scheme to eliminate AXE and to gain a monopoly on worldwide illegal drug traffic.

It wasn't until the third day, however, that I could do anything but play cat and mouse. On that day, we took a hostage. He was a wiry little thug named Lenny Shales, and he could not stand pain.

Shales had been left with another man to guard Lobell's apartment. We knew the apartment was being guarded, but we had to go back there to get ammunition Lobell had stashed in the wall of a bedroom closet. We couldn't get provisions through regular channels because Cronin's men had bombed the Amalgamated Press office on Staden.

Lenny Shales had gotten drunk on Lobell's well-stocked whiskey cabinet and had passed out on the couch. When we drew his partner out and shot him on the fire escape, we had only to throw Shales into the shower, under icy water, and then fill him up with coffee. Then, we drove him back to the inn near the airport for questioning.

Lenny sat in the chair, his hands tied to the wooden arms. His weasel eyes looked fearfully around the room, which we had darkened for effect. One lamp was lit, and it shone brightly in Lenny's scared face.

After a few preliminary questions which determined that

Cronin and Snyder, who had hired him, were out of Stockholm, I went right for the meat.

"Okay, Lenny, now tell me where they are right now. Where's their permanent hideout?"

He shook his head and went paler. "Jeez, I don't know that. Hell, they'd never tell me such a thing."

"For your sake," I said calmly, "I hope they did tell you such a thing and that you aren't going to be stubborn about passing it along."

"I don't know where they are," he cried. Lobell moved up to break his nose with the edge of his hand. Lenny Shales opened his mouth to scream, but Lobell stuffed a pair of rolled socks into it. What came out was a pitiful squeal and a grunt of pain. Lobell removed the sock.

Still he wouldn't talk. Lobell grew impatient.

"I brought along an eyepiece," Lobell said. "Why don't we pass up the bone-breaking session and get right to it."

Lenny Shales went stark white when Lobell mentioned using the eyepiece. A simple device invented in Italy at the turn of the century, the eyepiece consists of a leather strap that fits around the head, covering one eye. The strap has a hole in it, just over the eye. To this hole is attached a metal cup with a needle screw through its center.

When the strap is in place, the needle screw can be turned slowly until it pierces the eye; then, if necessary, the brain.

"All right," I said. "Put it over his left eye first. If that doesn't make him gabby, we'll go to the right eye."

"No," Lenny shrieked before Lobell shoved the sock back into his mouth. He squirmed in the chair, trying to break the nylon rope that held him. Sweat poured down his face and neck. He was wild-eyed. Even I felt a tremor shake my body as I contemplated the wickedness and the pain of the eyepiece.

Lobell methodically took the device from a small black case and spread it out on the table in front of Lenny Shales. He checked the buckle, then turned the screw to make certain it worked. All the while, Lenny watched every move he made. We were giving him plenty of time to consider what would happen once the eyepiece was in place.

Our deliberation paid off. Lenny began to nod his head furiously and to motion for us to remove the rolled sock from his mouth. He was ready to talk. I breathed easier.

"I'll give you everything I know," Lenny said in a burst of anxious breath when Lobell removed the sock. "It ain't much, but it's all I have."

"Start talking," Lobell said.

"They could be in one of three places," Lenny Shales began, "but I can't guarantee it."

"Don't play games with us, punk," Lobell said, jangling the eyepiece in front of Lenny's eyes. "It'll take only a few seconds to put this in place."

"I ain't playing games," Lenny said, shuddering as he looked at the torture device. "Nobody knows for sure. Mr. Cronin never says in advance what he's going to do or where he's going. But I know they're getting ready to ship out about six tons of heroin and there are only three places where they could have that much stored without government interference."

"Okay, we'll have to settle for that. Where are the shipping points?"

He named Tobruk, Libya, where heroin was collected and other drugs were manufactured in a factory I had blown up a few months ago; Bodrum, Turkey, another collection and manufacturing point, and Patrai, Greece. The latter was a remote resort town, so I doubted if Cronin would have the manufacturing facilities—or the safety—that the two other locations offered.

That narrowed it to Tobruk and Bodrum. Since I had blown up the pharmaceutical factory in Tobruk, I was convinced that Cronin and Snyder would be shipping the immense stash of heroin from the port city in Turkey. That is, until Lenny came up with his second bit of information.

"My guess is that they went to Bodrum in Turkey," he said, talking like a well-oiled mechanical doll now. "I think that's the new world headquarters."

"Why, because the factory in Tobruk has been destroyed?" I asked.

"Oh, the factory there wasn't completely destroyed," Lenny said. "Only part of it was gutted, but they got it rebuilt in a hurry. I figure they're using the Turkish place for headquarters because we got orders to go there for safety after we completed our assignments."

I thought about Bodrum and Tobruk. It seemed obvious to me that Cronin had set up some kind of sanctuary for his men in Bodrum, probably some well-guarded safehouse. But I knew that he also had his own yacht basin near Tobruk, in a tiny fishing village. And the villagers there protected him, for a price. Tobruk was the more logical place from which to ship heroin, because of the yacht basin and because it was easier to pay off Libyan officials.

And, logic told me, if Cronin was having his men make a beeline for Bodrum, Turkey, after completing their kill assignments, he wouldn't be there. He wouldn't have his men stream into his own parlor, so to speak.

No, my guess now was that Cronin was splitting up the danger. He had set up sanctuary for his paid gunmen in Turkey, but he was operating independently out of Libya.

And that was where I had to go.

I pulled James Lobell to the side of the room to discuss strategy. He would go to Turkey to pick off as many of Cronin's men as possible, while I would go to Tobruk, not only to kill Cronin and Snyder, but also to expose the largest shipment of illegal heroin ever assembled in one place. Lenny Shales, we would let him go. He would head directly for Bodrum, Turkey, to warn the others, thinking that we both would be coming there. His warning wouldn't help Lobell, but it might give me the edge in Tobruk.

To further throw Cronin and his people off guard, I decided against going directly to Tobruk. I needed new cover papers anyway, so I went to the one person who could get them for me in a hurry.

Raina Missou opened the door and her golden face broke into a wide, happy smile.

"Oh Nick," she said in her mellow, sing-song voice, "how in the world did you get here? They still have the Army and the Air Force out looking for you."

I slid into the room and closed the door. "It's nice to know that somebody wants me," I said with a grin. "I need another favor."

She smiled and came into my arms. After a long, sweet kiss, she backed away and shook her head. "You're impossible. But you still haven't told me how you got here."

"Easy," I said. "I commandeered a submarine and landed off the coast just before dawn. Nobody saw me."

I was telling the truth and I knew that she wouldn't believe me. I wanted it that way.

"I'm so glad you're still all right," she said, kissing me again. "I heard through the grapevine that three American agents were killed and I was certain that you were one of them."

"When did you hear that?"

"Just last night."

It was dangerous for me to go out on the streets again, but I couldn't make the call from her apartment. And I had to make the call. Raina went with me to the telephone exchange and watched for the military while I called the Washington office.

Yes, three AXE agents had been killed, presumably by Cronin's men, during the past 24 hours. Our men in London, Rome and Frankfurt had been riddled with bullets and dumped on the steps of American embassies.

Back in Raina's apartment, we made plans for a hasty departure to Tobruk. Raina had found a new source for illegal identification papers and could whip up a new batch for me by the following morning. Although the military was still searching for me, the search efforts were minimal. I was ready to try the airport again, unless I wanted to wait a few more days and try overland transportation.

I couldn't wait.

Cronin had apparently stepped up his plans to murder all AXE agents. The only way to stop the vicious plan was to stop the man behind it. It was imperative that I get to the factory in Tobruk as soon as possible.

The night with Raina was very special—and very productive. When I had been with her last, I had been less than whole, with the bullet wound in my side. Now, I was healthy and without pain.

We made love with all the strength and vigor we possessed. Then we slept while the world with all its troubles seemed far away.

But it was waiting for me when dawn came.

Things went so smoothly at the airport that I couldn't believe that I had been involved in a bloody gunfight there only a few days before. Military people filled the streets and concourse, but there were no high-ranking officers. I wasn't recognized in my dark gray suit, so went directly through customs to the plane, a gigantic 747.

When we landed at Tobruk, I gazed out at the wine-colored tarmac and at the low, sprawling wings of the terminal. There were no military people around and this lulled me into a sense of well-being. Even as I walked down the long corridor to baggage claim and customs, I sensed no danger.

But, as I reached the main doorway, with my suitcase in my hand and my mind convinced that I had nearly reached my destination safely, I heard the crack and thunder of a familiar voice:

"Hold it right there, Carter. I want to give you a proper welcome to Tobruk."

It was Dave Snyder, Agent N22.

As I spun around, I flexed the muscles in my right arm and snapped Hugo into my hand. But Snyder was expecting such a move. He was twenty feet behind me, his Luger drawn. He hit the deck and squeezed off two shots.

The twin explosions ripped through the concourse. People screamed. I jumped back against a stone pillar, reaching for my own Luger. A police whistle sounded, but I was already committed to a firefight. I whipped out Wilhelmina just as Snyder rolled behind a cluster of suitcases.

I leaped behind the pillar and fired three times into the suitcases. More people screamed and the police whistles multiplied and became louder.

I was preparing to fire again when Snyder threw a large suitcase toward me. Even as I ducked to one side, I saw him leap over the flight counter and slip through the little port where luggage was fed through on a conveyor belt to a back room. I fired twice at Snyder's retreating back, but I knew as I shot that he had got away.

Even before I could wonder how he knew that I could be at the Tobruk airport, police swooped down on me. Officers disarmed me and held me as a tall, handsome Fezzan strode up to me. He wore a neat, crisp khaki uniform, his chest bedecked with gaily-colored medals, and he carried a short riding crop which he slapped against his right thigh.

"*Monsieur* Carter, we have been expecting you," he said in excellent French. "I really don't know how you expected to get away with it."

"Get away with what?" I asked.

The big Fezzan policeman laughed and slapped his thigh with the riding crop.

"Really, *monsieur*," he said amiably, "I have heard that Americans have considerable gall, but you are the prize-winner. You come here for evil purposes and feel quite at home shooting up our people in an airport, hardly before your feet are accustomed to our soil. I cannot believe that—"

"Evil purposes?" I asked. "What evil purposes?"

He kept the smile, but did not laugh. "We have received unimpeachable information," he said slowly, "that you have come to Libya to assassinate our king. I am puzzled as to how you knew that he is in Tobruk and not in the capital, Bengasi."

I shook my head and grinned. Surely, Cronin and his men wouldn't use the same old chestnut of a story they had used to get me in trouble in Morocco. And surely the Libyans wouldn't believe him, as the Moroccans had.

"I know nothing about your king," I assured the policeman. "And I certainly didn't come here to do him harm. *Monsieur* . . ."

"Faichel," he said. "Emir Faichel, lieutenant in the King's Security Force."

"*Monsieur* Faichel," I said, "this is all a grave mistake. I have reason to believe that an international ring of drug peddlers is operating out of a factory in Tobruk. I came only to find out for myself."

He nodded, slapped his thigh with the crop. "I see," he said slowly. "And you came with a gun and a knife, just to see if drug peddlers were operating out of a factory here? By the way, *Monsieur* Carter, how did you get past airport security with such weapons?"

I grinned at him. "Airport security is pretty sloppy in this part of the world."

It was the wrong thing to say. His expression now was tight and lethal. He turned, slapped his thigh loudly with the crop and barked commands.

"Take him to the car and search him thoroughly. We will see how he lies after a time in jail. Take him now!"

The men hustled me out of the building and to a small, hidden parking lot near the terminal building. There, they found my gas bomb, leaving me without any defenses. Then I was shoved into a small black car, blindfolded and driven away from the airport.

After what seemed hours in the stuffy car, I was marched—still blindfolded—into a cool but foul-smelling building. I soon learned why it was cool and why it smelled so bad.

It was the central jail for political prisoners, housed in a granite building right on the waterfront. I was led down five sets of stairs, where the air was even cooler and ranker, and shoved into a cell. When I heard the door clank shut, I took off the blindfold. The men who had brought me were walking away into the dusky light of the cellblock.

"Hey, wait a minute," I yelled. "There's been a terrible mistake."

My protest was met with harsh laughter, the dripping of water and the scrambling sound of tiny feet. I turned toward the scrambling sound and saw two huge fat rats on a metal girder above my head. Their eyes were gleaming redly and, if I didn't know better, I would have sworn that their faces were wide with grins.

I had the terrible premonition at that moment that I would spend the rest of my life looking at those grinning rat faces.

Chapter Nine

The best that can be said about the jail in Tobruk is that I have been in worse places. The rats, I quickly learned, were to be the least of my problems. Cockroaches the size and ferocity of rabid mice shuffled across the floor, ceiling and walls around the clock. Dampness and cold chilled me to the bone and I could not sleep on the steel slab that served as a cot. The food, rotting and maggoty, was tolerable only because it came once a day and there was so little of it. The guard who brought it was either a mute, or the most dedicated of fiends. He never spoke or answered questions, and sometimes he would slide the tray of food in so violently that half my rations would slop onto the filthy floor. The other cells were empty, so I did not hear another human voice during the long days and nights.

At least, there was ample time to think and, gradually, I pieced together a semblance of order in recent events. I realized that Dave Snyder could not have known that I would be arriving in Tobruk unless he had been tipped off. Only two people knew that I was heading for Libya.

One was James Lobell and I refused to believe that he also had become a counter-agent. For one thing, he had plenty of opportunity to kill me when we were fighting side by side in Stockholm. It couldn't be Lobell.

The second was Raina Missou who had arranged papers and transportation for me from Casablanca. She had helped me a number of times in the past, so I found it difficult to believe that she was the spy divulging my plans. But there was still the mystery of why the Moroccan military people were waiting for me at the Casablanca airport.

As for Cronin and Snyder, I felt immeasurably frustrated at being unable to stop them. For the moment, I was out of the picture, barely surviving in the miserable steel-barred cell deep inside the granite waterfront jail.

If I didn't die from exposure, the rotten food would kill me. If I survived those, I might die from infection caused by rat bites. All in all, my situation was deteriorating with galloping speed. I had developed a wicked cough and knew that I was only a step away from pneumonia.

As for matters on the outside, I was tortured by thoughts of what might be happening. Even if Hawk were recovering from his injuries in the bomb blast to his automobile, death was waiting for him as soon as he was back on the street.

There was also the matter of AXE agents being picked off one by one. Cronin had failed with me and Lobell (at least, I hoped Lobell was still alive), but his men had killed agents in London, Rome and Frankfurt. Were others being murdered and dumped on American embassy steps while I fought the cold and the rats?

It was a very distinct possibility.

And there was the matter of the six tons of heroin being packaged and prepared in the factory on Tobruk's southern perimeter. Within the next couple of weeks, Cronin's yachts would sail out into the Mediterranean to make deliveries all through southern Europe and the Middle East. From there, the heroin, cut down and possibly laced with strychnine, would find its way into the streets of every major capitol of the free world. And it would bring to Cronin's coffers millions of dollars to be used for God-knew-what evil purposes.

Just as I was reaching the point of utter despair, I heard doors opening down the dark corridor, and the sound of many footsteps. It wasn't time for the daily maggot-infested slop to be thrown into my cell.

They were coming either to question me, or to kill me.

The same four burly cops who had brought me here appeared at the cell door and opened it. Without words, but with much gagging on the foul, stifling air, the four dragged me up the corridor to the stairs.

On an upper floor, the guards stripped off my wet, rotting clothes and pushed me into a cold shower. When I was reasonably clean, they made me dress in a suit of oversized khaki clothes and a pair of Army boots. I was taken then to a small, warm interrogation room.

After a half-hour wait, an Army major and two soldiers entered. The soldiers carried Russian-made Volshik automatic pistols. I knew the weapon well. It fired .45 caliber shells at a rate of twenty bullets a second. One burst could cut a man in half.

"I am Major Dieter Senussi," the short, squat officer said in a dull, unemotional voice. "I have orders to take you to the commandant of the King's Security Force at Fort Siwa. You will come with us and you will make no trouble. Is that clear?" The major handed me a pen and shoved a sheet of paper across the small desk. "This is a form stating that you have been well treated in our holding facility, and that your valuables have been returned to you. Sign it and we will leave immediately."

I wanted to argue on all counts, but I knew it would be useless. I signed the damn form and was surprised as hell when he gave me my watch and my solid gold card.

"May I ask the significance of the gold card?" the major asked. "It is blank."

"A lucky token, that's all." I said, shrugging. I certainly couldn't tell him that the card contained a great deal of information about me, written so small on the gold surface that it could be seen only through an electron microscope.

He nodded. "Let us depart."

The night air was like a warm tonic after more than a week in the wet, frigid cell in the jail's dungeon. Although I was half starved, I felt the rejuvenating effect of the fresh air and took in several deep breaths. Then I coughed violently and thought I was going to choke.

We entered a jeep just outside the jail, only it wasn't really a jeep. It was a Russian-made Courscur, almost an exact replica of the American jeep. It had a 20mm cannon mounted in the center, to be fired from the back seat, and a .50 caliber machine gun on its hood. Alongside the doors were pouches holding hand grenades and spare ammuntiion, plus automatic rifles strapped to the side of the vehicle. My hands itched with anticipation and I yearned to get my hands on just one of those weapons. The major apparently read my mind.

"You will sit straight and keep your hands in your lap," Major Senussi snapped as he climbed in and sat beside me in the rear seat. "If you so much as move a hand to pick your nose, the sergeant in the front passenger seat has orders to empty his machine pistol into your body. Is that understood?"

I coughed, mostly for effect, and nodded again. He seemed satisfied and leaned back in the seat, barking an order in Arabic to the driver.

The jeep lurched forward and soon left the waterfront area. We skirted the downtown section of the quaint old port city, but I caught quick glimpses of the old Arab quarters where men did business the way their great-great-grandfathers had done—by barter—and the gleaming new business section where computers were used to determine the latest price of oil and other commodities on the world market. In ten minutes, we were in the desert.

The warm desert wind streamed over the windshield and bathed my face and shoulders in a welcoming, soothing balm. My mind began to work and I wished that I could exercise the kinks out of my aching muscles or just quit coughing. I knew that the major was not taking me to Fort Siwa. He and his two soldiers had orders to take me far into the desert, execute me and to bury me in the sand. I was certain enough of that to know that I had to do something.

The major provided me with an entree into my plan. He took a familiar packet from his breast pocket and started to light up a cigarette. In the backlight from the headlights, I could see the gold-embossed monogram: NC.

"These are fine cigarettes, *Monsieur* Carter," the major said as he puffed contentedly. "Where do you buy them? I found only six extra packs in your suitcase and I'm almost out."

"It's a special Turkish blend," I said, yearning for one of my cigarettes. "I have them made for me."

Major Senussi grinned. "Pity there won't be more," he said, holding the cigarette up to look at it.

"Yes," I replied. "A damned pity. Of course, I could give you the name of my supplier. You could cable for them in Ankara."

"Good idea," the major enthused. "Here, I'll give you something to write the supplier's name on." He snapped his fingers and the soldier with the gun put down his weapon and rummaged in a glove compartment for paper and pen.

In that moment, I knew I had an excellent opportunity to make my move. But the major was watching me, holding his right hand on his holstered pistol. I would have to wait for a better opportunity.

I wrote slowly in the moving vehicle while the major and the solder watched closely. When I had written the supplier's name, address and cable code, I held the paper up so that the wind caught it. I let loose just before the major's hand was ready to close on it. The paper flew off into the night. I cursed as though I were disgusted.

"I'll write it again," I said with a friendly voice. "This time, I won't be so careless."

We were far from Tobruk now, beyond the lights that reflected on the clouds behind us. When the soldier passed back another piece of paper, I pretended that it was difficult to see what I was doing.

"Put a light on the paper," Major Senussi ordered. The soldier reached down at his feet and brought up a flashlight. He turned it on and I could see the paper vividly. Still, I wrote slowly, watching the soldier and the major from the corners of my eyes.

When I had finished writing, I noticed that the major's

hands were both reaching for the paper, and the soldier was still holding the flashlight, his weapon leaning against the seat.

It was now or never.

I threw the paper and pen into the major's face and then knocked the flashlight out of the soldier's hand. It flew into the air and out of the jeep. Before the men could gather their senses, I stood up and leaped sideways, knowing that I could break my legs—or my neck—when I landed on the macadam highway. I rolled myself into a ball as I sailed through the air and landed on my rump on the soft berm as the jeep hurtled on through the night, brakes squealing.

The landing knocked the breath out of me, but adrenalin was flowing rapidly through my body. I rocked to my feet and ran straight across the desert toward dark shadows of craggy rock formations. I stumbled and panted in the warm sand, but made it to the rocks by the time the jeep had stopped and turned to sweep the desert with its headlights.

I was no more than two hundred feet from the jeep, but I could hear Major Senussi's voice clearly on the desert air.

"Stay with the jeep, driver," he said crisply. "We'll fan out and get him. He can't go far because he's too weak."

Ah, but that's your big problem and my advantage, I thought as the major and the soldier climbed from the idling jeep. I don't intend to go far. I intend to wait for you.

The major took the right flank, the soldier the left. I moved slowly to intercept the soldier. When I was directly in his path, I lay behind a log-like formation and waited.

I could hear his footsteps in the sand, his breath panting from the effort of desert walking. As I lay waiting, I found a large stone in the sand and cupped it in my hand. When the soldier reached the far edge of rocks, I threw the stone as hard as I could toward the major far to my right. The soldier turned at the sound. At that moment, the major fired his pistol.

Now.

I brought the soldier down by the legs and slid one hand over his mouth and the other around his neck. I squeezed with all the strength left in me.

Without a sound, the soldier died in my hands. The major, recovered from his little scare, was probing among the rocks not a hundred feet away. The jeep's headlights revealed his short, squat frame as he crouched behind a rock.

I aimed the soldier's Volshik automatic pistol at the major. He made an excellent stationary target. But the soldier in the jeep would get away. I needed that jeep.

While the major stalked empty rocks, I retraced my steps in the dark sand until I was only a few feet from him. As he stepped through an opening between two rocks, I came up behind him. I gripped his mouth with one hand and jammed the automatic pistol into the small of his back. He dropped his pistol and stood silently trembling as I hissed:

"Call the driver. Tell him to come here."

The major shook his head and tried to break loose, but I tightened my grip, feeling my strength begin to ebb. If the major resisted much longer, I would have no choice but to shoot and lose the jeep.

"Call him or I'll pull the goddamn trigger," I ordered. He nodded and I parted my fingers around his mouth so that he could speak.

"Artesi!" he called out. "Come here. I need you."

Because of the burning headlights, we couldn't see the soldier in the jeep. We waited, then the soldier came around in front of the Courscur jeep. He stood with his automatic pistol at the ready and peered into the desert.

"What is the trouble, Major Senussi?" he called out.

I jammed the gun into the major's back until he almost squealed from the pain. He played it safe.

"Come over here," he yelled back. "I need you."

"Yes sir."

Sweat flowed down my face and soaked my shirt. My hands were wet and greasy from sweat, but I held the major and the gun tightly, knowing that my strength would not last more than a few seconds.

I felt my strength going, my hands slipping away from the major's head. Major Senussi sensed my growing weakness and started to turn. I didn't have a choice then. I could not wait for the soldier to come closer. I was about to lose everything for lack of another ounce of energy.

Reluctantly, I pulled the trigger and the burst from the machine pistol literally tore the major's body from my grasp. He flew away from me, let out one gurgling scream and crumpled to the dark earth. The soldier stopped in his tracks, fifty feet away. I fired and he went down.

Hunger gnawed at me like a persistent mouse. I searched the jeep, but found nothing but weapons and extra clothing. I stumbled back across the sand and searched the three dead soldiers, finding only a tin of American K-rations on the driver and a small candy bar on the major. I also found two fresh packs of my special cigarettes.

I glanced quickly at my watch. It was 11:20 p.m.

Before eating, I drove the jeep off the highway then turned off the lights and engine. I settled down near the body of the driver and ate the K-rations and candy bar. Thirst was my next problem, so I drained water from the jeep's radiator to drink. It was foul, but it was wet.

Then, with renewed strength, I pulled the bodies of the soldiers and the major behind the formation of rocks where I dressed in the major's uniform. With a farewell salute, I headed the jeep north again, toward Tobruk.

But I was not going to Tobruk, not just yet. A few miles south of the port city, I left the highway and struck out northwest, in the general direction of Darnah. I rode across the trackless sand, smoking one cigarette after the other—in nicotine heaven now that I had my own special fags back. Strangely, the smoke seemed to ease my cough.

On the coast, perhaps twenty miles west of Tobruk, I parked and gazed out across the dark Mediterranean. It was 12:30 a.m. Straight north across the ocean was Athens, Greece, where AXE kept a central message station. I had already planned to use the jeep's radio to get in touch with the station to find out what had been going on during my week-long incarceration in the Tobruk jail, but now I was reluctant to send out a beam. For the moment, nobody in the world knew where I was. But one radio message, picked up by the wrong people, could quickly change that.

I stood on the beach for a half-hour, trying to decide whether to radio the station. My desire to find out the latest about David Hawk—whether he was recuperating or whether he had been hit again by Cronin's people—was so strong that I knew I would make the call. But the risk was so great that I delayed as long as possible, breathing in the clean salt air of the ocean, gathering strength.

Even though I had eaten the food taken from the men who had been ordered to kill me, it wasn't enough. I was still hungry from long days of near starvation. There would be time, though, to stop on the way to Cronin's factory on the southern edge of Tobruk. For now, I had to find out about Hawk—and about what might be happening to other AXE agents.

I was also damned curious to find out what Lobell was doing. If he had gone to Bodrum, Turkey, as we had agreed, he might well be dead. We both knew that he would be walking into a virtual hornets' nest there.

Finally I turned on the jeep's radio, shifted to transmitting and took up the microphone. I dialed the frequency of the AXE station in Athens and pressed the mike button.

"N3 calling Athens," I said. "N3 calling Athens. Come in Athens."

"Athens here," a crisp male voice crackled above the low roar of the Mediterranean. "What is your code?"

I gave my radio code name and the voice came back, friendly now, and asked what I wanted.

"Require information on condition of nameless person," I said, gazing at the sky and wondering how many military aircraft were picking up this conversation.

"Recovering well," came the reply.

"Is he still hospitalized?"

There was a brief silence. "Negative," the voice said. "He is recovering at safehouse, according to latest report."

"Thank you," I said and breathed easier knowing that

Hawk was safe. "Require info on N36. Latest data."

After another brief silence, the voice came back with dismal news:

"N36 killed in Bodrum, Turkey, during raid on enemy."

"Any details on that?" I asked.

"Yes. Very strange report. N36 attacked enemy safe-house a week ago and was shot repeatedly. Immediately afterwards, safehouse and all occupants were blown up by mysterious explosion. Authorities have not learned source of explosion, but conjecture is that house was shelled by offshore battery of some kind. That is all, N3. Can you give location and describe current involvement?"

"Negative on that," I said. I shut down the radio and sat for a long time in the jeep, staring out over the dark ocean. Lobell was dead. He had been dead at least a week, and was dead all the time I was in jail. That confirmed that he had not been the counterspy ratting on my activities to Cronin. That left Raina Missou. And I grieved for both of them.

Chapter Ten

Much of the city slept. It was precisely 2:24 a.m. when I eased the Courscur-type jeep to a stop on a low hill just above Cronin's pharmaceutical factory on the southern edge of Tobruk. Stars dotted the black sky and light from the distant Arab section gave the impression of a false dawn. Directly behind me, wide streets of a tiny suburban development stretched across rolling hills.

The houses were all dark; the people were sound asleep. Once again, though, they were about to be rudely awakened.

Carefully and methodically, I attached the heavy magazine to the 20mm cannon mounted in the jeep's center. The magazine held ten shiny brass cartridges and copper-sheathed shells. Each shell, properly placed, could blow up the average-sized house. I had situated the jeep so that the shells would pour into the center of the factory. I had set the brakes on the jeep so that the recoil would not send me rolling back down the hill.

Next I loaded the .50 caliber machine gun with a 1,000-cartridge belt and put three extra belts on the seat beside me. Across my lap was a Volshik automatic pistol, with a reserve pistol between the seats. The major's .45 caliber automatic pistol was jammed into my trousers.

Also on the seat beside me were a dozen Russian-made hand grenades. In the back, in case I needed it, was a Russian mortar with fifteen shells. These weapons were for backup; the machine gun and cannon were far more accurate, and the hand grenades were only for closeup work.

It was 2:32 when I was ready. I sat in the jeep and sighted the cannon on a small ventilator housing in the center of the factory's roof. A light burned in the office, on the corner of the building nearest me, but I had the machine gun aimed at that spot. When the big gun commenced firing, men would come running out of that office.

I would kill those men and destroy their cars parked on a small lot near the office.

Even though I was ready, I waited, planning what I would do after the assault. There were two possibilities.

One, I would return to the remote beach between Tobruk and Darnah and radio for a submarine pickup. There was a good chance that my call would not be honored, or that my call would be picked up by Libyan military personnel. Either way, I would die on that beach.

Two, I would flee the area, circle the city, abandon the jeep and find a cheap hotel. I was wearing the major's uniform, so would have to dispose of that before trying to check into a hotel, no matter how cheap. Several hours had passed since I had killed the major and the two soldiers on the road to Fort Siwa. Chances were excellent that the whole Libyan Army was out looking for me.

Neither plan was very good, but I had no other.

There was also an excellent chance that Cronin and Snyder both were inside the factory just below me. It wasn't likely that they would be in the city, holed up in a hotel, while their incredibly valuable cache of heroin was out at the factory. No, I knew my enemies well. They wouldn't trust all that white gold to underlings.

They were in the factory, sleeping peacefully, believing that I was still rotting away in the stinking jail up on the waterfront.

Now I was ready and I put away all thoughts of anything except the coming battle. If I died in the effort, so be it. Time was running along and I couldn't wait until dawn's light to give the enemy a better chance of escaping.

I held my breath and squeezed the trigger of the 20mm cannon.

There was a thunderous boom and the entire jeep bucked under me as the shell whooshed away in the night.

Bull's-eye!

The first shell hit the ventilator in the center of the roof and a really tremendous explosion ripped through the quiet night. A tongue of flame spurted skyward and I squeezed the trigger again.

The second shell rammed in right on top of the first and the explosion seemed even greater. Swiftly, I adjusted the cannon's sight and squeezed the trigger again.

The whole center of the factory was in flames now. The light in the corner office became brighter and lights snapped on in adjacent windows.

I fired two more shells from the cannon, then gripped the mounted machine gun. I closed one eye and aimed at the door of the little office.

They didn't disappoint me.

Just as the fourth cannon shell burst near the center of the building, the office door opened and two men raced out, firing automatic pistols into the night. They didn't see me on the knoll above them.

I gripped the firing butt and squeezed the trigger. The big machine gun burped and rattled and bucked. The two men went down as fiery tracer bullets cut them in two.

While the first two men were writhing on the ground, not thirty feet from their dark cars, two others came out and, holding their pistols at the ready, began looking around frantically to spot their attacker.

I squeezed the trigger again, bright bullets creased the night and the men went down, firing their weapons at the sky.

Then, I took a few seconds out to readjust the aim of the cannon. I fired two more shells at the near corner of the factory, then raked the office and adjacent windows with the machine gun.

The roof of the factory was on fire now and the fire was spreading, inside and out. Light from internal fires shot from all the windows and I could see the shadows of men running about inside.

"Scurry, little rats," I hissed through my teeth. "Scurry around and collect your valuable drugs while death waits for you outside."

As though someone down there had heard me, four men came bursting out of the office, making a beeline for the cars.

Grinning, I fired the big machine gun and swept the entire parking lot with flaming bullets.

The men began to scramble and writhe as the bullets tore into their flesh. I moved the gun slightly and poured a withering blast into the line of cars.

One by one, their gas tanks ignited and exploded.

God, I was having the time of my life.

But it was all too good to last. Just as I had fired the entire magazine from the cannon and was attaching another, I heard the chatter of machine pistols behind me. I turned, surprised and frightened, to see two men on the roof of a house only fifty yards below the knoll.

Quickly, I swung the machine gun about and poured bullets into the house. In that moment, however, someone at the factory opened up with a heavy machine gun. The copper-plated bullets whanged against the jeep and sang around my ears.

If I had not decided to get out of there, the bullets made up my mind for me. The virtual hail of lead and copper convinced me that it was no place for a growing spy.

Ducking my head as hardware flew over me, I started up the Russian jeep, released the brakes and rammed the vehicle into four-wheel drive. With one hand on the steering wheel and the other working the cannon and the machine gun, alternately, I swooped down off the knoll blasting away at the factory and the men swarming out of it.

My brief attack down the hill took a devastating toll of Cronin's forces. Halfway down, the big machine gun from the factory stopped chattering at the same time a 20mm shell blew the hell out of the southeast corner. I knew that I had knocked out the gun. But there was ample fire from the many hand weapons scattered around the factory.

At the base of the hill, though, I saw bodies scattered

everywhere and knew that the jeep's machine gun had not been slapping bullets harmlessly off inanimate objects. I couldn't count the dead, there were so many of them.

I veered the jeep to the left just before reaching the line of parked cars. It was a dangerous turning, but a necessary one. If I had gone straight, I would have run into heavier fire. But turning sideways exposed a weak point to the men firing from the bright factory windows.

As I streaked along behind the parked cars, I started lobbing hand grenades at the men with guns. As the grenades began to explode and men to scream, I considered it only partial payment for what happened to James Lobell. The men were lucky that Lobell wasn't with me. If he were, he would *rain* hand grenades on them!

The jeep quickly reached the northern part of the factory grounds. Ahead was the city—and freedom.

But I couldn't leave just then. I spun the jeep around and emptied the cannon's magazine into the burning factory. Then, for good measure, I raked the factory with the machine gun in one long, continuous burst.

Only then did I head north again and speed away from the scene, leaving the factory a fiery shambles and Cronin's men a wasteland of twisted and grotesque bodies.

My only sadness, except for memories of Lobell, was that I had not seen Cronin or Snyder during my attack on the factory. Those slippery bastards had a special knack of avoiding my sting.

But the time would come.

I reached the main highway linking the suburb to the main part of the city, and sped along it for two miles, until I was among rows of low factories and skinny houses. Behind me, the sky was bright with the reflected glow of the burning pharmaceutical plant. I could hear low explosions, as though petrol tanks were exploding in the factory. And, far to the north where the city was beginning to awaken, there was the lonesome wail of police sirens.

After another two blocks, I got off the main highway and sped across the southern perimeter of the city to the coastal

highway. When I reached that long, curving stretch of
macadam that circumnavigated the city and cut the desert in
two, all the way to the Mediterranean, I settled down to an
easy cruising of about sixty miles an hour.

As I drove along, I reloaded the cannon and the machine
gun. I had not touched the Volshik machine pistols, but I
replenished my supply of ready hand grenades by taking
several more from the side pouches and placing them on the
seat, within easy reach.

Now, I thought, I'm ready for their pursuit.

But I had not reckoned with the Libyan Armed Forces.
After all, not more than six hours ago, I had escaped by
killing my three captors—three sterling representatives of the
Libyan Army—and I was still wearing the uniform of the
dead major. They would be out in force, looking for me.

As I sailed northward on the dark highway and left the
lights of the city, I saw tiny lights ahead on the highway. It
looked as though several vehicles were pulled up in a tight
cluster, blocking the way. I cut my headlights and slowed to
thirty miles an hour, then stopped. I took the major's binoculars from a bracket on the dashboard and surveyed the road
ahead.

Four military vehicles, including an armored car, were
spread across the road a mile ahead. Their headlights were
off, but their parking lights twinkled in the warm desert air.
And there were squat, silent figures moving about among the
vehicles.

Roadblock.

Somehow, I had to get through that roadblock. It was not
possible for me to hide out in Tobruk. I had no friends there,
no one to help me disappear from the prying eyes and guns of
either Cronin or the Libyan military. I had to make it to the
coast—undetected—and to radio for help. I hoped I would
get that help in the form of a submarine or perhaps even a
destroyer.

But there was no way to run the roadblock and escape
beyond it without pursuit from the military. I could not
possibly kill all the men waiting for me up ahead. The

survivors would hound me until all of us were dead.

Even if I crippled all four vehicles on the road, the soldiers would radio for help and a new roadblock would be established between me and the coast. In fact, there probably was at least one more roadblock beyond this one.

Although it went against my grain to avoid a firefight, I decided that discretion, as the sages say, is the better part of valor. I rammed the jeep into four-wheel drive and eased off the highway onto the dark desert floor. I struck off westerly, lights off, my eyes on the men at the roadblock to make certain I was not spotted.

I drove two miles to the west before turning north again. I found a narrow dirt road there and headed once again for the sea. I passed low huts of sleeping villagers and rumbled up and down sand dunes and rock formations. It was slow going, but at least I was moving forward, away from the pursuing thugs from the ruined factory.

And that was a satisfaction, knowing that I had truly ruined the drug factory this time. Before, I thought I had blown it to hell, but I had only destroyed a part of it. Cronin had rebuilt. This time, though, the lethal cannon on the jeep had destroyed much of it and set the balance on fire. Only a miracle could save the factory from total destruction. When I had fled, there was not even a hint of aid from the local fire department.

As for the six tons of heroin, perhaps I would never know if the drug had been salvaged. Perhaps a part of it already was being loaded on trucks to be taken out of the country. And, I thought with a chuckle, perhaps all six tons of it are burning with a bright blue flame back there in the factory.

Such thoughts threaded their way through my mind as I rumbled along the dirt road toward the ocean. But the main thought was escape. I would have to find a quiet cove to hide the jeep while I sent a radio message for help and then waited for that help. That should be easy, because the northern coast between Tobruk and Darnah was riddled with small, quiet coves hidden by stark cliffs of sandstone.

As I topped a high knoll and could smell the salt air of the

Mediterranean, I gave silent thanks to the military for setting up the roadblock that shuttled me off the main highway. Cronin and his men would use that highway to pursue me. But now I was reaching the ocean on a remote country road. There were many such roads along the coast, so it could take my enemies days to find out which one I took. By then, I would be safely on my way aboard a U.S. Navy vessel of some kind.

The first sign of big trouble came as I eased the jeep up a high bank and saw the dark, flat ocean far in the distance. The jeep engine sputtered.

"Come on, baby," I said aloud, pumping the gas pedal furiously. "Don't give out on me now."

The engine sputtered again and died. I looked down at the fuel gauge and knew that the engine would not start again.

The tank was empty.

Well, what the hell, I thought. The beach is only a mile or two ahead. I can hoof it the rest of the way.

As I climbed from the jeep and began to assemble a small arsenal from the weapons on the seat, I heard the laboring engines of more vehicles coming up behind. Fortunately, the jeep had stalled on top of a high bank. I had an excellent view of the road south. I whipped up the binoculars and scanned the horizon.

Two jeeps and an armed personnel carrier moved along the twisting road, single file, their lights off. At first, I thought the Army had found me, but as I examined the vehicles more closely I could see that they were not manned by military people. There were no insignias on the jeeps or the personnel carrier. And the man sitting high on the personnel carrier behind the massive machine gun wore an ordinary felt hat.

Cronin!

But my God, how had they tracked me?

It was now 4:18 a.m. I had attacked the factory at 2:41 a.m., less than two hours ago. And here were Cronin and his men, fully armed in undamaged military vehicles, hot on my trail. And I couldn't even move the jeep off the road to hide it.

However, I could leave the jeep and head across the sand

dunes on foot. By taking an oblique path from the road, I could reach the ocean in another half hour. But what then? I had no way to radio for help.

And, since the jeep was out of gas, my firepower was sadly diminished. I could swivel the machine gun to fire on my pursuers, but the cannon was stationary. It would only fire forward—and that meant the empty sea, not the vulnerable rear area.

Okay, so we fight with what we have.

I swung the big machine gun around and sighted on the moving column back down the road. A jeep was leading the pack, with the personnel carrier and machine gun right behind. Fifty yards behind that was the other jeep, probably carrying Cronin and Snyder, keeping well back from the line of fire.

If I waited and struck the rear jeep first, I might kill the leaders of the wolfpack, but I would not knock out the big machine gun. And, in a firefight, that was their most formidable weapon. I wanted to hit Cronin's jeep first, but knew that I would pay too dear a price for that delightful treat.

Then I remembered the mortar. I lifted it from its pouch on the door and set it up on the seat beside me. I aimed it as best I could and dropped a shell into it.

Just as it popped and whooshed through the air, I swung the big machine gun around, aimed for the men atop the personnel carrier and squeezed the trigger. The stuttering burst rent the night air like a huge knife tearing up canvas. Fiery tracer bullets coursed through the hot dark air.

The man in the felt hat let out a scream and literally flew off the top of the personnel carrier. His hat tumbled over and over in the air. But the mortar shell went far wide of the mark and exploded harmlessly on the desert, twenty yards to the left of the vehicle.

All three vehicles stopped, but I continued to pour in the fire. I raked the front jeep, then the rear one.

And then came the big surprise.

I saw the ball of flame from the front of the personnel carrier even before I heard the ear-shattering boom. A cannon, bigger than the one I had pointed toward the harmless ocean, had gone off, splitting the desert air like the crack of an earthquake tremor.

I heard the evil whoosh of the shell as it passed overhead, then felt the concussion as it exploded a hundred feet behind me, at the base of the knoll on which I sat.

Even as I cursed the foul luck that gave Cronin such superior fire power, the flame and the boom came again.

This time, the shell did not pass overhead. It struck the earth not twenty feet in front of me (and behind my stalled jeep). The explosion lifted the lightweight little Russian jeep off the earth and dropped it like a rock. I felt the impact deep in my vital organs. My jaw went slack and my mouth fell open, and my head felt as though it would split like an overripe melon.

Then, a virtual deluge of dirt and rocks and fragmented metal rained on me from the sky.

Before I could recover from the shock and sound of that tremendous blast, the air was filled with the husky chattering of the machine gun on top of the personnel carrier. Another man had taken the place of the first.

Hot bullets plunked into the jeep and sailed past me. One streaked between my right arm and my side, tearing at the khaki uniform and sending up the odor of burning cloth.

I bailed out of the jeep. I leaped backward and did a flip in the air. I landed on my knees in the soft sand and something slammed into my head, knocking me half unconscious. It was a hunk of metal from the jeep, torn out of the side like a piece of meat ripped out and spat away by a giant.

As I scrambled back toward the jeep to get an automatic pistol and some hand grenades, the big cannon boomed again. The shell hit just on the other side of the jeep and the impact lifted the jeep on its side.

God, it was tumbling over on me!

I reversed my movements and made a flying leap away from the jeep. I barely made it, and the jeep crunched down on its top, right at my feet. Strewn around me on the sand were a half-dozen hand grenades. I snatched one up and, just as a man came over the rise firing from the hip with a machine pistol, I pulled the pin on the grenade and lobbed it.

The explosion and his scream came simultaneously, and he disappeared in a grimy cloud of fire and dirt.

I had my finger in the ring of another grenade when something hit me—hard—in the back of the head, and the world was a kaleidoscope of murderous color.

Chapter Eleven

Sounds came first.

There was the soft roar of the surf, not far from where I lay.

There was the clinking of metal utensils on dishes. There were low voices whispering. There were the gleeful cries of children playing in the distance.

Then came the smells. Of fish and saltwater and wet sand. Of cooking food and of nearby outdoor toilets and of clothes worn too long without washing.

I opened my eyes and saw the rays of early sun slanting through the open window. I was on a hard little cot in a cramped room of a cottage. From the sounds and smells, I knew that I was in a fishing village somewhere on the coast. From the angle of the sun's rays, I knew that it was dawn, but not which dawn. Had days passed, or had I been out only a couple of hours?

The pain in the back of my head was intense, but it was almost matched by shooting arrows of pain through my shoulders, chest and legs. I wanted to run my hands over my body to find out why I hurt so much—and in so many places—but I had the sensation that I was being watched.

I didn't want them to know that I was awake until my mind was functioning far better than it was. I felt fuzzy.

I closed my eyes and used a kind of biofeedback to determine the extent of damage to my body. I sent messages to each part of my body, mentally searching for bullet wounds and broken bones.

The information came back and I was grateful. No bullet wounds. No broken bones. There were numerous bruises, as though I had been struck and slammed about, but nothing appeared to be serious. I would be sore for days, if I had that long to live.

My mind reviewed the scene on the road south of the coast, and I knew that I had been outgunned by Cronin and his men. If only I could have turned the jeep around to use the 20mm cannon, I might have knocked out the personnel carrier before their cannon blew me out of the jeep.

I pretended to awaken, slowly. Sure enough, someone was in the room, watching me closely. A small dark Arab fisherman stood up in the corner when I began to move my hands. He opened a door and called out in Arabic.

"He is awake now, Meester Cronin."

The little man disappeared through the open doorway which was immediately filled by the imposing figure of a large, portly man with gray hair and a gray mustache.

"We meet at last, Mr. Carter," Robert Cronin said, smiling down at me. He came into the room and sat on a stool beside the cot.

He was not what I had expected. Where I had expected a fairly young and dapper man in impeccably proper clothes, Cronin was almost the antithesis. His body was flabby and his clothes were almost shabby, although they had once been impeccable. His round face was highlighted by a red, bulbous nose, the inescapable sign of too much whiskey.

"Yeah," I said. "We finally meet. Where are we?"

"In the village of Isir, thirty miles east of Bengasi. Why do you want to know? Are you planning a small shopping trip into the city?"

"Something like that."

He pulled his fat knees up with clasped hands and stared at me for a long time. His eyes, once round and perhaps jolly, looked squinty and evil.

"You've caused me a great deal of trouble and cost me a lot of money," he said without rancor. "We shall have to repay you for all that."

"How will you repay me?" I asked. "With a twenty-dollar funeral?"

He laughed and his entire body shook and jiggled like a tattered Santa Claus.

"Oh, we can do much better than that," he said through his mirthless laughter. "I have a yacht ready, anchored a hundred yards offshore. We're making a little voyage to Palermo, Sicily, but I think you may find it to your liking to stop on the way."

"To stop?" I asked, knowing full well what he meant. "There's noplace to stop between here and Sicily."

He laughed again, with even less mirth. "I didn't say you would stop on land," he said, grinning with suppressed glee. "We're taking you to a very special funeral. Your hearse will be a million-dollar yacht. Your cemetery will be the entire Mediterranean. That, Mr. Carter, is several notches above a twenty-dollar funeral, don't you agree?"

"It sounds perfectly lovely, Cronin," I agreed, "but it hasn't happened yet."

"Oh, but it will. When we are fifty miles at sea, you will lighten our load considerably. We salvaged all of our valuable merchandise before my factory burned to the ground in Tobruk. So we will still have that load to carry on to Sicily. But we will enjoy that small chore, as we will enjoy seeing you make a brief detour to the bottom of the ocean."

I felt defeated then. I would mind dying, of course, but I could have faced it more easily if I had known that I had destroyed the six tons of heroin stashed in the Tobruk factory.

"Don't be so disappointed," Cronin said, laughing dryly again. "We'll have a delightful trip for the first fifty miles. Why, we'll have a party going all the time, and you'll have the wonderful companionship of an old and dear friend."

"Sure," I said. "You mean Snyder, of course."

"Of course," he said with a wide smile. He snapped his fingers and Dave Snyder, Agent N22, entered the room. He looked slightly sheepish, but tried to cover it with a scowl.

"Good morning, N3" he said. "Have a good sleep?"

"Up yours, you filthy bastard."

Snyder grinned, but his eyes narrowed and glinted with anger.

"Easy, Nick," he said, his voice tight and lethal. "We could just as easily bury you right here, you know."

"I know, but that still wouldn't change things. You'll be a filthy bastard all your life, no matter what happens to me."

Snyder grunted and rubbed his whiskered chin with his right hand. "If you had any sense," he said almost haughtily, "you would have thrown in with us a long time ago. Just because you risk your life for peanuts is no reason why I should."

"So your life is worth more than mine," I retorted. "How much are you getting to risk it? It better be plenty because you aren't long for this world, chum."

He laughed, but it was a tight, forced laugh. "It is plenty, and it's going to be plenty more when we get to Palermo and start unloading our latest treasure. Too bad you won't be there to see me become fabulously wealthy."

"Don't count on me not being there," I said. "Better still, don't count on you being there. A lot can happen in a four-hundred mile sea voyage."

"Yes," he said, nodding and grinning. "A lot can happen in that long a voyage. Unfortunately, you'll only be around for the first fifty miles. There's nobody to help you, Nick. We've made certain of that."

"Just how many of your former comrades have you helped kill?" I asked.

He shrugged. "They knew the risks," he said.

"How many?"

"Quite a number," Snyder said. "Of course, you learned about the men in London, Rome and Frankfurt, right?"

I nodded.

"While you were unconscious, several others went the same route. We took care of AXE people in Athens, Istanbul, Berlin, Paris, Vienna, Madrid, Lisbon, Oslo, Cairo and Bern. And, of course, the Stockholm guy, your friend Lobell, got it when he attacked our people in Turkey."

"And a bunch of your people also got it during that raid in Turkey," I said, grinning in spite of the hurt at learning of the death of so many of our agents.

"True," he said "but we have plenty of people to spare. Besides, we'll get even with the people responsible for blowing up our Turkish facility and killing so many of our crack agents."

"How can you get even," I asked, "when you don't even know who did it?"

He grinned and Robert Cronin grinned along with him.

"We have many ways of learning what we need to learn. You'd be surprised at how well we're organized."

I wasn't in the least surprised. Cronin and Snyder had known virtually every move I had made since receiving the assignment from Hawk to stop the plan to destroy AXE. Somehow, Raina Missou figured in their plans—I was convinced of that. But I wouldn't let them know that I suspected her. I was still hopeful of coming out alive. I would take care of Raina myself.

"I suppose I would be surprised," I lied. "I don't suppose you could tell me how you knew my every move, sometimes even before I made it."

Both men laughed. Cronin couldn't stop until he went into a coughing fit. Snyder leaned over and stared directly into my face.

"Hawk helped us," he said, breaking into laughter again.

"What the hell do you mean by that?" I demanded. I sat up on the cot and Snyder, still grinning, backed away a few feet. "Don't tell me Hawk is on your payroll."

"Hardly, Mister Carter," Cronin said, still coughing sporadically. "But he inadvertently made it possible for us to keep track of you. Oh, we still needed agents to tell us of your future plans, but we were able to keep track of you everywhere you moved."

"But how?"

Snyder leaned forward again and tapped the dark dial of the digital watch Hawk had given me several months ago.

"Your beloved leader put an electronic bug in that watch," he said. "He put one in a watch he gave me, as well as watches he gave to other AXE agents. I discovered mine after I joined up with Mr. Cronin and we found out that all the electronic devices worked on the same frequency. We merely tuned in on that frequency. You and other AXE agents have been walking signals, telling us exactly where you were at all times."

"You mean Hawk was using these watches to spy on us?"

"Precisely," Snyder said. "I suppose his rationale would be that he needed to keep track of you so he could help you when you most needed it. That would be his rationale, but the truth is that he was spying on you. You couldn't make a move without him knowing it."

I grinned, for the first time.

"What is so funny, Mr. Carter?" Cronin asked.

"If what you say is true, then Hawk knows where I am right now. He's out there waiting for you to make your move." I nodded toward the ocean.

"Hardly," Cronin said. "While you were conveniently unconscious back on the coast road, one of our experts removed the device from your watch. You no longer are a walking beacon, Mr. Carter. We no longer have use of that device because you are in our hands. As for Hawk, even if he knew where you were, he'd be helpless. We've wiped out just about every AXE agent within a thousand miles of here."

Suddenly, I felt very much alone. Lobell was gone and Hawk was helpless. As for Raina Missou, I began to feel guilty for the way I had concluded so readily that she had been tipping off Cronin about my movements. They had kept track of me through the electronic device in my digital watch, and through repeated checks with the AXE computer bank in Washington.

As for the Libyan military, help from that quarter would result in my death by firing squad. Some help.

I couldn't even pretend to be a traitor and join up with

Cronin and his men. They had virtually castrated AXE, the only threat to their plans, so they didn't need additional firepower.

"All right," I said with a deep sigh. "It looks as though I've come to the end of a long career. Why don't you shoot me now and get it over with?"

"And cheat us of the fun we plan to have at sea?" Cronin said, sputtering with laughter. "Oh, Mr. Carter, some of our people have waited an awfully long time to see the great Nick Carter walk the gangplank, stripped and beaten. They want to get a whack at you and then watch the sharks and other fish tear you to bits in the crystal clear waters of the Mediterranean. No, you'll be with us for a time, yet. Don't be so anxious to die. You can't imagine how much pleasure you're going to give all of us during the early part of our long sea voyage. Just you rest easy now. We embark shortly after lunch."

I went to the small window and looked out at the beach. Just outside were several armed goons patrolling back and forth. They were watching me like a hawk, so to speak. On the beach were stacks of wooden crates, and fishing boats were plying the water back and forth to a gleaming white yacht anchored well offshore. The fishing boats were hauling the crates—doubtless filled with heroin—to the yacht.

It looked as though Cronin had hired—or forced—the entire population of the fishing village of Isir to help ready his yacht for departure. The heroin must have been brought up from the factory in trucks so that the remote village could be used as a point of embarkation. That was smart. A yacht leaving Tobruk would probably be searched. When Cronin's yacht had left Tobruk it had not carried illegal cargo and so had been allowed to go to sea. Apparently, there were no checkpoint ports between Isir and Palermo—and the officials in Palermo would have been paid off.

I rubbed the back of my neck and felt every pain in my body bob to the surface as I stood watching the happy fishermen work at loading heroin aboard the big white yacht.

Intrepid, was painted in big white letters on its side.

The boat was flying an Italian flag which flapped in the morning sunlight. The scene outside was almost peaceful, but I knew it would explode into violence if I tried to make a run for it.

No, I would keep my place for now, waiting for the first opportunity to escape. I estimated the speed of the yacht at about six miles an hour. We would make fifty miles in just over eight hours. That meant that about 8:30 p.m., I would take my last walk, running the gauntlet between rows of whip-wielding thugs to a gangplank, and then into the open sea.

The minutes went by slowly and the sun crept higher in the North African sky. Heat built to the sweltering point in the little shack, so I peeled away the major's shirt and trousers.

By noon, the yacht was fully loaded and there were no more crates on the beach. My guards still patrolled outside the shack, and the boats were drawn up on the sand where they baked in the stifling heat. A lovely young brown girl entered the shack with a tray of food and sat near the door watching me eat. I was still hungry from my long fast in the Tobruk jail, so I didn't care that the food was foul, or that the girl—dressed in a tattered wrap that barely covered her ample breasts and wide loins—was watching me closely. Finally, though, my curiosity got the better of me.

"Can you speak English?" I asked. She cocked her head and smiled at me, but said nothing. I asked her if she spoke French, but she still didn't reply. Finally, I tried out my rusty Arabic. She nodded and replied in, of all things, a kind of pidgin Russian.

At first, I was surprised, then I recalled that Russia had had thousands of military and technical advisers in Libya for many years. Apparently, some of the more adventuresome Soviets had found their way to this remote village.

"Can you tell me what is happening out there?" I asked in Russian. "Why doesn't the white yacht leave?"

She laughed and tipped her hand in a drinking gesture. "The men fill up with white drink vodka," she said. "Would you like some vodka? Plenty for everybody.''

So they were turning the whole thing into a party. Well, I could do with a stiff drink to help ease the pain of my bruises.

''Sure. Why don't I just go with you and join the party?''

''No,'' she said, getting up. ''I bring vodka here. We have party alone. Right?''

I nodded and smiled. She darted from the room and came back shortly with a bottle of the potent clear whiskey. I toasted her health, then she toasted mine. We laughed and drank and I began to feel almost human. But I was careful not to drink much. If the others were having a party, perhaps they would all get drunk and become sloppy in their guarding of me. It was a slim chance, but I had no others at the moment.

The girl's name was Ansai. She had black hair, deep brown eyes and the most sensuous mouth I had seen in a long time. Her skin was pale brown. After three drinks, I felt mellow enough to forget about my aches, so began to look at the girl with aroused interest. She seemed more than willing to welcome my advances.

But my interest was more than sexual. I was fascinated by the Russian influence I had seen so far in Libya. First there were the Russian weapons, then the Russian-made jeep. Now came this girl who spoke a patois of Russian and Arabic and English. And the Russians had been involved in Libyan affairs for many years, beginning as far back as 1970 when Russia provided the military with tanks and weapons. Five years later, Russia sold more than a billion dollars worth of advanced military weapons to the tiny Arab country.

I was eager to learn if Soviet influence still applied in Libya and if somehow Cronin and his big drug deal had any Soviet implications. It certainly would explain why he was able to get away with so much without government intervention.

But first things first.

''Who sent you here?'' I asked Ansai.

''Village head man,'' she said with a sweet smile. ''Meester Cronin, he talk with head man and say you need company because come big delay in go-boat. I come see you, bring food, then bring white drink vodka.''

"Okay, company," I said reaching over to put my hand behind her head and draw her close. "Let's have that party you mentioned."

"Oh swell," she said with a chirping giggle. "I like party for drink and have ball."

I took the lithe little woman into my arms and kissed her noting for the first time that she was freshly bathed and perfumed. I thanked God that it wasn't Russian perfume. She returned the kiss, hungrily, and pressed her body against mine. We lay back on the cot and her hand went between my thighs to massage the hardness there.

"Fells great," I said. "Don't stop."

"Feels hard," she said and giggled again. "I'm not stop until you say so."

The dress pulled away easily, since it was tied with only one knot just below her breasts. I opened the bodice and kissed her breasts and felt giddy from the sensuous perfume—and, of course, the vodka. But I was far from inebriated or incapacitated. And the girl was ripe and ready.

We moved together and her strong young hands massaged my back and soothed the many aches there. In fact, I felt no aches at all, except the ache of need. It seemed years since I had been with Raina back in Casablanca.

Ansai was as good as Raina. She rose to meet me and guided me to the warm wetness of her sex. We came together smoothly and, very soon, the hot little shack was almost reverberating with our furious activity on the cot.

When it was done, I lay back and felt total relief. My aches and pains seemed to have disappeared far over the ocean's calm surface, leaving me with a contentment and a laziness that were most welcome.

"You like Ansai?" the girl asked, kissing the tip of my chin.

"Oh yes," I said, meaning it. "I like you very much. Are you coming on the white boat with us?"

She dropped her head and her fine, bright smile faded.

"No," she said. "I don't go on white boat. They say you will go far away and not come back. Men in stiff suits take you to distant land."

Suddenly, I was not so contented. "Ansai, what do you mean, 'men in stiff suits take you to distant land'?"

"Russians," she said. "You don't know about Russians?"

"What about the Russians?"

She shrugged and began tying her dress back in place. I took her soft shoulders in my hands and peered into her pretty face.

"What about the Russians, Ansai?"

"They come in big boat, I hear head man say. They meet white boat, say, fifty miles out in ocean and come take you on big boat to go to distant land. You not know all this? You not like to go to Russia?"

A myriad pieces fell into place right then. All along, I had thought that Cronin's men were lousy shots but they hadn't been out to kill me at all. Cronin realized that I was a valuable commodity—he was going to turn me over to the Russians for a price! I wondered if the Russians were involved with the six tons of heroin as well.

The biggest question now, though, was how I would escape before boarding the *Intrepid*.

Chapter Twelve

As soon as Ansai left the hot little room, Cronin, Snyder and two armed goons came in.

"It's half past one," Cronin said jovially. "We had an unavoidable delay, Mr. Carter, but we're ready to go now. Are you prepared for your final voyage?"

"I'm ready," I said with undisguised bitterness. "Are you ready to sell your soul to the devil?"

Both Cronin and Snyder looked puzzled, but Cronin recovered nicely with a hearty laugh.

"My dear fellow, I sold out to the devil many years ago. I don't understand your remark, but then I don't need to. You are my prisoner, not the other way around. Come, the yacht is waiting."

They marched me from the shack and through a crowd of men, women and children waiting near the beach. I saw Ansai standing beside a gnarled little man, presumably her father or the village head man. She smiled and waved to me. I started to wave back, but one of Cronin's goons whacked me across the forearm with his machine pistol. I noticed that it was a Volshik, but that didn't mean anything in particular. The damned country was full of those Russian babies, it seemed.

Arab fishermen rowed us out to the *Intrepid* and I was hoisted aboard by two burly thugs with machine pistols slung over their shoulders. I turned for a last look at the Libyan shore before I was hustled below to a cramped room that had obviously been used to store cleaning supplies. I could not lay down in the room—and it smelled of ammonia Janitor in a Drum.

We had been at sea two hours when the door opened and I was taken on deck. I could scarcely believe my eyes when I came up. There were a dozen goons on deck and all of them were sloshed on vodka. They were also very friendly. One came up to me and patted me on the behind.

"Ah, our hotshot guest," he said, breathing pure vodka at me. "Glad you could join the party."

"Get away from me, sucker, or I'll break your fucking head open."

He laughed, waving a bottle in one hand and his machine pistol in the other.

"My, but the fish still has his teeth," he roared. "Hey, Jonah, let's get him down and pull his goddamn teeth."

"That'll be enough," Cronin's voice craked over the laughter. "Come back here, Mr. Carter. Sit and enjoy the soft sea breezes. And have something to eat and drink if you wish."

Cronin, Snyder and two stiff-necked blond men I had not seen before were sitting in deck chairs near the stern of the yacht. Along the stern, on enormous white cushions, was a beautiful woman in a bathing suit. She looked as though she had never been in the water, and never would. Her face was heavily made up so that she would have looked far better in an evening gown instead of a bathing suit. I tagged her and the two men as Russians.

Russia stuck out all over them.

The goons released me and I walked across the deck and fell into a chair. My legs were still wobbly from being confined in the cleaning locker. As I sat, I glanced at the sea alongside the boat and guessed our speed at more than 10 knots an hour. We should be at the rendezvous point in about three more hours at this rate. I checked my digital watch and saw that it was 4:14. It would still be daylight when we met the Russian ship, but darkness wouldn't be far off.

I figured out another point then. The delay had been because of the Russian vessel. If we had left the beach earlier, we would have had to rendezvous with the Russians long before dark. The Russians wanted darkness to cover their departure after I was taken aboard.

Everybody waited for the Russians.

Ansai had been dead right about what was to happen to me, but I was curious as to why Cronin had invented that bit of fiction about dropping me at sea and going on to Palermo to sell the heroin. I knew the answer, or thought I did. He and Snyder knew how I felt about the way of life in Russia. If they had told me their plan, they figured I might try to escape, even if it meant certain death for me.

But I did know their plan and I would certainly try to escape. But I would not knowingly commit suicide, even to avoid being sold to the Soviets.

"I'll have that drink," I said as I gazed at Cronin, Snyder and the two stiff-necked men beside them. "And," I added with a wicked grin, "I'd like to buy a drink for the little lady back there."

Cronin and Snyder laughed, but the two blond men saw no humor in my remark. They acted as though the woman did not exist—certainly not there within a few feet of them, and in a bathing suit. While drinks were poured, though, Cronin acknowledged her presence.

"This is Mrs. Tolksen," he said. Then, he introduced the two men, but I didn't even catch their names, much less remember them. "We're giving them a lift, in a manner of speaking. You might say that they wore out their welcome in Libya."

"Funny," I said, taking a deep draught of the vodka to kill the aches in my body once more. "They don't look Sicilian."

Cronin began laughing again and the laughter grew until he was in the middle of a coughing fit.

"My good fellow," he said, slapping me on the shoulder so hard that pains shot up into my head, "we aren't taking them to Palermo. But I see that I am merely arousing your curiosity, so I'll let it drop there. You'll soon learn where everyone is going.''

"I already know," I said, deciding that I didn't want to leave with these jerks thinking I was totally stupid. I raised my glass in a toast. "Here's to a long and happy life in the mother country. *Prosit!*''

The two blond men nearly swallowed their glasses, but the woman merely smiled through her sunglasses.

She raised her glass.

"*Prosit,*" she said in a deep, husky, almost manly voice.

And that was the only word she spoke during the entire voyage.

''I should have known you would learn our little secret,'' Cronin said with his usual joviality. "But it doesn't really matter. You aren't going anywhere, Nick Carter. That is, until we meet our friends in about three hours. Pity we aren't going to make you walk the gangplank. I talked about that so much that I could almost see it happening. I would dearly love to see you naked and trembling up there, waiting to become fishbait. But, alas, you have value to us.''

"How much?" I demanded.

''Aha, you think your beloved Hawk would like to bargain for your hide? I doubt it, Mr. Carter. We have already spread the word that you are going willingly. As far as Hawk knows, you are the traitor to his cause, not Snyder.''

"Sure," I said. I tipped my glass, but did not drink. I kept the vodka, burning, in my mouth until nobody was looking, then spat it onto the deck.

Robert Cronin was a smart and able cookie, but he was letting his joy corrupt one major tenet of racketeering. He was allowing his people to drink too much. Whiskey doesn't mix with business, or anything worthwhile, and these galoots had been slugging down vodka since at least daybreak.

And I also noticed that, although a sumptuous buffet was set up on the starboard deck, virtually nobody was eating. So much booze on an empty stomach spelled double trouble. I kept on slugging at my drink and spitting in onto the already wet deck. The wind was coming up and the sea spray was wetting us all down.

And the dozen goons aboard the *Intrepid* were getting drunker by the minute.

"You certainly can hold your liquor, Nick." Dave Snyder said after the first hour. "At first, I thought you were faking it, but your glass just keeps getting empty."

Cronin and Snyder laughed, but the Russians just stared. I smiled and waved my glass for a refill, but I was thinking: If you weren't so goddamn drunk, traitor, you'd see that I've been spitting this crap all over your shoes. They're damned near as drunk as you are.

But I kept silent and kept on taking in vodka and waiting for an opportunity to let it slide to the deck. My mouth, though was getting numb as hell. But I let a little vodka go into my stomach every now and then. It seemed to provide strength, and it sure as hell provided courage. False courage or not, I needed all I could get.

When the time was right, I was going to turn myself into fishbait. I figured my chances in the open sea were better than they would be once I was taken aboard a Russian vessel. I have spent time in Russian prisons. I wanted no more of that.

The conversation turned then to wealth and what it could do for a man in the free world. The Russians took no part in the discussion, but they listened intently. The woman called Mrs. Tolksen sat smiling enigmatically, hiding behind her sunglasses, rearranging her luscious body on the soft cushions every now and then. I wondered how she would be in bed, and decided that she would be damned good. I had honestly figured that Ansai, in the little Libyan village, would be my last piece of tail on earth, but things were looking better. Even if I didn't excape and had to go to Russia, there was a chance that, someday, at some time I would be able to shack up with this glamorous number. Hell, perhaps she was assigned to be my guide while in the motherland.

"In about four or five years," Cronin said to the usmiling puppets in their stiff suits, "I should be as rich as Howard

Hughes was before he died. I know I'll be a billionaire by
then. The only question is, will I have two or three billion
dollars? I think I'll shoot for three billion. How does that
sound, Mr. Snyder?''

"Tremendous," Snyder said thickly. "A man just can't
have too much money."

"Correct," Cronin said, grinning at the mirthless bastards
from Russia. "With three billion, I can own half of Con-
gress. Instead of building airplanes or buying nightclubs, I'll
invest in pure power. I'll buy leaders and, before you know
it, the whole country will belong to me."

"And after that," Snyder said, waving his glass and
sloshing vodka on his already soused shoes, "comes the
whole fuckin' world."

"Please, Mr. Snyder," Cronin said, clucking his tongue
admonishingly. "There is a lady present."

"And I got my best girl's picture in my wallet," I said,
feigning drunkenness.

Cronin laughed until he nearly choked himself coughing. I
didn't know that old Army chestnut of a joke could still get
laughs like that. But whiskey can bring miracles sometimes.

Dusk came swiftly over the ocean, turning the crystal
waters murky. It started just after six and grew so fast that we
seemed to be heading into it. Actually, we were heading
northwesterly, almost into the teeth of the setting sun.

I calculated the time and our speed and reasoned that the
time was drawing near when we should catch sight of the
Russian ship. I had no idea what kind of ship would come. It
would probably be a gigantic fishing trawler, though. Not
even the Russians would send a warship out to pick up illegal
passengers and (probably) drugs. Or perhaps I only hoped it
would be a trawler, knowing that escape from a warship
would be virtually impossible.

For the past couple of hours, watching the men around me
get drunk, vomit over the sides, sleep it off and get up to
drink again, I had been rattling my brain to think of an escape
plan. I had given up on the idea of ditching at sea. If the
sharks didn't get me, distance would. I would drown before I

swam two miles in my present condition. At best, I could hope for only six miles—and we were more than forty miles from the nearest land.

My best bet was to make Cronin and the others think I had gone overboard to the sea's mercy rather than face a life of prison in Russia. The yacht was big and, if I could go over the side and somehow get back aboard unnoticed, I would hide out while Cronin's men searched the open sea for me. And I knew just where to hide—in that cramped little janitor's closet where nobody in his right mind would stay willingly.

Men had been going to the side to vomit overboard all afternoon, so I knew nobody would be suspicious if I did the same—or pretended to. From that undignified position, it would be a simple matter to flip overboard. From that point, I would be at the mercy of the sea and my own wits.

I would take my chances on that.

Now, all I had to do was wait for a better chance. I was almost the focal point, sitting there with the two Russians, Cronin, Snyder and the mysterious Mrs. Tolksen watching me. I also figured on waiting for a bit more dusk; it would be easier to pull off what I planned if the drunken gunmen aboard had the further disadvantage of poor visibility.

But dusk was coming slowly now as the sun seemed to hang like a big red ball over the western horizon. Soon the Russian ship would loom on the northern horizon and then it might be too late to try my gambit. No, I didn't need the added firepower of frantic Russians—who would be dead sober—to foul things up.

So I waited and sipped more vodka and spat it silently onto Dave Snyder's wet shoes and gazed at the lovely white skin of the Russian woman named Mrs. Tolksen. And listened to Cronin's grandiose chatter about wealth and power and world control. I could say one thing for the chubby and jovial crook: he didn't dream small dreams.

My opportunity came just as the sun was dipping into the sea, and it was better than I had hoped for.

Dave Snyder, slightly green from so much vodka and motion, got up and went to the side. He heaved his cookies into the ocean, then stumbled back along the deck, past the buffet table where rich foods were tempting my empty stomach, and sat in a deck chair, his head in his hands. Cronin and the Russians watched him, shaking their heads and clucking their tongues at the weakness of the man.

Hell, they hadn't seen anything yet.

I waited perhaps ten minutes, then made an urping sound deep in my chest.

"S'cuse me," I said thickly.

I got up, pleased that my actions brought a laugh from Cronin and a chuckle from the lovely Mrs. Tolksen. I hit the rail like a ramrod and bent double over the side, hiding my face from the onlookers. I made puking sounds and laughter rose behind me. Even the Russians were laughing now.

And then I pushed with my feet.

I heard a yell on deck, then the water came up and I hit in a straight dive. Just before I entered the water, I sucked in enough air to sustain me. I was going much deeper than an ordinary falling drunk might go.

I swam hard, knowing that bullets would soon come after me. I went straight down, feeling my lungs begin to hurt from the pressure.

When I was well below the keel of the yacht, I flipped over and swam horizontally, directly under the boat which had already cut its engines.

I had counted on that. I had no desire to be cut to bits by the twin screws that drove the *Intrepid*.

The momentum of the boat carried it past me and, when I came up, I was well to the stern. I swam silently, listening to the chattering of automatic weapons on the starboard side. The goons were shooting up the ocean near where I had gone over the side.

I reached the stern and clung to the rudder until I got my breath and strength back. Then, working swiftly, I yanked off my belt and wrapped it around the rudder, tying it so that, when the engines started up again, the boat would not be able to do anything but cruise around in a wide circle.

It might take them hours to figure out what the hell was wrong.

Then, I eased along the port side, clutching at portholes and the dock bolster to keep from falling back into the ocean. I reached midships and raised up to check the deck. It was empty. Everyone was on the starboard bow ogling the empty sea, looking for my presumably riddled body.

But I was wrong. Not everybody was up there.

Dave Snyder, the turncoat, came up a hatchway, still green around the gills and wondering why the engines had stopped.

I was on the deck so quickly that I marveled that I didn't strain a muscle getting there. Snyder turned just as I leaped at him. Sick as he was, he was still quick, from years of training with AXE.

I hit him with my body and we both tumbled to the deck. The impact carried us dangerously close to the gunwales, but I grabbed a cable running along under the main railing. With my left hand, I searched for Snyder's throat.

With a grunt and a superhuman effort, he thrust his body upward and broke my grip on the cable. My hand slashed out and caught him alongside the head just as the fingers of my left hand found his throat.

Snyder almost panicked then. Knowing that I would soon squeeze the life out of him, he thrashed and let out a loud roar. Thankfully, the roar coincided with the chattering burst of an automatic pistol as someone on the bow took an angry shot at the dark sea—and he hoped my floating body.

Snyder's thrashing, though, was his undoing.

We slipped under the cable and over the gunwale, and plunked in a single splash back into the ocean.

Down, down, down we went, clutching at each other, slashing, punching in slow motion in the water.

We were down there for what seemed an eternity. I became convinced, utterly and irrevocably, that I would die then. I made up my mind that Dave Snyder, Agent N22, turncoat and traitor, would die with me.

But slowly, we rose in the water and bobbed to the surface. I took a deep and welcome breath and ducked under again, pulling Snyder with me. And then I found his throat with my fingers.

He kicked out at me, but the kick went harmlessly past my legs and churned the dark water. I held on, waiting for him to stop thrashing, but he seemed to possess nine lives. The thrashing went on and on, and we were sinking slowly into the deep Mediterranean.

When I felt that I could no longer endure the struggle, the worst happened. My lungs were on fire and I had to let out the foul air that filled them.

When my breath went, we began to sink more rapidly. I gritted my teeth and squeezed as hard as I could.

But Snyder kept on thrashing.

And we both kept on sinking, faster and faster.

In a moment of panic, I almost let go to save myself. But years of training held me there with my deathgrip on the enemy.

Besides, I owed a hell of a lot to a lot of people, especially James Lobell.

Even if I died in the effort, I would kill this son of a bitch for him.

Chapter Thirteen

We must have been forty feet beneath the surface of the Mediterranean before I realized that I had to take a very big gamble or prepare myself for a suffocating death. I had both hands around Dave Snyder's neck, squeezing hard, but he was still struggling.

Somehow, I had to put him away for good.

I risked taking my right hand from his throat. I gripped his left shoulder and spun him around in the water. At the same instant, I released the grip of my left hand, then closed both hands about his head in a twisting lock.

I jerked swiftly and could not hear his neck snap as the bones broke, but I knew that the twisting had been fatal. Snyder went limp in my hands.

For good measure, I held on another few seconds, then released the turncoat agent. His body slid slowly down, past my own, and I began swimming frantically toward the surface.

At least, I hoped it was toward the surface.

Sharp pains rippled through my chest and shoulders and arms. The pains came from too much exertion and too little oxygen. My lungs were bursting and cells in my muscles were dying by the millions. My heart was slapping away like an out-of-control jackhammer, but my extremeties felt numb and cold as though they were not getting any blood at all.

In all my years with AXE, I have faced death on so many occasions that I've lost count. And I have been in worse fixes than I was at that moment, although I could not recall exactly when. Never, though, has my life passed before my eyes, as they say.

On the contrary, I could not remember anything of my life as I swam feebly through the dark water, aching for air and resisting the temptation to just open my mouth and take what came.

Although I was convinced that, this time, there was no way out of my predicament, I did not think about my past life, or even of death. I could think only of how marvelous it would be to take a good deep breath of fresh air.

I would have welcomed mouth-to-mouth resuscitation from a shark!

When I finally broke the surface of the calm ocean, I was nearly unconscious. I gasped several times, taking in small gulps of air and thrashing the water to keep from sinking again. Then, I realized that I was nearing a state of panic.

I calmed my nerves and began to tread water and breathe normally. And I took time to look around me.

There, a hundred yards to my left, was the *Intrepid,* cruising around in a circle. I remembered that I had tied the rudder so that it couldn't do anything but circle. Cronin's skipper had turned on running lights, so I was able to tread water and follow the yacht's course.

I realized that, if I waited where I was, the yacht would circle to within a few yards of me. I swam directly into its projected path, hoping to let it slide past in the darkness and to catch hold as it went by. If I missed, I would take the risk of being chewed up by the twin propellers.

After what I had been through, it was a rather paltry risk.

As I waited, I half expected to see Snyder's body come bobbing to the surface. But he had expelled all the air from his lungs, the same as I had. I knew that he would continue to sink, only to rise when his body began to decay and swell up with gasses.

Snyder would never cause me trouble again. Lobell had received partial payment for his life. I had to get aboard that damned yacht and make certain that my friend from Sweden would receive payment in full. Cronin's death just might satisfy the debt, but I doubted it.

The *Intrepid* approached, coming so fast in its tight circle that the boat listed to its port side, and I swam back a few feet so that I could be on its starboard side. I could hear the big engines throbbing and, above that, voices of men as they ran back and forth on the decks trying to spot me in the dark water. I could hear Cronin's voice, far from jovial now, haranguing the skipper about the jammed rudder. As tired and aching as I was, I chuckled out loud.

The boat came closer and I timed its speed at an even ten knots an hour. Miraculously, my digital watch was still working after all its time under water.

I had no idea what I would do once I caught hold of the boat, but I had no other choice. My desire to kill Cronin and finish at least a part of the job was high, but I was driven by another desire. The yacht seemed to be the only floating object within fifty miles and I could tread water only so long. Dangerous or not, I had to get aboard.

Fortunately, Cronin and all his men were on the port side of the yacht, searching the water inside the wide circle the boat was making. As the boat slipped past, I reached up and grabbed the thick docking bolster.

My hands slipped off and I was bumped harshly back into the water.

I came up spitting water and grabbed at anything I could catch. My right hand closed over a chrome cleat at the stern, but my feet were dangling in the water, dangerously close to the churning propellers. I pulled hard, trying to lift myself up, but my strength was almost gone.

I felt the swiftly-churning water on my legs and that gave me all the incentive I needed to try harder. The whirling screw of the starboard engine was about to amputate both my legs, and possibly other important items of my anatomy.

With the last ounce of my strength, I heaved myself up until my chest was hard against the bulging gunwale and my right foot had a hold on the bolster. I clung there for a few minutes, trying to regain enough strength to heave myself onto the deck of the *Intrepid*.

Then, as the yacht swept around to the west and headed southwest, I thought I saw the silhouette of something exceptionally large and imposing about a mile due west. But the eyes deceive you at night on the open sea. I could have seen a low cloud, or I could have seen nothing at all.

The distraction was enough to set off my danger instinct. I suddenly knew that, tired as I was, I had to get away from the circling yacht and trust my own recources in the open sea.

Reluctantly, but hastily, I loosened my grip on the cleat and plunked backward into the ocean. I began swimming away from the churning wake of the yacht.

When there was about a hundred yards' distance between me and the boat, a most incredible thing happened.

Brilliant lights, seeming to emanate from a high, broad tower, lit up the entire section of ocean. The gleaming white yacht was the focal point of the lights. I could see the boat's silhouette, see men running up and down its decks like frantic ghosts.

And then a voice, heavy and metallic and sounding like the crack of doom, filled the air:

"Cut your engines and throw away your guns."

There seemed to be a deep silence for the next few seconds, then the voice boomed again over a loudspeaker behind the bank of blinding lights.

"Ahoy, *Intrepid*. Cut your engines. Throw your guns overboard. You have ten seconds to comply."

The answer came swiftly. I heard the chattering of automatic weapons, then the shattering of glass. Four lights in the incredible bank of lights went out.

Whatever was out there did not frighten Cronin and his men. They were shooting at it, although it was obviously bigger and far more ominous than the yacht.

I waited to see what would happen next, but didn't have to wait long.

From behind the bank of lights came two long tongues of

orange flame, followed immediately by the crashing thunder of naval guns.

One shell landed just short of the yacht and sent up a tremendous geyser. The concussion nearly blew me out of the water and I felt my stomach, chest and groin go numb.

The second shell hit paydirt.

The shattering explosion was ear-splitting. The *Intrepid* sat motionless for a moment, silhouetted against the stark lights. Then, it seemed to fly apart from the center, shooting fiery embers and dark fragments of wood and steel and glass and human flesh into the air above the ocean.

This second explosion, when the boat went up in a billowing mushroom cloud, knocked out my hearing altogether and nearly crushed my chest.

I went under and tumbled over and over in the water as wave after wave hit me like spurting lava.

My lungs took in water and I coughed violently as I broke the surface again. And then the coughing stopped and I felt myself losing consciousness. Once again for me, the world went blank.

The dream returned and I was walking down a sunny street into a soft, washing breeze. My feet were moving, but they were not touching the sidewalk. I felt very good and a sense of well-being seemed to emanate from the sunlight and fresh, warm air.

And I knew why the dream kept recurring.

My subsconscious was telling me to get the hell out of the espionage racket, to find a quiet place in the country, to take long, safe walks down sunny streets—to live happily ever after.

But, even as I began to awaken, my mind was on my business.

All I could think of as I came around was that six tons of heroin, representing many millions of dollars in street sales—plus many millions of agonies for the people who made the buys—had been blown to smithereens and were now a permanent part of the blue Mediterranean. It didn't

matter to me that Cronin and his cronies had also been blown
to bits, or that Snyder the turncoat was feeding the fish on the
bottom of the sea.

They all were destined for death the minute they made the
decision to get rich from the miseries of other people on this
sometimes unsavory planet.

I was still thinking of the lost heroin, and its effect on the
sea life near where the yacht had been blow up, when I
opened my eyes and recognized the familiar surroundings of
a ship's hospital. A Navy corpsman smiled down at me.

"Glad to see you awake, sir," he said. "You need to get
something solid in that stomach of yours."

As if on cue, my stomach rolled and lurched with hunger. I
saw the tube then, leading from a suspended bottle to a
bandage on my right wrist. They had been feeding me in-
travenously.

"How long have I been here?" I asked, my voice still a bit
shaky.

"Couple of days. You're aboard the *USS Alabama*."

I nodded, although I had not known which American
warship had picked me up. Then, I remembered the bright
lights and the horrendous explosion that had sent me tumbling head over heels in the water.

"Are you the guys that blew the *Intrepid* out of the
water?"

"Yep. We're also the guys that shelled a factory in Turkey
a few days ago."

"I figured that," I said. "A good friend of mine was killed
during that shelling."

The corpsman shook his head. "No, he was dead before
we commenced firing. I heard that the captain and a special
guest aboard talked with him by radio when we heard shooting on the shore. He was mortally wounded and told us to
fire. When his radio went dead and the skipper couldn't
establish contact again, the ship opened fire."

I opened my mouth to ask about the special guest, but the
corpsman stopped me.

"No more talking until after you eat."

He raised the head of the bed and plunked a tray of food on my lap. I ate ravenously, unaware even of what I was putting into my mouth. It was far better than the usual Navy chow. As I ate, the corpsman chatted.

"That special guest with the captain wants to talk to you as soon as you're able," he said. "He's a heavyset man with a tweed jacket and a big black cigar. I guess you know him, right?"

"Right," I replied through a mouthful of food. "You might as well let him know now. I'm as able as I'll ever be."

The corpsman shifted from foot to foot, acting a bit uneasy.

"There's also a woman aboard and she has been waiting right outside the whole time you've been in sick bay. She begged me to let her see you as soon as you woke up."

"Do you know her name?"

He shook his head. "She came aboard one night when we were laying off the coast of Morocco. I think it was Casablanca. She had kind of golden skin and . . ."

"Raina Missou!" I said, feeling considerably better than I had felt for some time. "Hell, sailor, let her in."

He still shifted nervously. "I don't know, sir. The captain said I was to let him know right away. I think the man in the tweed jacket wants to talk to you first. But the woman is so damned beautiful, and so insistent."

"Look, it's all right. The woman is an old friend. Let her in for a few minutes and we won't tell a soul about it. Okay?"

"I don't know. If the captain ever got wind of it, he'd—"

"He won't get wind of it," I said, anxious to see Raina and to apologize for ever suspecting that she was one of Cronin's people, or had reported my movements to him or to anyone else. The bug planted in my digital watch proved that Snyder was the one that had been tracking my movements. Raina was innocent, but I had been ready to head back to Casablanca and kill her, based on suspicion alone.

"All right," the corpsman said. "I can let you have five minutes alone, then I'll have to ask the woman to leave so I can report to the captain that you're awake. You have to promise not to tell him or his guest that I let the woman in to see you."

I held up my right hand. "Scout's honor," I said, smiling in anticipation of seeing the beautiful Raina Missou. "Nobody will ever know."

The corpsman nodded and smiled. He went out and I heard him talking to someone in the doorway. The door closed and Raina came up beside the bed. She was smiling and her golden skin and lovely figure were like a beacon in the night. Her rich perfume filled the antiseptic hospital room and I felt warm and horny all the way down to my toes.

"How are you, lover man?" Raina said in her lovely, delicate sing-song voice.

"Just great," I said. "How are you, Raina?"

She smiled and bent down to kiss me. Then, she stood above me, the smile fading from her face as lines hardened around her eyes and mouth.

"You seem to have a hundred lives, Nick Carter," she said in a strange, flat voice. There was no sing-song quality to it now. "But I think you've used up the last one."

"What are you talking about, Raina?" Danger signals jangled in my head, but even the signals seemed to sense that it was too late.

Raina backed away and pulled a small revolver from between her full breasts.

"Raina, what's this all about?"

She smiled crookedly and leveled the gun at my head.

"Remember the safehouse you attacked on Corsica several weeks ago when you were fighting an organization called NOTCH?"

"Yes, sure, I remember it."

"Everyone in that house died from poison gas you somehow managed to put into the ventilation system."

I nodded. "I had guessed that," I said, "but this is the first time I've received any confirmation. How do you know about that?"

"My father was one of the last twelve NOTCH leaders in the sub-basement of that house," she said. "You and I met a long time ago, Nick, but only because my father wanted me to get to know you and to keep him informed of your activities. He was a top man in the NOTCH syndicate and you all but destroyed it. You killed him. And, my lover friend, I am going to kill you.''

I gazed incredulously at Raina Missou as she stood not five feet from me with the little pistol raised in one golden hand. I had to force myself to remain calm, and it sure as hell wasn't easy.

''Raina, you've had plenty of chances to kill me since I destroyed that syndicate—and your father, as you say. Why did you help me so many times when you carried such a grudge?''

She smiled the crooked smile again. ''Cronin was my father's worst enemy for years,'' she said easily. ''I was helping you because I knew you would kill Cronin. Once that was done, I would get my own revenge.''

''But how did you arrange to be here with Hawk, on an American battleship?''

''That was easy,'' she said. ''I contacted your agent in Rabat and he put me in direct touch with your boss. I told the man with the smelly cigars how I had helped you in Casablanca and that I was in love with you. When he said that he was on the way to help you, I begged to come along.''

I almost chuckled, thinking of Hawk and how he might react when a girl like Raina Missou came on strong. But my musings were brief; I was in one hell of a lot of trouble.

''Raina,'' I said, using a soft and easy approach with her, ''you don't want to get revenge like this. As soon as you fire that little popgun, they'll kill you, you know.''

''I know. I'm ready for it.''

''No you aren't. Nobody is. Raina, put down the gun and let's forget this whole thing. Nobody knows that your father was a member of NOTCH. We can take you back to Casablanca and you can go on with your life there. You—''

''No dice, Nick,'' she said. ''You didn't kill the syndicate bosses. A couple of them are alive and they know that my father had been stealing from them over the years. He stashed his fortune away in Switzerland and I'm the only one who knows where it is. The syndicate wants me. After they get the information they need, they'll kill me. You see, Nick, I had to get out of Casablanca when I did and I used you and your boss to achieve two purposes. I got away from the syndicate and I now have a chance to avenge my father's death. You can't beat that, especially when I'm already marked for death.''

"Raina, we can help you, protect you.''

She shook her head and her long, dark hair bounced on her shoulders and trailed down to the smooth golden cleavage. God, she was beautiful.

She was also lethal.

"The corpsman said I had five minutes with you,'' Raina said, gripping the pistol more tightly. "The time is about up. I plan to shoot as soon as someone opens the door.''

I knew then that it was useless to talk to the girl. Apparently, she had been quite close to her father, whose name I didn't even know, and she was dead set on revenge.

I couldn't let the corpsman open that door and have her blow a hole in my head.

Slowly, I worked my left hand under the tray the corpsman had placed on my lap. Under my breath, I counted to three. On the count, I flipped the tray and sent it flying toward Raina.

She fired.

The bullet struck the tray and ricocheted off the ceiling. At that precise moment, the door opened and two big Marine MPs rushed in and grabbed Raina.

Right behind them was David Hawk, puffing viciously on a black cigar. His right arm was in a sling. As the Marines dragged Raina's sagging, sobbing body out of the room, Hawk eyed me with a kind of contempt.

"I'm ashamed of you, N3,'' he snapped as he pulled a chair up beside my bed and sat in it. He put a tape recorder on his lap and held the microphone in his hand. "After all these years, you still trust women too much.''

"That's true, sir," I said, feeling weak from the close call with death. "Women are my weakness."

I didn't point out that women apparently were his weakness also or he would not have let Raina Missou talk him into bringing her along. I felt bad about Raina. I had once suspected her, then had felt guilty about that suspicion. In my own way, I had loved her. It was painful seeing her dragged away by Marine guards, seeing her broken in spirit.

And then I realized that Hawk had not succumbed to Raina's charms. He apparently knew about her all along, but figured that I had gone soft on her. The only way to prove to me that she was an enemy was to bring her along and let her confront me.

Christ, what a way to prove a point. I could have died and the truth would not have helped me a damned bit.

But that's the way Hawk works.

"Yes," he said. "Women are your weakness. Remember that the next time you meet someone like Raina Missou. N3, I've been chasing all around the world cleaning up after you. I had to strike in Turkey and again here in the middle of the Mediterranean. I don't like to get involved this way. I expect my agents to handle things a bit better."

"Yes, sir," I said, "but you have to admit that this situation was different. We've never had an enemy try so diligently to kill you and all our agents. Not even Killmaster could have handled this case alone."

"And why not?"

I shrugged and suddenly felt very sleepy. I also felt nauseous from the swirling cigar smoke in the little room.

"I think the corpsman put something in my food to make me sleep," I muttered, closing my eyes and wanting very much to drift away to dreamland.

"He did," Hawk said crisply. "You'll sleep for at least another 24 hours. By that time, we'll be in Italy where I can get a plane back home. There's a great deal to be done, N3. We have to recruit and train a lot of new agents. They pretty much ripped us to pieces as an organization."

"Yes, sir," I mumbled, feeling heavy sleep wash over me like a soft, warm wave.

"Meanwhile, I need some information from you. I know where you have been, but I don't know everything you've done."

I perked up a little just then. "By the way, sir," I said. "How did you know that I was in Libya and on board the *Intrepid*? Cronin found the tracking device you put in my digital watch."

"They found one of them," Hawk said. "The one I wanted them to find. I had a second one, disguised as a battery, embedded in the works. Any more questions?"

I felt the wave of sleep again, but I did have another question. Even in my groggy state, I remembered that Cronin had planned to meet with a Russian ship and to sell me to the Russians. And I remembered the two stiff-necked blond men and the glamorous-looking Mrs. Tolksen who presumably were blown up with the yacht.

"Sir, I don't think you know this," I said, stifling another yawn, "but Cronin's yacht was supposed to rendezvous with a Soviet ship. They were going to sell me—and probably the heroin—to the Russkies."

"I assumed all that," Hawk said, "when I saw the big trawler. It arrived just after we hauled you aboard."

"So there *was* a ship," I said. "I'm sure glad you got there first. I wouldn't want to be on that trawler, heading for the mother country."

"You wouldn't be heading there," Hawk said. "You would be on the bottom of the Mediterranean."

"Sir? Do you mean that . . ."

"Let's just say that there was an accident at sea," Hawk said firmly. "Now, anymore questions?"

"No, sir," I said, feeling an irrepressible wave of sleep again. "I just want to sleep and . . ." I drifted into sleep, but Hawk's crackling voice jolted me awake.

"You can sleep later, N3" he snapped. "Right now, you have things to put on record."

"Please, sir," I mumbled, straining to keep my eyes open,

and to keep from vomiting from the sickening cigar smoke.
"I just want to sleep."

I heard the click as David Hawk turned on the tape recorder, then heard the crisp, cool, authoritative—and quite
familiar—command:

"Report."

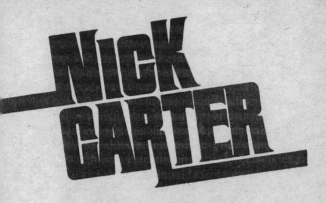

DOUBLE IDENTITY

CHARTER
NEW YORK

AWARD BOOKS ARE PUBLISHED BY
UNIVERSAL-AWARD HOUSE, INC.
DISTRIBUTED BY ACE BOOKS
A DIVISION OF CHARTER COMMUNICATIONS INC.
A GROSSET & DUNLAP COMPANY

Chapter One

PEEP SHOW

From modern Peking Airport to the center of the ancient Forbidden City is about forty kilometers. That is the linear distance. Reckoned in terms of time, or in any other possible fourth dimension a traveler might conjure up, it could as easily be forty millenniums! Once through the busy Outer City where tall chimneys belch clouds of smoke and long rows of new apartments remind one strangely of Los Angeles—white stucco and red tile—the traveler can enter into the comparative peace and quiet of the Purple City. Beyond this, at the very center of the great yellow web that is China, is the Imperial City. Or, as the masters of China today prefer to call it, the Tartar City.

Wang-wei, Chief of Coordination of Chinese Secret Services, glanced impatiently at the watch on his slim wrist. It would never do to be late to *this* conference! The Celestial Twins—upon occasion Wang-wei permitted himself a sense of humor—the Twins themselves had summoned him. Mao and Chou.

Wang-wei glanced at his watch again and muttered impatiently to the driver of the small, black, Russian-built sedan, "Faster! T'ung-chih!"

The driver nodded and prodded the car. Wang-wei's well-manicured nails played a busy tattoo on his pigskin breifcase, that inevitable badge of officialdom. He was a neat little man in his early fifties with a thin, sardonic copper-skinned face. He wore dark trousers and handsome British-made shoes and a black high-buttoned blouse in the para-military style. Because of the nip in the bright October day, he was wearing a conservative sport jacket. He was hatless, his graying hair neatly *en brosse*. Wang-wei was handsome and well preserved for his age, and he was vain of it.

The black car sped through a series of gates and came to T'ien An Men, the entrance to the Tartar City. Here, sur-rounded by golden-tiled roofs, was a large public square. The driver slowed and glanced back at Wang-wei for instruc-tions.

For a moment Wang-wei paid him no attention. He was thinking that it would be a pity if he could not see his mistress, Sessi-yu, while he was in Peking. His eyes nar-rowed and he felt his loins stir as he thought of Sessi-yu and her Golden Lotus! What a Lotus it was—almost a thing apart from herself, an entity well versed in the tender arts, rich with the lore of ten thousand years of exquisite venery.

The driver grunted something, and Wang-wei returned to the mundane world. He had best keep his wits about him for the next few hours. Soon now he would find out what the Celestial Twins wanted with himself—and with his prize Turtle.

Across the square stood two drab government office build-ings. Between them was a compound fenced by a high, blue-painted wall. Wang-wei left the car and entered the compound through a wooden gate guarded by a soldier of the Security Troops. The man carried a tommy gun slung over his shoulder. He scowled at the pass Wang-wei showed him, but waved him in.

It was very quiet in the compound. An ancient house, three-storied with a tiled roof and curved eaves in Old China style, stood in the center of the compound. For a moment Wang-wei stood and surveyed the house with an enigmatic little smile. Even had he not been quite familiar with it, he would have known from the style of architecture and the curvature of the eaves that it was a house of felicity. Many spirits had been consulted before it was built in this exact spot.

Another tommy-gunbearing guard came down a graveled path to meet him. Wang-wei displayed his pass again, after which he was escorted into the house and upstairs to a small anteroom on the third floor.

Because he had been ushered to this particular room Wang-wei knew that something very special was up. The main room, just beyond the sliding door of saffron paper, was a very special room indeed. Wang-wei had visited it many times before on both business and pleasure. It was, in a very real sense, *his* room! A mainstay of his work when he was in Peking. That the Twins had chosen it for this meeting meant that something of vast importance was afoot!

Wang-wei allowed himself to guess. Counter-espionage? Wang-wei permitted himself a small dry smile. What else? His Turtle, Turtle Nine, had also been brought to this place. Was probably downstairs at this very moment. Turtle Nine, so carefully groomed for so many years. So well trained. So meticulously indoctrinated and brainwashed. And, less than a year ago, the skillful plastic surgery! Wang-wei permitted his smile to become full blown. He was right. He *must* be right. They were going to use Turtle Nine at last. Use him on the one mission for which he had been trained for years.

The saffron paper door slid back with a hiss. A high ranking officer crooked a finger at Wang-wei. "Come," said the officer in a soft Cantonese accent, "you are wanted." He closed the paper door after Wang-wei, but did not follow him into the large rectangular room.

Wang-wei hesitated a moment at the entrance, clutching his briefcase to his narrow chest. He glanced down at the floor and felt the same start of surprise he always did, even though he had been in the room many times. The floor was of clear glass, looking into a large apartment below. It was, in effect, nothing more than a huge two-way mirror of the type used for peep shows—and spying—the world over. From below it appeared that the ceiling was a mirror intended for obvious uses.

At the far end of the room two men sat in comfortable chairs. On a low table between them were tea things and a bottle each of whiskey and soda. There were glasses and ashtrays, but neither of the men was smoking or drinking. Both of them stared at the newcomer with interest.

The oldest of the men, a round little fat man with the bland face of a Buddha—which, in a modern version, he some-times supposed himself to be—waved to a third chair and said, "Come, Wang-wei. Sit down. Things are about to start. We have only been waiting for you."

As Wang-wei sank into the armchair he was aware of cynical amusement in the dark eyes of the other man. He had not yet spoken, this man. He was younger than the Buddha type, thinner, healthier looking. His dark hair was thick and glossy and blazed at the temples with a tinge of gray. Now he leaned forward, well-kept hands on his knees and smiled at Wang-wei. "So—it is the little Master of the Turtles! And how are all your slimy charges keeping these days, com-rade?"

Wang-wei's answering smile was nervous. He knew that Chou had never liked him, that he questioned Wang-wei's competence for the high and important office he held. And that name—Turtle Master! Only Chou ever dared to taunt him with that. But then Chou could do pretty well as he liked—he was heir apparent.

Wang-wei kept his face impassive and, with an inward prayer that Mao's decaying kidneys would hold out forever, he snapped open his briefcase and extracted a thick sheaf of papers. As he did so he glanced down through the glass floor into the apartment below. There was activity down there now, but nothing important. Merely a servant turning on soft lights and arranging bottles and glasses on a little bamboo bar in one corner.

Chou saw his glance and chuckled. "Not yet, Master of Turtles. The fun hasn't started yet. I hope you're up to it. It might be a little bloody, you know. And if the blood turns out to be your Turtle's—"

The Buddha type waggled a fat finger at Chou. "Enough!

Save you jokes for later. With all that I have on my shoulders I have come, in person, to see this thing. I am almost convinced that it will work—almost, but not quite. So let us get on with it." He turned to Wang-wei. "What of this Turtle Nine of yours?" The fat little man tapped some papers on the table. "I know much of him already, but I wish to hear it from your lips. It is you, after all, who bears the ultimate responsibility."

Wang-wei did not like the sound of that, nor the glint in Chou's obsidian eyes, but he was helpless. It was *not* his plan, only his Turtle, yet he was to be held responsible! With an inward sigh of resignation he riffled through his sheaf of papers. He began to read in his harsh, clipped north China accent:

"Turtle Nine—name is William Martin. Born and raised in Indianapolis, Indiana, USA. Nineteen when captured in Korea. Now thirty-three. Listed by the Americans as dead in action. Death insurance paid his widow, who is now remarried and lives in a town called Wheeling, West Virginia. There were no children. This Turtle has always had Number One status, has always been highly cooperative. He is considered completely trustworthy and—"

"Considered trustworthy by whom?" Chou leaned to stare at Wang-wei, his mobile lips curled in a half-smile.

Wang-wei flushed. "By me, sir! This Turtle has been a prisoner now for fourteen years and, though I have not had charge of his training all that time, I will stake my life that he is the best Turtle we have."

Chou leaned back in his chair. "That is exactly what you are doing, little Master of Turtles."

Mao made an impatient gesture. "Never mind all the details, Wang-wei! Get on with it. This Turtle has been subjected to all the usual procedures?"

Wang-wei ran his finger down a typed page. "Yes, Comrade Leader. He has been completely re-educated! That, of course, was done long ago. He is now politically reliable, has been for years."

Chou crossed his legs and lit a long Russian cigarette. He

winked at Wang-wei. ''What the Americans crudely describe as brainwashed?''

Wang-wei ignored him. He focused his attention on the Buddha, the father figure of all China. The fat man was frowning now. He plucked at a petulant little mouth with a finger. ''There is something I do not understand—why has this Turtle Nine never been used before? As I understand it you number these Turtles in the order of their capture? So this particular Turtle, this William Martin, was the ninth American soldier captured in Korea?''

''That is true, Comrade Leader.''

Mao frowned. ''Then I ask—why has he never been used before if he is so reliable? Nineteen fifty-one was a long time ago—you must have taken many Turtles since then, yes? One is a little, er, surprised at the life span of this Turtle.''

It was a tight bind and none the less so because Wang-wei had half-expected the question and had prepared for it. Turtle Nine *had* been around a long time. The plain truth was that Turtle Nine was a handsome and superbly built specimen and had long ago taken the eye of a very high ranking official in another department. This aging official, enamored of the young man, had made it worth Wang-wei's while to keep Turtle Nine at home and safe. As simple as that, really, yet it was not a thing he could tell the Buddha figure. Hardly. Mao was a strict puritan; he had had men shot for lesser perversions.

Wang-wei launched into his prepared story. Turtle Nine was of much value in instructing other Turtles. He had, also, suffered a series of illnesses. Lastly, and most important, Turtle Nine had been saved for a really important job, a mission of the first rank, such as that now at hand.

Mao appeared to accept this. Chou shot an ironic glance at Wang-wei with his dark eyes and contented himself with saying, ''One sometimes wonders if you allow yourself to become attached to the Turtles, Wang-wei?''

Wang-wei forced a hard laugh from his thin lips. ''With all proper respect, Comrade, that is ridiculous!'' He made a little *moue* of distaste. ''They are, after all, Turtles!'' It was enough, his expression seemed to say. In China there is nothing lower than a Turtle! It is a mark of disgrace and a deadly insult, to call a man a Turtle. It was quite natural that the captured Americans, those chosen for re-education and brainwashing, should be so called. At the moment Wang-wei had over a hundred such Turtles in his cage.

Mao consulted his papers again. ''Turtle Nine has undergone deep hypnosis, yes? He is a good subject?''

Wang-wei nodded. ''The very best, Comrade Leader. He is in hypnosis at the moment. He will not be so again until he reaches Peshawar. Only our agent there, Turtle Nine's control, can trigger him. She is now awaiting his arrival to put Segment One of Dragon Plan into operation.''

Chou grinned at Wang-wei. ''Our agent in Peshawar is a woman?''

''Yes, Comrade. An American girl. A member of their Peace Corps who is sympathetic to us.''

''But why a woman?'' Mao stared intently at Wang-wei, a frown on his chubby features.

Wang-wei explained, his coppery face intent, ignoring Chou's knowing smile. ''We thought it best, Comrade. For many reasons. First the American woman is on the spot, the most strategic spot, exactly where we want her—in Peshawar at the mouth of the Khyber Pass. She *really* works for the Peace Corps—she is quite genuine. Another thing of importance is that she is known to be promiscuous, she has had many lovers, and one more will excite no comment. But most important is that Turtle Nine's hypnosis has been sexually oriented. He will, er, react only to commands given in a certain manner and in a certain place.''

This latter had been Wang-wei's own idea and he was quite proud of it.

Chou, always a little faster on the uptake than his master, looked at Wang-wei with a grin. ''What could be more secret than a lady's bedroom, eh?''

''Exactly, Comrade.''

Mao held up a hand for silence. He picked up a sheet of paper and looked at it. ''So much for that. I presume you people know what you are doing. You had better! Now—this Turtle Nine has also undergone extensive plastic surgery in the past year?''

''True, Comrade Leader.''

Mao stared at Wang-wei with round, cold little eyes. ''It was a success, this surgery? And also the special training? The personality indoctrination? This Turtle Nine now is a double for the AXE agent, Nick Carter? He looks and walks and talks like Nick Carter?''

Wang-wei hitched his chair a little closer to the throne. He was on firm ground now. ''Comrade Leader,'' he said, ''Turtle Nine even *thinks* like Nick Carter! He thinks he *is* Nick Carter! The one called Killmaster. At the moment, that is. Before he starts his journey he will, of course, be decontrolled. Until he reaches Peshawar. Our agent there, the American woman, will be able to trigger him back into full hypnosis at any time. He will then assume, as planned, the full identity of Nick Carter, of this Killmaster.''

Mao picked at his mouth. ''Just how familiar are you with the details of Dragon Plan?''

Wang-wei shrugged in a courteous manner. It was not wise to appear too knowledgeable. He could guess most of it, naturally, but that was kept to himself.

He said: ''My own part mostly, Comrade Leader, as is natural. I have had Turtle Nine under close personal supervision for the last six months. He has studied films and pictures of the real Nick Carter. Also records of the man's voice which we had to beg from the Russians—they did not wish to share with us.''

Chou, in a malevolent voice, said, ''The Russians—they are also Turtles!''

Wang-wei continued, ''Turtle Nine now dresses as Nick Carter. In what the English call conservative good taste. His haircut is the same, and all his personal belongings, as nearly as we could come. He has been trained in the use of this agent's weapons—a 9mm Luger, stripped down, and a throwing stiletto which the real Nick Carter carries in a sheath on his right forearm. He will, under the controlled hypnosis, be as ruthless and as deadly a killer as the real AXE man.''

"And that," interrupted Chou, "is as deadly as you can get. The man is a fiend, I hear. Nothing of paper about this one! If your Turtle can kill him, Wang-wei, you will be doing all of us a great service. The Russians, those fools, have been trying for years without success."

Again Mao lifted a pudgy hand. "That is all true, of course. This Nick Carter is worth a dozen divisions to the West. He must be killed, naturally. That is Segment Two of Dragon Plan. But Segment One is still the most important— the war between India and Pakistan *must* go on! There must be no cease-fire! If, despite all our efforts, there *is* a cease-fire it must be continuously violated—by both sides. That, of course, is the essence of Segment One of Dragon Plan—to keep the pot boiling! When both India and Pakistan have exhausted themselves, then we will know what to do."

Chou said, in a soft voice, "And Segment Two, I believe, is to lure the real Nick Carter? To draw him into following the double, the Turtle, and then kill him? Dispose of Killmaster once and for all?"

Wang-wei nodded. "That is so, Comrade. At least we hope so. We are counting on the AXE organization's learn- ing that their precious Nick Carter has a double who is working against them. We think that then AXE will send the real Carter to find the double and dispose of him—only we hope it will be the other way around."

Chou smiled. "I hope you are right, Wang-wei. For your own sake."

The Buddha type played patty-cake with his fat hands. "That should be amusing—Nick Carter killing Nick Carter! Too bad that it will probably take place in some obscure corner of the world where we cannot watch it."

Wang-wei smiled and nodded. Then he pointed down through the glass floor. "They are starting, Comrade Leader. Now you will see my Turtle Nine in action. Four men will try to kill him as he makes love to a woman. My Turtle knows nothing of this, of course. He thinks this is routine, all a part of his privilege day for good behavior. My senior Turtles, you know, have a day off every week for, er, for relaxation.''

Chou gave an oily chuckle. ''You are indeed a great one for euphemism, Turtle Master. And I will tell you something else, my little friend. You are a liar and a hypocrite! You have staged these peep shows many times in the past—and always you pretend to be bored with them. You even seem to disapprove of your own methods, as though they were not quite moral.'' Chou lit another of his long cigarettes. ''Do you know, Master of Turtles, that I do not believe in your little act? I think you enjoy these little shows—as much, for instance, as I do.'' Chou leaned back in his chair, crossed his long legs, and blew smoke at Wang-wei with a crooked smile. ''Now—get on with it!''

Mao, the bland fat little Father of China, gazed from one to the other. His frown was slight but his voice was cold. ''Yes—get on with it. And I give you two a warning now— this dissension between you will cease! I do not know the cause of your quarrel, nor do I wish to know, but if it continues I will take steps! The People's Republic cannot afford *your* bickering. Is that clear?''

Chou said nothing. He leaned back and closed his eyes. Wang-wei nodded anxiously to the Leader. He had just realized. It had just come to him in a blinding flash of intuition—Chou coveted Sessi-Yu! What a fool he had been to introduce them . . .

Mao pressed a button on the table. A servant glided unobtrusively in to draw the jalousies and turn off the single light. Each man made himself comfortable in the darkened room. Wang-wei shot a furtive glance at Chou and saw him unfasten his collar and wipe his high forehead with a clean white handkerchief. Wang-wei reached to unhook his own collar. He had noticed that he had a tendency to sweat during these peep shows.

The apartment below was like a brightly lit stage, every detail of which was visible from above. It was much used, this apartment, and the setting could be changed at will. Wang-wei had never been in New York and never hoped to be—even in its most absurd flights the Propaganda Ministry had never suggested that the United States could be physically invaded. But Wang-wei had read the script. The apartment into which he was now staring was supposed to be in an expensive and swank Park Avenue hotel. Small but elegant, with a luxurious décor.

At the moment the apartment was empty. Then a door opened and a man entered. Wang-wei stiffened with something akin to pride. It was Turtle Nine. His Turtle—his own exquisite handiwork! He leaned forward, his head between his knees, and stared down through the glass floor at this creature which he, and fourteen years of captivity, had wrought. As a schoolboy he had read *Frankenstein* in translation and he thought of it now. He, and of course many others, had created this thing that now walked to the little bar and poured itself a drink. A Scotch and water, Wang-wei noted. The real Nick Carter usually drank Scotch.

The man at the bar was wearing a light gray tweed of conservative and expensive cut, made to order in one of the best establishments in Regent Street, London. The shoes were also British, tan, hand-lasted and boned. The shirt was a Brooks Brothers button-down. The tie, a dark wine knit, had cost twenty dollars. Beneath the beautiful suit, Wang-wei knew, his man was wearing boxer shorts of crisp Irish linen. Five dollars a pair. Wine dark socks of Scottish wool—eight dollars. Wang-wei would have made a fine merchant—he had a memory for such details.

Mao broke the silence. "Your Turtle *looks* like the pictures I have seen of this Nick Carter, Wang-wei. That I admit. But I cannot see his face closely. Have the surgical scars healed?"

"Nearly so, Comrade Leader. There is a little pink tissue still—but one would have to be very close to him to notice it."

"Such as, perhaps, being in bed with him?" Chou's little laugh was oily.

Wang-wei could not help wincing in the gloom. He was thinking of his elderly compatriot, he who had been enjoying

Turtle Nine's favors and paying so well for the privilege. Chou, of course, was not alluding to *that*. Nevertheless Wang-wei felt a dew of perspiration creeping out on his forehead.

But his voice was steady as he agreed. "Exactly, Comrade. But he will go to bed with no one until he reaches Peshawar. Our agent there, the American girl—"

Mao shushed them. He sounded impatient. "When does this little show begin, Wang-wei? There *are* a few other matters which demand my attention today."

Wang-wei dabbed at his brow with a handkerchief. "Soon now, Comrade Leader. I wanted you to have a good look at the man alone first."

"Then let us be quiet," said Mao petulantly, "and watch!"

The man at the bar sipped at his Scotch and water. He snapped open a silver case and lit a long cigarette with a golden tip. An East German agent had salvaged a butt two years before in a Berlin hotel and sent it on. You never knew, in the profession, when little things would prove important.

The man at the bar sat in an attitude of seeming relaxation, yet his eyes roved ceaselessly and the body beneath the expensive suiting gave the impression of a powerful spring coiled for action. He was a trifle over six feet with not an ounce of fat on him. The shoulders were a great muscular wedge tapering to a slim waist, the legs long and sinewy beneath the well-fitting trousers.

As the three men watched from above the man at the bar took out an automatic pistol and inspected it with the ease of long practice. He took out the clip, thumbed cartridges onto the bar, and tested the feeder spring. He inspected the clip for flug and grease, then reloaded it, and snapped it back into the pistol. He put the weapon into a plastic holster which he wore on his belt and buttoned his coat. There was no tell-tale bulge. The jacket had been properly tailored.

Chou broke the silence.

"Let me understand this properly. This man we see, this

Turtle Nine, is now under hypnosis? He believes himself to be Nick Carter? He really thinks he is Killmaster?''

"Yes," said Wang-wei. "He is convinced of it."

Mao hissed at them. "Quiet! Watch this—the man is as fast as a snake."

The man below, seemingly bored, had left the bar and taken a stance about twenty feet from a cork dart board fixed to one wall. With a barely perceptible movement he lowered his right shoulder, flexed his right hand. Something shiny dropped from his sleeve into the hand. So fast was the throwing motion that Wang-wei could not follow it—but there it was, the little stiletto, quivering near the center of the dart board!

"Admirable," chortled Mao. "Very near the bull's-eye."

Wang-wei sighed and kept silent. No use telling the Leader that the real Nick Carter would have *hit* the bull's-eye. His Turtle would have to work a little on the knife throwing. After all, if matters arranged themselves properly, his Turtle would have to go up against the real Nick Carter.

Below them the apartment door opened and a girl entered. Chou sighed audibly. "Ahhhh—now we can get down to it."

The girl was tall and slim and exquisitely dressed in Western style. She wore a chic little hat and suit and her legs were smooth perfection in dark nylons and high heels. Around her slim shoulders was a mink stole.

There was no audio from the apartment below—it could be turned on at will, but at the moment was inoperative at Mao's wish. The Leader did not care what was said. Only what was done. This was nothing more than a test of Turtle Nine's efficiency and readiness for his job.

Wang-wei could hear Chou's breathing thicken as they watched the intimate tableau unfold beneath them. He had to admit that it *was* exciting. He *did* enjoy these little shows, and not always in the way of duty. Chou was right about that! For a moment Wang-wei permitted himself fleeting thoughts of Sessi-Yu and her Golden Lotus, then he forced himself to pay attention. This love making now going on below them, while exciting to the more vulgar senses, was of no real importance. The real test was yet to come. When Turtle Nine, in a very real sense, would be fighting for his life.

The girl had taken off her little hat and flung the mink stole on a sofa. She refused a drink. Her slim arms coiled around the tall man's neck and she pressed her lithe body hard against his. They stood kissing for a long time. The girl had her eyes closed. She raised one neatly shod foot from the floor, then the other. She began to wriggle and undulate against the man.

"She knows her work," said Chou in a stifled voice. "Who is she?"

"Her name is Hsi-chun," said Wang-wei. "Of no importance. A prostitute we have sometimes used. She is not even Chinese. Half Korean, half Japanese. But you are right—she is most efficient."

"Most," said the fat Leader. "But in a matter of this sort—is she discreet? Can she be trusted?"

Wang-wei nodded, though realizing they could not see him. "I think so—but it does not signify, Comrade Leader. We take no chances. When this is over Hsi-chun will be disposed of."

The couple below had gone into the bedroom. The girl stood laxly, arms drooping by her sides, as the man disrobed her. Her head was thrown back, her narrow dark eyes staring at the mirrored ceiling, as the man slipped off her little jacket, her blouse, and kissed her tawny shoulders as he removed her bra.

Wang-wei felt a slight pang. She was a lovely little thing, even though a whore. She seemed to be staring directly at him now. Almost as though she knew he was there, knew what was going on, and was begging him to help her.

Wang-wei sighed. It did not do to get sentimental over whores. Still—maybe he could help her a bit. He would have to see. Perhaps she could be shipped south to the troops along the Vietnamese border. It would, he supposed, be a little better than death!

The girl stood now in only garter belt and dark stockings. Her long legs were the color of honey. The man kissed her breasts, small and round and firm as little melons. She smiled and ran her slim fingers through his close-cropped dark hair, caressing the well-shaped head. She appeared to be enjoying her work, thought Wang-wei. And why not? Turtle Nine, now the complete double of Nick Carter, would naturally be a fine lover. The real Carter's prowess as a lover was well known to Chinese Intelligence.

The man and woman were on the bed now, deeply engrossed in the hot preliminaries of love. The lithe body of the woman contorted in passionate arabesques. Her little red tongue flickered like a lizard's as she sought to arouse the man further.

"Part of her instructions," whispered Wang-wei. "She is trying to make him forget everything but her."

"She seems to be succeeding," said Chou dryly.

"Not altogether," said Wang-wei. "Watch!" There was a note of pride in his voice. Turtle Nine had learned his lessons well.

The man below pulled himself away from the woman's embrace. His lips moved in a smile. She pouted and sought to hold him, but he shook her off and went back into the living room. He was naked except for the stiletto in a sheath attached to the inside of his right forearm.

The three watchers saw him try the door, checking the lock. He went to each window and checked it.

Mao hissed in the darkness. "He is very careful, your Turtle. You are sure he does not suspect what is coming?"

"He suspects nothing, Comrade Leader. These are merely routine, elementary precautions that the real Nick Carter would take in such a situation."

Chou said: "Who are the men who are going to try to kill your Turtle? Not good Chinese, I hope?"

"They are Chinese," answered Wang-wei, "but not good. They are all criminals who have been sentenced to death. They have been promised their lives if they win."

Chou laughed softly in the gloom. "And if they do win—if

they kill your prize Turtle? What will you do then, Wang-wei?''

"Find a new Turtle and start over, Comrade. It only requires patience. You should know that."

"I know that I grow impatient with this chatter," barked Mao. "Be quiet and watch!"

The pseudo Nick Carter had taken a ball of twine from his jacket pocket. He fastened one end of the twine to the chain pull of a tall lamp near the door. Then, placing a chair in the proper position, he brought the twine down vertically to the floor, beneath the chair legs and across the door to yet another chair where he tied the end of twine. The twine now formed an ankle high trip-line just inside the door. The man tested the trip-line once or twice to make sure it worked, then left the room in darkness and returned to the small bedroom where the girl lay impatiently stroking her soft breasts.

"Clever," acknowledged Mao. "But the door is locked. How will your men, the criminals, get in?"

"They have a passkey, Comrade Leader. Just as a real enemy might have. They will be coming soon now."

Wang-wei heard the rustle of linen as Chou mopped his face. "I am glad I am not in your service," he told Wang-wei. "There are too many precautions to take—how does one ever find time to enjoy anything?"

"It is necessary," the little Intelligence man told him. "Otherwise an agent would not live long enough to enjoy anything."

They watched as the man sank on the bed beside the woman. He took the stiletto from its sheath and plunged it into the bed near his right hand. The Luger was placed beneath a pillow near his left hand. A radio, which must have been playing on a bedside table, was snapped off. Just before the man covered the woman with his stalwart body he reached out and snapped off the single light.

Mao moved in the darkness. He pressed a button on the table and the audio came alive. First only a low electronic buzz, then they began to make out the individual sounds.

Chou cursed softly. "Why did he have to turn out the light!"

Wang-wei felt a little superior. "It is necessary, Comrade. So if the outer light is tripped on he will be at an advantage in the dark."

Mao shushed them again. They sat and listened to the varied sounds coming from a loud-speaker in the wall of the room.

A gentle twanging of bed springs. A muffled cry from the woman. A sudden high panting sound from the woman, then her long groan of pleasure . . .

The lamp in the living room went on. Four Chinese, all wearing blue coolie suits, stood for a moment blinking in surprise. Above them Wang-wei felt his own heart give a great leap. This was the real test!

Not a tenth of a second passed before the coolies, recovering from the sudden shock of light, went into action. They all carried long cruel knives. Two of them had revolvers. One, in addition to his knife, wielded a deadly little hatchet.

They scattered about the room, calling softly to each other, and began to converge on the dark bedroom. The watchers above saw only a faint shadow of movement in the room. The woman's scream was abruptly stifled. The Luger spat flame at the coolies from the protection of shadow, the slapping reports loud in the speaker. One of the coolies who had a revolver stumbled and fell sprawling, his blood soaking the carpet. The revolver spun from a dead hand across the floor. A coolie leaped for it. The Luger snapped again and the man fell.

The remaining armed coolie crouched behind a sofa and sent a fusillade of lead into the bedroom. The coolie with the hatchet dropped to his hands and knees and, under his companion's covering fire, began to crawl around the walls toward the bedroom door. These were desperate men, with their lives doubly in the balance, and they were not giving up easily.

The Luger snapped again and again from the bedroom.

Tufts and chunks of the sofa flew through the air but the man with the revolver was not hit. He kept firing into the bedroom. The crawling man with the hatchet was near the door now. He glanced up, saw a light switch, and shouted to his companion as he stood to click it on. The lights flared on in the bedroom.

Wang-wei's Turtle Nine came through the bedroom door like a naked bolt of lightning. In his right hand was the stiletto, in his left the flaming Luger. The coolie with the hatchet gave a little cry of rage and triumph and flung his weapon. It glinted in the bright light, spinning end over end. The thrower was an accomplished tong killer—for which he was to die—and had never been known to miss.

He did not actually miss now! Turtle Nine ducked swiftly and the spinning hatchet passed over him. The girl, her soft mouth wide open in a scream, took the little axe squarely between the eyes. She sank back on the bed, the hatchet embedded in her lovely face.

Turtle Nine was thinking like the automaton he was. He ignored the hatchet man for the moment and leaped toward the sofa, weaving and ducking. He fired twice and the Luger went dry. The coolie behind the sofa fired once and missed and his gun also clicked empty. He stood up and leaped to one side, thinking to avoid the rushing Turtle Nine.

But Turtle Nine did not rush. His arm went up and back and something sang through the air. The coolie stood by the sofa, gazing stupidly down at the stiletto pinned to his heart like an ornament. Slowly he toppled, clutching with both hands at the stiletto in his flesh, caressing the shiny hilt with bloody fingers.

The remaining coolie had had enough. He leaped for the door with a cry of terror. Turtle Nine smiled and threw the empty Luger. It clipped the man at the base of the skull and he fell stunned.

Turtle Nine walked slowly toward the writhing figure. He stood over the man for a moment, contemplating him, then raised a bare foot and delivered a deliberate and vicious kick to the side of the man's neck. The watchers above heard the spine break.

For a little time there was silence in the glass-floored room. Then Mao said: "I think your Turtle is ready, Wang-wei. Even for Nick Carter, Killmaster. You will put Segment One of Dragon Plan into operation tomorrow morning."

Chapter Two

SEEK OUT AND DESTROY

They had left the foothills and were climbing steadily into a gorge that would, eventually, funnel them into Karakoram Pass and then down a long tortuous glissade into Kashmir. Nick Carter paused to catch his breath and comb particles of ice from his three-day growth of stubble. He hadn't had a chance to shave since leaving Washington. Now he tried to breathe the thin air and gazed back of him, to the west and south, where the snow-covered tips of the Himalayas were beginning to gather and reflect the sunset in a fan of superb color.

N3, senior ranking **KILLMASTER** for AXE, was not in the mood for aesthetic appreciation. He was pretty damned miserable. There had been no time to acclimate himself to the altitude and he carried no oxygen. His lungs were paining him. His feet were clods of ice. Everything but his thermal underwear—his chief, Hawk, had graciously given him time to collect *that*—stank of yak. He wore yakskin boots and a yakskin cap and face-hood and, over a padded suit which some Chinese soldier must have inhabited for years, a greatcoat of yakskin.

Nick swore fervently and kicked the shaggy little pack pony, Kaswa, in its shaggy little rear. The impact stung his half-frozen foot and served only to annoy Kaswa. The pony cast a reproving look at Nick and continued to amble at his own pace. Nick Carter swore again. Even Kaswa was some kind of a nut! Kaswa was really a camel's name, or so the guide Hafed had informed him with a gap-toothed grin.

Nick kicked the hardy little beast again and glanced up the broad defile leading into the pass. He was falling farther behind all the time. Hafed, who was trekking point, was a good quarter of a mile ahead and well into the shadows of the pass. Behind him, strung out at intervals, were the five Sherpas, each with a shaggy pony akin to Kaswa.

"But faster," Nick told his pony now. "Much faster! Get a move on—you slab-sided, wall-eyed, hairy little monster!"

Kaswa whinnied and actually increased his pace. Not because of the foreign devil's kicks but because it was near feeding time.

The guide Hafed called a halt where the trail narrowed between two towering cliffs. A frozen waterfall, an intricate frieze of cold lace, dangled from an overhang and they made camp behind it. By the time Nick came trudging up, the other ponies had been fed and the Sherpas were consuming bowls of hot yak-buttered tea prepared over carefully shielded Coleman stoves. Hafed, a jack of all mountain trades and, seemingly, all languages, had been uneasy all day. He was afraid of encountering a Chinese patrol.

Nick and Hafed shared a Blanchard tent. Nick found it already pitched behind the frozen waterfall. He got his pack off Kaswa and sent the beast on its way to fodder, then spread his sleeping bag in the tent and fell on it with a long sigh. He was beat, utterly beat. He itched intolerably all over. Along with the dead Chinese soldier's uniform he had also inherited a few fleas.

It had grown dark now. There would be no moon or stars. It was growing colder by the minute, a misty chill that was bitter to the bones, and wind was beginning to move in the pass. Nick opened his eyes and saw a few snowflakes drift past the ten opening. Fine, he thought wearily. That's all I need—a blizzard!

Nick nearly dozed off as he listened with half an ear to

Hafed getting the men and ponies bedded down for the night.
Hafed was a jewel, no doubt of that. He looked like a bandit
and he smelled bad, but he kept things going. He seemed to
have a smattering of every language in this part of the
world—Chinese, Tibetan, Bengali, Marathi, Gujerati—
even some very fractured English. N3 suspected that Hafed
was employed by the CIA, though nothing had been said. But
Nick knew that when the Chinese had invaded Tibet the CIA
had also moved in as best it could, considering the formidable language and physical barriers.

AXE, of course, had also moved into Tibet in a small way.
That was why he was here now, aching and flea bitten and
feeling rather nauseated. The chief AXE agent in Tibet had
been murdered—by a man calling himself Nick Carter. A
man who looked and acted like Nick Carter! But his *Doppelgänger* was a murderer, which the real Nick certainly
was not. Killer, yes. Murderer, no. And that, thought N3
wearily now, had been his double's first real mistake.

Hafed came and squatted in the entrance of the tent. It was
too dark to see but Nick could visualize the guide's face,
swarthy and button-nosed and slant-eyed and covered with a
curling, greasy beard. The smell of Hafed came to him now
in the gloom.

"How is it going?" Nick queried tiredly. "The men still
going to quit?"

Hafed moved farther into the small tent. "Yis—they not
go any more than this place. They are Sherpa and this not
their country, you understand? They also much afraid of
Chinese soldiers."

Nick struggled to remove the yakskin coat, then fumbled
in the pockets of the quilted suit for cigarettes. Hafed lit them
from a faintly glowing punk-cord. "Better not to show
light," he said. "Chinese soldiers have very sharp eyes, I
think."

N3 cupped his cigarette in his palm. "What do you think,
Hafed? Are there any Chinese around?"

He could sense the man's shrug. "Who knows, sar?

Perhaps. But it is *karma*. If the soldiers come, they come—
that is all. We can do nothing."

"On the map," Nick said, "this area is marked as having
an undefined border. I don't suppose that means anything to
the Chinese!"

Hafed chuckled grimly. "No, sar. Nothing. Is better for
them—in such places they put their flag and say so sorry but
this now our land. It is their way."

N3 smoked his cigarette and brooded. He didn't give a
damn for the Chinese at the moment, except as they were
behind, must be behind, this *Doppelgänger* bit! Anyway he
was too tired to think; his head felt light, like a balloon that
might detach itself and float away any minute.

Hafed went away for a moment and came back with a huge
cup of tea heavy with *tsampa*. "Better you drink this," he
commanded. "I think you not feel good, sar? I watch all day.
You sick."

Nick forced some of the tea down. "You're right," he
admitted. "I feel lousy. And that's bad—I can't afford to get
sick." He grinned feebly as he spoke. Hawk wouldn't like it.
An AXE man never allowed illness to interfere with a mission.

"Is all okay," Hafed said comfortingly. "You just have
mountain sickness—all foreigners have it, I think. Is the
altitude is all. You be all right in two, three days."

They smoked for a time in silence. Nick fished a bottle of
Scotch from his pack and spiked their tea. The warm, peaty-
tasting whiskey made him feel a little better. Hafed spread his
bed roll beside Nick and lay down, scratching vigorously. He
gurgled contentedly over his tea and whiskey. Outside the
wind was beginning to howl like a great white wolf after
prey. The cold began to pry into N3's marrow, and he knew
there would not be much sleep for him that night. Perhaps it
was just as well. He needed time to think, to catch up with
himself. Since Hawk's phone call had pulled him away from
a warm bed and a hot woman he had been going at a frantic
pace. Rather absurdly the refrain of an old Gilbert and Sulli-

van tune ran through his brain. In parody. *An AXE agent's lot is not a happy one!*

Perhaps not. But it was the lot he had chosen. And, despite all his bitter griping at times, he knew it was the life he wanted and loved. So why complain when he was hauled from between a pair of velvety thighs in the dead of night and sent to Tibet!

An AXE jet had gotten him from New York to Washington in less than an hour. It had been a crazy chaotic night. His boss, Hawk, was livid and tired and disheveled and in a rage. AXE headquarters, behind the innocent façade on Dupont Circle, was in an uproar. Hawk, an unlit cigar rolling in his tight mouth, had spoken with Nick betweentimes as he shouted into half a dozen phones.

"You," he snapped, pointing the cigar at Nick, "are somewhere in Tibet right now. You are on official business, top secret, and you contacted our head man in Tibet—a Buddhist monk by name of Pei Ling. You milked him for all the information you could, but then you made a mistake. There was something you didn't know—your own Golden Number!"

N3 had long ago shaken away the daze of sleep and the drug of Melba O'Shaughnessy's kisses. His icy mind was clicking like a computer.

"So that's where the imposter slipped up? He didn't know his Golden Number?"

Hawk had grinned a little smugly. "He didn't even know there *was* a Golden Number! Chinese Intelligence is good, I admit, but we still have a few secrets. And the Golden Number, thank God, is one of them. They're smart enough to know that they couldn't foresee everything, but I doubt if they expected their man, this phony Nick Carter, to be blown so soon. It's a hell of a break for us—now you can get right on his track. I don't have to tell you the orders—seek out and destroy! You leave in half an hour—there will be no time for briefing and no time to arrange a cover. You'll have to work naked, as yourself. On your own. By guess and God. Find this bastard, son, and kill him before he can do a lot of irreparable damage."

"It could be a trap," said Nick. "To draw me within killing distance."

Hawk's false teeth clamped on his cigar. "You think we haven't thought of that? Of course it's a trap! But that is probably only a part of it, boy. They wouldn't set up an elaborate deception like this just to kill you. There has to be something else—something bigger. You've got to find out what that is—and you've got to stop it."

Killmaster lit one of his gold-tipped cigarettes and watched Hawk with narrowed eyes. He had seldom seen his boss so upset. Something really big was brewing, no doubt of that.

Hawk was at a wall map, pointing. "This phony you is heading due east. We're projecting, of course, guessing if you like, but I think we're right. If we are, and he does go east, then there is no place to go in that desolation but the Karakoram Pass. And *that* leads into northern Kashmir. You begin to get the picture?"

Killmaster smiled and crossed his long legs. "All I know is what I read in the papers," he said. "And I read tonight, on the way down here, that India and Pakistan are getting ready to sign another cease-fire agreement. U Thant seems to be making a little headway."

Hawk went back to his desk and sat down. He put a pair of scuffed shoes on a leather-backed blotter. "Maybe there will be a cease-fire and maybe there won't—there certainly won't if the Chinese have anything to say about it. Right now we're doing a lot of wild guessing, I admit, but it is almost certain that this phony agent is being sent into Kashmir, or India, or Pakistan or wherever, to keep the war going. The Chinese Reds have *got* to keep that pot boiling—they stand to gain a lot. Just *how* they plan to do it we don't know—that's your job to find out." Hawk fixed Nick with a hard little smile. "It's really not at all complicated, son. Just find this double of yours and kill him! That will clean up the whole mess.

Now you'd better go and talk to Transportation—you leave in twenty minutes. You'll have everything behind you, as usual. The CIA, FBI, the State Department, all of them. Ask for anything you want. If you have time, of course. There's not much of that. And stay out of trouble—don't get mixed up with any foreign police. You know we can't acknowledge you. You're completely on your own in this one, my boy. *Carte blanche*. A free run—so long as you don't involve this government.''

Hawk tossed Nick a thick brown envelope. ''Here are orders and traveling instructions. No time to read them now. Read them on the plane. Goodbye, son. Good luck.''

There were times, though the world was never allowed to see it, when Nick Carter, as realistic and hard-boiled as the two-legged tiger he was, felt like a motherless child.

He had time, barely, to call Melba in New York. She was still in his bed in the penthouse. Warm and sleepy, but with an icy edge to her voice. Nick knew what the trouble was, but it was not a thing you discussed on the phone. He had left Melba hanging again, and not for the first time. When Hawk called you moved—and Hawk called at the goddamndest times! It was too bad, really. Melba was a doll. But she wanted a man there when she needed him. Nick, as he hung up and walked to the waiting jet, had an idea that he wouldn't be seeing Melba again. Not in bed, anyway. He sighed as they strapped a chute on him—what matter? It would be the same with any woman. AXE was his real true love.

AXE planes took him as far as Mandalay, where he was turned over to the Air Force. The next stop was in Thimbu, in Bhutan, where the plane fueled at a secret airbase which, it was hoped, neither the Russians nor the Chinese knew about. Then over the Hump—Everest was pointed out to him—and he was dropped in a black parachute onto the Soda Plains in the midst of a magnificent wilderness. Hawk, with his shouting and his phones, had wrought a logistical miracle. Hafed, with his Sherpas, was there to meet him. Killmaster did not examine the miracle. He was content to accept it. You dropped into the night, twelve thousand miles from home, and there was Hafed awaiting you. Sherpas, ponies, smell and all. *Formidable*!

Hafed's odor filled the tent now and Nick lit another cigarette against it. He was still nauseated and light-headed and each of his arms and legs weighed a ton. The mug from which he drank tea and Scotch must weigh at least ten pounds. Actually N3 was much sicker than either he or Hafed knew; high altitude is a killer of men if the exposure, without oxygen, is long enough. A lesser man, without Nick Carter's superb body and razor-edge condition, would have been raving and helpless long before this.

Hafed finished his tea and whiskey and put down the mug. "Is also big storm coming," he said. "That scare men too. Is first snow of winter—is not so bad, I think, but men not like. Anyway is excuse. Maybe they not be here when we wake up in morning, I think."

Nick was too tired and sick to care much. There was, however, the mission to be considered. He couldn't accomplish much if he were stranded in a Himalayan pass in a blizzard. In these parts they didn't even send around the St. Bernards with a cask of booze.

Hafed sensed his concern and said, "Not to worry, sar. They will leave us ponies and supplies. Sherpas honest people. Take only what is theirs. Anyway the lamasery— what you call convent—is only maybe five, six miles up the pass. We be much okay there until storm over."

"That's nice to know," said Nick wearily. "I hope the girls there have learned about tubs and hot water and soap. I've got a few guests I'd like to get rid of."

As though on cue Hafed began to scratch. His cigarette glowed in the little Blanchard tent, double-lined against the wind and cold. Hafed's next words were a blunt question. "Why you go to Lamasery of She Devils, sar?"

N3 considered for a moment. Hafed was probably to be trusted—most likely was working for CIA—yet he could not be sure. Nick could not afford to give anything away.

Nick tapped the breast of his quilted jacket. "Orders. That's all I know, Hafed. I'm to go to this place—the Lamasery of the She Devils—and make a contact with someone called Dyla Lotti. A woman, I guess. Probably the High Priestess or whatever they call her. That's all I know.''

It wasn't quite all he knew, but it was enough for Hafed to know.

Hafed appeared lost in thought for a moment. Finally, ''How much you know about this place, this lamasery? About this woman, Dyla Lotti, sar?''

Nick lit a cigarette and tossed the pack. ''Nothing. Not a damned thing!'' Again this was not quite true. Dyla Lotti was, in fact, working for AXE. It was she who had gotten the message through to Hawk about the murder of the AXE man in Tibet.

Hafed's cigarette sparked in the gloom of the tent. Outside the men and ponies had bedded down for the night and the only sound was the rising wail of the wind down the pass.

''It is a bad place, this lamasery,'' said Hafed at last. He sought for his English. ''Is real reason the men will not go on—they are afraid of the women there. They are all bad women!''

Nick, in spite of his aching head, felt interest kindle in him. What was Hafed trying to tell him?

''How do you mean—bad? The place isn't a prison is it?''

Again Hafed hesitated before answering. ''No—not real prison. But is place they send bad girls—priestesses who go with men. Is against religious law, to be with man, but these girls do it anyway and so they are sent to this place for punish. To Lamasery of She Devils! You see now why my men not want go there?''

N3 had to chuckle. ''Not exactly, Hafed. Seems to me they *would* want to go there—with all those bad girls running around loose!''

Hafed made a sucking noise with his lips which Nick interpreted as Tibetan for disapproval. ''You not understand, sar. My men all good men—much married. You notice little leather boxes they all carry on string around neck?''

''I've noticed. Charms of some kind, aren't they?''

''Yis—good charms. Usually only Sherpa woman wear

them—but when men go away for a long time they take *dablam* with them. Is like—like taking spirit of wife with them. You see, sar? Spirit of good wife watch over man—he can do nothing bad then? Understand?''

Nick laughed. ''I understand. They're afraid they might be tempted in a lamasery full of loose women?''

Hafed joined in the laugh for a moment. ''Is maybe part of it, sar. But is more—lamasery have bad name for happenings. Is no men there, you see, only women! And are many stories also—sometimes when men stop there, travelers, they do not leave again. No one ever see them more. That is bad, no, sar?''

As sick as he was Nick still had a bit of impishness left. ''Depends on your viewpoint, Hafed. Some men I know would consider it a lovely way to die! And maybe they don't die—maybe the girls just keep them in cells, or something, and use them whenever they feel like it. It might not be such a bad life—while it lasted!'' Nick smiled in the dark. He could think of a dozen old jokes based on just such a situation, but it was no use wasting them on Hafed.

A thought struck him. ''How come *you're* not afraid to go to the place of the She Devils, Hafed?''

''Not married,'' said the little man succinctly. ''Not have *dablam* with spirit of wife in it. I not afraid of yellow priestesses. Maybe even I like! Goodnight, sar.''

In a moment or two Hafed was snoring. Nick lay and listened to the menacing voice of the wind and knew that he had been right—he would not sleep much tonight. To pass time he checked over his weapons, working by feel in the dark—he could field strip and reassemble the 9mm Luger in just under thirty seconds, working by touch alone. He did so now, patting the weapon affectionately. Wilhelmina, as he called the Luger, had been living a quiet life of late. As he slipped the pistol back into the plastic holster on his belt Nick thought that perhaps things would liven up soon. Certainly, when he caught up with the impostor, there would be work for the Luger.

Or maybe he would kill his double with the stiletto, Hugo.

He shook the needle-sharp little weapon from the chamois sheath on his right forearm down into his hand. The hilt was smooth and as cold as death. As N3 hefted the deadly little weapon in his palm his mind grasped at a curious irony— Chinese Intelligence was most thorough—suppose they had outfitted his double with the same weapons he himself carried. Nick's grin was sour. It would make for a most interesting showdown—Luger against Luger, stiletto against stiletto!

But there was one weapon the impostor would not have—Nick unbottoned the quilted trousers and fumbled for Pierre, the little gas bomb which he carried in a metal case between his legs like a third testicle. Pierre was as deadly as a viper—and much faster. One inhalation of the gas and you knew instant death! Nick doubted that the Chinese had tumbled to Pierre—and even if they knew about the bomb they wouldn't be able to reproduce it. The gas was a well-guarded secret of the AXE labs.

Nick replaced the little gas bomb carefully and adjusted his pants. Pierre might just give him the edge over his opponent.

By now the whiskey had worn off and he was beginning to feel very ill again. He yearned for more alcohol but did not reach for the bottle. He wanted to be as bright as possible when he met this Dyla Lotti on the morrow—a hangover would never do.

N3 lay for a time, suffering and listening to Hafed snore. He left the tent to relieve himself and was nearly knocked down by the force of the wind. The narrow gorge where they had camped was a blinding whorl of snow. The ponies, their shaggy hides white, stood patiently with their rumps into the wind. Two snow-covered mounds marked the tents where the Sherpas slept.

N3 lingered for a moment behind the stalactites of the frozen waterfall, staring into the snow-dervish haunted gloom. It was easy to imagine things out there. Chinese soldiers creeping up. His double, as anxious to kill as he was himself. The women from the lamasery, perhaps, raiding the camp and carrying away the screaming men—a ludicrous reversal of the Sabine bit.

Nick forced himself to laugh at the pictures blurring through his aching head. He was sick, that was all. Nevertheless he found that he had to fight and to hang on to reality. Things were fuzzy and limpid and unreal—like one of Dali's canvas fantasies.

It was only the altitude, he told himself. He was sick, after all. Yet he felt the cold clamp of an alien hand reaching for him out of the darkness of this place, so near the top of the world, where She Devils lived and magic was commonplace.

Nick shook himself and went to the tent. Nerves. Better watch it or he would be seeing the *yeti* next—the Abominable Snowman! Sherpa mothers used the image of the *yeti* to frighten their children into being good. Nick grinned to himself as he re-entered the tent. It would be fun, at that, to catch a *yeti* and send it to Hawk. Maybe he could train it to become an AXE agent!

Hafed was still snoring gently. Nick envied the guide his slumber. The night ahead would be long and cold.

Suddenly the words of his old *guru*, Rammurta, who had taught yoga at the AXE Special School, came back to him.

"The mind can conquer the body always," old Rammurta had taught, "if only it knows the technique."

As N3 began his breathing exercises he thought how strange it was that yoga had not occurred to him before. It had stood him in good stead so many times. And here he was, not many miles from the birthplace of yoga, India, and only belatedly did he come to it. The altitude sickness again, he thought. There was no ignoring the brutal fact—he was not his usual self. And that could be extremely dangerous—for him. He *had* to snap out of it.

N3 squatted on his sleeping bag and assumed *Siddhasana*, the perfect pose. He sat staring straight ahead, his eyes open but growing gradually opaque as his senses turned inward. He no longer felt the cold. His breathing slackened and flattened out to a mere whisper. His chest barely stirred.

Slowly, imperceptibly, he slipped into the state of *pratya-hara*. It was a complete withdrawal of consciousness. Nick Carter sat like an image, an idol. He might have been one of the bronze effigies which decorate every Tibetan temple.

The guide Hafed snored on, blissfully unaware of what he would have regarded as an *avatar* crouched beside him. The guide did not awaken, nor did Nick Carter stir, when the Sherpas awoke early and stealthily departed down the gorge. They were going back to their homes and away from the Lamasery of the She Devils, the spirits of their good wives still safe and dominant in the leather *dablams*. Going softly, the tinkle of pony bells muffled by the wind, the Sherpas faded away into the blowing snow. They took only what was theirs. Hafed had paid them in advance.

Chapter Three

THE SHE DEVIL

The chamber, even though the massive, nail-studded door was barred on the outside, could hardly be called a cell. It was much too comfortable, of whitewashed brick, high and spacious and hung with priceless rugs. There were also rugs on the hard-packed, earthen floor. Nick, who was no rug merchant, recognized one of them as a Samarkand, worth at least a thousand.

His bed was on the floor, consisting of half a dozen thin mats piled atop each other. The sheets were of purple silk and the coverlet of rich brocade. A large brazier in the center of the room sent out waves of charcoal heat. Beyond the brazier, set against the far wall, brooded an enormous brass statue of a monkey. The beast was sitting on its haunches, the handlike forepaws raised as in supplication to strange gods. It was an enormous idol, reaching nearly to the ceiling, and Nick had taken an immediate dislike to it. The eyes, for one thing. They were hollow and once or twice, in the weak yellow light of the butter lamps, he had seen a glitter of white in the empty brass eyes.

So he was being spied on occasionally. So what? It wasn't the first time. Nick arranged the wooden block pillow beneath his head—it was covered with felt and rather comfortable—and wished the High Priestess, Dyla Lotti, would get on with things. He really had no time for the usual

Tibetan amenities—yet he recognized that they must be observed. Protocol must be observed, especially in this place of women. N3 grinned in resignation and lit a cigarette from the one pack he had been permitted to keep. He blew smoke at the brass monkey and thought back over the events of the day. It had been a long and hectic one . . .

He had emerged from the yoga trance to find Hafed there with the inevitable cup of tea. Nick was feeling slightly better, stronger, and after a breakfast of tea and biscuit and pressed beef they packed the two remaining ponies and plunged eastward into the pass. The blizzard was in full fury by now.

There was no time for talk and no need for it. Hafed did not have to explain—either they made the Lamasery of the She Devils before their strength gave out or they died in the rugged confines of the pass. N3, head lowered into the icy wind, was content to slog along behind Kaswa. The pony knew what it was about, and stuck close to Hafed and the other pony. The trail narrowed steadily until, at one point, it was a bare twelve inches wide with an overhanging cliff to Nick's right and a mile fall-away to his left. The one factor that saved them, that made the trail passable, was the savage scouring of the wind that kept it free of snow. The going was unmitigated hell. Nick clung to Kaswa's shaggy tail and hoped for the best—one slip and the mission was all over.

By mid-afternoon they were past the worst of it. About four, as early darkness was clamping down, Hafed stopped and pointed up through the swirling snow. "There, sar! The lamasery. You see all the lights—they are expecting us."

Nick leaned on Kaswa and caught his breath. Now and again the snow curtain lifted enough for him to catch a glance of the lamasery. It was perched precariously on a great flat shelf of rock jutting out from the cliff. A clutter of low buildings built of stone and brick, all of which were a dull red-earth color. Ahead of them, perhaps a quarter of a mile, stairs cut into the living stone of the cliff twined upward.

The lamasery was indeed ablaze with light. Must be a thousand butter lamps going, Nick thought.

He went forward to where Hafed was resting by his pony. He noted that even the guide was blowing hard. Nick gave him a cigarette which Hafed accepted gratefully and lit skillfully in the wind with his glowing punk-cord.

"How could they see us coming in this gale?" Nick asked. "Most of the time I can't see five feet in front of me."

Hafed cupped his cigarette against the wind and puffed. "They know, sar. They are She Devils, remember? Much powerful magic!"

Nick only stared at him, saying nothing. He was tempted to tell Hafed that he could drop the simple Tibetan act, now that they were alone, but he kept silent. Let the man play it his own way.

Hafed, with a hint of sheepishness, went on to say, "Anyway they always keep lookouts, the She Devils. They say they look for stray and lost travelers, to help them." Hafed grinned at Nick, showing black stumps of teeth. "This I do not believe—I think they look for men. I think they would let a woman traveler freeze to death in this pass. Listen, sar!"

The wind brought them a braying of great horns and the resonant clangor of a single huge gong. The myriads of butter lamps flickered through the storm like beckoning candles in the windows of home. Hafed gave Nick an odd glance.

"We better get on, sar. They not like to be kept waiting, the She Devils. Very impatient people."

As Nick started back to his pony he chuckled. "I'm impatient, too. For a hot bath and a clean bed and some sleep."

Hafed's laugh was borne to him on the wind. "Not count on it, sar. Bath and bed okay yes. Sleep I doubt, I hope you are feeling stronger, sar. You will need all strength tonight! Also me!"

They found crude stables cut into the rock at the foot of the stairs and left the ponies there. The attendants were all old women in coarse robes of a dirty orange color. Their heads were shaven and they glistened with a pungent oil. They stared at the two men and chittered like monkeys among themselves in some strange Tibetan dialect.

They began the long climb up the rock stairs. High overhead someone was clashing cymbals. It was fully dark now
and the stairs were poorly lighted by butter lamps set in
niches.

As they climbed Hafed explained. "Most of hard work is
done by the old devils. Young devils spend all time keeping
pretty and making love."

"I thought you said there were no men?"

Hafed gave him what Nick could only construe as a pitying
look. "Not always need men," the guide said curtly. "Other
ways!"

Nick saved his breath for the climb. It had been a foolish
question, he admitted. Naive. Lesbianism was bound to be
rampant in a place like this. Probably as second best, he
thought. After all, these priestesses, or She Devils, had been
sent to this place because they had transgressed with men.

N3 thought he could detect a certain impatience in Hafed's
manner now. Either that or the guide was in incredible
shape—he was fairly leaping up the steep stairs. Nick
grinned a little sourly. Why not? Hafed carried no *dablam*
with a wife spirit in it. He was looking forward, it seemed, to
a hot time in the old lamasery tonight! Nick sighed and
struggled upward. Judging by the women he had seen thus
far—Hafed could have them.

Their entry into the Lamasery of the She Devils was a
triumph played to farce. They were met at the top by a throng
of priestesses carrying torches and beating cymbals. They
were escorted through a huge gate to an inner courtyard of
hard-packed earth. The women stared at them and waved
their torches and giggled amongst themselves. Several of
them pointed and made suggestive motions with their bodies,
but none of them ventured close. They all wore orange robes
and tight-fitting yakskin boots with curled-up toes. Their
heads were shaven, but nevertheless Nick saw some beauties
among them. Mostly, however, he noted the odor that per-
meated the courtyard and the remote crevices of the lamasery. The smell of a thousand women living in close quarters.

At first it bothered him, but in a matter of minutes he found it not unpleasant—a compound of oiled hair and perfumed bodies and a natural female musk.

Hafed and Nick were immediately separated. Hafed appeared to find this natural. After a short discourse with an elderly priestess who was built like a Sumo wrestler, in a language that seemed to consist of squeals and grunts, Hafed turned to Nick. "You are to go with this old one, sar. She speaks only their dialect, so you will not be able to talk with her. Maybe planned so, I think. Anyway she take care of you and later maybe you will be permitted to see the High Priestess—Dyla Lotti."

"Permitted, hell!" Nick was tart. "I've *got* to see her—right away. This is no goddamned pleasure jaunt, Hafed. I—"

Hafed leaned close to whisper. Around them the circle of orange-robed women watched and whispered among themselves.

"Better do just like say," Hafed muttered. "Remember I tell you, sar? Can be dangerous if not handle right. She Devils are own law here. You see big ones around—those with clubs and knives?"

Nick had noticed them, muscular women with red arm brassards and carrying spike-studded clubs and long knives thrust into their girdles. He nodded. "Yes. What are they? MPs?"

Hafed grinned. "Sort of, sar. Much tough. You go now do like they tell—we not want trouble. I think Dyla Lotti come and see you maybe tonight soon!"

So Killmaster followed the fat old priestess down a series of long cold corridors lit by butter lamps. Finally they entered a room where it was actually warm and a great cauldron of water boiled. Here more old women were in attendance. Overcoming his initial resistance with deft skill and much chatter, they had given Nick a bath. Eventually he relaxed and enjoyed it. They bathed his private parts with no more ado that if he had been a piece of meat on a butcher's hook, though one old crone did tickle him and cackle something that made the others laugh. Nick thought it was probably uncomplimentary.

He managed to retain his weapons, but only after a fierce struggle and much altercation. One of the old priestesses was sent to check—presumably with the High Priestess herself—and came back with word that the weapons were permitted. At least they gave up trying to snatch them from him.

On the lighter side was the awe with which the elderly priestesses regarded Pierre, the little gas bomb he carried between his legs in a metal cylinder. This occasioned as much cackle as a fox in a chicken run! They stared at him and spun prayer wheels at a great rate. Here was a foreign devil with three balls—and one of them of metal! N3 could almost hear the rumors starting, and visualize the clack that would run through the lamasery that night . . .

Now, as he fretted on the soft bed, he wondered about the barred door. Was he a prisoner, as he had thought at first, or was the barred and locked door to keep the younger She Devils out? He grinned. Once they had heard about his third testicle they might come looking, if only out of curiosity.

He lit another cigarette from his butt, stubbing the butt out on a couple of thousand dollars worth of rug. There were no ashtrays. He stared at the monkey again. Was that a glint of white behind the brass eyes? A watcher? Nick yawned and hitched the orange robe closer around his big frame. It was coarse and scratchy, but it was clean. God only knew what they had done with his clothes. All he had left was the robe and a pair of yakskin boots and his weapons.

He was about to field strip the Luger again, for lack of something to do, when he heard the door being unlocked. Hastily he thrust the pistol beneath the covers. If this was Dyla Lotti he didn't want to meet her with a gun in his hand. Might violate protocol or something.

It was only another old woman, one he had not seen before. She bowed and cackled and handed him a large bowl of warm milk. She made drinking motions and stood waiting. To get rid of her Nick drank the mixture. Warm yak's milk to which something had been added, something he could not recognize, at once tart and sweet. A mildly pleasant taste.

The old crone smiled with approval as he finished the milk and handed her the cup. She thumped one withered breast, over her heart, and gummed words at him that sounded, vaguely, like "make well." She left and Nick heard the door being barred and locked again.

Almost immediately he began to feel drowsy. A lovely warm euphoria stole over him. His heart, which on the final trip up the lamasery stairs had been about to burst his chest, slowed to a stready normal beat. N3 closed his eyes and sank into delicious deep contentment. Whatever dope he had been given it was certainly effective. She Devil's Own Home Remedy—maybe he should try to get the recipe and bottle it for sale in the States. It beat any six martinis he had ever drunk.

N3 had no idea how long he slept. He did not come awake instantly, alert and ready, his usual manner of wakening. Instead he drifted back to consciousness slowly on a pleasant pillow of dreams, only just aware of where he was and who he was. It was very quiet in the lamasery now. It must be late. Most of the butter lamps had gone out; the remaining few shed a thin tawny light that wavered fitfully. The charcoal in the brazier was a sullen red glow.

Flickering lamps! Strange. They had burned with a clear straight flame before. Nick pushed himself up on the bed, fighting off lethargy, and glanced across the room at the great statue of the brass monkey. It was moving away from the wall, swinging slowly around on a pivot. A chill little draft invaded the room, causing the butter lamps to flicker again. N3 felt for his weapons with a touch of panic. Then he relaxed. They were all there—Luger, stiletto, and Pierre the gas bomb. He was not defenseless!

The brass monkey was still swinging out from the white brick wall. When it was at right angles to the wall it halted with a little click. Nick rubbed his eyes, trying to rid them of sleep. He still felt drugged and fuzzy, yet he did not mind. He felt good. Fine! As though he were neatly wrapped in some downy insulation, shielded from any impact of reality. He was aware, too, of one other thing—he was immensely ready for physical love! And that, some yet undrugged part of his mind told him, is just plain absurd. Ridiculous. At this moment in time and space, just beginning what could be the most chancy and dangerous mission of his life, that he should suddenly become a raging stud . . .

He saw her then. There was a black oblong in the brick wall, where the brass monkey had been, and a figure was standing there now. A waft of perfume came to Nick. More absurdity. No rare Tibetan perfume this—he recognized it immediately. Chanel No. 5!

The figure stepped out of the black shadows into the room. Had he not been drugged, N3 probably would have exclaimed. As it was he took the apparition in stride—nearly. Even the drug could not ward off entirely the sudden chill and feeling of evil present in the room.

Without speaking the figure came into the room and halted by the brazier. Behind it the brass monkey slid silently back into place. Some kind of automatic counter-weight, Nick told himself furiously. He was fighting the drug tooth and nail now, struggling to clear his mind. This must be Dyla Lotti. The High Priestess herself whom he had been instructed to contact. Why didn't she take off that damned leering mask!

The devil mask was hideous enough to chill the blood of any man. They eyes were terrible red slits, the nose a purple hook, the mouth a grin of sheer horror. Serpents twined instead of hair. This was nightmare stuff!

Killmaster summoned all his will. He flipped a casual hand at the bed side. "Come and sit down. I've been expecting you. Sorry about the chairs, but you people don't seem to run to them. You know who I am, of course? Why I'm here?"

From behind the mask a pair of narrow dark eyes regarded him. Still she did not speak. She wore the traditional orange robe, but it was of silk instead of rough homespun and was belted in at the waist. This revealed just enough of her body for Nick to guess that it was superb. On her feet were tiny yakskin boots with silver tassels on the curled-up toes. Around her neck, below the mask line, he saw a long string of wooden prayer beads.

By now Nick knew he was fighting a losing battle against the drug. God—that milk must have been loaded. He fought to keep the weird devil mask in focus. The whitewashed walls kept folding and wrinkling and realigning themselves. And he was still aching, hurting, with the physical manifestations of love. And that, he thought dimly, is sure as hell not protocol. If I let myself get out of hand I'll louse up the whole deal.

He fell back on a simple, inane remark. "Think you'll know me again?"

Dark eyes flickered behind the devil mask. She had not moved. Now she took a single step toward him. Her voice was soft, well modulated, speaking English with hardly an accent—the good, grammatically pure English of one who has studied it assiduously as a second language. The soft tones, coming from behind the grotesque mask, gave Nick Carter a second shock.

"I must be very careful, Mr. Carter. As you must. Only a week ago another man lay on that same bed and assured me that *he* was Mr. Nicholas Carter. He looked exactly like you. He spoke exactly as you speak now."

Nick swung his legs out of bed and pulled the orange robe about him, fighting off languor. Wilhelmina, the Luger, was snug in her plastic holster in the waistband of his shorts. Thank God the old crones had left him those.

Nick said: "This other man—this phony Nick Carter? You say he was *exactly* as I am? Think hard now, Miss—er—what do I call you?"

Had the dark eyes twinkled behind the mask? He couldn't be sure. There was something familiar and reassuring about the Chanel No. 5 now. This was, after all, only a woman. And he was Nick Carter—the real one. He could handle it.

"Call me Dyla Lotti," she said. "That is my name. And yes—he *did* look exactly like you. Except, possibly . . ."

She took a step nearer the bed and peered at Nick. "Possibly the eyes—his were a little colder. But that is an emotional, a subjective judgment. But he was enough like you to pass any but the most severe test."

"He fooled you? You thought he was the real Nick Carter? At the time?"

The devil mask moved in negation. "No. I was not fooled. I pretended to be, but I knew that he was really a Chinese agent posing as you, Mr. Carter. I had been warned, you see."

Nick fumbled with his remaining cigarettes. "You mind?"

A tiny hand, daffodil yellow, appeared from the copious sleeve of the robe. It waved assent. Nick saw that her nails were long and curving and stained a blood red.

He lit a cigarette and arranged the robe again. He was a little more at ease, a bit less excited now that they were down to business, but desire still haunted him.

He exhaled blue smoke and said, "We're a little blurry on that at AXE, you know. You'd better put me straight for the record—just how were you warned? This agent, this Chinese phony, killed our man Pei Ling in Kaitse—that's in central Tibet. There are a helluva lot of mountains between here and there. How could you get word about Pei Ling's murder so fast?"

He saw the dark eyes widen behind the mask. She approached another step, her arms crossed now over her breast. Firm, full breasts, Nick guessed. Must be strapped down now. The scent of Chanel was stronger.

"You sound as though you do not entirely trust me, Mr. Carter." Was there a hint of mockery in the voice?

"It isn't a question of trust, Dyla Lotti. Just a matter of mechanics. I want to know how it could happen. I want, I've got to know, as much about this thing as possible. Some little matter, something you think of no importance, might be vital. You understand?"

"I understand, Mr. Carter. You will have to excuse me—I am very new at this sort of thing. I am a High Priestess, not a spy. I only agreed to work for you, for your people, because the Chinese are in our country and I want them out. It is against our creed to hate, Mr. Carter, or to preach hatred—but I am a sinner. I hate the Chinese! They are swine. Dogs!"

N3 felt more relaxed. The drug was still working in him, but now he felt his urgent desire for a woman, any woman, fading away. His mind was clearing; the room, the woman in the mask, everything was coming through clear and sharp again.

Somewhat to his surprise Dyla Lotti went to the opposite side of the bed and sat down. Primly, he thought. He twisted to face her, grinning. "Wouldn't you be more comfortable if you took that thing off—the Halloween bit, I mean? It looks heavy."

The mask swayed toward him and he was aware of the close scrutiny of the dark eyes. There was an odd note in her reply. "I prefer to keep it on for the time being, Mr. Carter. Perhaps—later? You must sleep again, and drink more medicine—and then I will return to see you. Then I will take off the mask. You agree?"

The formality had lightened. Nick smiled and lit another cigarette. "I agree—but I don't know about the medicine bit. That last blast of yak's milk was loaded! What did she put in it, anyway?" He glanced furtively down at his now quiescent loins. "It—er—it has some weird effects."

If Dyla Lotti knew what he meant she made no sign. Yet her voice was warmer, more friendly, when she said, "It is *sanga* root—a sort of wild mushroom that grows on the mountain tops. Very rare. You *must* take it, Mr. Carter. I know. I have had the altitude sickness myself. The *sanga* root eases the strain on your heart—otherwise it will wear itself out in this thin air."

N3 eyed the devil mask. "It has certain side effects," he said with an innocent expression.

There was no doubt about it this time—the dark eyes flashed and twinkled. "Perhaps," Dyla Lotti admitted. "And perhaps the side effects are beneficial also. But we must get back to business, Mr. Carter. Soon I must go. I have my duties, you know."

Nick wondered what those duties could be, well after midnight in a lonely and storm-besieged lamasery, but he did not ask. He listened, interrupting only now and then to ask a question.

A week before, one day before the fake Nick Carter had arrived, a runner had reached the lamasery. He bore a chit of paper in a cleft stick and he died from exhaustion half an hour later. But he had been a Sherpa, with incredible lungs, and he had come all the way from another lamasery at Kaitse. The message he bore was scrawled in blood—a dying man's blood. The Chinese agent had made another mistake—after shooting Pei Ling he had not checked to see that the Lama was quite dead.

Nick asked, "You still have the message?"

Dyla Lotti took a coarse sheet of paper from her wide sleeve and handed it across the bed to him. Their fingers touched for a moment and Nick felt as though an electric current had jolted him. He raised the note to eye level with fingers that trembled faintly. God—he must be careful! The yearning was coming back!

He could make nothing of the note. It did seem to be written in blood, by a dying man, a wobbly scrawled mess of chicken tracks. He got the impression that it was meant to be read from right to left. He handed it back to Dyla Lotti with a baffled expression. "Afraid you'll have to read it to me."

He could not see her smile behind the devil mask, but he sensed it. "It is in Urdu," she explained. "A high form of Hindustani—educated priests use it at times. It does not say much—he had no time left. Just that he was killed by a man posing as you, Mr. Carter. A Chinese agent. He asks me to communicate this to your people—to AXE—and warns me that the Chinese agent would probably stop here on his way through the pass into Kashmir. He also suggests that I pretend ignorance and, how do you say it—?"

"Play along—go with the gag."

Her nod was doubtful. "Yes—I suppose something like that. I did so. In due time the imposter arrived, looking exactly like you, Mr. Carter. I, er, played along. He asked many questions. So did I. I think he trusted me—he did not suspect that I knew the truth—but I do not think he told me anything of importance. Neither did I tell him anything that he did not already know, or could easily find out. My reason was simple— I did not *know* anything that would have been of interest to him. As I told you I am a High Priestess, not a spy or a secret agent. My role was to be secondary, passive—I was to pass on information from time to time if I thought it important. That is all. But Pei Ling was dying and had no one else to turn to—so he sent the runner to me."

"And you sent it out to us—that means you've got a transmitter here in the lamasery!"

The devil mask nodded. Her voice sounded reluctant. "Yes—there is a transmitter. Well hidden. I was warned never to use it except in case of grave emergency—there are always Chinese patrols around and some of them have machines—whatever it is that they use to locate hidden transmitters?"

"DF—directional finding equipment," said Nick. "Yes, the bastards—they would have those. But you seem to have gotten away with it, Dyla Lotti. You haven't had any Chinese callers?"

"Not yet. I hope I never do. And I will be glad when this is all over—I am not well equipped for this work. I am a woman and I am afraid!"

"You've done fine so far," N3 told her. "Great—we'd have been lost without you, Dyla Lotti. Really in a mess. We wouldn't have known anything about this fake agent but for you—at least not until he had done a lot of damage. As it is I'm not too far behind him."

"He left four days ago."

"Through the pass into Kashmir?"

She nodded. "Yes. He had a guide and ponies and five or six men. They did not stay here at the lamasery—the weather was good then and they camped in the gorge. I think they were Chinese soldiers without their uniforms. But that is only a guess—they kept to themselves. They would not even have anything to do with my girls, which is most unusual for soldiers.'' Dyla Lotti permitted herself the slightest chuckle. Nick also thought he detected a note of slyness in her voice, but he ignored the opening—if it was that—and kept determinedly to the business at hand.

He rubbed his eyes; he was feeling drowsy again. Then he said: "So you didn't tell him anything—you couldn't. But what did *he* tell *you* ? I've got to know that."

"Not much. Only that he was going from here to Karachi on a highly secret mission. He did not say what it was, naturally. I pretended to believe him and I did not ask too many questions—I was afraid he would become suspicious and I did not wish to join Pei Ling."

Karachi! Pakistan! N3 remembered Hawk's words now. The Chinese Reds might attempt to put a finger into India-Pakistan pie. Keep the pot boiling. It began to look as though Hawk had guessed right. Unless, of course, it was a deliberate plant, a feint, to draw Nick out of the way while the real monkey business was consummated elsewhere.

Somehow he thought not. Admittedly he wasn't thinking too clearly at the moment, drugged as he was, but he agreed with Hawk that part of this business, at least, was a trap to draw him within killing distance. If that were true the phony agent would leave a clear trail. Another thing was that the agent, and his bosses in Peking, wouldn't have expected their subterfuge to be discovered so soon. They would know that the CIA, and AXE, apparatus in Tibet was crude and primitive at this stage. They must have been gambling a little, depending on luck, and it had failed them.

Aloud Nick said: "I'm only four days behind him. I'll get him. Thanks to you, Dyla Lotti."

She rose and came around the bed to stand beside him. Her fragile red-tipped hand reached to touch his and lingered for a moment. Her skin was cool.

"I hope so, Mr. Carter. Now I must go. And you—you must take your medicine again and remain quiet."

Nick found that he was clinging to her hand. "You said you would come back, Dyla Lotti. And can't you stop calling me Mr. Carter? Nick would be better—more friendly."

The long dark eyes regarded him through the slits in the devil mask. "I keep my word—Nick. I will come back. In an hour or so. But only if you are obedient and take your medicine—you will never catch this Chinese devil if you are ill."

Nick grinned and let go of her hand. "Okay—I'll take it. But I warn you—that potion of yours is pretty deadly. You may be sorry you made me drink it!"

She was at the opening in the wall now. She turned and again he could sense a smile beneath the mask. "I will not be sorry," she said softly. "I know about the *sanga* root. And you must not forget, Nick, that if I am a High Priestess I am also a woman. I will return to you."

As she was disappearing into the wall Nick said, "How about my guide, Hafed? I hope you're taking good care of him."

She laughed and the sound was like silver bells in the chamber, thin but resonant.

"*I* am not taking good care of your guide, Nick—but my priestesses are. I do not forbid it—they are also women. Young women. They drew lots and there were ten lucky winners."

She disappeared. There was a faint grind of machinery and the brass monkey began to swing back into place.

N3 lay back on the bed and contemplated the ceiling. Ten lucky winners! Good God! He hoped Hafed was in form.

Minutes later the old crone came to him with another large mug of yak's milk. Nick drank it down without dissent. Might as well play along, go the whole route. He knew, now, that *sanga* root, whatever else it was, was also an erotic drug. An aphrodisiac. Probably they had fed Hafed some of the same stuff. No wonder the girls were lining up.

He examined his professional conscience—the only sort he ever bothered about—and found it clear. He had done everything he could do for the moment. He had made his contact. He knew what there was to know. Not even Hawk would expect him to push through Karakoram Pass in a blizzard.

So bring on the music and the dancing girls, N3 told himself as he relaxed and watched the old priestess heap more charcoal on the brazier. He had nothing to lose but his virtue and that was more than a little tattered as it was. Yes—it looked like quite a night ahead. He never doubted for an instant that Dyla Lotti would return—the promise had been in her voice.

One tiny itch remained in his brain. She had shown him no sort of identification and had asked for none. She could not be expected, of course, to know about the Golden Number, but still—

He dismissed the thought. Dyla Lotti was an amateur, a novice, who had been pulled in in an emergency. Not to worry about it. Anyway he had his weapons and his wits—

Or did he have his wits? He found that he was laughing and rolling on the bed. The old priestess looked at him and smiled benignly and left, locking him in again.

Nick was aware of a high hyena sound in the chamber. His own laughter. If only Hawk could see him now! Probably he would get a lecture on morals and the dereliction of duty! Nick went off into another peal of laughter. His head was a feather pillow floating on his shoulders. The room was soft and fleecy and warm and snug—and what was the world outside to do with him?

"I must just decide to stay here forever," he told the room. "Never leave! A thousand man-hungry women!" Ye Gods! He and old Hafed could have the ball of their lives!

It occurred to him that he had no idea what Dyla Lotti looked like. He couldn't have cared less. She was a woman, soft and curved and perfumed. Maybe that hadn't been a mask after all—maybe it was her real face! He still didn't care. A man could learn to love a face like that in time—and the way he felt right now it wouldn't take long!

Nick Carter stuffed one of the covers in his mouth to stifle his giggles. He felt so good—good—good . . .

Chapter Four

THE SWEET DEATH

Nick dozed off but awoke immediately when he heard the brass monkey swing on its pivot. He sat bolt upright on the bed, dimly understanding what was happening to him—and caring nothing for it or any consequences. Lust simmered in him.

A single butter lamp flickered in the chamber. The brazier glared with a great red eye. Dyla Lotti came into the room and the monkey creaked shut behind her. She advanced to within a few feet of the bed and halted. Unspeaking, they gazed at each other.

Even without the devil mask she was tall. She would come nearly to his chin. She wore a single sarilike garment of translucent jade silk. Beneath it her skin, well oiled and scented, glistened with the shimmer of old ivory. A delicate pale yellow. Her hair was a burnished mass of black silk caught high and held with amber combs. Her mouth was small, a moist crushed rosebud, and when she spoke at last her teeth glinted white in the semi-gloom.

"You like me, Nick?" There was a tease in her tone.

"I love you!" said Nick Carter. "Come here."

"Not yet. Do not rush me." Her smile was languid. "One does not hurry love—one lingers with it and enjoys it more."

Desire welled in Nick. Such impetuosity might ruin everything—yet he could not control himself! He had to have her. Now! This minute—this second! He leaped from the bed and dropped his robe and slipped out of his shorts.

His lungs hurt with the effort of speech. "Come here," he croaked again. "For God's sake!"

Dyla Lotti gasped at the sight of him. Her red mouth formed a round O of surprise. She laughed, "You were right, Nick, dear. The *sanga* root *does* have side effects!"

Nick took a step toward her. Rage flared in him. What the hell—if this pale yellow bitch turned out to be a tease after all the buildup he—he would strangle her! So help him he would!

Dyla Lotti pointed a long scarlet fingernail at him. "Sit down on the bed," she commanded quietly. Nick found himself obeying. It seemed right that he should obey her. Without question. His anger of a moment before faded and was lost.

N3 sat naked on the bed and stared at her. Dyla Lotti approached him slowly. He noted for the first time that she was wearing a pair of red high-heeled slippers. At the moment they did not appear incongruous.

She halted a scant twelve inches from him. He could see the gleaming fire of a huge sapphire, affixed to her navel, shining through her diaphanous gown like a beckoning eye. Her belly was flat and taut and the color of rich cream. It was cool and velvety when he leaned to kiss it.

Dyla Lotti put her hands on his shoulders and pushed him gently away. She kissed him on the forehead with moist hot lips, then drew back a little. She raised her arms and the garment fell away, a slithering froth washing the long perfection of her legs. N3 gazed at her in awe. Every pulse in his body clamored for her. This was perfection in a woman at last! The ultimate—the *plus*! What every man, in every time, had dreamed of and yearned for! For a moment doubt and fear struck at him—she was not real! He was dreaming her—under the power of the drug he was only dreaming her!

Dyla Lotti cupped her hands beneath her breasts and leaned to him, extending those succulent melons for his caress. "Kiss!"

Nick Carter obeyed. It was no dream. Her breasts were warm and cool and firm and soft. The perky small nipples were heavily rouged. They were aromatic with scent which stole into his nostrils as he kissed and laved them with his tongue. He noticed, almost without conscious perception, that she had painted spirals of gold around each breast. It did not seem particularly odd. Nothing was strange now—it was all perfection, all just right and as it should be.

Dyla Lotti stood with her fine legs wide apart, her head and shoulders back, her flat pelvis thrust forward. She ran her fingers through Nick's smooth hair. She moved her pelvis in an undulating circular motion. She permitted the greedy search of his fingers. She moaned and moved closer to him, writhing and twisting as his hands sought out every secret.

Suddenly, with a breathless exclamation, she fell across him on the bed. Her long legs clamped him in a vise of velvet flesh and he was powerless to consummate his fierce desire, to loose the awful red tension that was tearing him to bits. When Nick began to curse, to protest bitterly, she closed his mouth with her own.

Her mouth was avid, even cruel. It sucked at his and her tongue went crazy, lashing his desire even higher. She kissed him with a vampire's eagerness and her fragile small hands toyed with him. It was beyond bearing! Nick reached for her. Enough of this damned nonsense!

Dyla Lotti was too quick for him. Like a wraith her slippery oiled flesh slipped from his grasp. She put a finger on his lips. "Lie quietly," she commanded. "Lie quietly and listen, my lover. I desire you as much as you desire me—but it cannot be! I am a High Priestess—I have taken vows of virginity!"

"This is a hell of a time to think of that!"

She touched his lips again with her finger. "I said to be quiet! I will talk. I will explain—and you will not be sorry, my Nick. Only be patient. There are other ways, you know, ways that can give great pleasure. You must remember where you are, my dear one. This is not the United States where everything, even love, is done in a great hurry. This is Tibet and we are very near to India—have you never heard of the Kama Sutra?''

N3 fought his way out of the drug haze long enough to say that he had indeed heard of the Kama Sutra, that he had read it, and he was damned if he was interested in Hindu erotic literature at the moment!

Her tongue was a sweet lance of honey in his mouth and she was whispering, ''The Kama Sutra mentions alternatives, Nick. Other ways. So you see I am not going to disappoint you—so now be quiet and be patient and come with me into the perfumed garden. Close your eyes, my dear one, and think no thoughts. Do not try to understand what I do—only enjoy it. I will take you to Paradise!''

Nick Carter stared at the ceiling. It appeared to move in the faint light of the single butter lamp. Dyla Lotti left him for a moment—he heard the faint *slip-slip* of her bare feet—and the odor of incense began to permeate the room. She had thrown it into the brazier. The stuff had the pleasant pungency of burning wood, only much lighter and sweeter and with the barest suggestion of a flesh smell.

''Breathe deeply,'' the woman whispered. ''Breathe deeply—it will aid your pleasure.''

Nick obeyed. Somehow he knew that he would always obey her now. Dyla Lotti was the High Priestess—*his* Priestess! He would always obey her. He must! In return for obedience she would lead him into the perfumed garden and show him such pleasures! It was really all rather cut and dried, he thought. Fated! Karma! He was fulfilling his destiny at last—why else had he come so many weary miles to this place to do—to do what? He had quite forgotten.

Dyla Lotti settled herself at his feet. He could feel her slim buttocks against his feet, feel her slender fingers tracing up his thighs. Higher and higher—fingers that were skilled and patient and evoking. Nick felt himself begin to tremble ever so slightly.

It was a war between his sensual being, now being so exquisitely stimulated, and his intellect. And his instinct. The tiniest of bronze gongs was beating somewhere in the

back of his brain, warning him. Against what? He did not
know and, almost to the point of peril, he did not care.

He began to feel a strange tenderness, mixed with an
unexplained enmity, for this woman who was ravaging him.
For the moment, he thought, no matter how it turns out, we
are lovers! It was a caught instant of time when all else was
forgotten and there were only the two of them in the world. It
was the drug, of course. The drug working to destroy the will
and intellect of Killmaster, he who was a masterpiece among
agents, who was as near perfection in mind, body, and will as
a secret agent can be and still remain human.

And Killmaster was very, very human.

He also sensed that, for the moment at least, he was losing
this battle. Perhaps this time he had taken on more than he
could handle. The drug was so powerful and, at the moment,
he was so weak. Yet he must somehow retain his sanity, even
in this sweet ordeal through which she was now putting him.
He heard her moan for the first time then, and sensed that she
shared some of his feeling of passion.

He could not move. Could not speak. For the moment he
was a floating island of tranquillity *sans* all desire. He was
alone in the universe. He was nothing. Did not exist. He had
at last achieved the Hindu goal of perfection—Nirvana.
Nothingness!

Chapter Five

RUDE AWAKENING

When N3 awoke some hours later he was alone. All the butter lamps had been replenished and the chamber was a blaze of tawny light. He lay for a moment, trying to fight the drug, trying to get clear in his mind who he was, and where, and why. It was useless. He could think of but one thing—women! Dyla Lotti if possible—if not then any woman.

Nick had no concept of time—no idea how long he had been in the lamasery. It could have been minutes, hours, days, months, years—it was not important. There was a cup of the familiar yak's milk beside the bed and he drank it down to quench a gnawing thirst—knowing it was drugged and not caring. He paced the narrow confines of the chamber, as naked as the day he was born. The drug was goading him. He must have relief.

It soon came. Half an hour later the old crone ushered in three giggling young priestesses. They were washed and perfumed and pretty enough in their Mongol way—and as avid for relief as he was. They wasted no time. They surrounded Nick and bore him down on the bed under a smother of thrashing brown limbs and firm young breasts. They spoke not a word of English and the man from AXE had no Tibetan, scholarly or otherwise. It mattered nothing. The four of them invented their own language, a *lingua franca* of laughter and giggles.

When Nick flagged, as he did eventually even with the

drug in him, the youngest of the priestesses—she couldn't have been much over sixteen—produced one of the famous silver clasps from a pocket of her robe and, with many giggles, instructed Nick in its proper use. It made, literally, a new man of him! Later he was anointed with a strange red powder, well rubbed in, which drove him into a new frenzy. Young, isolated, confined in a wilderness, yet these She Devils appeared to know every artifice of love. The orgy, though Nick did think of it as such, went on for hours. There was no food or drink and no one disturbed them. At times two of the little priestesses would leave Nick alone with the third, while they made love together, all sharing the same bed.

None of this seemed in any way strange to Nick Carter. He knew he was drugged, admitted it. Loved it! Desired it! Lovely thing—*sanga* root. He could never get enough of it! He had been born again—he was free and swinging on top of the world, had long ago passed Cloud Nine and was approaching Cloud Ninety-Nine!

N3 never quite knew when the She Devils left him. One moment they were straining on the bed with him—the next moment he was alone, awakening in a daze and staring around. He felt cold and his nerves were jumping. There was the cup of yak's milk by the bed and he was reaching for it when the brass monkey began to swing open.

Nick raised the cup to his lips and was about to drink. He smiled at the dark oblong in the wall. "Dyla Lotti! I thought you would never come back. I—"

Hafed came rapidly into the room. Before Nick could stop him he seized the cup and poured the yak's milk on the floor. "Best not drink more, sar. You plenty doped now, I think. Much bad. Come—we go out of this place fast. Much danger here!"

Nick sat on the bed, naked, scratching at the stubble on his face and grinning at the guide. Hafed was a good joe, a swell guy, but he was getting a little above himself. He shouldn't have poured that milk out. Now he would have to ask the old crone to bring him some—

Hafed handed him a small vial containing a greasy yellow

liquid. "Drink, please. Is what you call antidote, I think. Kill drug. Drink fast, please. We not have much time, sar. Get out this place hubba—I think Chinese soldiers come. They be here now but for storm."

Nick Carter staggered erect. To please good old Hafed he drank the contents of the vial and began to retch—the stuff smelled like urine and probably tasted like it, too.

"Ughhhh!" He wiped his mouth on his hand. "What in hell is that?"

Hafed smiled briefly, "Yak piss, sar. And other things. You can walk now, yis? You come with me hubba? I show you important things."

"Walk? Of course I can walk. What do you think I—" Nick took a few steps and tottered, nearly falling. Damn! He was as weak as a kitten.

Dismay registered for a moment on Hafed's swarthy features. "I was afraid of this," he told Nick. "*Sanga* root do it—much bad if you have too much. And you already sick anyway—never should take *sanga*."

N3 collapsed on the bed with an idiotic grin. "That's just what my sainted old mother used to tell me, Hafed. 'Never take *sanga*,' she said. A thousand times she said it— 'Stay away from that *sanga* root, boy!' "

Hafed scowled. "Not funny, sar! Chinese soldiers get here I get my head chopped off number one fast. Maybe not you, but me. You try hard to walk, yis?"

Nick tumbled on the bed laughing. Suddenly everything was uproariously funny. "To hell with walking, Hafed! I'm never going to walk again! I'm never going to do anything again but stay in this bed and fornicate! That's it, old buddy! I'm gonna stay right here and fornicate my stupid life away! Care to join me, old buddy?"

Hafed unleashed a string of curses that ranged from Chinese to English through Tibetan and Hindustani. "Goddamn son bitch," he said at last. "I maybe should run away and leave you, sar, but I not do. You good man."

Nick Carter put his head in his hands and began to weep softly. "You good man too, Hafed," he sobbed. "A real buddy. I love you!"

Hafed stepped close to the big AXE agent and slapped him hard across the face. "I sorry, sar. But must do! Not much time!"

N3, who could have broken the little man in pieces with one hand, kept on crying. Hafed was not a friend after all—Hafed had come to invade his perfumed garden! Hafed was destroying his Paradise! Vaguely, as the antidote began to take hold, Nick saw Hafed as an emissary from the cruel world of reality. Come to remind him, Nick, of such wearisome matters as job, mission, duty! He hated Hafed! He would kill the interfering little bastard.

The antidote struck his guts a hammer blow! He rolled off the bed and began to spew. Oh God—he was sick! For ten minutes he lay in his own vomit, unable to lift his head, retching and spewing and devoutly wishing for death.

Finally he was able to climb to his feet and don the coarse robe. He discovered, without surprise, that his weapons were missing. All of them gone—Wilhelmina, Hugo, Pierre!

Nick sat on the bed and rubbed his forehead. His eyes were pits of flame and an anvil was bouncing about in his skull. He looked sheepishly at Hafed. "Sorry—guess I've been away for awhile. What time is it? What day? And weren't you saying something about Chinese soldiers?"

Hafed plucked at his sleeve. "You come now. Make fast! I show you what I find—we talk then."

Nick followed Hafed through the wall behind the brass monkey. The passage was narrow and high and surprisingly warm. It led steadily downward. Butter lamps in iron sconces showed them the way.

"I sleep with many She Devils," Hafed explained as they went. "Some talk, some not. One talk a lot. After she go to sleep—sleep now. She take *sanga* root, I do not. I not need root. While she sleep I think what she talk—some very funny business go on. Is good time for looking—so I look. All She Devils at prayers and meditation now, you see. I find this place."

"Good for you," grunted Nick. He sounded surly, was, and instantly regretted it. This loyal little guy had gotten him out of a hell of a jam! Was trying to, at any rate. They weren't

out of it yet! N3 was coming back fast now and the enormity
of his lapse was growing on him. He had been sick as hell, of
course, but that was no excuse. Not in an AXE man. He
cursed himself briefly, then his jaw took the familiar jut and
he moved back into command. What was done was past
repairing. Now he must salvage what he could—forget everything but the future and the mission.

They rounded a sharp turn in the passage and came to an
iron door. It was half open. Hafed pointed to the door. "In
there, sar. Most interesting."

It was a small room well lit by butter lamps. There was a
table and chairs. On the table lay Nick's weapons. He inspected them. They seemed intact, in working order. As he
was checking the Luger Hafed said, "Maybe you look in that
door, sar. Also most of interest." He pointed to another iron
door set into the far wall of the little room. Nick went to it and
pulled it open. Instantly the sickening odor of decaying flesh
smote his nostrils.

N3 took a step backward, grimacing. He had seen too
much of death for it to hold any terrors for him, but this was
nasty! Over his shoulder he said, "Who is she?"

Hafed's voice was soft in the little room. "I think maybe
the real Dyla Lotti, sar."

The open door revealed a space not much bigger than a
closet. Chained to the wall was the near skeleton of a woman.
Leathery shreds of flesh still clung to the fragile bones and
her hair was white. The eyes had rotted, and most of the nose,
and the flesh around the mouth had fallen away to reveal long
yellow teeth fixed in an eternal grin. Nick closed the door,
remembering the youthful perfection of Dyla Lotti's body.
Dyla Lotti? But Hafed had just said—

Nick dropped his robe and began to strap the chamois
sheath on his right forearm. His face was rigid, hard beneath
the stubble. "Tell me," he ordered Hafed. "What's your
idea about all this—what makes you think that"—he nodded
toward the closet—"is the real Dyla Lotti?"

Hafed squatted, his back to the open door leading into the
corridor. He produced a murderous looking knife and began
to whet it on a calloused palm.

"I hear many thing while making love to She Devils," he explained. "I already tell that. Last one I have, she now sleeping, hates Dyla Lotti. Talk about her a lot. But she talk of *old* woman!"

Hafed pointed to the closet. "She old! And all She Devils say have not seen Dyla Lotti in long time—she much sick and stay in her own rooms. Lamasery is run by Number Two She Devil—name of Yang Kwei! That Chinese name, I think. I ask—find that Number Two Abbess is half Chinese. Not here long. My She Devil say that real Dyla Lotti get much sick as soon as Yang Kwei come—they never see her again. Stay room. Yang Kwei fix all meals, take care of old woman."

Hafed jabbed his knife into the floor. "You see, sar?"

"I see." N3's face was grim. What a dope he had been—in more ways than he cared to think. Yang Kwei had posed as the real Dyla Lotti. It had been easy enough. He was a stranger, following a most tenuous lead, and he had been secluded. He spoke no Tibetan, had no means of communication with the other She Devils even if they had been permitted to speak with him.

Nick pointed to the door which concealed the dead old woman. "Poisoned her, eh? Anyway weakened her and then brought her down here and chained her in there to die. Nice girl!"

"Chinese," said Hafed. As if that explained everything.

Nick, re-armed now, shrugged back into the orange robe. He must find his clothes. And get the hell out of the Lamasery of the She Devils—but not before he had another little talk with the phony Dyla Lotti!

"We've got to get her," he told Hafed. "Get her and make her talk! So lets—"

The guide's answer died in a little hissing sound. Nick swung to face the door. Dyla Lotti, or Yang Kwei, was pointing a small automatic pistol at them.

"Put your hands up," she said in her lilting, soft, too perfect English. "Carefully, Nick. I do not wish to kill you now. After all the trouble I have gone to—to keep you for my friends. They will be here soon to collect you, AXE man!"

Nick put up his hands. Wait and see what developed. He

had a little time and he was too far away to grab her gun. He glanced at Hafed. The guide was still sitting on the floor, his knife sticking in the floor before him. He had raised his hands.

The girl also glanced at Hafed. Her red lips curled in a snarl. "You, animal have been too lucky! I will not mind killing *you,* so be very careful. I would prefer to have the soldiers cut off your head, in public as an example, but I would not mind killing you. So keep your hands high! Try nothing!"

Hafed nodded humbly. He kept his hands high. "Yes, High Priestess. I obey. I will do anything—anything! Only do not kill me! Please do not kill me!" Hafed's voice fell into an abject whine. He spat toward Nick. "I only helped the foreign devil because he pays well, High Priestess. I would be most glad to work for you instead. Only give me a chance! I know much of this fool's private business!" Hafed squirmed and groveled on the filthy floor.

Yang Kwei regarded the guide with contempt. "You are a Turtle!" she snapped. "And a stupid Turtle at that. Do you think you can fool me with such idiot's talk? I know that you have worked for the Americans, for the CIA. But you will not again. Now be quiet, Turtle!" She turned her attention to Nick.

"They will be very pleased with me in Peking," she told him. "And very glad to see you—they will ask you many questions, Nick. All of which you will answer—in time!"

"Maybe," said N3 quietly. "They do say that no man can stand up to torture for long. And I don't carry a cyanide pill, either."

The girl regarded him with a mean smile on her rosebud mouth. "I thought not. I searched you while you slept and I did not find one. You are the big, brave, murdering American gangster type, Nick. I have heard all about you. But you will not be so brave when they finish with you in Peking."

Nick risked a glance at Hafed from the corner of his eye. What was the man up to? He was easing one foot from a yakskin boot. Slowly, almost imperceptibly, Hafed was drawing his foot out of the boot. The knife was still jutting from the floor in front of him. His hands were stretched high over his head. What the hell? What did the man think he could accomplish with one bare foot?

Hafed's right eye, the one with a slight cast in it, caught Nick's and the AXE man saw the faintest of winks. Keep her busy, Hafed seemed to say.

Nick Carter nodded toward the closet behind him. "You kill her?"

Yang Kwei showed her pearly teeth in an unpleasant smile. "I had to. She was taking much too long to die and I had to have her out of the way before you arrived. We were expecting you, but not quite so soon." She shifted the little automatic from her right hand to her left, as though her hand was tiring. Nick shot another glance at Hafed. His foot was nearly out of the boot now. Absurdly, considering the moment, Nick noted that Hafed had had a bath.

His eyes roamed back to Yang Kwei. She was wearing the same orange robe of silk, belted in between her slim hips and the full-pointed breasts. She was wearing boots again instead of the red slippers. Her head, without the black wig, was closely shaven. Somehow the absence of hair in no way detracted from her beauty. Her eyes were narrow and dark, sparkling dangerously now, and her nose was delicate. Her skin had the sheen of slightly aged porcelain. Not a wrinkle marred it. Nick studied that small vivid mouth and remembered what it had done to his body. It was really going to be a shame to kill her—she was, after all, only fighting for her country as he was for his. Then he remembered the thing in the closet behind him! In that fleeting moment he became both judge and jury and tried her and found her guilty. He sentenced her to death—after she talked!

Something of his composure, his confidence, communicated itself to the woman. She frowned at him and her finger tightened on the trigger of the pistol. She scowled at him. "You are thinking that you will win after all. You goddamned Americans are all so superior! Like the British bastards used to be." The profanity had an odd sound, coming

from that small red mouth. Nick grinned, relaxed and con-
temptuous, trying to anger her further. Distract her. Hafed
had the boot off now.

She caught Hafed's motion and whirled, the pistol jutting
at the guide, her trigger finger whitening with pressure. A
hair trigger would have killed Hafed then.

"What are you doing? Remain quiet, dog, or I'll kill
you!"

Hafed shrank from the lash of words. He rubbed his bare
toes and whined, "I am sorry, High Priestess. I did not
mean—it is that my feet hurt so badly. They ache. I must rub
them. I—"

"Quiet, fool!" She spat at Hafed. "You are an idiot! You
and your stupid feet! Annoy me again and it will be the last
time!" She turned back to Nick. He had nearly jumped her
gun while she berated Hafed, but had decided against it.
Hafed was working toward something. Wait and see.

He saw. Hafed's toes were long and slender and nearly
prehensile. Nick got it then. The man had a foot like a
monkey! And Hafed, while scratching and groveling on the
floor, was working his bare foot nearer the knife. So that was
it. N3 readied himself.

The small black eye of the pistol was steady on his belly. In
a soft interrogative tone Yang Kwei said, "I wonder why I do
not shoot you now, Nick? Shoot you in the stomach and
watch you suffer for a long time."

"Your natural kindness of heart," said Nick. "You
couldn't hurt a fly—maybe an old helpless lady, but not a fly.
It might bite you back." He watched Hafed from the corner
of his eye. Now!

Hafed slid his long toes around the upright knife. He rolled
backward on his shoulders, his leg coming high, the knife
flashing in an arc. He spun the knife at Yang Kwei, screaming, "Get her!"

She tried to duck and fire at the same time. The instinctive
movement ruined her aim. The little gun flashed and spat.
Hafed grabbed his arm with a curse. Nick was across the
room like quicksilver. He smashed at the pistol with a thick

forearm. It flew from Yang Kwei's hand to the floor. Hafed scrabbled for it.

The girl writhed and twisted in Nick's grasp, squirming and fighting like a demon. A knife appeared from the pocket of the robe and she slashed at him. He crunched her wrist in a great hand and she screamed and dropped the knife. Her hot sweet-smelling body slumped against his big frame. Nick pushed her against the wall and held her pinioned with one hand around her throat. He looked at Hafed. "You all right?"

Hafed was already binding up his shoulder. "Is flesh wound, I think. Not much. What we do now, sar? I say get out this place hubba-hubba! I think she not lie about Chinese soldiers."

Nick looked at the girl. Her lips were drawn back in a defiant snarl and he was reminded of the devil mask. "Maybe not about the soldiers," Nick agreed. "But I think she lied about certain other things—like a certain phony going to Karachi?"

He watched her expression closely. She spat in his face. He slapped her hard with his open hand. She spat again, saliva dribbling down her chin.

Hafed said, "Not make her talk that way. I do! But we must hurry—I by damn not want head chopped off! Come—I show you something else I find."

Nick pushed Yang Kwei ahead of him down the passage, following Hafed. A few steps and they came to another room. It was larger and a brazier glowed in the center. In one corner was the green steel console of a radio transmitter and receiver. Hafed opened the door of a closet very similar to the one that had concealed the skeleton of the real Dyla Lotti. Nick whistled softly. This closet contained stacked rifles, half a dozen tommy guns with clips of ammo, musette bags filled with grenades. There was even an old Browing Automatic Rifle.

N3 pushed her against a wall. "No lamasery's complete without an arms cache, eh?"

Yang Kwei stared at the floor, her face sullen. She did not

answer. Nick turned to watch Hafed make his preparations. He knew immediately that he wasn't going to like it—but he would go through with it if he must. The sooner Yang Kwei talked the sooner they could be on their way. He hoped she wouldn't prove too stubborn. He had no desire to see that lovely body torn apart. Killing was one thing—torture was quite another. But the matter was in Hafed's hands now and he would have to go along with it. The guide, as an Oriental, would have different ideas about such matters.

A long black beam supported the low ceiling. From it dangled rusty chains and manacles. Hafed wasted no time. He was obviously thinking of his own head and he was in a tearing hurry.

He laid his long knife in the coals glowing in the brazier. Nick, watching Yang Kwei closely, saw her begin to tremble. A smell of heated metal began to fill the room. Hafed looked at Nick. "Let me have her, sar."

Nick pushed the girl toward him. She stumbled and half fell and Hafed caught her. In two seconds he had her in the chains, strung to the rafter, her toes barely touching the floor. Hafed ripped off the orange robe and flung it aside. The girl swayed naked before them, clutching at the floor with her toes. Her splendid breasts rippled and jounced with the movement. Her small brown nipples were erect and hard, as though she were expecting a lover's kiss instead of the searing metal. Nick, watching her intently, thought he detected a hint of tears in the narrow black eyes. Could he let Hafed go through with this?

Hafed took his knife from the coals. The tip was white and smoking. He stepped toward the girl. "She talk now, sar. Damn quick you bet."

"Hold it a minute!"

Nick went close to Yang Kwei. He stared into her eyes as they lifted to meet his gaze. She was trembling and tiny beads of sweat were greasing her body, but the dark eyes were defiant. Nick felt sad and helpless. Yet he had to try.

"I don't want to do this, Yang Kwei. Don't make me. All I want is a straight answer to one question—where was my double, the phony Nick Carter, really going from here?''

Her eyes dared him. "Karachi," she said. "I told you the truth. Karachi! He *wanted* you to know!''

Instinct told Nick she was telling the truth. It figured. If it was a lure, a death trap for himself, it figured. The impostor *would* want him to follow. But he couldn't take any chances—he had to *know,* to be absolutely sure. He was already four days behind the man—five by now, due to his own drugged insanity, and he couldn't afford to lose more time.

Hafed was waiting with the glowing knife. "This is the last time I'll ask," Nick told the girl. "Is it still Karachi?''

She nodded. "Karachi—I swear it! That's all he told me. Karachi.''

Nick stepped back and motioned to Hafed. So be it. If she still said Karachi under torture—

Hafed was very businesslike. He jammed the flaming knife against the girl's left nipple and twisted it. There was a tiny flash and a hiss and a smell of roasting flesh filled the little room. The girl screamed in a high-pitched agony that ripped at N3's guts. He caught at Hafed's arm. He confronted the girl again, the question in his eyes. She tried to spit at him, but had no saliva. Her eyes hated him even through their daze of pain. Her left nipple was a seared red scar.

"Karachi—" It was a bare whisper. "I—I can't—he went—Karachi!'' She fainted.

Hafed stepped forward again, the knife newly heated, and was about to apply it to her right nipple when Nick stopped him. It must be Karachi, then. In any event he couldn't stand any more of this—if she had been a man, if she could have fought back, it would have been different.

"That'll do," he snapped to the guide. "Now we get the hell out of here. Get two of those tommy guns and plenty of ammo! Then I've got to find my clothes—I suppose our ponies are all right down in the stables?''

Hafed said that the ponies would be waiting. No one in the lamasery knew what really went on. Nick's clothes would undoubtedly be in the wash room or the laundry—and now couldn't they get the hell out before the Chinese soldiers came?

Nick rubbed his chin and stared at the limp form of Yang Kwei dangling in the chains. "What'll we do with her?"

He knew he should kill her, but at the moment, in cold blood, he could not summon the resolution. He excused himself. He was still pretty weak and sick.

Hafed solved that problem also. "I fix," he said. Rapidly he took the girl down and carried her out of the room. Nick heard vague sounds coming from the passage. Meantime he busied himself. He took the steel front plate off the transmitter and kicked the set into small bits. He smashed the rifle butts to pieces on the floor.

Hafed came back and picked up two of the tommy guns and as much ammo as he could carry. Nick did not ask him what he had done with Yang Kwei. He thought he knew.

Nick tossed the remaining tommy guns into the brazier and watched the wooden stocks begin to burn. He thrust four of the grenades into the pockets of his robe. Hafed fretted at the door. "Hurry, sar! Hurry!" Nick could see that the man was afraid. Couldn't blame him for that. Hafed was torture minded—he knew what the Chinese would do to him if they caught him!

As they passed the iron door Nick glanced in. Something lay in one corner, covered by the silk robe Yang Kwei had worn. Nick caught a glimpse of brittle white hair on a yellow skull. The door to the little closet was closed and locked.

"Maybe Chinese find her," said Hafed as they hurried down the passage. "Maybe not. Is Karma, yis? She get same as she give old woman, yis? Is justice, no?"

Nick Carter had to admit that it was. He put Yang Kwei out of his mind. He found his clothes freshly laundered and got dressed. Then he and Hafed left the Lamasery of the She Devils. No one paid them much attention, except for a sly glance now and then. One of the She Devils stared at Hafed and made an obscene gesture and laughed, but for the most part the life of the lamasery was proceeding much as usual. It was true, apparently, that the rank and file did not suspect what went on. They took orders and asked no questions and waited patiently for men. They had no inkling that, at the moment, they were without a leader. They would find out eventually. The Chinese would see to that. They would undoubtedly install another of their sympathizers as the new High Priestess. Nick filed that little tidbit away for later use—Hawk and the CIA would appreciate the tip.

As they hurried down the steep stairs in the cliff he was surprised to see it growing dark again. He had been more than twenty-four hours in the lamasery. So Hafed informed him. Otherwise, N3 thought grimly, it could have been twenty-four days! Even twenty-four years! He had been in a hell of a state there for a time. Someday, when he had the time and inclination, he would investigate that chaos of diseased memories.

Right now they had new trouble. Bad trouble. Chinese trouble!

The ponies, fed and rested, were being led out of the stables. Hafed grabbed Nick's arm and pointed. "Look, sar. She not lie okay—soldiers come now! Better we make fast, I think."

"I think you're right," Nick agreed. "Damn it!" He glanced to the east along the snow-choked pass. "You think the ponies can make it through that?"

Hafed, with a choice assortment of Oriental curses, said that the ponies would. They'd better or he and Nick had had it. He did not phrase it exactly so, but it was the gist. He was speedily packing his pony. Nick did likewise, wasting no time. It was growing darker by the second—that might save their lives.

He took a pair of binoculars from his pack and trained them on the soldiers. There were about fifty of them in the patrol with twenty or so heavily laden ponies. Metal sparked in the dying sunlight. Several of the ponies were carrying long tubes. Mountain guns! Mortars!

Hafed saw the mortars too, with his naked eye, and swore again.

"Is very bad place we must pass—much narrow. Good for

big guns. They know, too. Come, sar! Not time to waste!''
He was already kicking his laden pony east into the pass.

Nick lingered for half a minute. He caught a flash of sun on
lenses and saw a Chinese officer watching them through
binoculars. On impulse he put his thumb to his nose and
waggled his fingers. He saw the officer snap a command and
soldiers were running to the ponies bearing the mortars. Nick
made a rapid estimate of the distance—a little over half a
mile. He smiled. They should be safe enough. The mortars
could range it easily enough, but they weren't likely to be
accurate in this poor light. He kicked Kaswa and took off
after Hafed, already vanished around a bend in the pass.

N3 couldn't have been more wrong. He had forgotten that
the Chinese were familiar with this country. In all probability
they had the narrowest section of the gorge zeroed in, had
firing stakes planted along the way.

It was his lagging behind that saved N3. He was three
hundred yards behind Hafed when the first mortar shells
came in. *Sssshhhhhss—shssssss—shsssssss—shsssssss*—a
clutch of four whispered into the narrow waist of the gorge
and exploded with a whanging bang. Nick grabbed the
pony's bridle and led it into the shelter of an overhang. Four
more mortars exploded. Rock chips whined through the air,
mineral shrapnel as deadly as metal.

The trail crooked just ahead. He could not see Hafed.
More mortars poured into the gorge. Nick crouched and
cursed and waited for the deadly fire to cease. They *must*
have this spot zeroed in—they were firing blind and yet
pinpointing the narrow gut with devastating precision.

It grew darker. The mortars ceased to whisper in the
chilling air. Nick waited ten minutes, then kicked Kaswa into
life. He doubted the Chinese would come after them in the
dark, but he could take no chances. And Hafed would be
waiting, impatient and afraid, crouching in some hole just as
Nick was.

Hafed would wait a long time on this desolate slope of the
Himalayas. Nick found him lying in a great splotch of blood
on the snow. The same burst had gotten both Hafed and his

pony. The pony was gutted, its pink entrails smoking in the crisp air. Half the guide's head was missing.

Kaswa nosed at the dead pony and whinnied, a plaintive sound. Nick tugged him out of the way and began heaping snow over the blood and bodies. There was no time to do more. The snow would protect Hafed's corpse from the wolves at least until spring—then perhaps the She Devils would find him and bury him. Or the Chinese. It did not really matter.

Yang Kwei had taken her revenge after all. Part of it! She had held them just minutes too long. Nick gazed into the darkness of the pass leading east—he still had a far piece to go. He was alone now. Five days behind his quarry.

His face began to stiffen in the wind and he pulled the yakskin cover over it and chucked to the pony. He would make it. He had to make it. Death was in the wind that was rising, but not for him. Not yet. He had a job to do first.

He had lost the first round. But there would be a second— and it would begin in Karachi.

Chapter Six

DEATH COMES COILING

Karachi was blacked out!

The sprawling city on the Arabian Sea was as black as the future of Operation Deuce. Nick Carter had talked to Hawk from the airstrip at Ladakh and had learned, along with a great many other things, that his mission now had a name. DEUCE. It was a great help! N3 couldn't see just how—his mood was exceedingly bitter at the moment—but it only proved that even in AXE red tape and bureaucracy sometimes prevailed. Right now Nick would have settled for something more practical than a mission tag—say some first-class diplomatic immunity!

He was wanted for murder!

Now, in what was even for him a new low in harbor joints, he skulked in a dirty corner and buried his face in a tattered copy of *The Hindi Times*. It helped not at all that his own picture—blurred but fully recognizable—was on the front page of the paper.

His Hindustani was not fluent, but he could make out the gist of the caption: *Nicholas Carter, murderer and suspected secret agent, wanted for murder and escape!*

Nick sighed and ordered another bottle of Pakistani beer. It wasn't good but it was cold. And he needed an excuse for hanging about the place. So far he hadn't seen any cops—maybe the owner was paying off—and he needed a haven for the next few hours. He had to figure out his next move. Quickly! And when he had it figured he had to move just as quickly. He would have to venture out of this safe hole— defying the curfew—and he would be damned conspicuous in the deserted streets. But there was no help for that. He had to get out to the Mauripur district, where the murdered man had lived, and do a little on-the-spot investigating. It should be most interesting to know *why* his double, the impostor, had killed again! This time his victim was an American: Sam Shelton, confidential attaché to APDP—Arms Procurement and Distribution Program. It had been Shelton who had implemented Washington's order to shut off the flow of arms to the Pakistanis when the war with India flared. High policy, that, and Sam Shelton only the tool! Only carrying out orders. Yet the fake Nick Carter had killed him! Why?

Nick lit a Goldflake—American cigarettes were unobtainable in Karachi's cheap *boîtes*—and glanced furtively around. No one was paying any attention. Or so it seemed. You never knew.

The dirty little bar was situated in the Malir-Landhi district on the muddy Indus River near Karachi Airport where, a few hours before, Nick had said a hurried goodbye to the crew of the Hercules C-130 who had flown him in from Chushul Airstrip in Ladakh. They had been a nice gang of young Americans, bent on raising a little hell in Karachi—maybe visiting one of the infamous bathhouses where the entertainment was varied and continuous before, during, and after your bath. Nick would have liked to have accepted their invitation to join them—even though their youth and effervescence made him feel a thousand years old.

He hadn't, of course. Mission Deuce lay heavier on him by the passing second. He was a good week behind his quarry now—or so he had thought at the time. He had a man to find and kill and he had best be getting on with it. He said goodbye and plunged into darkened Karachi, improvising now and doubtful about his next move. It had been sheer luck that he had picked up a discarded copy of *The Hindi Times* and found that he was wanted for murder and escape! There it

was, his picture, on the front page. It was, of course, a
picture of the phony Nick Carter—but the Karachi cops
didn't know that!

Nick finished his beer and lit another cigarette. He kept his
face shielded by the paper and again surveyed the bar. It was
jammed and smoke-filled now. Most of the patrons were
men, though here and there Nick saw a prostitute in cheap
Western finery. The men were a polyglot crew, mostly river
and harbor workers with a scattering of lean Pathan tribesmen wearing pajama-type trousers and dirty turbans. The
stench of unwashed bodies was overpowering.

From the rear of the place came the sudden twanging of
stringed instruments playing—to Western ears—a most un-
melodic dance tune. There was a great surge by the crowd
toward the music and Nick found himself and his corner
deserted. Suited him fine. He stared down the bar and,
through the mob, could see a fat woman wriggling her belly
in a very basic version of the *jhoomer*, a Pakistani folk dance.
The folk, N3 thought, would never recognize it! The layer of
fat just above the woman's scant covering wobbled and
gleamed with sweat as she gyrated. Little cries of encouragement came from the crowd of men, most of whom were
drunk. It was strictly a Moslem crowd, Nick noted with a
sardonic little smile. What else? You didn't see many Hindus
around Karachi these days. If they were around at all they
kept well out of sight.

He glanced at his AXE watch—it had survived the terrible
passage out of the Karakoram Pass better than he had, his feet
were still aching from frostbite—and saw that it was a quarter
after twelve Karachi time. No point in stalling around here
any longer. He was only postponing the trouble. He had to
get out to Mauripur, find Sam Shelton's house, and see what
he could find in the way of a clue. Probably nothing—yet he
must try. Reluctantly he began to push back from the table,
dreading the empty streets, when he saw the incident at the
bar. N3 remained in his chair, watching, as a hunch began to
grow and develop in his quick brain. The man at the bar
sounded like an American.

Certainly he was angry—and drunk. And broke. That was the real trouble. The man was broke and the bartender, a huge fellow in a dirty purple-striped shirt and a red fez, would not serve him. As Nick watched the bartender reached across the bar and shoved the smaller man brutally. The man fell amidst a clutter of butts, waste paper and spittle, his head nearly in an old petrol tin serving as a spittoon. He lay there for a moment, unable to rise, mouthing a string of foul curses in Hindustani—Nick caught the word *bap*, father, coupled with what seemed to be a species of incestuous monkey. Then the man on the floor swung into English. Americanese, and the result was delightful to hear. Nick grinned openly and enjoyed it, thinking that even Hawk could learn a word or two from this derelict!

N3 made his decision and acted immediately. It was his way. He had little to lose and possibly a great deal to gain. Even a bum like this must have a home of sorts—someplace to hide for the night. Anything was better than a hotel, even the cheapest, where he would have to show identification—and where sharp eyes would spot him as a wanted man.

He went to the fallen man and pulled him up roughly. The bartender looked on without interest, his swarthy face conveying his boredom and impatience with Yankees who were broke and on the beach. They were pigs! Useless pigs! One never *got baksheesh* from such as these. They drank cheap beer only and did not patronize the whores and—

Nick tossed a 100 rupee note on the bar. "Bring whiskey. Good whiskey—American if you've got it! *Tez!* Hurry up!"

The barman was immediately servile. He had misjudged, then. This big one had money after all! And something else—an air of authority that was not to be trifled with. And yet another thing! The bartender pondered as he fumbled for the single bottle of precious American whiskey—had he not seen the face of this big one somewhere before? Recently—quite recently! The bartender summoned his assistant and conferred with him for a moment in rapid Pashto. Both he and the assistant were Afghans.

The assistant studied the face of the big American who by

now had gotten the drunk back to his table and succeeded in propping him up. "No," said the assistant, "I have never seen him before. But if he is a friend of the Bannion, of that one, how can he be anyone important or worth anything? You are mistaken, boss. He can be of no consequence. I doubt they have a *naye paise* between them." He went back to watch the belly dancer.

The owner crumpled the 100 rupee note in his pocket and took the whiskey and two dirty glasses to the table. His assistant was, in fact, supposed to be a junior partner—but if he did not find out about the 100 rupees so much the better. And Ali could be wrong, too. He would keep an eye on this big American with money—just in case.

There was a folded copy of *The Hindi Times* on the dirty table. The owner used it to brush away the flies and ashes. The big American reached to take the paper from his hand. "Mine," he said. "I haven't finished with it yet."

"*Dwkh,*" said the owner. "My sorrow, sir. Will there be anything else? You wish perhaps to view the dancing? I could, er, arrange a private performance!"

Bannion, the derelict, raised his head from the dirty table. He stared at the owner with red-rimmed eyes. "Get lost, you greasy fat son of a bitch! Who needs you? Beat it!" He turned to Nick. "Better watch him if you got any money. He's a thief. They're all thieves!"

The owner retreated a step, but did not lose his servile expression. He dry-washed his hands and stared at Bannion with disdain. To Nick he said, "I must warn you against this one, *sahib*. He is worthless—for many years now. He is a cadger, a dead beat! I—"

Bannion tried to struggle out of his chair, his face working with rage. "You're gonna be a dead Afghan son of a bitch if you don't get that lousy fat carcass out of here!" he collapsed into the chair again.

Nick Carter nodded to the owner. "Leave us alone."

When the man had gone he studied the man called Bannion. Pretty far gone, he thought. Way down in a deep hole.

At the bottom of the ladder. Hopeless. Still he might prove useful.

Bannion was on the short side, squarish in build, with a little pot belly. His three- or four-day growth of stubble was reddish mixed with gray. What was left of his lank hair, around a smooth pink tonsure, was of the same color. His eyes, as he stared back at Nick now, were watery and inflamed. He looked like a bad case of pinkeye! He wore a filthy old GI field jacket covered with grease stains and a pair of equally disreputable OD pants. Beneath the field jacket a ragged tee shirt was the color of dirt. Nick, very deliberately, making a thing of it, glanced down at the man's feet. He wore old Army shoes, one with a heel gone. He was sockless.

Bannion said nothing while this scrutiny was going on. He scratched at his red beard and narrowed his inflamed eyes at Nick. Finally he grinned. Nick was a bit surprised to note that his teeth weren't bad.

Bannion said, "Inspection over?"

N3 nodded curtly. "For now."

"I pass?"

Nick restrained a smile. This was a cocky little bastard, no matter that he was down and out.

"Barely," he said. "I really don't know yet. You're really a mess, aren't you?"

The little man grinned. "You can say that again, mister who-ever-you-are. I'm the bum to end all bums! I'm a derelict and a hopeless, no-good bum! But all that's pretty obvious, isn't it? So why bother with me? Why pick me up and bring me over here with all this good whiskey that, as far as I can see, is going to waste. You don't look like a do-gooder to me. And you aren't carrying a prayer book and a tambourine, either. So what goes on, mister? And, while you're telling me, can I have a shot of that panther pee you're paying for?"

Nick shoved the bottle toward him. "Help yourself. Only stay on your feet, please. I think I might have a little job for you later. Not much later, either. Just how drunk are you now?''

The man seized the bottle and poured with a fairly steady hand. He jerked his head toward the bar. "Not as drunk as they think I am. That's an act I put on sometimes—these bastards like to see a white man drunk and making a fool of himself. Makes them laugh—and when they laugh they buy drinks. Simple as that, mister.'' He drank his shot in one gulp and hastily refilled his glass, then shoved the bottle toward Nick. "Thanks. Been a long time since I've tasted real American booze. Mostly I drink beer or Karachi rot-gut. Now, mister, what's your angle?''

N3 felt a tinge of pity. He repressed it immediately. There were millions of these men in the world, all with a hard luck story, and he had neither time nor inclination to listen to another one. Yet this man might prove valuable in just this situation—it remained to be seen.

He replied to the question with another question. "What's your name? I'd like to know something about you before I go on with this—not much, but a little. How you happen to be stranded in Karachi, for instance?''

The little man reached for the bottle again. "Mike Bannion,'' he said. "Michael Joseph, in full. I used to be a newspaper man. In the States. In the world, for that matter. All around and about! That was ten years ago—when I landed here in Karachi after a story. I got the story—but I also got drunk. I've been drunk ever since. I'm going on being drunk as long as I can manage it. And you're wrong about one thing—I'm not stranded. I've got a home, believe it or not. I've also got a wife and nine kids. I married a native—Moslem girl. Her old man hates me and disowned her. She's fat and ugly now—having all those kids—but when I married her she was something. Now she takes in laundry to feed the kids and pay the rent and I shift for myself to get drink money. And that's it, mister, the story of my life. Or all of it that you're going to get—I don't care how much money you pay me!''

Bannion took a deep breath, another shot of whiskey, and

stared with covetous eyes at Nick's pack of Goldflake. Nick shoved the cigarettes across the table. "Help yourself."

As Bannion lit up Nick studied him carefully. He must make up his mind in a hurry. Now. He decided to go through with it. It was a risk, but then he was used to taking risks. One more couldn't make much difference. He took the copy of *The Hindi Times* from his pocket and opened it to the front page. He shoved it across to Bannion.

"Take a good look at that. Read the story if you can—then I'll ask you a few questions. If you give the right answers, and are still interested, I think we'll be in business."

Bannion's expression did not change as he studied the picture. He glanced at Nick once, then back again to the paper. Obviously he read Hindustani well. Finally he folded the paper and handed it back to Nick. He nodded slightly back of him toward the bar.

"If they spot you you're in trouble. I notice there's a reward for you—and these characters would sell their mothers for a plugged rupee. Unless they thought they could blackmail you first."

Nick put the paper back in his pocket. His grin was faint, quizzical. "Perhaps that thought has occurred to you, too?"

Bannion grinned in return. He poured himself a drink. "It was the first thing that struck me, Mr. Carter. But we'll see. That your real name?"

"Yes. But this is not a picture of me. It's the picture of a man who is posing as me. *He* killed the American, Sam Shelton. I didn't. It's a very complicated story and I'm not going to try and explain it to you now. Maybe never. It's all very top secret stuff. You'll be working blind, with only my word for anything. Still interested?"

Bannion nodded over his glass. "Could be. I wasn't exactly born yesterday, you know. And I couldn't care less whether or not you killed this guy—I only want two honest answers out of you! Have you got money—lots of money?"

Nick smiled faintly. "Uncle Samuel is behind me all the way."

Bannion brightened. "Good. Second question—are you

working for the Commies? Because if you are, and I find it out, the deal is off! I might even get mad and lose my temper. There are some things even a bum like me won't do."

Nick grinned across the table. There was something likable about this little redheaded wreck of a man. Not his odor, or his looks certainly, but something!

"Just the other way round," he said. "I'm agin. That's all I can tell you."

The bloodshot eyes regarded him steadily for a long time. Then Bannion reached for the bottle again. "Okay. I'm in, Mr. Carter. Short of murder, I'm in. What do we do first?"

Nick poured the drinks. "This is the last," he warned Bannion. "I want you as sober as possible. After this one we leave—and we'll need transportation. Got any ideas about that?"

"I've got a jeep outside," said Bannion surprisingly. "The oldest jeep in the world. Name of Gae—that means cow in Hindustani. She still runs—barely. Where do you want to go, Mr. Carter?"

As they left the man from AXE said, "Call me Nick when you must call me anything—and don't use my name anymore than you must. Never in front of other people! Right now I want to go to the Maurpiur district—to Sam Shelton's house. You know the district?"

"I know it. I even know the house—it's on Chinar Drive. I used to drive a beat-up taxi around town until the Paks got sore and spoiled it for me. They don't like white men working at their jobs."

Nick followed him to a dark lane near the Indus. The night was clear and cool, with a hanging yellow lantern of moon, somewhat spoiled by the smell of mudflats and dead fish. In the faint light Nick could see ghostly *dhows* drifting with the current down to the Arabian Sea.

Maybe it wasn't the oldest jeep in the world. Perhaps, Nick thought as he climbed in, it was only the second or third oldest. You couldn't say that the paint job was bad—there was no paint. There was no glass in the windshield. The tires were worn down to the cord. The single headlight was wired on and bounced alarmingly.

Bannion had to crank—the starter having long ago gone to buy whiskey, he volunteered without shame—and after an anxious moment Gae began to cough and wheeze and hawk up great blue gouts of stinking smoke. They took off cautiously as Bannion babied the tires. A coil of spring nipped at N3's backside as they rattled and clanked and clunked down every dark alley Bannion could find. And he seemed to know them all. He carefully skirted the modern downtown section of Karachi. They came to a maze of miserable huts thrown together from every kind of material—packing crates, bamboo, mud blocks and logs, flattened oil and beer cans. The stench was appalling. They wound through this desert of misery by means of a single-lane knee deep in greasy mud. The ancient jeep huffed and puffed valiantly. The hovels, and the smell, covered acres.

Nick Carter put a handkerchief over his nose and Bannion snickered. "Rough, huh? Refugees from India in here—no place else to put 'em. It's a hell of a mess—even I live better than these poor devils."

"Speaking of places to live," said Nick, "after our little excursion tonight I'm going to need a place to shack up—a safe place where I won't be bothered by cops or anyone else. Your place should do?"

"Perfect," Bannion nodded and smiled, his teeth flashing through the red beard. "I thought you'd come to that! You're welcome—part of the deal. The cops never bother me. I know most of them in the neighborhood and anyway I've been around so long they take me for granted now. I'm just the American bum!"

"Your wife? And nine kids?"

Bannion shook his head. "Not to worry. I'm bringing home some money, so Neva—that's my wife—will be happy with me for once. The kids do what I say! No problem there, though you'll have to keep out of sight. We're one big happy neighborhood and the wives gossip something fierce—but we'll worry about that later. Speaking of money—I'd better have some to show Neva.''

Nick fumbled in his wallet and handed the man a thousand rupee note. ''That's for now. There will be plenty more if we get along. If you do a good job and don't let me down I might be able to do something about getting you out of this hole.'' He let it go at that. Bannion made no answer.

They reached Drigh Road and headed west. It was a modern highway, four lanes, and well marked. Bannion pressed down on the gas and the old jeep sputtered and picked up speed. The speedometer didn't work, but Nick guessed they were doing at least forty-five.

''This is the tricky bit,'' Bannion said. ''They patrol this pretty well. If we're stopped it'll be along this stretch.''

Nick glanced at his AXE watch. It was a little after one.

He heard a sound of planes overhead and glanced up. They were old prop jobs. Far across the city he watched lances of brilliant light spring to life and sweep the sky. There came the distant popping of anti-aircraft fire. Two of the searchlights caught a plane in their apex and held it for a moment, pinned to the black sky like a moth to cork. The plane slipped away. There came the remote crash-thud of a bomb exploding.

Bannion chuckled. ''Hit-and-run raid. Tomorrow the Indians will officially deny it ever happened. The Pakistanis are probably raiding Delhi about now—and they'll deny it too. Some war! A two-bit deal that neither of them wants.

N3 remembered Hawk's words—somebody wanted this war. The Red Chinese!

They were getting into the Mauripur district now. Well-paved streets and large estates and compounds surrounded by thick-growing *chinar* trees. A delicate fragrance of cashew-nut bushes scented the crisp night air. The AXE man noted the street lights, dark now because of the blackout.

''This is where the money lives,'' said Bannion. ''And most of the foreigners. The place you want is just up here.''

Bannion slowed the jeep to a crawl. Even so the old engine

made a fearful racket in the quiet night. "Turn it off," Nick ordered quietly, almost whispering. "Park it someplace where it won't be noticed by a patrol, then we'll walk."

Bannion switched off the engine and they coasted. They left the jeep in the clotted shadow of a towering Persian oak, and Bannion led the way down a strip of blacktop. He stopped in the shadows just short of where a white gate gleamed in the gibbous moon. At that moment, from afar on the outskirts of the city, a jackal wailed.

"They come in close looking for food," Bannion said. "Tigers not a hundred miles from here."

Nick told him to shut up and stand quietly. He was not interested in tigers, other than himself, and the only jackals he cared about were the two-legged variety. He whispered his instructions to Bannion. They would remain in the shadows, and stark still, for twenty minutes. If anyone was watching they should betray themselves by then. In the meantime Bannion, whispering into N3's ear, was to fill him in on a few matters. Bannion obliged.

He had followed the Nick Carter case in the papers, of course, but only with cursory interest. Until tonight his interest in spies and secret agents had been nil—his chief concern being the next drink. Now he probed his alcohol-ridden memory as best he could.

Nick Carter—the man who looked like and was posing as, Nick Carter—had been arrested because of the alertness and loyalty of Sam Shelton's maid, a Hindu girl. Hindus who worked for Americans were fairly safe in Karachi. The maid had admitted the man calling himself Nick Carter and had left him alone with Sam Shelton. Shelton, she told the police later, had appeared puzzled at first, but glad enough to see the man. They had gone into Shelton's private office. Later the girl heard angry words and peeked through a keyhole just in time to see the stranger stab Shelton with a small stiletto. The girl had used her head, had not panicked, had called the police immediately from an upstairs phone.

By luck there had been a police car nearly on the spot. They captured the killer after a terrific struggle in which a policeman was badly hurt. Once taken, however, the murderer had given no trouble. Not in the ordinary way. In another way he had been enormous trouble. He had identified himself as Nicholas Carter, an American agent, and had cheerfully confessed to killing Sam Shelton. Shelton, the man claimed, was a traitor who was about to defect. He had been killed on orders from Washington. To top it all off the killer demanded diplomatic immunity.

The real N3 whistled softly as he heard this latter. Clever devil! He wondered if the story had been rehearsed, or if the guy had simply made it up as he went along? Anyway it was fiendishly confusing—as the man had meant it to be. The cables and air waves between Washington and Karachi must have been blazing. Nick grinned sourly now as Bannion talked. He could almost smell the mutual distrust. And Hawk—his boss must be nearly out of his mind.

The best—or the worst—was yet to come. Day before yesterday the fake Nick Carter had escaped! Had been delivered from jail by a gang of masked and armed men who left three dead cops behind, plus one of their own. This man had turned out to be a Hindu thug well known to the police, which helped matters not at all.

Into this mess Nick Carter had walked! Unsuspecting. Hawk hadn't known the details in time to warn him. Might not have warned him anyway—Nick had a job to do and he was on his own. It was a thing his chief was capable of—withholding information that might only complicate matters. It was a judgment call—and Hawk never erred on the side of making things safer and more comfortable for his agents. It was his theory that such solicitude only made them lax.

Nick could find but one small crumb of comfort—he was only two days behind the impostor now. It occurred to him that the man might still be in Karachi.

The twenty minutes were up. The moon ducked behind a cloud and it was very dark. Nick, walking on the grass, went to the white gate and vaulted it. Bannion was just behind him. "What do you want me to do?"

"Stay and watch," Nick whispered. "Be careful. I don't

expect you to take any risks or get in any trouble for me. But if anyone comes snooping, a police car, or anyone, I'd appreciate a warning.''

"I whistle pretty good.''

Nick remembered the jackal. "Whistling's too obvious. How's your jackal howl?''

Bannion's teeth flashed in a grin. "Not bad. I scare the kids with it sometimes.''

"Okay then. That's it. After you signal, and if you think there is any danger, you take off! I don't want you caught.'' Bannion would talk, of course.

"I don't want to *get* caught,'' Bannion agreed. He chuckled. "Not until I get the rest of the money anyway. But every cop in Karachi knows my jeep.''

"We'll risk that,'' said Nick. "Now keep quiet and hide. I'll be as quick as I can.''

The house was low and rambling, much like a ranch house in the States except that one wing had a second story. Maid's room, Nick thought as he studied the house from the shelter of a hedge. It was dark and quiet. He wondered briefly what had happened to the maid. Cops still holding her? Gone to relatives in India?

A tiny censor in his brilliant, superbly trained brain began to click and glow. But for once he ignored it, so intent was he on his purpose.

Nick moved across a cement porch without sound. He found a French window open, the jalousie raised. A second censor clicked in his brain. This time he paid heed. How come the window so conveniently open, so beckoning? Sloppy police work when they had sealed the house? Could be. Or could not be. So—he was being paid danger money for this mission.

N3 checked his weapons. Pierre, the gas bomb, was safe in the metal cartridge between his legs. Surely, he wouldn't need Pierre tonight. Hugo, the stiletto, was cold against his forearm. Sam Shelton had been killed with a stiletto, remember!

N3 checked Wilhelmina, the Luger. He jacked a cartridge

into the chamber, muffling the sound beneath his borrowed airman's jacket, and flicked off the safety. He went into the dark room beyond with a single fluid motion that was without sound.

Nothing. A clock ticked dutifully away, though its owner had no more use for time. It was blacker than a dictator's sins! Nick felt his way along a wall, his fingers detecting flocked wallpaper.

He reached a corner and halted, counting the seconds, listening. After two minutes he dared the pen light he always carried. The thin beam disclosed a big desk, files, a small safe in another corner. He was in Shelton's office.

Cautiously he approached the desk. It was bare except for a blotter, a telephone and some sort of an official form pad. Nick held the light close and scanned the pad. It was a new one with only a few sheets missing. Nick picked it up gingerly—he had no means of knowing how clever the Karachi police were with fingerprints—and read the small black lettering. It was in gobbledy-gook. Officialese! U.S. Lend Lease style. It was a pad of requisition slips.

The dead Sam Shelton had been special attaché for APDP—Arms Procurement and Distribution Program. There was a huge transshipment depot on the Indus northeast of Karachi.

N3 scanned the pad again. He turned it in the air so the little beam of light played across the top sheet at an angle, bringing up indentations, the impression of what had been written on the preceding sheet. Even without special technique he could make out a long list, written in a small hand, and at the bottom the heavy swirl of a signature. *Sam Shelton.*

Excitement began to build in the AXE man now. He thought he was getting close—close to finding out what the fake Nick Carter was after. He twisted the pad this way and that, trying to make out more of the writing. He was positive that one of the faintly limned phrases was—*Consigned to—*

Damn! He needed a heavy pencil, a soft lead, to brush over the impressions and bring them up. The desk top was bare.

Nick found a drawer, the top drawer, and slid it softly open. There should be—

For a micro-second the man and the snake stared at each other. It was a krait, eighteen inches of instant death! Cousin to the cobra, but much deadlier. Death in less than a minute and no serum could save you.

Both the man and the snake struck in the same instant. Nick was just a shade the faster. His action was spontaneous, without thought. Thought would have killed him. His nerves and muscles took over and the little stiletto flashed down to pin the krait to the bottom of the drawer, just below the obscene flat head.

The krait lashed in a furious death agony, still trying to strike its enemy. Nick Carter gave a long sigh and wiped sweat from his face, watching the fangs still flickering a half-inch from his wrist.

Chapter Seven

DOUBLE TROUBLE

His nerves went back to normal before the krait stopped writhing. Careful to avoid the still feral mouth the man from AXE found a soft pencil and brushed it lightly over the pad. It was a trick every kid knew. As he stroked in the soft graphite, words began to appear. Soon he could read most of what was on the pad. N3 pursed his lips in silent speculation.

Sam Shelton, acting by the authority of his office, had turned over a lot of arms to the Pakistani Army. Evidently on orders from the fake Nick Carter. It didn't have to be that way, but Nick had a sinking feeling that it was. His double had taken the top sheet from this pad. A requisition and consignment slip releasing arms to the Pakistanis. Dated day before yesterday.

Nick slanted his light on the pad and read a note scribbled on the bottom—the arms to be shipped up the Indus, by boat, to the Lahore front! That would look just great in the newspapers! Washington favoring Pakistan over India—breaking its own edict! It wasn't true, of course, but that was how it would *look*. If it got out.

N3's handsome, saturnine face crinkled in a wolfish grin. It wouldn't get out—not if he had anything to say about it. It was just one more angle to this job—find that arms shipment and stop it! That must take priority even over killing his other self.

He scanned the paper again. Rifles—and Mls at that! Light and heavy machine guns. Grenades. Bazookas and light anti-tank guns!

Five million rounds of ammunition!

Nick Carter heard it then. A faint sliding sound somewhere in the house. In one rapid motion he flicked off the light, snatched the stiletto out of the dead krait, and ran on tiptoe to a wall near the study door. He liked something solid against his back.

The sound was not repeated. N3 waited, tensed and ready, breathing noiselessly through his open mouth. Not one of his superb muscles so much as quivered. He was an unseen statue—the perfect hunter doing what he was best at—the waiting stalk.

Five minutes passed in utter silence. The clock's insistent voice was metronomic in the dark. Nick could count his pulse as it thudded in his temples. He began to realize what he was up against. A man who was supposed to *be* himself—and who was just as patient, as cunning, and as deadly! And that man, the impostor, was somewhere in the house now! Waiting, even as Nick was waiting. Waiting to see who made the first mistake!

N3 understood something else—his enemy had purposely made that noise. It had not been a slip, a mistake. His enemy had *wanted* Nick to know that he was in the house. That single small sound had been a challenge. *Come and get me!*

That, N3 admitted, was the hell of it! He had to go after the other man. The fake agent had all the time in the world— Nick had none to spare. The double had come back to this house because he had reasoned that Nick would come here! And he was confident, sure of himself, else he would not have signaled his presence. He had an organization behind him, too. A clear escape route laid out. Help within the sound of his voice. N3 had none of these things. He stood alone but for the growing anger and determination in him. The confrontation had come sooner than he had expected.

One other thing was clear. The arms shipment must be on its way. The Chinese agent had attended to that first, then doubled back to ambush Nick as he followed the trail. What queer bravado could have prompted the man to make a sound, to give himself away? A kind of twisted pride—or stupidity? Over-confidence?

Most unprofessional, Nick thought as he went back out the French window in a silent gliding motion. Unprofessional and dangerous. It's going to get him killed!

For a moment he lingered in the shadows of the porch, listening. Nothing stirred near the house or in it. The planes had gone and the searchlights vanished. A *pi* dog howled dismally from far off—it sounded nothing like a jackal. Nick thought of Mike Bannion and hoped the little man was obeying orders and wouldn't come snooping. And wouldn't get hurt if, indeed, the man inside had helpers about.

He left the porch and moved silently through grass on which droplets of dew were beginning to gather. He had replaced Hugo in the sheath and went with the Luger ready and eager. He would like to do this job silently, but that might not be possible.

There was a low garage attached to the house by a latticed breezeway. Nick waited patiently for the dying moon to show, then saw that he could get to the upper floor, to the single wing of the house, by means of the latticework. He studied the layout intently in the brief light. He would have to do it by touch in the dark.

The moon sailed behind a dark cloud. Nick pushed cautiously through a low hedge of Indian cactus and tested the lattice. It held his weight. He went up like a monkey, using only one hand, the Luger alert in the other. The lattice was new and strong and did not creak, though it bent and swayed alarmingly.

There was a narrow strip of gutter and roof between the top of the lattice and the window which was his target. N3 stepped forward lightly and ducked below the window level. This was the only upstairs room in the house—he had figured it to be the Hindu maid's bedroom—and whether he was right or not didn't matter. What did matter was that it was the obvious way into the house. For that reason he had chosen it—his enemy might not be expecting the obvious.

Or again he might. Nick Carter swore gently to himself. The bastard had the advantage for the moment—he was in there somewhere and he could afford to wait. He *knew* that Nick had to come to him.

And so Nick did! But N3 had a healthy sense of fear, or what Hawk called intelligent caution, which had kept him alive for a long time in a very precarious profession. Now he huddled beneath the sill of the window and considered if he should take the gamble the window represented. It was another of the moments of truth he must continually face.

Nick peered up at the window. It was closed but the jalousies inside were slitted open. Nick flexed the stiletto into his hand and reached up, using the weapon as a pry-bar. The window moved a fraction. Not locked on the inside. Nick pondered that for a moment, then pried again with Hugo. The window shifted upward a half-inch. Nick re-sheathed the stiletto and got his big fingers into the crack and lifted. The window went up with a faint grating noise.

Sweat glistened on Nick Carter's face and stung his eyes. He had been half expecting a blast of gunfire in his face, or a knife between the eyes. He breathed out a sigh of relief and kept going. The window had made enough noise to be heard anywhere in the silent house—his man would know at once what it was. And where Nick was! It might draw him, but Nick doubted it. The bastard could afford to wait.

He held the faintly rattling jalousies aside and legged over the sill. The room was dark but he caught the smell immediately. Blood! Fresh blood! The moon flashed for an instant and he saw something on a bed—it looked like a crumpled pile of dark rags through which something light glimmered. The moon went out.

Nick scuttled on his hands and knees for the door. His fingers told him it was locked. *On the inside*. His enemy was in the room with him!

Nick held his breath. Absolute dead silence pervaded the

room. When at last he had to breathe—yoga exercises had
built his lungs to where he could do without air for four
minutes—nothing had changed. Still the deadly, frightening
silence and the smell of fresh blood. Whose blood? Who, or
what, was the thing on the bed?

N3 breathed soundlessly by mouth and did not move. he
began to doubt his senses. He had not thought there was
another man in the world who could go as quietly, as steathi-
ly, as himself. Then he remembered—this enemy *was* himself in a sense! The Chinese had trained this impostor well.

There is a time to wait and a time to act. Nobody knew the
adage better than Nick. So far he was behind. He was losing.
The enemy knew he was in the room—but Nick did not know
where the enemy was. Force his hand. Put on the pressure.

N3 began to crawl around the wall, thinking hard, trying to
see the ultimate trick if there was one, expecting any moment
the blinding flash of a light in his eyes. The smash of a bullet.

His brain worked furiously as he moved. Had he somehow
been swindled, tricked? Or tricked himself? Had the door
somehow been fiddled with so that it only *appeared* to have
been locked from the inside? Sweat chilled on him at that
thought—if it were true and his double had men with him
then Nick was in a trap! They could guard the window and
door and kill him at their leisure—or merely hold him prisoner until the police came. That didn't bear thinking about.
The cops would think they had the real killer again! It would
take weeks to disentangle the mistaken identity mess and
Nick would be ruined as an agent for a long time to come.

His hand touched cold metal. The bed. He raked under it
with the stiletto, the Luger ready, his own nerves beginning
to fray ever so slightly now. Damn the waiting, lurking
son of a bitch! He wanted it that way. He was playing it that
way.

There was nothing under the bed. The smell of blood was
thick and sour-sweet in his nose now. He went beneath the
bed and emerged on the far side, his fingers tracing up. It was
a box spring and the mattress was thick. His hands touched
something on the floor which he could not understand—bits

of soft, fluffy stuff like waste or cotton. What the hell? The stuff lay thick on the carpet.

His fingers came away damp and sticky. Blood. Blood all over his fingers now. Nick put them to his nose and sniffed. Fresh, all right. Not yet fully congealed. Whoever it was that was dead on the bed had just been killed.

He moved away from the bed, wiping his fingers silently on a dry stretch of carpet. There were two danger spots. A closet—there must be one—and the bathroom if it opened off the bedroom. His man could be lurking in either spot.

By this time N3 was having to use his will power to keep his nerves under control. Seldom had they been so tested! He felt a sudden overwhelming urge to find the light switch and flood the room with brilliance—shoot it out with the bastard face to face! He killed the urge with a grim inward chuckle. That would be playing the other man's game. He was doing too much of that now.

Yet he had to relieve his tension somehow. He found the bathroom and went into it like a tornado, not caring for poise, ripping and flinging about with the stiletto and the Luger. He tore down the shower curtain and demolished the medicine cabinet. Nothing!

He found the closet and gutted it. Nothing!

No sound. No movement. Only darkness and a strange corpse on the bed and the growing awareness that he was being completely outsmarted. Being made a fool of! And time leaking away relentlessly. There was not even time for a halt, for a cool and logical reappraisal of what was beginning to look like an impossibly insane situation. Either he was all wrong—or he was losing his marbles!

The bed now began to draw him like a magnet. There was something about the bed—something that glimmered in his brain and tried to fight through to him and couldn't quite make it. N3 scuttled back to the bed like a big crab and stabbed beneath it again with the stiletto. Still nothing. And then something very peculiar happened to Nick Carter, to Killmaster. For the first time in his career he found himself verging on real panic. This whole thing was crazy. He must be losing his mind. The guy had to be in this room and yet he wasn't! No man could go so long without breathing—and sooner or later breathing was bound to give you away in dead silence.

Wait a minute! The body on the bed! The blood was real enough, warm and sticky, but blood could be *brought* into a room and splashed about.

Cautiously, very slowly, conscious that his hand was shaking a bit, Nick began to explore the surface of the bed. His fingers touched soft flesh. Cool velvet beneath his fingers. Nearly cold now. He touched a tiny button of flesh. A nipple! He was touching a woman's breast.

So much for that idea. The corpse was real enough. A woman's body. His still roaming fingers plunged into a deep wound squarely between her breasts. No weapon, but Nick could guess at what had killed her. Stiletto!

The phony agent had taken his revenge on the Hindu maid. What a fool she had been, what fools the Karachi police, to let her stay on in the house. Probably she had figured she would be safer here than elsewhere in this angry Moslem city. Sad irony!

Her single filmy garment had been pulled up over her head and tied, so his sensitive fingers told him. Nick scowled in the blackness. It was easy to imagine what else the man had done to her. He had spiced his revenge, his waiting, with a little rape. Cold, clever, heartless devil! The krait in the drawer was proof of that, if more was needed. He had known that Nick would prowl that desk. Only that hadn't worked and—

The moon came out again and sent a glancing bright beam through the slats of the jalousies. It saved Nick Carter's life.

He saw the flash of the stiletto just in time. A savage silver glint in the bad light, aimed at his leg just above the knee. A hamstringing stroke! The crippling stroke came from the bed, *beneath* the dead girl! In the same instant Nick heard the *pock-pock* of a silenced gun. Two shots. One of the slugs nipped at his thigh, but by that time he was in action, a

cyclone attacking the figure still struggling out from under
the dead girl.

The phony Nick Carter was just a trifle awkward at the
wrong moment or the real Nick would have died then! As it
was he felt flesh sear over his left ear as the gun *pocked* again.
He dove at the bed, stabbing with his own stiletto, saving the
Luger for a target he could see clearly. He was met by the
flung body of the dead girl. The limp and bloody arms and
legs cloyed about him like a net of flesh. The moonlight was
fainter now, cloud shadowed, and Nick saw his man roll out
of the bed on the far side. He was wearing something on his
face, something ugly and snoutlike. A respirator! That was
how he could breathe under the girl in the nest he had cut in
the mattress!

The gun in the man's hand *pocked* at him again. Miss.
Nick went over the bed in a long sprawling dive, still not
using the Luger. He wanted it to be the stiletto—or his hands
on the bastard's throat!

He cleared the bed but slipped to his knees. The man
kicked him in the face and tried to aim with his gun at close
range, trying to shoot Nick in the head. Nick came up
roaring, his desire for silence forgotten. He smashed the gun
aside with one arm and ripped his stiletto around in a vicious
circle. His enemy skipped nimbly back, yet gasped in pain.
Nick went boring in, the stiletto in front of him like a lance.
The moon blacked out.

N3 leaped forward and was met by his enemy coming at
him. The collision was great, both men shaken and gasping,
grunting and sweating, as they locked and swayed. Both
forgot the stilettos now and tried to bring their hand guns to
bear. For a full minute they stood locked in a deadly embrace, each clutching the right wrist of the other, each trying
to bring his weapon to bear and keep the other's at bay.

The enemy was a perfect match for Nick in everything but
strength. He was as tall, as wide, as lean and ferocious, but
he lacked Nick's rock-ribbed muscles. Slowly, painfully,
Nick began to bend the other's arm down. His finger tensed

on the trigger of the Luger. He had no silencer and it was
going to make a hell of a noise and that would bring the man's
companions and he just didn't give a damn. He was going to
kill this son of a bitch as quickly as he could. He was going to
spread his nasty guts all over the room. A belly shot—the
whole damned clip right through the big gut!

Slowly, inexorably, hating and sweating and yearning, he
brought the Luger down. His other hand held the man's gun
wrist in a vise of steel. There could be no tricks now—he had
him this time. He had him now! Vaguely, through his red
daze of rage and frenzy, Nick Carter knew that he was doing
this wrong. He should try to take the man alive, to take him
prisoner and try, somehow try, to get him back to
Washington. He would talk, this one, and he could tell them
many things.

To hell with it! Kill!

The fake agent broke. His wrist and forearm collapsed. He
squealed and tried to pull away from the Luger now digging
into his belly. Nick pulled the trigger.

Nothing! Nick pulled the trigger again as the man fought
like a maniac to break away. Nothing. Nick swore and got it
then—somehow the safety had gotten knocked on again! He
had done it—the phony! His sly fingers had found the safety
and fiddled it as they struggled. Slimy clever bastard! But it
wouldn't do him any good.

But it did! As Nick flipped the safety off again his con-
centration wavered. His enemy slashed down with his freed
hand at Nick's left which was holding him prisoner. The
savage blow broke Nick's grip at last. The man dove for the
open window and went through it in a crashing welter of torn
jalousies. Nick cursed and forgot all caution and let the Luger
spit through the window, the reports thunderous in the little
bedroom. He leaped to the window in time to see a shadow
roll off the roof and crash through the breezeway. Nick let the
whole clip go with a lousy feeling that he was hitting nothing.
He felt sick with failure. He had had the bastard—and let him
get away! It was more than professional failure—it was

personal failure! And, worse, the man had damned near killed *him!*

Time to go, he told himself. Go fast. Nothing more to do here. I bungled it good!

A jackal howled nearby. The sound had a strange note of urgency, one that is not commonly associated with jackals. Nick grinned without a hint of mirth. Mike Bannion was getting nervous—and maybe was in trouble. Better go see.

He started to leave by the window, then thought better of it. They might still be about, though he doubted it. That phony had had enough for one night. As he went down the stairs in the dark house Nick had to admit, although grudgingly, that the fellow was tough. Good. But then why not— was not imitation the sincerest form of flattery?

Mike Bannion was already at the wheel of the jeep. He was nervous and with cause.

"There's a patrol snooping around down the street," he said as they swung away. "We're lucky they aren't on our necks now. Maybe they think all that shooting was Indian commandos or something—probably they're mapping a battle plan. I hope they don't hear this heap."

"They can hear this heap in Chicago," Nick said sourly.

Bannion patted the battered dashboard. "Maybe—but she'll get us home if they give her a chance."

Nick Carter yawned. He hurt all over. His feet were killing him and the flesh wounds were smarting, but the worst was the hurt to his pride. He had failed. That there would be another time, must be, was of no consolation now. He forced himself to think of it as a professional must—some you won and some you lost! It was a mark of his caliber that never once did he think of how near he had been to losing everything.

Wearily he lit a cigarette and gave the pack to Bannion. They were well away from the Mauripur district now, running down black and smelly alleys, and the danger seemed to be over. For the moment.

Bannion said: "What in hell was going on in there? It sounded like a shooting gallery."

Nick was curt. "Part of the deal is that you ask no questions. You see anybody come out? See anyone at all?"

"Not a soul."

N3 nodded. Maybe the man hadn't had friends after all. Maybe he was a loner, like Nick himself. That would be in character.

"It was a tie game," he said savagely, almost to himself. "I'll get the bastard the next round!"

Chapter Eight

THE LONG BLOODY TRAIL

In late afternoon of the same day N3 lay in a rope bed—no thick mattress here to conceal an assassin—and pondered the immediate future. One thing was certain—he must get out of Karachi that night. The police had found the Hindu girl's body and a new hue and cry was on. The afternoon papers had it, along with another picture of the phony Nick. There had also been a flash on the radio. The murdered girl was a Hindu, and of no importance, but the Karachi police were nettled. They had been made to look bad!

Only one thing about the entire situation really pleased Nick Carter—his double would have to leave Karachi too. He wouldn't dare hang around with all the heat on. The man had made one try at killing Nick and had failed—he would try again—but Nick was sure it would not be in Karachi. He wouldn't *be* in Karachi if his luck held. If it didn't he would be in jail—charged with *two* murders!

He finished the last of his tea—cold now—and gnawed at a slab of *nan*, the flat circular bread of the country. Bannion's wife, Neva, had fed him well since his arrival. There had been *birayni*, rice, and a blistering mutton curry called *keema*, and all the goat's milk he could drink.

Nick lit a cigarette and lolled back in the uncomfortable rope bed, more like an oversize hammock than a true bed. His feet were high and wrapped in dirty bandages on which

Mrs. Bannion had smeared some vile smelling salve. It did seem to help. His feet were a mess, still chafed and peeling from frostbite, but he would just have to make do on them. The Air Force in Ladakh had issued him socks and a pair of shoes two sizes too big, and that helped. His feet still hurt like hell!

The minor wounds he had gotten in the scuffle last night were nothing! Mere bullet burns which Bannion had patched up with iodine and plaster. He hoped his double was feeling worse than he was—he had gotten the man once with the stiletto for sure—and maybe again with that flurry from the Luger. He could hope! Anyway the fellow had gotten away—the police had found only the butchered corpse of the maid.

Thinking of his feet, of pain, made Nick think again of his journey through the Karakoram Pass after Hafed had been killed. That had been a narrow thing. Close. After the pony, Kaswa, died of exhaustion Nick had been in one of the tightest binds of his fantastic career. He was very close to the end of that career when the Carter luck returned and he stumbled into the camel caravan. Normally the caravan—it was the last from Sinkiang Province into Kashmir that year—would have been on its way the day before, after sheltering from the blizzard, but a camel had taken sick and they had lingered to treat it.

Nick had made it to the camel camp, but he could have gone no farther. The caravan had taken him with them, on the back of a shaggy bactrian, into Leh where they had turned him over to the U.S. Air Force.

It was strange, Nick thought now, to owe your life to a sick camel!

He snapped a piece of bread at a gecko which was staring at him with beady eyes from a rafter. He felt himself getting restless again. Mike Bannion should be back soon. He had been gone all day, following Nick's orders and spending AXE's money. True the man had a million things to do, but he should be back. Nick damned his own impatience and hobbled to the single window to peer out, keeping well back

out of sight. It would be dark soon and he and Mike Bannion
could leave. He mustn't be spotted now.

The backyard on which he gazed was a slum in the midst of
even worse slums. There was a mango tree full of monkeys
and kids and the incessant chitter-chatter of both. There must
be a million kids, he thought, all dirty and ragged and some
nearly naked. N3 lit another cigarette and grimaced. Even
with all his own problems, with the sour taste of failure in his
mouth, he could feel for the kids. Poor little bastards! Not
much future for them. Mike Bannion should have his drunk-
en ass kicked for bringing more of them into the world—with
no means of caring for them.

The door opened and Bannion's wife came into the room
to get the tea things. She nodded to him but did not smile.
There was no communication—she had no Hindustani and
Nick Carter spoke no Urdu—and Nick had wondered if she
could be trusted. Certainly Mike thought so, but then husbands didn't always know everything about wives. Especially husbands like Mike.

Nick glanced at his watch. It was after five and no police
yet. So she could be trusted. He watched moodily as she
gathered up the tea things and, after nodding again, left the
room and closed the door softly behind her. He heard a bar
fall into place. That was a precaution against nosy kids.

Nick went back to the rope bed and stretched out again. He
flipped his butt at the gecko still fixing him with its evil glare.
Goddamn it, Bannion! Come on!

He was not afraid of Bannion betraying him. The little
drunk had visions of *lakhs* of rupees to come. He would not
throw money away. But he could have been picked up by the
police for routine questioning. Suppose his ancient jeep had
been noticed in the Mauripur district last night? Nick felt
cold. Bannion would talk in the end, however reluctantly.
Sweat prickled on N3's neck—all that money Bannion was
carrying! If the cops got him they would never give up until
he explained it—and if he did that he would have to betray
Carter! A fury raging in his big, outwardly calm body, Nick
forced himself to be calm and think of other things. If it

happened that way it happened. Karma!

Karma. Tibet. The Lamasery of the She Devils!

N3 scowled at the tiny lizard on the rafter. So the Chinese soldiers had found Yang Kwei in time. Must have—and had relayed her information on to the impostor—else the man wouldn't have known Nick was coming to Karachi. Wouldn't have been able to set the trap which had so nearly caught the AXE man. Nick cursed under his breath and wished the She Devil a short life and an unhappy one. Then he remembered her sexual technique and almost relented— she'd be okay if she would get out of the profession, out of agentry and politics, and make somebody a good wife! He had to grin at his own whimsy, then forgot the She Devil. Where in the everlasting hell was Mike Bannion?

The object of his concern entered the room a minute later, bringing with him the smell of good whiskey. He had shaved, and gotten a haircut, and donned clean clothes. He was, as near as Nick could tell, still sober. He did not look quite like the same man except for his grin. Once again, briefly, Nick wondered why and how the man had gotten stranded in Karachi. His speech betrayed him as an educated man, and he did not lack intelligence. Why? Whom had he betrayed, sold out, murdered?

Bannion tossed a carton of American cigarettes at Nick. "Behold! Black market. Many rupees. I got a case of Scotch, too. I know you like it and I don't care what I drink."

Nick had to smile. The little man was irrepressible. "I hope you were discreet—spread the buying and spending around?"

Mike sank into the room's single chair and elevated his feet to a battered table. He was wearing new shoes of the heavy duty type. He winked at Nick. "I was most circumspect, boss man. I spread it around. I hit a lot of the second-hand merchants and the surplus stores—you can even get World War I stuff from them, and I was careful. I didn't even get new tires for Gae—got used ones, but they're in good shape. Got a used battery, too, and some spare gas cans. In fact I got everything on the list you gave me. You're ready to roll, Nick, and so am I.''

Nick broke open the carton of cigarettes. He had been down to his last pack. "You've decided to come along, then?" Until now Bannion had not committed himself past a willingness to help Nick get ready for the trip.

Mike Bannion shrugged. "Why not? I can help you—and God knows I need every *pice* I can make. In any case I've already helped you—so now I'm in as deep as you are. As the Limeys say—in for a penny, in for a pound. Anyway I *like* doing this—been a damned long time since I did anything worthwhile.''

Nick left the rope bed and hobbled toward the table. Mike gave him the single chair and Nick took it without question. "How are the feet today?" Bannion asked as he helped himself to a pack of cigarettes and threw one short stocky leg over a corner of the table.

"Murder," Nick admitted. "But never mind the feet—if you're coming with me we've got to have an understanding. Now! About the booze.''

Bannion's eyes held his steadily. "As I said, Nick, I'll watch it. One bottle a day, no more. I have to have that or I'll fold—have the DTs and the screaming meemies! I wouldn't be *any* good to you then.''

N3 regarded him for a long moment, his eyes steel hard. Finally he nodded. "Okay. You're making a bargain. Better stick to it. If you louse me up God help you—I won't! I'll leave you out there to die. I mean it, Bannion!''

The little man nodded. "I know you do. You don't have to threaten me. I know how tough you are. I suppose you have to be in your—er—in your job.''

N3 stared at him. "What is my job?''

"I don't know," said Bannion hastily. "I don't want to know, either. I'm in this only for the *baksheesh*, remember? Now hadn't we better be getting on with it—I've got the stain and the makings outside. It's almost dark now.''

"Do that," Nick said curtly. "You get a map? Did you scout the arms depot?''

Bannion went to the door and bellowed for his wife to

bring in the bundles he had left outside. He turned back to
Nick with his grin showing again. "I went out to the depot
and snooped about as you told me. I wasn't even noticed—
I've been there before looking for work and I pulled the same
routine again today. No work, of course. They won't hire
white men for coolie labor. But I kept my ears open and got
what you wanted—a big shipment of arms went upriver
yesterday by steamer. Under guard, of course. Half a company of Pakistani soldiers. That do it?"

N3 said: "That does it! I can tell you this much, Mike—
that shipment is headed for the Lahore front and I've got to
stop it. It's a mistake—it should never have been sent!"

Neva Bannion came in with her arms full of small boxes
and packages which she piled on the table and around it. Her
wrists and ankles were still delicate, still fine, though the rest
of her had gone to fat. Her light copper-colored skin was
smooth and unblemished. Though she was not in *purdah* she
wore a long shapeless *burqa*, without the hood and eye-slits,
which covered her from neck to toe. Her glistening black hair
was piled high on her head and held with a cheap, factory-
made comb. Nick conceded that she must have been attrac-
tive once—before Mike Bannion and the children.

She left without speaking. Mike winked at Nick. "I'm in
pretty good at the moment. Food and money in the house,
you know. If I was going to be here tonight I could
probably—"

Nick broke in. "The map?"

Bannion produced a small-scale map of Pakistan and
spread it on the rickety table. He tapped with his finger.
"Here we are, in the Goth Bakhsh sector of Karachi. If
you're really going after that shipment all we can do is follow
it up the Indus and try to catch it. Though I don't know what
the hell you think we can do against half a company of
Pakistanis."

N3 was studying the map intently. "Leave that to me," he
murmured.

Bannion gave a mock salute. "Gladly, sahib. Mine not to

question why, huh? Okay, I won't. I'll just have a little shot instead." He left the room.

Nick shook his head as he pored over the map. It wasn't good to have to use, to trust, a drunk like Mike Bannion. But there was no help for it. He needed the man—both for his knowledge of the country and as a part of his new cover. He was starting on this venture as a Eurasian oil prospector, a free lance. Mike Bannion was his guide. There was just one big hitch—they had no papers!

N3 shrugged and went back to his map. So they would have to do it on the cuff, without papers. And hope his luck held.

The country through which they were traveling was some of the most rugged terrain in the world. That should help Nick thought now. It would be scantily patrolled. He traced the northeasterly course of the great Indus with his finger: to their right would be the arid Indian Desert, to their left was a series of rugged mountain ranges running parallel to the river and joining the Himalayas in northern Kashmir. Except for the narrow strip watered by the Indus it was nasty country.

Bannion came back with a bottle of expensive Scotch and two plastic tumblers. He showed the bottle to Nick. "Two drinks gone, see. This will get me through until morning—and I'll even buy you a drink out of it. Okay?"

N3 nodded. The Scotch tasted good. He pushed the map across the table to Bannion. "This is your department, Mike. How about it? Can they take that shipment all the way to Lahore by water?"

Bannion rubbed his bald spot and frowned at the map. "No can do. The Indus goes west of Lahore. Anyway it isn't navigable beyond Bhakkar—not this time of year. They'll have to go overland from there."

"Maybe that's where we can catch them," Nick said. "Two men in a jeep, even *your* jeep, should be able to catch a convoy."

He did not think it necessary to explain that, if and when he caught up with the arms convoy, he hadn't the slightest idea what he was going to do. He would have to figure that out later. All that was important now was—if that shipment of arms was used against the Indians and the world found it out, then the U.S. was in trouble! And the Chinese would see that the world found it out! Maybe that was the whole point of the impostor's foray into Pakistan—to get those arms by trickery and turn them over to the Pakistanis. Then claim the Americans had given them and beam the distorted facts to the world.

N3 pondered that very briefly, then dismissed it. No. It had to be more than that—something bigger. Bigger even than trying to kill him! But what?''

Mike Bannion broke into his thoughts. ''I don't know if it's important or not, but maybe you'd better know. I saw something today at the arms depot that sort of put a chill in me.''

Nick began to take off the OD shirt the Air Force had given him. It was time to get on with the make-up job.

''Such as what?'' He was anxious to get going now while Mike was sober. He hadn't much faith in the man's promises.

Mike began to smear brown paste on Nick's face and neck. ''Such as a mullah preaching a jehad, a holy war! A lot of the workers at the depot are Pathans, you know. Tribesmen come down out of their hills to make a rupee or two. They're rough bastards, Nick. Savages. And they were listening pretty good to this old guy today. He got them worked up into quite a lather.''

N3's first impulse was to forget it. This deal had enough angles now without looking for more. His immediate job was to find that arms shipment and hope the man he was after was somewhere near it. If not, and after he stopped the shipment—how?—he would have to use himself as bait again to lure the double.

Yet he listened. In his job no small thing could be overlooked without danger. Bannion's next words drove a fertile wedge into Nick's alert mind.

''The mullah was yelling at them in Pashto,'' Bannion said. ''I understand a little. Not much, but enough to know that he was promising them the world if they'd go back to the hills and wait. He was shouting about food and new uniforms and plenty of guns and ammunition and—''

Bannion broke off what he was doing and stared at Nick. "Hey! That arms shipment! You don't suppose?''

Nick did not look at the little man. He shook his head. "No. I don't suppose. That shipment is headed for Lahore. Under guard. You just told me that, remember? Half a company of the Pakistani Army!"

Bannion shook his head. "That wouldn't stop the Pathans if they wanted the guns. My God! A jehad is all we need now around here. A holy war!''

All the relevant facts were sparking through Nick's computer mind now and he didn't like the mental cards he was pulling. Bannion *could* be right. Could have stumbled on the key to this whole complicated intrigue. But why—why would the Chinese Reds want to aid the Pathans, the Afghan tribesmen, in launching a jehad? What could they gain? The Reds were, nominally at least, on the side of the Pakistanis.

And yet they always enjoyed fishing in troubled waters, the Reds. What had his boss, Hawk, said—that they must keep the pot boiling. The Chinese had been losing a lot of face lately and they were getting desperate. They were in trouble in Africa and Cuba and Indonesia, and in Vietnam. The United States tiger had turned out not to be paper after all!

But a jehad! A war in the name of Allah against all infidels! What in hell could the Chinese hope to gain out of that? Unless, of course, they could *control* the jehad. Bend it to their own uses. But how?

Nick gave it up for the moment. He started to dress. He was dark enough to pass for a Eurasian and he would think of a cover name when it came time. A name wasn't too important anyway—they had no papers to support a name. They would have to slide through on luck, if at all.

Two hours later they were chugging up the Indus in an ancient freight boat that had never decided whether it was a dhow or a felucca. There was no wind and the big lateen sail

was furled, but the rusty, two-cylinder engine was taking
them up the broad shallow river at a steady four miles an
hour.

The boat was covered amidships with matting which concealed the jeep. The old vehicle was loaded to the collapsing
point with their gear. Nick and Mike Bannion remained out
of sight as much as possible, stretched out on jute mats near
the jeep. They had blankets in the jeep but neither bothered
with them. Mike had gotten them a heavy sheepskin coat
each, and a bush hat with the wide brim pinned up in the
Australian fashion.

They dozed, silent, watching the tiny spark of the boatman's cigarette at the stern. Nick had elected to bring the
owner of the boat along, though he knew he might regret it.
Yet he had to risk it. The man, a dirty fat fellow in a red felt
hat and long shirt and baggy pants, was deckhand and en-
gineer and sailor and cook all in one. Neither Nick nor
Bannion knew much about dhows or whatever this old tub
was. There was always the possibility that he would have to
kill the man later, to shut him up, but N3 did not allow
himself to dwell on the thought now.

So far Mike Bannion had kept his promise. He was drinking slowly. His bottle was still more than half full and it was
after midnight.

Nick was checking his weapons, Wilhelmina, Hugo, and
Pierre, when he heard the gurgle of the bottle in the dark
smelly hold. The boat's last cargo apparently had been fer-
tilizer.

Mike said: "I said in for a penny, in for a pound, and I
meant it—just the same I hope we don't have to tie up with
any Pathans. They're a lot of bloodthirsty bastards!"

Nick smiled in the gloom. "I think you're worrying about
nothing. I remember my Kipling and Talbot Mundy—aren't
the mullahs always preaching a holy war? Just part of their
routine—down with the infidels!"

A match flared as Bannion lit a cigarette. He was not
grinning. Nick realized that the little alcoholic was really
worried.

"They're devils from Hell!" said Bannion. "They torture their prisoners. Jesus—the stories I've heard! I've seen pictures, too, of what they've done to patrols they've ambushed on the frontier. Only a couple of months ago there were some pictures in *The Hindi Times*—the tribesmen ambushed a Pakistani patrol in the Khyber Pass. They didn't kill all of them—the survivors they impaled on bamboo stakes. Ugh! It made me sick. They take off the poor bastards' pants and then lift them and slam them down hard on a sharp stake! There was one picture of this guy with the stake all the way through him, coming out of his neck!"

The bottle gurgled again. To soothe him Nick said, "You sure that was a Pakistani patrol? Not Indian? The Pathans are Moslems, aren't they?"

More gurgling sounds. "That don't make a damned bit of difference to the tribesmen," Bannion whispered. "Especially when some mullah had got them all heated up. All they care about then is blood and loot! I don't mind admitting it, Nick—I get the crap in my blood when I think about the Pathans!"

"Take it easy on that bottle," Nick warned. "And let's try to get some sleep. I don't think we're going to meet any tribesmen. I'm a hell of a lot more worried about Pakistani patrols that I am Pathans. Good night."

Three days later he found out how wrong even Nick Carter could be!

The kites and vultures gave the first warning. They were soaring in great circles over a bend in the river. It was a desolate, barren stretch halfway between Kot Addu and Leiah. The boatman saw the vulturous diners first. He pointed and sniffed at the air. "Something dead there. Many, I think. Many birds—cannot all eat at once."

Nick and Mike Bannion ran to the prow. The river was shallow here, curving in a great bend from west to northeast. There was a long sandbar in the middle of the bend. On the bar they saw the gutted, blackened, still smoking wreck of a small river steamer. An old rear-paddle wheeler. It was

covered with a wriggling, flapping, obscenely moving mass
of vultures. As their boat approached the wreck the cloud of
birds rose in a multi-colored swarm, croacking harsh com-
plaints. Some of them were barely able to get airborne
because of sagging, heavy bellies.

Nick got the odor then. A battlefield smell. He was familiar with it. Beside him Bannion cursed and took a huge
revolver from his pocket. It was an old Webley he had
somehow managed to buy in Karachi.

"Put it away," Nick told him. "There's nothing alive
there."

Mike Bannion peered beyond the wreck to the westerly
shore of the river. The barren land sloped sharply up to
rounded, blunt-topped khaki hills. "Maybe they're still up
there, watching. I told you, Nick. I had a feeling. It's those
sonofabitching Pathans—they ambushed the steamer and
grabbed the arms shipment. Jesus—that old mullah wasn't
kidding! They *are* starting a jehad!"

"Calm down," Nick told him. "You're jumping to a lot
of conclusions. Anyway we've got to check it out—if it was
the tribesmen we'll soon know."

They soon knew. They beached on the sand bar. The
boatman would not accompany them. He was in a state of
terror. Nick and Bannion made their way through the stink
and the sprawled bodies to the steamer. It was a shambles.
Blood and brains and decaying guts everywhere. Many of the
Pakistani soldiers had been beheaded.

Mike Bannion turned a corpse over with his foot. The face
had been shot away, but the turban and dirty singlet, the
baggy trousers, were enough to identify it.

Bannion cursed. "Pathan, all right. Stripped, too. Took
his bandoliers, rifle, knife, everything. Even his shoes.
That's Pathan for you—they never leave anything behind but
stiffs! So what do we do now, Nick?"

N3 covered his nose with a handkerchief and explored the
gutted steamer thoroughly. It had been a massacre, all right.
The Pakistanis had somehow been caught napping and had
been wiped out. The arms were gone. Where? To start a

jehad? Probably, he admitted. Bannion was right. The tribesmen were off and running, screaming bloody Allah. They would have their jehad. They would have it—but who would *own* it?

Very clever, he admitted. Trick the arms out of Karachi and have your boys waiting in ambush. He ticked the list of arms through his mind again, the list he had read in the murdered Sam Shelton's office.

Rifles—light machine guns—heavy machine guns— grenades—bazookas—anti-tank guns! Five million rounds of ammo!

Nick Carter's smile was grim. You could have yourself quite a jehad with all that!

Mike Bannion joined him. He was carrying the giant revolver in his right hand and frowning. "They took some prisoners, Nick. I'm sure of it. At least I counted the dead Paks and they don't make half a company. They must have taken prisoners. I don't understand it. They never do!"

N3 glanced across the river to the western shore. Even at that distance he could see the broad trail the tribesmen had left leading up into the stubby hills. Pretty sure of them- selves. Not afraid of retribution. That figured—the Pakistani Army was busy fighting India at the moment.

An idea moved in his brain. Could there be another reason for that broad trail? An invitation, perhaps?

He turned to Bannion. "Let's get unloaded. Better hurry before our friend there loses his nerve entirely and shoves off and leaves us."

Mike Bannion avoided Nick's eyes. He said: "You're going to follow them?"

"Yes. I've got to. No way out for me. You don't have to go—you can go back to Karachi with the boatman. But I'll have to take the jeep and the supplies. Well?"

Bannion took his bottle of Scotch from the deep pocket of his sheepskin coat and tilted it. He drank for a long time, then put the bottle down and wiped his mouth with his hand. "I'll go with you. I'm a damned fool, but I'll go. Just one thing!"

Mike's grin was a little sheepish. "If anything happens—

to me—and you get out of it okay, will you see if you can get a little of Uncle Sugar's dough for my wife and kids? They got nothing.''

Nick smiled. ''I'll try. I think I can swing it. Now let's get cracking—that character is going to shove off any minute!''

It took the Luger to persuade the boatman to put them ashore on the western side. They unloaded the jeep and supplies where the Pathan trail left the river.

Bannion nodded to the boatman and looked at Nick, the question plain in his eyes. The man would talk, of course, as soon as he got back to Karachi.

Nick hesitated a moment, then shook his head. Why kill the poor devil? By the time he got back to Karachi it would be too late for anyone to stop them. It occurred to him that by that time he might be glad, overjoyed, to see Pakistani troops.

Nick watched the craft disappear back downriver as Mike Bannion checked over the jeep. The vultures had returned to their meal.

''Come on,'' Bannion told him. ''If we're going let's go. This old heap is as ready as she'll ever be.''

A mile inland they found the first Pakistani soldier buried in earth up to his neck. He was dead, his throat slit, and his eyelids had been cut off. Something white glimmered in the gaping dead mouth.

Mike Bannion took one look and was sick over the side of the jeep. He would not go close to the dead man. Nick walked to the grotesque bloody head sticking out of the sandy soil and studied it. He leaned down and took a bit of paper from the mouth. Something was scrawled on it—Chinese ideographs!

His Chinese was rusty but in a moment he made out the message.

Follow me. The way is plain. You will find one of these markers every few miles. I look forward to meeting you. Again!

It was signed: *Nick Carter.*

Chapter Nine

KHYBER PASS

A limpid warm rain was falling on Peshawar, that ancient
and historic city in the narrow mouth of the blood-stained
Khyber Pass. It was a weekend and many of the tribesmen,
Afghans, Pathans, and Turkomans, had brought their women
into town to shop in the bazaars. While the women gossiped
and did their trading the men gathered in the teahouses and
kept the samovars boiling. Most of the men were lean and
fierce, each with a cruel knife thrust into a colorful sash. The
subject of conversation, when police or strangers were not
around was—jehid! Holy war! The time was coming!

It was not a monsoon rain—they were over for the year—
and Nick Carter found the moisture pleasant on his face as he
peered from a dark archway in the Street of the Story Tellers.
It was a narrow, cobbled lane stinking of garbage and human
filth, but N3 was too impatient and anxious to pay heed to the
smells. Mike Bannion had been gone a long time. Too long!

Nick fidgeted. He had already been twice noticed by
whores, one who hadn't been a day over twelve, and he knew
he'd better move on. The luck had been incredible so far—if
it was luck—and he didn't want to spoil it now.

To his left, at the end of the street, he could see the
looming mass of Mahabat Khan mosque. Directly across
from him was a well-lighted shop where leather workers
were busy—Nick could see sandals and cartridge belts on
display. The belts were of the old-style bandolier type, worn

crossed over the shoulders, and N3 wondered, rather grimly, if Ml ammo would fit them.

He retreated back into the dark arch and lit a cigarette. He leaned against a rough stone wall and pondered, covering the cigarette with a big hand and frowning. He didn't like the setup. Not at all. But he had to play it—play the cards the way they fell. He, and the ever more reluctant Bannion, had come boldly into Peshawar that afternoon. Four days from the Indus. The old jeep had somehow made it—and the trail had been clearly marked as promised. There had been no more notes—only the milestones, the corpses of Pakistani soldiers buried in earth to their necks. Throats cut. Eyelids gone. Noses cut off in some cases.

Nick inhaled deeply and held it. This was a real weird, kooky setup. They'd left the jeep in the camp on the outskirts of Peshawar and walked in. The rain had started about then. No one paid them much attention, which in itself was not unusual—from ancient times the Khyber Pass had served as a gateway, and invasion route, between east and west Asia. Strangers were no novelty in Peshawar. At first the only ones to pay any attention to the two men in their cocky bush hats and sheepskin coats were the beggars and the kids, and the shopkeepers—and, of course, the inevitable prostitutes.

They had been in Peshawar only half an hour when Nick Carter spotted his double. It was still light, the rain gentle, and he had seen the impostor in the Street of the Potters. There was a woman with him. An American girl. A beauty!

It was all incredible and too easy, and N3 knew it, but he took it in stride. He ducked into a spice shop and whispered a few hurried commands to Mike Bannion. Mike was to follow the couple and report back when he could do so without losing them.

Mike had come back once to say that they were now in the Street of the Coppersmiths. The girl had purchased some Benares brass and gotten into a hassle with the merchant. Nick and Bannion had left the spice shop and had walked to his present place of concealment. Then he had sent Mike back to spy some more. That had been over an hour ago.

A bullock cart creaked past the archway, its dry axles squealing like stuck pigs. Nick Carter flipped his butt away in disgust. He'd better go find Mike. It meant breaking cover and the possibility of being spotted by the man he was after, but it couldn't be helped. Yet he was reluctant. He had a feeling about this one—they were expecting him, they knew he must come, and his double was not likely to be caught off guard. So be it. Yet this was a tactical situation at the moment, not strategic, and he thought he had a little advantage. They—his man would not be alone, this time—they did not know Mike Bannion! Nick could use the little drunk as his eyes and ears for a time—or so he had hoped. But now? Mike was running scared and admitted it. He was keeping his promise, drinking only one bottle a day, but now that the pressure was getting heavy? Nick smiled wryly and prepared to leave his shelter. Mike might have decided to toss in the towel—might be taking cover in a brothel or a hashish den.

He heard the footsteps then. A moment later Mike Bannion paused at the arch and peered in. "Nick?"

"Yeah. Where are they?"

Bannion stepped into the gloom. "At the Peshawar Hotel right now. In the bar. They looked like they were settling in for a time, so I took a chance."

"Good man," said Nick. "I was just doing you an injustice in my thoughts."

He heard Bannion tug at the bottle in his coat pocket. Then the gurgle. He couldn't see the impish grin, but he knew it was there. Mike Bannion was afraid—Nick Carter knew fear when he saw it—but so far the guy was bearing up well.

Mike said: "You think I'd taken off for the boondocks?"

"It occurred to me."

Gurgle. "I won't let you down," Bannion said. "I'll try hard not to—but I wish the hell I knew what went on. That guy I was following—I damned near soiled myself when I got a closeup of him That's *you!*"

"I know," said Nick. "It's a little confusing. Don't try to figure it out, Mike. If we get out of this maybe I'll tell you about it."

"If we get out of it?" *Gurgle.*

"I warned you it might be dangerous," snapped Nick. "Now lay off the booze! We've got work to do. I think things are going to break tonight—and break fast. We mustn't lose them, whatever happens. What do you know about the woman with him?"

Mike Bannion lit a cigarette. He was letting his red beard grow again. "Only that she's a doll, a real dish. Blonde, in her late twenties—maybe thirty—swell legs and a pair of knockers that makes a man ashamed of his thoughts. Beautiful face, too!"

"You didn't miss much," said N3 dryly. "I'm surprised you didn't ask her for her autograph."

"I did better than that! I found out her name." Bannion paused to gloat a moment. He was, Nick considered, as drunk as he'd been since they started. But as yet he was holding it well enough.

"Fine work," he praised. He tried to sound enthusiastic. "How'd you do that?"

"I told you I knew a little Pashto. When they left the coppersmith's stall they went to a tobacco shop. The guy—you—got to looking through some magazines, Russian and Chinese, and I had a little time. I cut back to the coppersmith and slipped him some *baksheesh.* The woman's name is Beth Cravens, as near as I could make out. She's an American. Works for the Peace Corps here—helps with the schools. The old guy was a talker but that was all I had time for. I didn't want to lose them."

"Amen to that! Let's get back to the Peshawar Hotel. They have a car?"

"She does. An English Ford. It was in the lot behind the hotel when I left."

"Come on!" N3 was curt. "And lay off that sauce from now on—until I tell you different!"

"Yes, sahib."

"It's for your own good," Nick told him dourly. "There's nothing funny about a shiv in the back!"

"I couldn't agree more," said Bannion. "Don't worry.

Every time I feel the urge to get blotto I think of those Paks
buried in the ground with their eyes and noses gone. It's a real
soberer-up!''

It was getting close to eight as they made their way through
the narrow crowded streets toward the Peshawar Hotel. As
they skirted the spacious square in which the mosque
Mahabat Khan stood, Nick said: ''I want you to give me your
impressions of the man, Bannion. Right off the top of your
head. Don't think, don't embroider it. Suppose you didn't
know *me*. Didn't know I had a double. What would you think
of him then?''

Bannion scratched at his red stubble. He was nearly running to keep up with Nick's long strides.

''Impressive,'' he said at last. ''Damned impressive.
Good-looking bastard. Handsome without being pretty, if
you know what I mean. Big, tall, lean. Looks like he's made
of concrete. Looks tough, too, Like he could be very mean.
Graceful. Moves like a tiger.''

''You're a good observer,'' N3 admitted. He was a little
flattered and admitted it. He also admitted the Chinese had
done a good job—a number one, excellent, first-rate, professional job. His double was so near like himself it was a little
frightening.

''I can tell you something else about him,'' said Bannion.
He snickered. ''The guy is a real heller with the women. At
least with this one—she's all over him! When I left she was
playing with him under the table in the bar!''

N3 said nothing during the rest of the walk. His thoughts
were busy with the girl. Beth Cravens. The Peace Corps!
Jesus—where would the rats gnaw into next?

It had already occurred to him that the woman might be an
innocent dupe. It was quite possible. The Chinese agent had
fooled Pei Ling in Tibet and Sam Shelton in Karachi. Fooled
them at first—for some reason both of them had had second
thoughts—and doubts. They had been killed.

So this Beth Cravens *could* be innocent. The man had
introduced himself as Nick Carter and she had believed him.
But why: What in hell was Nick Carter, the real AXE man,

supposed to be doing in Peshawar?

His heart, his intuition, whispered the truth. The woman was a Red agent. Another American who had sold out! A spark of anger moved in N3—another lousy traitor! Somehow it seemed worse because the treason came wrapped in a lovely package.

From a doorway across from the Peshawar Hotel they could see into the little bar. The quarry was still there. No monkey business under the table now—they were openly holding hands and the girl was gazing at the big man with adoration. If it's phony she's a good actriess, Nick Carter admitted.

A sudden thought struck him. A hunch so overpowering that he would have almost bet his life on it. He turned to Bannion. "You sober enough to go into the hotel and act like a gentleman? Like you're looking for an old friend?"

"Sober as a judge," averred Bannion. "Some judges I've known. Why?"

"Go in and throw your Pashto around and see if you can get a look at the register. I think he's staying there. Just look at the last half-dozen names."

Bannion was back in five minutes. "You're so right. *You're* staying there! Big as life—signed in as Nicholas Carter. On business."

"Dirty business."

Nick pulled the collar of his sheepskin coat up against the rain. He pulled down the Aussie type hat. Now that the phony had established himself, *he* mustn't be seen. Especially by cops or the military. It would only engender confusion and he wanted no more of that. Get the thing over with and get out.

"Go get the jeep," he told Bannion. "Find a *tonga* if you can and don't let him spare the horse. If you can't find a *tonga*, run for it—get back here as soon as possible. I'll be in the back someplace—you say she drives an English Ford?"

"Yes. It's black. Nearly brand new."

When Bannion had gone trotting off Nick went around the hotel to the parking lot. The Ford was there, shiny with rain. The only other car was an ancient Chrysler with a flat tire.

N3 stood in deep shadow and let the rain soak him. It was coming down a bit harder now. He studied the Ford—it had a luggage rack on top. If worse came to worst, and Bannion didn't return in time with the jeep, maybe he could—

A moment later the decision was forced on him. The woman and the false Nick Carter came around the corner of the hotel and headed for the Ford. Nick retreated a bit more into the shadows. Damn! What now? He just couldn't afford to lose them. For the moment he had just the faint edge of advantage and he didn't want to lose that, either. But unless he took them now—too early for his liking—he would have to let them drive away. Nick automatically checked his weapons. The Luger was ready to snarl. Hugo lurked in his sheath. Pierre, the gas bomb, was as lethal as ever. But to what purpose? He could kill the man, certainly, and maybe make the woman talk. Maybe! But he had no time to fool around. That arms shipment had come into Peshawar, or through it, and then vanished. Nick had to find it. With the guns and ammo as his ace he could go to the Pakistani Government and start clearing matters up. Without it—

As it turned out he needn't have worried. They weren't going anywhere for the moment. He watched them climb into the car. The back seat! Curtains were pulled. The English still put curtains or shades in some of their cars!

In a few moments the little car began to rock gently. N3 could hear the faintest whisper of springs. Just like the good old States, he told himself with a hard little smile. Every car a traveling boudoir!

He made his decision without hesitation, praying that Bannion would not show up now with the noisy jeep. It would spoil everything. What they were doing in there shouldn't take them long—then they would be off to somewhere, perhaps to the arms cache, and Nick Carter was going to be with them. Bannion would just have to look out for himself.

N3 tiptoed carefully across the parking lot. The car was still swaying gently and he could hear the low mumble of voices. They wouldn't have heard the Trump of Doom!

Carefully, slowly, with each movement carefully gauged in advance, he climbed on top of the Ford and flattened himself. He accomplished it in utmost silence, as stealthy as Death creeping. Not once did the couple within break their lubricious rhythm.

It was pitch dark now and rain was slanting down in black wet ropes. In such visibility Nick thought he had a good chance of going undetected as they drove through the streets of Peshawar. The rain would drive people inside.

The test came sooner than expected. The scrabbling within the car ceased and Nick heard them talking. In Chinese! His last doubts about the woman, about Beth Cravens, vanished. She *was* a traitor.

The door opened and the man got out. He stopped to kiss the woman and said, still in Chinese, "I'll see you later, Beth. At your place. I want to check with my people who are watching that bastard's camp."

"All right, my love. Oh, Nick, how marvelous you are! I am so happy. You will be careful? This man is dangerous. Even for you, Nick. He may be in Peshawar right now!"

"Maybe," said the man. "Maybe, but I doubt it. These Chinese agents are stupid. He'll run pretty true to form, I think. Anyway my men are watching the camp and the jeep is still there, I hear. This fake Nick and the redhead will have to go back for it, and to make their plans. That's one reason why I want to stay around the hotel for a time—he may even have the gall to come in and register as me. As Nick Carter! I hope not, it would cause complications, but at least I would like to study him for awhile. Figure out how best to kill him."

There was an odd note of command in the woman's voice as she spoke, "You're forgetting again, darling! You're not going to *kill* him. The plans were changed, remember? You're going to take him prisoner, take him back to the States for questioning. Try to remember, my love."

For a moment the man hesitated. He appeared to be thinking, to be struggling to get something clear in his mind. Then, "Of course. I did forget. Capture, not kill! New orders from Washington. All right, then—I'll see you at your place later. Goodbye.''

"Goodbye, sweetheart, I'll be counting the minutes. If I'm not there wait for me. I must go to the fort and talk to Mohammed Cassim. He says the tribesmen are becoming impatient for action.''

"Handle him gently,'' siad the man. "Remember he's Number One with all the tribes, the Wali. We need him right now. Later it won't matter.''

"I will, love. I know what to say. But now that they've got the guns they're fighting the bit. I'll be so glad, Nick, when this is all over and we can go back to the States and get married.''

"And me, Beth, love! Goodbye now.''

The big man, Nick Carter's double, stalked away into the rain without looking up or glancing back. Nick kept his face against the roof of the car. The man turned the corner and was gone. Rain still slatted down.

Nick could hear the swish and rustle of feminine garments being adjusted. A faint curse. An impatient tug. When she got out of the back and climbed behind the wheel N3 noted a briskness, an alertness, about her actions which belied the dreamy after-love mood she was supposed to be in. She was humming to herself. *When the Saints Come Marching In.* It hardly seemed to fit the occasion.

The car started with a lurch. She was a poor driver. Nick clung precariously to the rails of the luggage rack.

She found a narrow alley, deep in mud, and slid the car through it onto a deserted street. Good. She was not going through the main part of town after all. She appeared to be avoiding it as much as possible.

Nick Carter wondered, for just a fraction of a second, about his own sanity. Or at least his hearing. Then he smiled in the rain and shook his head—*he* was all right. The man *had* said those things and the woman—playing along with the gag?—had been right with him.

Nick Carter. Chinese agent. The bastard's camp. New

orders from Washington. Not kill but capture. Back to the
States and get married.

The car hit a nasty bump and Nick hung on for life. He let
the whole conversation he had just heard swirl about in his
brain. One thing he was beginning to understand—this
phony didn't *know* he was a phony. Not at the moment,
anyway. The guy thought he really *was* Nick Carter.

Somebody, thought the man from AXE, is crazy. And it
isn't me. But wait a minute! Just a minute—maybe not so
crazy after all. He recalled the odd moment when the man
had been confused and the woman's voice had changed, had
been both wheedling and hard.

Nick grinned in the rain. It could be. It just could be. You
had to hand it to the clever rat bastards!

The man was hypnotized!

Chapter Ten

THE FORT

Today there are three routes through the Khyber Pass, a modern blacktop road with two lanes, a railroad, and the caravan trail which has been there for thousands of years. Shortly after Beth Cravens left Peshawar she swung off the blacktop and down a steep, rutted decline to the ancient trail. The going was rugged and Nick Carter's big frame was battered unmercifully. He comforted himself with the thought that the lady couldn't be going far.

He was right. The Ford swung off the caravan trail and began to climb a winding drive. Gravel crunched beneath the tires. The darkness was total except for rain-filled tunnels of light cast by the car; Nick got a fleeting impression of stunted trees and dense undergrowth and a bald, flat-topped hill.

The little Ford toiled around the last spiral and stopped. The lights went out. Nick huddled in the rain, fighting a sneeze, and heard the door open and slam. She was not humming now.

Footsteps going away. Another door opened and shut. The moment he heard the door close Nick was off the car and running for a blob of shrubbery he had noted before the lights went out. He crouched in the wet bushes and waited.

Lights flicked on in the house. Nick saw a small stone patio, a water tank, metal awnings, a neat wooden fence. The Peace Corps lady lived pretty well! By reflected light he saw that the house was of stone, long and low and comfortable looking. Another light came on and he saw her move across a window. Bedroom? He crouched and ran softly through the pelting rain.

A damp raincoat lay across the bed. The girl was in the act of pulling her damp rumpled dress over her head as N3 peered in the window.

He saw immediately why Mike Bannion had been so impressed. She was a stunning creature. Rather tall, with long legs and large hard breasts. She dropped the dress to the floor and stared at herself for a moment in the mirror over the vanity. She leaned to lipstick her wide mouth, then ran a strong, capable-looking hand through her damp blonde hair. She was wearing only long beige stockings, gartered nearly to her hips, and black bra and panties. N3 noted the play of the good muscles in her smooth pale back and shoulders. A big, strong girl. Fine body. Lovely face. Too bad she was a Red. A traitor. She wasn't going to look so well in prison garb!

Nick decided not to kill her unless he absolutely must. A living corpse, wasting a life away behind bars, was a better warning and example than a dead body.

The woman swung toward the window and he ducked. She went to a closet and came back with heavy slacks, a fur-lined jacket, a sweater and an old Army fatigue cap. Nick watched as she donned these things, and put her slender feet in a pair of Wellington boots. The lady had business. He recalled the conversation in the parking lot—she had to see a certain Mohammed Cassim, the local Wali,—leader—and calm him down. The tribesmen were impatient.

That makes two of us at least, Nick thought grimly as he left the window and went back to his dripping bush. I'm impatient, too.

He had not long to wait. The lights went out and a door closed softly. He did not hear her lock it. It figured. If lover-boy came before she returned he could get in— probably into bed and wait for her. The idea flashed in his brain then but for the moment he stowed it away. First things first!

He lurked in the bushes until she passed him. He let her take a little lead. She was off guard, unaware, made no effort to conceal her passage. She went noisily, swacking at the bushes with a little stick. Nick followed her with the stealth of a tiger.

Thunder rumbled like distant cannon on the horizon and there was an occasional stroke of pale lightning. Nick blessed the lightning. It was blacker than Satan's gut!

Beth Cravens never once looked back. She went steadily, surely, and the following AXE man thought that she must have made the trip many times. At last they climbed out of a valley—he saw her silhouetted for a moment on the ridge—and reached a wide plateau. Nick guessed that it would overlook the Khyber Pass at a narrow sector—probably it was one of the old forts built by the British in the last century. The Pathan tribesmen had always been trouble and the English had never really conquered them.

Nick came up a narrow path to the ridge too fast and was nearly caught. He heard the girl speak to someone and ducked behind a huge boulder just as lightning flashed again.

The girl said: *"Ynfalla jehad!"* If God wills a holy war.

A coarse male voice replied, *"Lahewl.* Pass, memsahib. They are waiting for you."

N3 huddled behind his boulder and thought fast. Lightning had given him a glimpse of the huge crumbling old stone fort. And the Pathan guard. Big man. He would be well armed and tough. There would be many others in sound of his voice. This was going to be a little delicate. Nick flexed his right arm and the stiletto, Hugo, dropped into his hand.

The girl had vanished through a small postern in the old wall. N3 stepped from behind his rock and walked steadily toward the same spot. The challenge would come in a moment.

It came. "Who is that? Halt!" The Pathan's voice was fierce and suspicious.

Nick Carter sauntered coolly onward. He had to get closer. There must be no sound. He gambled. "Comrade Carter," he said in Chinese. "Comrade Nick Carter. Has the lady passed in yet?'' He had no Pashto and was betting that his double hadn't either. The Chinese should identify him, or at least confuse the guard.

The ruse worked. The Pathan hesitated long enough for Nick to get in close just as lightning tore the dark sky apart. The man sensed something wrong and stepped back. His rifle came up. Nick Carter sprang.

Nick got in close and put the stiletto into the man's throat. The murderous blade tangled in the thick beard as it went deep into flesh. Nick ripped it across, severing the jugular and turned quickly aside to escape the spurting blood, leaving the blade in the throat to prevent an outcry. The man died quickly and Nick eased him to the wet ground. He yanked out the stiletto and wiped it on the man's goatskin cloak. He pulled the body out of sight behind some boulders and went back to the postern gate and stood listening for a moment. From deep in the fort came the faint rise and fall of voices. It sounded like a heated discussion.

N3 went through the postern like a drifting shadow. Inside, to his right, a guttering oil torch was thrust into a rusty iron ringbolt. A stink of mutton oil was heavy in the narrow, bricked passage. To his left the floor sloped upward and he could see the reflection of another torch just around a bend. The voices came from that direction.

To his right the passage sloped downward. Nick followed it, guessing that it would lead to the old casemates, thick-walled and iron-doored cells where the British had stored their powder and shot. If what he was looking for was in the fort at all—it should be in the casemates.

The musty dank passage led down and down. Presently he saw another oil torch glimmering where the brick tunnel ended in a cross-passage. He went soft footed, hardly breathing, the Luger in his right hand with the safety off.

N3 peered around the corner into the cross-passage. To his left was a blank wall. To his right he could see tall iron doors on massive hinges. They were nearly closed, just the thickness of a man's body separating the iron lips. From within the dungeon they guarded came a faint murmur of voices. N3 ran as lightly as a huge cat to the doors and flattened himself against them.

The men in the casemate kept murmuring in subdued tones. Nick could make out an odd slip-slapping sound. It was a moment before he caught on. Then it came—they were playing cards! He applied a furtive eye to the crack between the iron doors.

There were two of them, swarthy and bearded and turbaned. Both were burdened with heavy leather bandoliers and their rifles were standing against a packing case nearby. N3's quick eye missed nothing. The rifles were old Krags—so the new arms had not yet been doled out?—and the stenciling on the packing case said GRENADES.

This was it. The end of the arms trail.

One of the sentries laughed harshly and slapped down a card. "*Rona*, fool! Weep! I win! And is it not time for our relief? Where is that misbegotten son of a sick camel? My belly gapes!"

The other man flung his cards away with a curse. "You have the luck of Shaitan himself! Wait, Omar—wait! Smell that? Is it not—"

Nick Carter cursed softly and fumbled with his trouser. Pierre, the terrible little gas pellet, slipped from his fingers and tinkled on the brick floor. Blood had made his fingers slippery. And blood had given him away to the Pathans. They could smell blood a mile away!

Both men leaped for their rifles. Nick scooped up the gas pellet, twisted the dial, and flung it into the casemate all in one fluid motion. He threw his weight against the great iron doors and strained with every muscle in his powerful body. God—they were heavy! Immense! But they were moving. Slowly. Very slowly.

The guards had time for one shot apiece before they died. The slugs flattened themselves against the iron doors and whined back around the chamber. N3 stood with his back to the massive doors and breathed a silent little prayer—if those shots had been heard—

Five nervous minutes passed and no one came to investigate. Nick breathed a little easier, but not much. A relief was due soon. And soon enough the body of the other guard would be found. There was not a minute to lose. He had made his move now, launched his attack, and he was off and running for his life. Hesitation, a single mistake, a goof of any kind, and he was a dead man. If he was lucky he would die quickly. If not—well, he remembered the buried Pakistanis. N3 shrugged his big shoulders and pried the doors open again. *Karma—Kismet—Inshallah!* You name it. It all added up to Fate and luck and it never did any good to worry once the battle had started.

He took a deep breath and plunged into the casemate. From that moment on he was too busy to worry.

The Pathans lay on the brick floor, mouths open and eyes staring. Both had ripped at the clothing about their throats as they died. Pierre was not a kindly death.

Nick, still holding his breath, picked up the lantern and went rapidly around the huge brick chamber. Stacks of boxes and crates reached to the ceiling, each one neatly stenciled. It was the arms shipment that his double had tricked out of Karachi. No doubt of that.

Nick dared to breathe now. The fumes of the gas pellet had dissipated, gone. And with them one of his chief weapons. He had no spare. He had only the Luger and the stiletto—and his wits. Nick gazed around at the room crammed with deadly weapons and grinned. They wouldn't do *him* any good. Brute force wasn't going to win for him against half the Khyber tribes. And a couple of shrewd operators like the woman and the impostor. He had to out-think them or he was finished—this little romp was just beginning.

In a corner of the chamber he found open boxes of uniforms. He pulled a couple out onto the floor and part of the puzzle fell into place. Became clear as sunlight. Indian uniforms! *And* Pakistani uniforms! Both sides. Change at will. Raid into India and then raid into Pakistan. Keep the pot boiling and the war going.

Clever, these Chinese!

Nick picked up one of the old Krag rifles and smashed

open a box of grenades. As he worked his lean face was as taut and grim as a death's head. Nasty folk he was dealing with! His double and the woman were arranging a jehad— once it got started the Indians would retaliate with thier own version of a holy war—*dharmayudha*. Anyone who had ever cracked a history book knew about religious wars—the most bestial of all. And the Chinese were ready to unloose *that* on the world to gain their ends.

N3 worked now with fury and frenzy. The relief was due any minute. He tore a dozen uniforms to shreds and twisted them into a long thick fuse leading from the doors back into the center of the chamber. He cursed softly as he sweated. Usually AXE agents were the best equipped in the world. He had nothing. It was improvise and hope.

He wiped his hands on a uniform to get the blood and sweat off and took the detonators from a dozen grenades. His fingers were rock steady but sweat streamed down into his eyes. One mistake here and—

Nick emptied the explosive from the grenades around the end of the fuse that led into a packing case of M1 ammunition. Along the edges of the fuse he laid more uniforms, ripped and torn so they would burn more readily. He wanted a good hot fire in here—and maybe even then it wouldn't work. Might not explode. It was not as easy to set off properly packed ammo as some TV writers depicted.

By the end of the fuse near the doors he placed the oil lantern. It was, he thanked God, a fairly modern version. An old railroad lantern. He placed it solidly on a box and turned up the wick as far as it would go. There was only about half an inch remaining. It would have to do.

Now for the really dangerous part. Nick Carter twisted the pin from a grenade and held it tightly. If he released it now the lever would fly off and the place would go skyward. He gripped the grenade in one big hand and fished for his shoe lace with the other. He had already loosened it and it came out readily. He wrapped it twice around the grenade to hold the firing lever in place and knotted it with his teeth and the fingers of one hand. He was breathing hard when, satisfied it would hold, he put the grenade gingerly down a foot from the lantern. He admitted, grudgingly and for the first time, some respect for generals who went around with taped grenades all over them.

He twisted a small, thin fuse out of a coat lining and tied it cautiously to the string around the grenade. Then, very carefully, he laid the free end of the cloth fuse across the base of the lantern, against the wick and little more than a quarter of an inch below the flame. He weighted the fuse in place with a coin and stepped back.

It was done! When the lantern wick burned down to the fuse it would fire it and the flame would travel along the fuse to the string holding down the arming lever on the grenade. The string would burn through and release the lever and whammo—

He hoped. There was no way of really knowing. Along the way something might fizzle out. But if things worked out he was going to have himself one hell of an explosion.

His time *had* run out. As he left the chamber and sweated the huge doors together he heard footsteps and voices coming from the far end of the passage. Damn! Another few seconds and he'd have been out of there!

Nick called himself a fool. The relief guards had to go too—otherwise they would spread the alarm. Damn again! He had better start thinking straighter than this.

He had time to get the doors together and chain them and snap a huge padlock into place. He found a chink in the brick wall and pushed the key deep into it. He could hope there was draught enough in the casemate to keep the lantern burning.

They were nearly on him now. Nick Carter ran on tiptoe down the passage toward the turning. They would be around the corner in a second. As he ran he writhed out of his heavy sheepskin coat and wrapped the garment around the Luger. A silencer!

As the two relief guards rounded the corner he shot them both at close range, firing at the face and head so they would die quickly and without sound.

The sheepskin silencer worked better than he had ex-

pected. The clatter of heavily armed men falling on bricks
made far more noise than Wilhelmina. Both died as quickly
as he had wished.

N3 hovered over the bodies for a moment, then saw a
shallow niche in the wall across the passage and toward the
blank end. It would have to do. He dragged the bodies there
and left them. On his way back he took the torch from the
sconce and stamped it out on the floor. He felt his way in
blackness back toward the postern.

His luck was holding. He could still hear voices and see
lights at the far end of the passage, away from the corridor
that had led him to the casemate. No alarm as yet. Nick
slipped through the postern and out into the rain-swept night.
The fresh air felt good on his sweaty body. He ran for the
sheltering boulders and stopped for a breather. What now,
friend?

He had to admit that he didn't exactly know what now. All
he could do was keep going, taking every target of opportunity, keep battling and hoping and raising all the hell he
could. Something would give. Maybe himself. But he didn't
think so.

N3 was still lurking in the boulders when Beth Cravens
passed ten minutes later. She was humming again. This time
it was *Lover Come Back to Me*. Nick's little smile was mean
as he wondered if the tune was prophetic.

He went stealthily after her, back along the way they had
come. She seemed happy, unconcerned. So far, then, he had
gotten away with it. Nothing had been noticed. Five men
dead and not yet noticed. Pathan organization and discipline
was a little lax. Thank God.

No use worrying about his bomb in the casemate. He had
done all he could. It might not work at all; it might partially
work; it might smolder for hours before the big bang came.

Meantime there was Beth Cravens to attend to. Maybe he
could talk her into coming back to the U.S. A few years in an
American prison would be better than what would happen to
her when the Chinese Reds got finished with her. They
offered no second chances.

Nick Carter thought he knew how he could convince her—if only the impostor, the lover she was expecting, hadn't shown up yet.

He hadn't. Nick watched as the woman showered and prepared herself for what she imagined would be a night of passion. N3 was not above peeking into the bathroom window and observing some very intimate preparations of the sort an experienced and knowledgeable young woman takes when she is expecting a lover. Nick wondered what she had used in the car behind the Peshawar Hotel. Maybe she carried them in her purse!

A sound alerted him and he disappeared from the window like a ghost. His double was coming. Second encounter!

Chapter Eleven

BEDTIME STORY

This time it was no contest.

Nick took his *alter ego* from behind with a vicious chopping blow across the neck. The man went down like a stone, out cold. Nick dragged the inert body into the shelter of dripping bushes and began to strip it. The only light in the house now was a soft rosy glow from the bedroom. How nice. Like a candle in the window. She must be getting impatient.

Won't be long now, baby, N3 promised as he stripped the man. He was hoping to take Beth Cravens by surprise, in the dark, but if she did turn on a bright light he wanted to be able to pass as himself. Himself! Nick shook his head. This mixup was making him screwy.

He risked the pencil light to inspect the unconscious man's features. He felt a little sense of shock—it was like looking in a mirror. The man was so damned near a perfect ringer—if you missed the tiny pink surgical scars and a certain mean cast in the mouth that Nick did not normally have.

Dressed well, too. Nick slipped on the expensive suit, a bit wet and muddy now, and the fine shirt and tie, the good shoes, the fawn Burberry. He transferred his black plastic holster to the new belt, put the Luger in it, and was ready to go. He left the impostor bound with Nick's belt and strips torn from his old OD shirt and trousers. Should hold him long enough.

What to do with the man's weapons was a problem for a moment. Nick ran the flash over them quickly. Duplicates of his own. A 9mm Luger, stripped down, and the stiletto— a trifle longer than his own. No one was perfect. He took the clip from the Luger and slipped it in his pocket, then flung the weapons as far as he could into the night. Metal clanked on the stony hillside.

As he started for the house the light in the bedroom went out. Nick whistled a little tune deep in his throat. He felt good. Keyed and on edge. Ready for anything. He was looking forward to this—he remembered how she had looked before the mirror.

He didn't want to kill her, though she deserved it. She was a betrayer of her country—but such a lovely creature. He knew the Chinese would be merciless with her for failing, and he hated to think how they would deal with her. He must give her a chance to consider defecting. But he would have to do it fast. Climb into bed with her before she could get suspicious. That it would be dangerous he took for granted, as he always did. She might shoot him on sight—or later. A little grin crinkled Nick's mouth—what a hell of a way to get shot. And he must be careful not to betray himself until the last moment—he could not hope to keep up the deception forever, of course. A single error might give him away. He didn't know the layout of the house, didn't know about doors or closets or the kitchen or where anything was. It would be like running a strange obstacle course in the dark.

His voice would pass, he thought. At the parking lot the man had spoken nearly like himself—Nick had wondered at the time where the Chinese spy masters had gotten the recordings or tapes. That might bear looking into—if he ever got back.

He went in a side door, the way Beth Cravens had. He used his tiny light, shielding it with his hand, hoping she wouldn't see it from the bedroom. He couldn't afford to fall over anything—be a dead giveaway.

The woman called from the bedroom. "Nick? Darling? What took you so long? I've been waiting for ages."

In his own voice, blurred just a bit by what he hoped she would think was alcohol, Nick said: "I've been waiting for that turtle bastard at the hotel—he never did come. I spent too much time in the bar, too. I think I'm a little drunk, honey." He slurred his words.

Beth Cravens laughed, but her voice sharpened. "That wasn't very smart, darling! You know you shouldn't drink too much until this job is over. We can't afford to take chances with this man."

Nick was oriented by now. He headed for the bedroom and her voice, taking off his clothes as he went. "I'm not that drunk," he said, hoping she would think he was. He laughed loudly to cover the sound of his clothes coming off. "I'm not as drunk as you think I am!"

"Well—I hope you're not *too* drunk. You know—"

"I'm not." He was naked now, carrying the stiletto and the Luger. He stooped and shoved them under the bed. What a woman—it hadn't been over two hours since she had been bouncing around in the car. Now she was avid again!

"You sound sort of funny," Beth said. He heard her twist and reach for the bedside light. He slid beneath the cool sheets and pulled her to him, clamping his mouth over hers. For a moment she was tense, questioning, then her flesh betrayed her and she slid her tongue into his mouth.

He wasted no time on preliminaries. Not only were they dangerous, but there was so little time.

Beth Cravens welcomed him. She lifted herself to engulf him. Without a trace of tenderness, and yet without hate or malice, he took her. Perhaps a little brutally, but Beth did not appear to object. It was she, in the end, who turned to frenzy and began to inflict pain in her ecstasy.

She began to whimper and claw at his back. He felt her nails rake him, scraping away flesh. She followed his every movement, her moist body glued to his as though she could never bear to part with him.

To Nick she seemed insatiable. She was a trial even to his

great endurance. But at last Beth Cravens gave a long convulsive sigh and ceased to move. But not for long. She reached up and wrapped her soft arms around his neck and smothered his mouth with moist kisses. It was, he guessed, her way of telling him not to go away—the best was yet to come.

He knew it was dangerous to linger. He must talk to her now.

Suddenly the bedside light went on and she was staring at him with what might have been fear and awe and amazement—and gratitude? The little automatic in her hand was rock steady on his muscle-corded belly. She had had the gun under her pillow!

"Who are you?" Her voice trembled but the gun did not. She was sitting up, naked from the waist, the fine white breasts bobbling as she fought to control her breathing. Her blonde hair was in wild disarray and her red mouth swollen and smeared. Her face was pink, but the gray eyes were cold. Nick could see the wild beat of a pulse in her milky throat.

N3 smiled at her. He felt relaxed and good and sure of himself. Let her think she had the upper hand. Anytime he felt like it he would take the pea-shooter away from her.

"I'm Nick Carter," said Nick Carter. "The real McCoy. Not an imitation. Surprised?"

She took it in her stride. He admired her nerve and intelligence. She believed him at once. Then she smiled and moved away a little, her finger tense on the trigger of the little black pistol. "So you did come. I thought you would but I couldn't be sure. I only know what the turtle tells me—and he's not very reliable when he's under hypnosis. He's really not such a good subject."

Nick grinned at her. "I bet they think so in Peking."

"Yes, but they were wrong. They did it under lab conditions—I have to do it in the field." She was wearing a little silver locket on a fine chain. Absently she began to twirl it, her gray eyes huge and steady on Nick.

The man from AXE stretched luxuriously. "You're wasting your time, sweetheart. I don't hypnotize." No AXE man did. It was a rudimentary requirement for the service.

Her smile had a tinge of pseudo-sweetness in it. The eyes were not quite so cold. But the pistol was as steady as ever. "This is really better than what we had in mind at first," she said. "My orders have been changed. Peking doesn't want you killed now—they want you taken alive. They've got big plans for you."

"How considerate of them. I'll bet I can guess, too. Why fool around with a fake Nick Carter when you can have the real thing, eh? Get me and brainwash me and turn me loose again in about five years. I'd play hell with Uncle's security then, wouldn't I? That it?"

Her perfect teeth flashed. "About. No matter. I've got you—now I can stop playing house with that other fool. That's what gave you away, you know." Her smile was sly and tinged with lust. "You're terrific! My God—the Turtle was never like that. In a way it's a shame that I have to turn you over to *them*."

Nick was enjoying himself. Fun while you wait. If it was coming the explosion should be any minute now.

Nick gave her a maddeningly slow smile. "What if I don't go with you? You really wouldn't want to shoot me. Peking wouldn't like it. Also, I'm afraid you're going to be disappointed. There's not going to be a jehad. Your tribesmen are not going to use those two sets of uniforms to keep the war going. And if you're expecting help from your Turtle—don't. He's a bit tied up at the moment." He leaned toward her. She moved away and pushed the pistol at him. "Stay away!"

Nick went on. "I'm going to make you a proposition—give you a chance. You'd better take it. All hell is due to break loose around here. You'll be in the middle of it, with a lot of mad Pathans after your lily white hide. You would be smart to come with me. Right now. I'll get you back to the States and you can stand trial. After I kill your boy, of course. The Turtle. Well—think fast, Miss Cravens. I'm a temperamental guy—I may withdraw that offer any time."

She spat at him. Sudden hate glared in her eyes. "You

lousy, crummy superior bastard! You come in here, throw your stinking weight around and think you can bulldoze and fast talk me into going back to the States. That stinking idiotic country! I'd die first!''

"You might at that. If the Pathans get you afterwards."

"After what?" she screamed. "After what? Y—you moron! I've got the gun, remember. Jesus—I wish I dared kill you now!"

Nick waggled a finger at her. "Ah-ah—Peking not like."

He had her mad enough now. Raving. But why didn't the goddamned fort blow? Come on, grenade! Come on!

As if in answer, it started right then. A gradually rising, high keening blast superimposed on the basso of the explosion. The cottage twisted on its foundation. A giant hand lifted it and put it down askew. Walls cracked and big chunks of ceiling came down. A small chandelier came down with a crash.

Beth Cravens screamed. Nick reached and flicked the little gun out of her hand. He made a fist and tapped her behind the ear, hard but not too hard. She slumped on the bed. He gazed at her for a moment, feeling no pity now. Next stop a Federal prison. He didn't suppose they would shoot her. Not in so-called peace time.

"Get your hands up! Drop the gun!"

N3 dropped it. It was no good to him anyway—not enough gun to handle *this* situation. He put up his hands and stared coldly at the man in the doorway. His double. The Turtle. And he was carrying a shield—Mike Bannion!

The impostor was behind Mike, one brawny arm around the little man's throat to hold him in position. It wasn't difficult. Mike was very drunk. His eyes rolled wildly and his knees sagged.

Mike's old Webley was in the double's hand. It was sighted firmly on Nick Carter's naked belly. God damn it! To come so far, to be so close, and then be destroyed by a well-meaning drunk! Mike must have been looking for him, to help, and had somehow stumbled into the phony agent.

The Chinese agent held Mike in a vise of muscle that so

nearly matched Nick's. He looked at the unconscious girl. "You kill her?" His eyes were clear and his voice firm and he looked every inch the killer. Nick guessed that he was out of hypnosis—it had worn off or the man had been shocked out of it.

"She's not dead," he told the man. "just knocked out. You intend to kill me?"

"What else?" The eyes, so very like Nick's own, were cold and empty. The only expression in them was that of wariness.

Cautiously, not moving, thinking furiously, Nick said, "Won't it be sort of like killing yourself?"

The Webley did not waver. The man watched Nick with cold contempt. The AXE man could see the final decision to kill arriving in the man's eyes.

He nodded toward the girl. "She told me that Peking wants me alive."

"So I made a mistake. I got the orders wrong. And for God's sake cut the crap—don't try to con me! We're both pros and you lost, so shut up and die like a pro." The finger tightened on the trigger of the Webley.

Nick Carter's admiration was not all feigned. "You're a hard case," he said. "Where are you from in the States? You still got any people there?"

"None of your screwing business!" The finger moved on the trigger.

Mike Bannion began to squirm and thrash around. He was helpless, held by the massive arms of the impostor as though he were a rag doll. But the struggle prolonged Nick's life for another second. The man applied a powerful pressure to Mike Bannion's throat. The little man tried to fight back, tugging and pulling at the muscular arm that was throttling him. His eyes found Nick for a moment and he tried to grin and panted, "I—I shorry, Nick. I found him—thought he you! I be good guy, untie and now . . . I so shorry . . ." He passed out.

His double grinned evilly at Nick. "Let that be a lesson to you! Never hire drunken help. Now you get—"

Nick clasped both hands. "If you're really going to kill me I'd like to pray for a minute. Surely you won't deny me that—no matter what you are now. You were once an American. I'd guess you were a soldier once. You must have had buddies who died in battle. You wouldn't deny a man the right to a last prayer?"

It was corny and he knew it, but he was gambling for his life. He *had* to get off the bed and on his knees. The Luger was under the bed, at the foot, where he had dropped it when he climbed into bed with the woman.

Contempt flickered in the other man's eyes. He scanned the bedroom rapidly. If he looks under the bed, Nick thought, I've had it. I'll have to jump the gun and this time I won't make it.

The cold eyes came back to Nick. The man tightened his grip on the sagging flesh shield that was Mike Bannion. It was the shield that finally decided him. He couldn't see how Nick could get at him.

The man said: "I'll make a bargain with you, Carter. You want to pray? So pray. But first you answer a question—and if I think you're lying I'll kill you right now. Bang! No prayers. Okay?"

"Okay. What's the question?"

The man's smile was as mean as Nick's own could be. "I had to kill a couple of guys because I couldn't come up with something they called a Golden Number. At first it was just routine—they didn't even ask me until after I had what I wanted—but after, when I couldn't come up with that damned number, they got suspicious and I had to kill them. So what's the Golden Number? If I can take that back to Peking it might help square me for this mess." The Webley twitched at Nick. "You talking or you want to die noble? Without prayer? Tell the truth and I'll let you pray. Maybe a whole minute."

"I'll tell you." It was another gamble. If he lost now he would louse up a lot of other agents. Get them killed. Nick decided not to lie, though he was good at it. In this bind he simply couldn't chance it.

"It's the number of the year in the old Metonic Cycle. That's nineteen years. So the number can be anything from 1 to 19. Every agent's number varies, depending on who is asking the identifying question. The contact gives the agent a year, any year, and the agent identifying himself adds one to it. Then he divides by nineteen. The remainder is the Golden Number. Nineteen is the golden number when there is no remainder. Simple?"

His double scowled. "Like hell it's simple. No wonder I couldn't come up with it. Okay—you can pray now. One minute."

"Thanks."

Nick Carter slipped off the bed to his knees, as near the foot of the bed as possible. He kept his hands clasped and well in sight. He closed his eyes and began to murmur.

The phony agent said: "Just one sign of monkey business, just one, and you get it. Then I'll kill your friend here. Be good and die with no trouble and I might let him go. He's just a lush—no reason I should kill him."

Liar. An obvious play to Nick's own feeling as a decent American. The innocent shall not suffer. When would they realize that the Americans could play just as rough as they could.

Somewhat to his own surprise Nick found that he really was praying after a fashion. For the success of this crazy gambit.

Then it was go! He rolled to his right, snatching the Luger from beneath the bed and kept on rolling across the floor as he fired. He got in the first shot. Then the Webley roared at him. Nick never stopped moving, rolling, crouching, scuttling. He let the clip empty into Mike Bannion's chest.

The din of Death was stilled. The room was hazy with smoke from the Webley's old-fashioned cartridges. Mike Bannion lay near the door, across the body of the man he had not shielded from death after all. The Luger, at such murderous range, had put slugs through Mike's body and well into Nick's double. The Webley lay on the carpet, halfway to the bed, where a dying hand had tossed it.

Nick slipped another clip into the Luger. Wilhelmina was hot. He inspected the bodies. Both stare-eyed dead. He lingered for a moment over Mike Bannion. "I'm sorry, Mike. I'll keep that promise—see that your wife and kids get some of Uncle's sugar."

He went to the bed. Damn it! She would never serve her time now. One of the double's wild shots had gotten her right in the face.

Nick dressed rapidly and turned off the lights. Bannion must have come back to the Peshawar Hotel, found him gone, and somehow found out where Beth Cravens lived. He had come out to help, poor little bastard. Loyal enough in the end. Drunk, too.

But it meant that the jeep should be someplace around.

Nick found it parked on the old caravan trail. Most of their gear was back at the camp but he couldn't worry about that now. Time to fold his tent and softly fade away. There was a sweetish stench of high explosive in the air and from the direction of the old fort he could see flames staining the rainy black sky. Sooner or later officialdom would get around to investigating—and sooner or later, probably sooner, the Pathans would come for their revenge. Best be gone when they did.

He was about to climb in the jeep when a thought struck him. A devilish, typical Nick Carter thought. Why not? It was crazy as hell, but again why not? Sort of garnish the salad as it were. He went back to the blast-racked cottage, found a mattress cover in a closet, and set to work. As he worked he pondered the possibility of bringing it off—this wild scheme. He should be able to do it if the luck held.

He could skirt Peshawar and get out of the Khyber and head for Rawalpindi. It was about a hundred miles. No sweat if the old jeep held up and there was still plenty of gas.

Sooner or later he was going to run into a Pakistani patrol. So be it. He was in the clear now, or would be when he got out of the Pass, and he could probably sweet talk them into letting him contact the Air Force in Ladakh. They would remember him. Through them he could contact Hawk in

Washington. Once he explained matters Hawk would start pulling wires and making his famous phone calls.

He was sure his Chief would go along with the gag. Hawk's sardonic sense of humor was much the same as Killmaster's.

Nick Carter picked up the body in the mattress cover, threw it across his shoulder, and strode out of the cottage.

Chapter Twelve

RETURN OF THE TURTLE

The first light snow of the year had drifted down on Peking during the night. It was nothing much, merely an October frosting, and Wang-wei did not even notice it as he drove to the house in the Tartar City. His thoughts were on something other than the weather and they were not easy or happy thoughts. He had not liked the tone in which Chou had summoned him to this meeting.

He did not, in fact, like Chou. The man might be heir apparent, but he was also a thief. No less! He had indeed taken Sessi-yu and her marvelous Golden Lotus. The fact that Wang-wei had already found a new concubine did in no way assuage his hurt. He had nearly loved Sessi-yu.

As he left his car and entered the compound he was admitted by the same guards. As he climbed the stairs to the anteroom. Wang-wei knew that it was not *déjà vu*—this had all really happened before. Of course. Not much over a week ago he had sent his Turtle on the mission, put Dragon Plan into effect. New uneasiness stirred in the little Chief of Secret Services. There had been nothing from Peshawar now for two days.

Yes, he had certainly been here before. Many times. But as he entered the long room with the mirrored floor Wang-wei had a strange premonition. He would not be here again!

Chou and the Leader were waiting for him as before. There

was the same table and chairs, the same refreshment on the table. Only this time the Leader did not offer him a drink or smoke. His tone was curt as he pressed a button and lights went on in the apartment below.

"Your Turtle is back," said the Leader in his cold small voice. "I thought you would like to see him—since it so intimately concerns you."

Wang-wei stared at them. "Turtle Nine? Back so soon—I—I had not heard. He did not report to me."

"He did not report to anyone," said Chou. His voice was mean, nasty. "He came by way of the British Trade Commission. Well sealed and packaged. I am convinced that the British did not really know what they were delivering—they did it as a favor to the Americans."

"I do not understand."

"You will. Watch."

A door opened in the apartment below and four coolies entered. They were carrying something. Wang-wei felt the sweat start on him. A coffin! A plain pine box.

"Take a good look," said Chou softly. "It is the last time you will ever see your favorite Turtle. Turtle Nine! Remember how you bragged of him?"

Wang-wei could not answer. He automatically loosened his collar as he stared down through the glass floor. It was his Turtle, right enough. Turtle Nine. The perfect double for Nick Carter. Now pale and still in the box, his hands crossed on his big chest.

"He was even embalmed," said the Leader crossly. "Courtesy of the American Air Force. How they must be laughing at us!"

Wang-wei wiped his sweaty face. "I—I still do not understand! I have heard nothing. I—"

Chou leaned to hand him something. A small slip of paper with a gummed back. A seal of some kind. "Perhaps this will enlighten you, friend Wang-wei. The coffin was sealed with many of them. All signed. Read it."

Wang-wei stared down at the little paper seal in his hand. It bore the AXE symbol—a murderous little hatchet! Across the seal, scrawled in a bold hand, was: *Worst wishes, NC*.

"Phase One and Two of Dragon Plan have failed," said the Leader. "We shall have to think of something else."

Wang-wei mopped the inside of his collar. He couldn't tear his eyes away from the coffin. "Yes, Comrade Leader. I will begin planning at once."

"Not you," said the Leader.

To Wang-wei the words sounded oddly, and terribly, like a firing squad.

"NICK CARTER OUT-BONDS JAMES BOND."

—Buffalo Evening News

"Nick Carter is the oldest surviving hero in American fiction. In his latest Killmaster incarnation, he has attracted an army of addicted readers for the Nick Carter series that has been published in a dozen languages, from Dutch to Japanese. . . . Nick Carter is super-intelligence par excellence . . . [his] penchant for sex and violence seems to have universal appeal."

—The New York Times

"America's #1 espionage agent."

—Variety

"Generation after generation of readers has been drawn to Nick Carter."

—Christian Science Monitor

"Nick Carter has emerged as America's most popular, most resilient and most imitated fictional character! . . . Nick Carter is extraordinarily big."

—Bestsellers